# Designer Genes

## "The Boyfriend Cut"

a novel by

harley brooks

Designer Genes—"The Boyfriend Cut" © 2013 Harley Brooks
ALL RIGHTS RESERVED

**The Cataloging-In-Publication Data for** *Designer Genes—"The Boyfriend Cut"*
**is on file in the Library of Congress.**

**ISBN: 978-0-9856598-2-0**

Cover Design © Kelli Ann Morgan
Inspiration Creative Services
www.inspirecreativeservices.com

Editing by Lynne Harter
Word Nerdy Editing Services
http://www.wordnerdyediting.com

Interior book design by Bob Houston
http://about.me/BobHouston

Printed in the United States of America

# Dedication

For renowned author,

**Ivy Ruckman**

who told me one rainy afternoon four years ago,

"Designer Genes" would be published.

Thanks for believing in me.

## Love is supposed to be a choice made by the heart ...not the government.

Born with the genetic markers the government seeks, an unassuming seventeen-year-old girl is dropped in the middle of a covert cloning program where her future is secretly decided. Marli Davis wants out of the government's clutches until she meets her destiny...and his twin brother.

Over six feet of lean muscle, lips that should be registered as lethal weapons and the perfect link to Marli's genetic code, Jordan Mason's only strategy is to fulfill his government contract, not fall in love. His heart, however, changes the game plan and when jealousy spins everything out of control, he chances losing Marli forever.

Jesse Mason offers Marli the one thing Jordan can't give her. Freedom. All he asks in return? Her heart—a price she's not sure she can pay.

Is a life without love, or Jordan, a sacrifice Marli's willing to make? Is Jordan's love for Marli strong enough to fight for her, or strong enough to let her go?

A choice ruled by the heart. A destiny ruled by the consequence.

# 1
# CHOSEN

Red. A powerful color demanding immediate attention, yet foreboding and suggesting danger—*proceed with caution*. The total opposite of what I intended to do, but not alone.

Overhead, the spring sun burned with the same impatient intensity vibrating within me. I drummed my bare toes against the warm concrete stairs and picked at a piece of mortar between the bricks. Fifteen minutes had passed since the courier delivered the envelope and I'd launched a panicked call for help.

"Hurry up," whispered across my lips delicate as the brush of dragonfly wings, while *save me* thundered inside my rattled brain. My eyes dropped to the bold letters on the label.

*April 10, 2072. Interview Request for Candidate 5846—Selection A for Candidate 2255.*

The heartbeat in my ears thrummed louder. I'd never received a red envelope—a request for an interview—one for my possible assigned genetic link: *mate*. If I listened closely, I heard the sound of my normal life skidding to a halt and felt the tentacles of The Program reach for me, leaving the edges of my dreams to fray until they disappeared.

Chosen at age fourteen, my selection for candidacy met with mixed reactions. A child accepted into The Program signified prestigious standing and guaranteed special benefits. To my father, however, it meant letting the government decide his child's destiny—something he refused to allow.

Scheming behind his back, my grandmother, aided by my mother, secretly enrolled me without my father's knowledge. When he discovered the personal betrayal, the resulting chain of events forever altered my world.

Powerless to change things, Dad forbade the government's interference before I turned seventeen. It seemed the moment I blew out the candles on my last birthday cake, queries flooded my cyber mailbox from compatible candidates. Today, however, I received the first request for an interview.

A soft whirring sound started up the block and seconds later, a solar car holding the two people who'd shared almost every major moment in my life, parked at the end of the walk. Alex, who appeared pixie-like with her tiny build, mischievous eyes and spiky hair, bounded up the sidewalk first. She tugged at the cropped neon-green fabric that barely qualified as a skirt, while twisting her celestial bleached stalks into fine points. A yellow band circled her wrist allowing her the freedom to live life on the edge and not under the confines of The Program. The problem, however, was Alex believed consequences happened to others, not her.

"Your *cheeks* are showing," Brittany stated in her usual judgmental tone.

A tall, lithe figure with a mane of glistening black hair edged at her waist, Brittany Johnson, or *Brit*, probably had the most common sense in our trio. Raised by strict parents who held fast to their Asian background, she policed everyone's moral conduct. Nonetheless, her comment didn't faze Alex. Nothing did.

"Maybe I mean to expose a little tush."

I tipped my head toward the house across the street. "I'm sure the neighbors appreciate the show."

"Old man Baxter probably needs something to kick-start his heart. He's got to be like a hundred." She turned and purposely waved as if he watched.

"You're impossible, Alexandra Nichols."

Brit tapped the red envelope. "So that's it?" I nodded. "Wow. Guess I expected more—diamond crusted or something spectacular by the way they describe the 'honorable request.' Did the thing at least come on a satin pillow?"

I laughed. "No, but the delivery guy did bow before handing it to me. I should have checked for wings tucked inside his shirt, or a halo hanging off the handlebars of his scooter."

"More like a retractable pitchfork in his back pocket if he was a messenger from The Program."

"So…are you going to open it?" Alex asked.

"I don't know. Dad will have a come-apart if I do."

Brit drew a deep breath. "You're only reviewing—not accepting, right?"

"Right," I said aloud while inside an emotional war waged. Curiosity plagued me, but once I inserted the pod in my computer registering I'd received the request, I crossed a point of no return. I'd activate my candidacy, officially entering the clandestine world surrounding The Program.

Without my father's permission.

Brittany's voice pulled me from my thoughts. "When does Rick get home?"

"In about an hour, depending on how late he's running with patients."

Alex scoffed. "Patients? Marli, they're cats and dogs."

Veterinarians fell into the same category as street sweepers in some people's eyes. Saving animals' lives didn't hold the significance as saving humans, until one of society's elite needed to give "Fluffy" a tenth life. Then vets were considered *gods*.

I tugged hard on a bleached spike.

"Ouch! Fine. *Patients*. Either way, we better hurry."

I opened the front door and paused. "So we're clear? We look at the pod then reseal it. Dad never knows and you two take this secret to your graves."

Upstairs in my bedroom, Alex sprawled across my bed, head propped on a pillow against the footboard. Brittany perched on the edge of the desk, close to the computer. I passed them each a candy straw from my junk food stash and folded one knee on the chair, keeping a foot on the floor. Half of me grounded, the other half uncertain and frightened. I inserted the pod, no longer feeling a breath exit my lungs or a heartbeat in my chest.

A bead of moisture prickled my upper lip. Dad would have a meltdown of epic proportion if he knew what we were doing. At this moment though, I only cared about Candidate 2255—my supposed assigned "link." I rolled the cinnamon candy stick between my lips and shoved the image of my father's enraged face to the back of my mind.

A tall, well-built boy walked into view and perched on a stool against a white screen.

"Oh. My. God," Alex whispered.

Brit's chin dropped and she braced her arm on the desktop to lean closer. I slumped onto the chair, mouth bone dry, the candy straw stuck to my tongue.

"Hi."

The tone of the voice on the video feed sounded gentle, kind. The single word—a friendly greeting, felt intimate, and an unexpected blush tingled across my cheeks.

"I'm Candidate 2255."

A shiny bronze curtain of waves followed his jaw line and hid his face when he lowered his head. He scraped at the corner of a fingernail before smoothing his hands down his thighs. Shifting a hip on the stool, he flipped his head, sending his wayward locks swinging neatly back in place. His mouth pinched, a deep breath drawn and held as if weighing a decision.

"I know it's against protocol, but I hate being referred to as a number. My name is Jordan Mason and…I'm really nervous."

Mesmerized, I watched him push the sleeves of his light blue sweater to just below his elbow as if the simple gesture was the most incredible thing I'd ever witnessed. The corner of his bottom lip tucked into his top teeth for a second before slowly slipping back into a heart-shaped mouth. A *kissable* mouth. When his fingers slid through his thick hair, a nervous flutter wiggled in my stomach. I pulled my legs tight to my chest and dangled my toes off the edge of the chair.

"Okay—" he continued on a rush of air, "—about me. I attend Cornell University. I'm in the second year of their accelerated medical program." He rubbed the back of his neck and a sheepish grin scrunched his mouth. "I, uh, graduated high school early."

An immediate grimace twisted my face and I dropped my gaze to the pink bracelet adorning my wrist. *Four diamonds and a whopping seventeen years old.* My unimpressive portfolio didn't even include a high school diploma yet.

A light chuckle rumbled over the speaker and the voice, smooth as warm caramel, continued. "Wow, I sound pretentious. Something I hate, by the way. So what do I like? That's easy. For one, I love animals. Dogs, especially. They're happy if you simply scratch behind their ears."

I snapped to attention. On my twelfth birthday, a robin hit the living room window, breaking a wing. Dad and I nursed the bird until it took flight one morning. Ever since, I wanted to follow in his footsteps and become a veterinarian.

*Could I possibly be assigned to someone who'd allow* my *dream to come true?*

A slight curve pulled Jordan Mason's mouth and dimples bracketed the corners. "Next would be water, whether sailing, encased inside a huge wave, or sitting nearby on a beach, I love it." His eyes twinkled, his expression animated as he wandered in his thoughts. "Surfing is one of my passions. In fact, I'm a fan of the old-fashioned long board—had one custom made. It catches a wave perfect every time."

Hmm. Water sports. An embarrassing memory flickered. I tried surfing a couple of times with my brother and his friends when we lived in California, but rather than "catch a wave," I spent most of the time under one.

Jordan laughed, the sound wrapping and holding me in a dizzying vice. His eyes glittered with excitement. "Cars are another obsession. I love them fast and flashy. My Porsche, *Sweet Sally,* is my best friend. She's taken me on lots of road trips. I know, not 'environmentally acceptable,'" he air-quoted. "I love the open road almost as much as I love flying. Another favorite hobby. I'm a licensed pilot—personal aircraft and helicopters."

Alex sneered. "Of course you are."

Brit reached over and smacked the top of her head.

"SHHH!" I hissed.

This time, two hands scrubbed roughly over his scalp and another sigh ruffled his mouth. A weird feeling rushed through me like hot and cold water running side-by-side. I pushed my fists into my eye sockets to stop watching.

"There I go again, bragging. Sorry," he said, the lilt unnerving. "What I really mean to say is I love doing anything that makes me feel free."

*Freedom.* Not a lot of that in The Program and I sensed a connection to Jordan Mason right then. Like me, he always fidgeted with his bracelet. His body language, the harsh angles his expression suddenly took, revealed being a candidate and required to jump whenever the government asked, might be something he didn't like either.

I stared as he fingered the blue band around his arm, unaware I touched my own. When the light above sparked the diamonds on his bracelet, I gasped. *Five* diamonds. Crap! The cinnamon stick dropped off my lip to the floor.

At age thirteen, the government issued colored bands representing your life status. Outside of The Program, yellow, orange, and green were the three major colors. If my dad had his way, yellow would still surround my wrist, but the pink ring I wore served as a constant reminder he'd lost…and so had I.

The special blue and pink bands issued to candidates had diamonds representing status, and five diamonds symbolized the highest—the elite. Four diamonds sparkled on my wrist, but the fifth one on Mr. Mason's band made him the equivalent of royalty in The Program. He out ranked me.

"Stop!"

The computer paused at my voice command. I shoved away from the desk and paced, twisting my hair tight enough to break it off at the roots. "There's been a mistake. His band has five diamonds, not four!"

Alex's forehead twisted. "I don't get it. That's a good thing...isn't it?"

Brittany, also a candidate, her pink band trimmed with four diamonds like mine, understood immediately. "Not really. It means he can claim Marli."

Alex kneeled in the center of the bed, waving her candy straw like a magic wand. "So? The guy's hot."

"It's not that simple. If he claims me, I don't have a say in my own future."

She pointed at the handsome face frozen mid-sentence on the screen. "Hell of a 'future.' What's your problem? Someone who's smart, obviously rich, and beyond sexy, wants you."

"Exactly. Why me? His assignee should be a politician's daughter, or a wealthy heiress. Not some ordinary teenage girl from Ohio. I'm-I'm—" I leaned on my knees, breathed deep to get my lips to stop tingling. "—scared."

I backed against the wall, pressed a hand to my squirming stomach. The computer beeped, possibly alerting someone on the other side of the cyber-curtain. Before Jordan Mason's video request could open, I had to sign into The Program's database using my candidate identification number, allowing the government access to *my* computer.

Brit's brow rose when it chimed again. "Marli, do something."

"Go!"

"One last thing," Jordan said gently, "I know this whole setup is about an assigned mate, but you should know honesty is important to me. I need a girl in my life who's real. Someone sincere, compassionate, and funny. A sense of humor is important, if we're going to survive this."

*Survive this?*

"Stop!"

Alex threw her hands in the air. "Now what?"

I parked on the window seat and stared at the stilled close-up image. I knotted my T-shirt in my fist and tears choked my voice. "I can't do this. I'm only seventeen. What about college? A career?"

Alex fell back on the bed, her head hanging off the side. Her wide eyes looked at me upside down. "Davis, you're messed up." She pointed at the computer. "Look at him!"

I had no argument. Jordan Mason could be the finest example of the male species ever, and he seemed sincere—trustworthy. The computer started the countdown beep. I checked the screen. The camera shot had closed in on Jordan's face and my heart pushed my ribs.

"Alex, you don't understand."

She rolled over and crossed her legs behind her. "I understand that you get to have sex with that hunk."

Suddenly, my brain felt like it might explode. "Sex?"

"Duh? Do the math, Marli. 'Perfect boy plus perfect girl equals perfect baby.' That's what your stupid Program wants, isn't it? Outside a petri dish, there's only one way that's happening."

I stared at my bed as if seeing it for the first time. The mattress you laid on, the pillows your head sank into, the sheets you'd slip between *naked*. The computer chimed another warning. I glanced at the monitor. His eyes watched intently as if reading my thoughts. I swear I imagined his mouth twitch.

Brittany dropped beside me and pulled my fingers away from my mouth. "Quit biting your thumb." I traded thumb for lip. "And your bottom lip."

"I can't help it. I'm freaked out." I stared into the black eyes mirroring my fear. "Brit, I don't even know him."

She smoothed my hair. "You know The Program doesn't care about the emotional stuff. It's all about fulfilling a contract."

"While doing *IT* with *that* guy!" Alex razzed.

She lost her virginity to the backseat cushions of her boyfriend's car on her sixteenth birthday, and loved sharing her ideas on how Brittany and I could release our pent-up hormones.

"Shut up, Alex," I scolded, harsher than intended. Her cocky grin faded and she moved off the bed.

"Whatever. I'm just saying you could do worse. I'm going down to the kitchen. This sanctimonious crap has bored me to starvation."

The computer dinged a final warning. I faced a crossroads and as much as I wanted my friends here at the beginning, right now I wanted to be alone.

"Brit, do you mind going after her? I need to think."

"Don't do something stupid. Remember this is your freedom we're talking about. Don't let some dreamy-looking boy take it away. You're more than someone's genetic link."

As soon as the door clicked shut, I rushed to the computer. "Go," I softly commanded, noticing the skipped beat in my chest. I settled my chin on crossed arms, close to the electronic cage holding my destiny.

*But I'm his link.*

Jordan Mason's thick lashes swept against pinked cheeks and a ghost of a smile parted his lips. When his eyes lifted, his expression took on a boyish innocence. His voice dropped, soft and timid.

"Hope you accept my request."

At that instant, nothing else mattered. Something about him…that look, tugged my heart strings. A shiver slipped beneath my skin sending thousands of electrified pulses rushing through me. My stomach floated with excitement, my palms sweaty, and permanent teeth marks welted my bottom lip.

My finger hovered over the keyboard as if sensing the turmoil churning within me. For some reason I pretended it could never happen—me, "chosen." I held onto the fantasy I'd live life unscathed…unnoticed…normal.

But now? Candidate 2255, the heartthrob on my screen, wanted *me*. The thought petrified me, yet for some inexplicable reason, I felt drawn to him. I pressed "Accept" and released the breath I held captive. Jordan Mason disappeared, replaced by a confirmation number blinking in blinding red and some form with blank spaces requiring information.

A shimmer of stars twinkled behind my tightly squeezed eyelids. *Did I really just surrender my destiny to a boy in designer jeans?* The voice of reason deep in my brain fell silent—a loud confirmation I had.

Numb, I stumbled down the stairs, slithered along the wall and grasped the handles on the refrigerator as if blind. Brittany's eyes filled her face. My friends knew how to read me and the answer, undoubtedly, radiated on my face. However, I couldn't be certain if my expression showed joy or terror.

Brit's brows knotted. "What did you do?"

"I accepted the interview."

Alex punched the air with her fists and pranced around the kitchen singing the praises of my moral demise. "Wahoo! You're going to have sex with the hot guy!"

Brittany dipped her tea bag with so much force the tea sloshed over the rim of her cup. "Rick is going to kill you."

I tossed her a rag. "Probably." A smile pulled my mouth. "What's scarier? I don't care."

Or so I thought, until the next morning.

## 2
## THE INTERVIEW

Saturday. This morning I'd board a private jet bound for Florida while my friends headed to the mall to shop for dresses for Senior Ball, or to the beach to soak up some rays and color their winter-white bodies. They were free. They could spend hours in teenage bliss, ending with new clothes or a golden glow, but they wouldn't face anything life altering.

Unlike me. Today, I interviewed for my assigned mate.

Dad drove through the security gates to the private aviation area of Lorain County Regional and followed the painted arrows until we arrived at Hangar 4-B. A white Lear jet's nose pointed our direction and a flight attendant descended the stairs.

He scowled and tapped the dash several times. "For the record, young lady, I still don't approve of this. Swear *this* time you won't agree to anything until we talk?" He rubbed his stubbly chin. "Why do I bother? You've ignored my warnings so far."

Another argument brewed. We'd barely spoken the past two days. When I'd joined him for breakfast the morning after I'd watched the pod, the wrinkled red envelope sat next to my plate of waffles.

"You opened it," he'd snorted, the irritation in his tone unmistakable. "I hoped you'd let me return it to the courier service on my way to the clinic." His fork plunked loudly against the plate. "Marli, I thought we decided to discuss decisions regarding your candidacy together. The Program owns your future once you get involved. Do you understand this at all?"

I said nothing, picked at my food and stared at the still shot of Jordan Mason I'd downloaded on my pocket digital pad. Dad snatched the pad from my fingers.

"I'm talking to a hormone-filled brick wall. *Boys*," he grumbled.

Up to that point, my interest in the opposite sex stayed limited to an on-again-off-again relationship with my high school boyfriend, Sam Jenkins. Romance hadn't been a priority in my life. But that was before Candidate 2255.

I remember nervously clearing my throat a dozen times, trying to hide my excitement before making the fateful announcement I'd accepted the request for an interview. Dad's explosive response had resulted in a broken plate and sticky syrup spattered across the floor.

"You *what?* But you're still in high school. Dammit Marli! How could you do something so foolish?"

At the time it didn't feel that way, but reflecting back and facing the private plane taking me to Florida today, "foolish" might be a mild interpretation. I prided myself in being levelheaded, not impulsive, and certainly not impressed by superficial things like drop-dead gorgeous boys. Apparently, I didn't know myself at all.

Anxiety crept over me. "Dad, can we not fight? I'm nervous enough and don't want to leave with bad feelings between us." I worried my thumbnail, feeling the edges of my eyes burn. "I'm sorry, okay?"

He grabbed a handful of my hair and gave a playful tug to get my attention. "Don't cry. You'll mess up your pretty face." He brushed the hair over my shoulder. "I'm sorry, too. Your old man isn't ready for you to grow up, and I'm certainly not happy about turning you over to some boy the government's chosen."

"It's just an interview, Dad. You're not getting rid of me anytime soon." A light knock tapped the window to the side of my head. "I have to go." I opened the door and he caught my arm.

"Be careful, Marli. I love you."

The brass wall of the private elevator felt cold against my back and I pressed tighter, wishing I could disappear into one of my many reflections. The numbers quickly scrolled on the way to some stranger's penthouse, each floor passing on a delicate ping. Above the touch panel, a digital clock tapped out the time.

By now, my friends had gathered at favorite hangouts for lunch. The girls would babble on about dresses, jewelry and shoes, and the boys would watch their lips, waiting for the moment they could latch on and shut them up. Kiss away the chatter.

Their decisions from this point, depending on the kiss, would give them a hint on how Saturday *night* might turn out. They only had to worry about one night, not a lifetime; the choices made theirs—not the government's. Now that I'd accepted the interview request, I danced to whatever marionette string my puppeteer pulled.

The metal carriage bumped slightly when it reached the top floor. The elevator doors opened to a foyer with a pale, colorless floor polished to a high sheen, and walls painted a faint shade of apricot. The ceiling sparkled with tiny lights set inside mirrored panels. When I stepped over the threshold under the radiance, I wondered if I'd actually crossed into another dimension. Beneath my feet, the floor glowed in bright fuchsia pink and if I lifted my foot, the color vanished, reappearing under my next step.

A security camera hummed, slowly sweeping over the foyer. An eerie feeling shimmied up my spine knowing someone was already evaluating me. I twisted a lock of hair tightly around my finger as if the silken lifeline could keep me from falling into an unknown abyss. Fingering the pink band strangling my wrist, I fought against the panic bubbling in my chest.

At the end of the hallway stretching before me, two intricately carved doors guarded the penthouse. Fear locked my feet to the floor as if held by imaginary magnets, unable to move closer to my worse fear, possibly poised behind the beckoning gates. Until a week ago, I never knew Candidate 2255 existed. Jordan Mason. Confident, boldly honest, and the most incredible looking boy I'd ever seen. Me? Candidate 5846: Marli Davis. Seventeen and scared to death.

Fifteen glowing pink footsteps ended at the penthouse entrance. When prompted, I scanned my wristband over the identification monitor, announcing my arrival. The floor returned to a ghostly gloss and the doors opened.

An older gentleman stood in the entry, his cheery wink crumpling one eye easing my anxiety. I followed him to an elegant sitting room, self-conscious of the loud echo trying to catch us as my heels tapped the granite floor.

A delicate vanilla scent settled on the air in the spacious surroundings. Two white leather couches framed a low table with an arrangement of fresh orange lilies in the center. I caressed the armrest of one sofa, the supple leather soft as velvet. Only the wealthy could afford such fine quality leather.

Across the room, a wall of windows spanned ceiling to floor. In the distance, the harbor glistened, the wharfs lined with numerous vessels. A few sailboats drifted lazily on the azure waters. Almost a serene scene, if dark sinister ships didn't frame the outskirts of the bay.

Border patrols.

Not since the year 2040 had anyone traveled outside this country without undergoing rigorous government screenings. I figured that if you were rich enough you could probably bribe your way through the hassle. Otherwise, you had to be involved with the government, or have a candidate in The Program. Another perk or trade-off.

In an attempt to quell my nerves, I wandered to a black baby grand piano in the far corner. Eighty-eight polished keys glistened in the afternoon sun. I held down the left una-corde pedal with my foot to soften the sound before depressing Middle C.

I recognized the waxy feel of the real ivory key versus a slick manufactured one, the tone rich in the belly of the piano, even with the lid closed. I was nine years old the last time I played a piano with ivory keys. The upright tucked against the dining room wall at home had the plastic keys, even though it was close to forty years old. The piano before me had to be a family heirloom, although it looked as if it had barely rolled off the assembly line.

I closed my eyes, my fingers exploring the naturals and accidentals. I depressed D…then E…ventured to F and dropped back to C, carefully repeating the two measures. The image of Grandma Adams patiently teaching me to play flashed in my mind and I felt myself fall into the childhood memory, forgetting where I stood. Until my toe tapped the right sustain pedal and I hit the high F, ready to launch into my favorite piece of music: Tchaikovsky's "The Dance of the Sugar Plum Fairy."

The note rang out in the spacious room, piercing my daydream and stealing my breath. Quickly I released the pedal and stilled, waiting for someone to scold me for touching the piano in the first place before kicking me out altogether. No one came and the room fell silent again.

Cautiously, I rounded the side of the piano. Several silver framed pictures dotted the closed lid. A surprised breath caught in my throat. Apparently, my assignee told the truth about his so-called "passions." He stood next to a racecar in one digital print. In another, the photographer captured him under the canopy of a deep, aquamarine wave on a surfboard. The third framed image showed him sitting on a rock against a blazing sunset with a guitar resting on his knee.

I brought the picture closer for inspection and discovered the silhouetted boy was not my assignee, but ran a close second on the gorgeous meter.

"That picture was taken last summer."

Startled, I slammed the frame down, knocking several others over. When I twirled to face the voice, my foot rocked to the side and the boy from the picture caught my hand.

"Sorry, I didn't mean to scare you." His chocolate brown eyes slowly swept over me. "So you're Jordan's candidate." He turned my wrist and examined the pink bracelet holding me captive. "Only four diamonds? From what I see, you're definitely worth five."

A flash of heat crawled up my neck and an unsettling sensation awakened with his questioning...or maybe it was how my hand felt inside his. I pulled away, but the feeling remained. He reached around me and righted the toppled pictures. When he glanced sideways, he caught me staring and the glimmer in his eyes spiked my inner thermostat.

"What's your name? The only reference I've seen is your number, '5846.'"

"Who are you?"

A striking resemblance to my assigned candidate, almost a *duplicate*, but science hadn't mastered human cloning. Sandy blond hair, lighter and longer than my assignee's, swept away from chiseled facial features kissed golden by the sun. Black shorts and a white T-shirt with a surfer hologram, stretched tight over a muscular chest. A smug grin pulled the corners of his mouth at my obvious, although brief, eye roll over the length of his body. The burn intensified on my cheeks.

"Doesn't matter who I am. You're not here for me. Damn shame, though. After seeing you, I'm regretting some past choices."

I checked out the band circling his arm. Yellow—not blue.

He shook his wrist. "Not the royal blue you're destined for, but *yellow* at least allows me to have a life."

The strange boy wandered to the keyboard, completing the refrain I started. "Tchaikovsky? You play the 'big guns.' Sugar Plum Fairy, correct?"

"Yes, it's my favorite piece. Sorry, I shouldn't have touched the piano. It's so beautiful, and the ivory keys...I couldn't resist."

He pulled the lid over the keyboard while his eyes held my gaze, a direct "hands off" gesture. I tried not to let my embarrassment show, but I knew my skin already mottled with red patches from the heat stinging behind my eyes.

"My grandfather's. He played piano in nightclubs to pay for college. My grandmother gave him this piano for their twenty-fifth wedding anniversary. When they died, the piano became ours."

The curious part of me wanted to know what happened, but being a stranger, not to mention having experienced a recent death in my own family, I knew unless the information was volunteered, questions shouldn't be asked. I gave the standard reply, realizing now it's something said more out of respect than honesty.

"I'm sorry for your loss."

He stepped forward before I could react, his face close enough I could see gold flecks in the irises of his eyes. His thumb gently traced over my cheek and I flinched, moving away.

Confusion, fear, and an unexpected thrill twisted inside my stomach. Even if he wasn't my assigned candidate, I figured he probably shouldn't be here. Nor should I have felt tingling sparks when he touched my skin.

"Strange floor in the foyer," I said, changing the subject.

"Security floor—instantly senses a person's emotions. So, are you really afraid?'"

I stared, confused.

"Pink. Yellow is happy, red means angry, and pink equals fear. Your footsteps flashed bright. *Very* scared." His brow tweaked upward. "Then there's purple."

"Purple?" I asked, taking another backward step.

He followed my retreat. "Passion."

"Passion? Really?" I questioned the fact a floor could judge hormonal overload.

"Supposedly. I think my parents had the thing created to tattle on us when we came home past curfew—kind of like an electronic 'chastity meter.'"

I laughed, immediately covering my mouth. "*Parents*. They can be a pain sometimes."

When he smiled, the dimple in his right cheek deepened. "More often than not. I don't understand how the floor works. Something about thermal readings…scientific 'voodoo.' As long as it doesn't flash green."

"Green?"

He shifted his gaze to the ceiling. "Chemical or alcohol consumption."

"I'm guessing that's happened to you?"

His shoulders shrugged, a sly grin twisting his mouth. "I'll never tell." He stepped into the space I vacated and pulled a strand of my hair through his fingers. "Damn, you're a knock-out. Jordan's one lucky bastard."

Mr. "Yellow Band" frightened me and yet, I couldn't move away. A surprise twinge of anxiety squeezed my chest. I didn't want to move away.

"Jesse! Step away from her." The woman's sharp voice slammed my heart to my toes, and I teetered again on my four-inch spikes. He caught my elbow and she glowered. "What do you think you're doing, young man?"

"Leaving, what else." He gave her a dismissive salute and disappeared, but the warmth on my arm from his touch lingered.

Right then I decided Jesse was dangerous—and forbidden.

"I'm sorry for that unfortunate display."

She stood in the doorway leading to a formal dining room, her slender frame silhouetted by the shaft of light behind her. Wisps of gray threaded through the dark blonde hair bordering her face. I dropped my eyes against her hard stare, realizing she also assessed me.

She gestured to the leather couches, omitting any introduction. Not required. Candidates weren't allowed to meet, let alone conduct their own interviews. Too risky. Personal emotions couldn't play a part.

"Judgment can be clouded by emotional attachment," explained my counselor. *Shelve the heart and you won't get hurt*, according to me.

The cushion I settled on cradled like a soft cloud. I watched her readjust the same pictures Jesse had before gracefully perching on the opposite sofa. An awkward silence captured the moment. Trying to be subtle, I turned my head slightly. No sign of Jesse, but I felt certain he remained close.

"I apologize for my son's inappropriate behavior. I don't understand him, sometimes," she sighed. "Jesse is Jordan's twin, although they're not identical. I suppose it's all right to tell you that. I'm new at this. Jordan is our first to proceed this far." A slight smile flickered on her mouth. "Oops. I suppose I just let my identity slip. I'm their mother, Eva Mason."

She sucked a deep breath. "Jesse was also in The Program, but circumstances changed his course. He's now pursuing a career in music."

"So, Jesse's musical ambitions? Classical or modern?" A snicker echoed from somewhere down the hall.

She considered my question, leaned forward and lowered her voice. "Unfortunately, modern. He's in some new age rock band."

"Is he any good?"

Her demeanor changed instantly. "I think we've discussed Jesse enough. After all, you're here to interview for Jordan." Her brusque reminder sent a wave of heat over my face once again.

She concentrated intently on the contents of the digital file framed in her hands, a finger tapping her bottom lip. "According to your records, your father is a veterinarian. I assume you were raised around animals?" Her nose wrinkled for a second as if she smelled something bad.

"Animals have always been a part of my life. I love them. During the summer, I work at Rick's, *er*, my father's clinic."

Her rose painted lips pursed. "Rick?"

"'Rick' is my dad's name. I called him that before 'daddy,' according to my mother. Sometimes, I slip."

"It's unusual." Her curt tone told me she didn't approve. "Speaking of your mother, your file indicates she currently serves with our military overseas. Is that correct?"

"Yes. I believe she's stationed somewhere in Greece."

"You *believe?* You're not certain of your own mother's whereabouts?"

We'd hit a touchy subject. My mother and I hadn't been on the best of terms since she and Grandma Davis hijacked my life. My candidacy opened the door to a military job my mom had wanted for years, only there happened to be a captain standing behind it my father didn't know about. I wasn't sure which I felt angriest at her for—deceiving me…or Dad.

"I haven't had much contact with my mother since she deployed," I quickly offered. "To be honest, I seldom hear from her."

Jordan's mother's eyes dropped, her tone sharp and the next comment, I suspected, not directed at me. "Yes, well government jobs can sometimes be very demanding." She quickly scrolled to another page. "Your brother, Daniel, also served in the armed forces?"

"Yes." My answer drifted out on a whisper and I braced myself for what always followed. Hearing the words, however, opened the painful wound.

"It states here he was killed in the line of duty." Her eyes found mine when I grew quiet and I looked away. "I'm sorry for your loss," the words bouncing back, borrowed from the air where I'd left them earlier. "His death must have been difficult for you."

The salty sting of tears burned behind my eyes. The pain still felt raw and the flashback served up the same haunting nightmare.

*...Always the black military shuttle pulls in front of the house. Two officers appear at the door. They hand me a small metal box containing what is left of my brother's "personal effects." Only one thing prevents me from toppling off the porch. Muffy, my Great Dane, who for once in her life stands absolutely still and holds me against the brick wall with her weight, until the shuttle disappears from my sight...*

I blinked away the mental keepsake and returned to the present, but my emotional reaction didn't pass unnoticed.

"Miss Davis? Are you all right?"

I straightened, fighting back sudden tears, but a couple dripped over my cheek. She reached into her pocket and handed me a lace edged handkerchief. A deep breath restored my voice. "It's only been a few months since the funeral. Daniel and I were close. I really miss him."

"You're still grieving, aren't you? If I'd known it was so recent, I certainly would have been more delicate." Her gaze drifted, her voice diminishing. "Losing someone close is heartbreaking."

She placed the digital file on the corner of the table. "Let's change the subject, shall we? First, may I call you Marli?" I nodded absently. "Good. Marli, tell me your reasons for accepting Jordan's request for an interview."

What sounded simple was, in fact, the opposite. The reasons I accepted this interview, and in particular Jordan, could either win me over in her eyes, or send me packing. No second chances with interviews.

"Jordan said he loves animals. I'm planning to become a veterinarian, so my future has to include someone who likes them as much as I do."

Declaring my intentions for a future other than doting on her son was risky, but a stand I needed to make known. It was more than becoming a vet—it was about me controlling my own destiny.

Mrs. Mason grabbed my file again, her brows tangling as she scanned the pages. "Jordan likes animals? This is news to me. Maybe when he researched your data file he saw your interest in working with them and said so to impress you?"

I bristled at the accusation. "No, actually he couldn't have. There's nothing on my profile about my passion for animals. That's why he impressed me. It was the first thing Jordan mentioned when he talked about things he liked."

She placed the electronic pad on the sofa cushion to her side, then leaned forward, hands folded tightly. "Marli, you know Jordan is in medical school. He's also being groomed for the research team specializing in human cloning. You should rethink a technical career—something more suiting a prime candidate, not to mention socially acceptable as Jordan's life partner, should he choose you. Leave the animal doctoring to those outside The Program."

Anger sizzled. "Animal doctors," in my opinion, were every bit as respectable as brain surgeons and just as I was about to argue the point, Mrs. Mason brought me up short with an even more shocking statement.

"Of course, you could become pregnant right away, which would also serve the greater purpose, and in fact, be preferable to all parties concerned."

All thoughts of animals vanished. Panic shoved my anger aside immediately. "*Pregnant?* No way!" My heart clamored in my throat. No one prepared me for this particular line of questioning, and my unruly answer came as a gut reaction.

She steeled her anger only slightly. "I'm sorry. Do you have a problem with producing Jordan's child? I thought you understood, Miss Davis. That is the purpose of your candidacy and the fundamental reason you're here."

*It is? No, it can't be!*

Suddenly, I wanted to bolt from the room, but I pretended to be unaffected by her announcement and picked my words carefully. "I know what's expected, but I'm not rushing into being a chosen breeder. I'm accomplishing something for me, first."

After my disrespectful outburst, Jordan's mother abruptly ended the interview. What miniscule of warmth shown me earlier, iced. I'd botched things, big time. Maybe she'd remember something redeeming before everything went sideways.

Not likely.

If I couldn't think of one, neither would she. As the moderator, I knew her opinion weighed heavily on whether to choose me. Ultimately, the decision would be Jordan's, which left me little hope.

I never met Jordan.

# 3
# HIJACKED

Discouraged, I sank into a chair near the front doors of the lobby to wait for my car service. I retrieved my cell receptor from my purse to check messages, finding an instant readout from Sam.

*Hey babe, coming back to me? Miss you.*

I entered a quick *call you later* and shut my receptor off. My thoughts were a mess and I couldn't handle more guilt. Sam wasn't in The Program. We could date until my candidacy activated as long as we never crossed a certain line, physically. An entire page in my contract with The Program dictated I remained a virgin. *No contaminating the gene pool.* Losing my virtuous status would get me kicked out.

It would also set me free.

Even though it seemed almost everyone I knew outside The Program had experimented with sex by my age, I didn't feel ready. Maybe it had something to do with my parents' screwed-up relationship, or Alex always freaking out if her period didn't come on time, but I figured it had more to do with wanting to fall in love first—real love, not *lust*.

I pulled out my pocket data pad with the intention of working on the assignment due Monday in my Human Relations core class, a prerequisite for candidates, centering on the psyche of relationships. Instead, I opened the file labeled "Fantasy."

The digital image of Jordan Mason I'd downloaded filled the screen. I drew an imaginary line down the bridge of his nose with my finger. The small bump in the center humanized him. A simple flaw on an otherwise perfect face someone else might find unattractive, to me erased any trace of vanity.

*Does he have a sense of humor or take life seriously?* A definite brainiac if he graduated early and already involved in some accelerated medical program. My finger continued along the line of his jaw. *Maybe he plays a musical instrument like his brother. The piano like me?* His hands looked strong. *What would my hands feel like tangled in his?* I touched his mouth. He had an amazing smile—the way it curved those full lips, marking the dimples on each side. *I wonder if his lips are soft or firm when he kisses.* Too bad I'd never find out, given how the interview ended.

I shut the display off. At least I didn't have to worry about his first impression of me anymore. Nope, I could cross Jordan Mason off my nightly "dream team" and return back to my boring life in Ohio. Romance was overrated. At least that's what I told myself. Still, I couldn't help the emptiness I felt. Spending a lifetime getting to know Jordan Mason seemed like the ideal happily-ever-after, even if within the confines of The Program.

The doorman hailed me when a silver Mercedes stopped at the curb. He'd barely shut my door before the car rocketed into traffic.

"Miami International, please."

The driver gave an affirmative nod. A few minutes later, however, the airport exit sign passed. "Excuse me, but you missed the turn off." No response. All the air inside the car seemed to disappear and my palms turned sticky. I spoke louder. "You need to turn around. I can't miss my plane." A fearful shakiness appeared on the last word.

"Your flight is delayed, Miss Davis." The voice sounded familiar. I slid to the center of the backseat to see the driver's face in the rearview mirror. When he glanced up, I recognized the dark brown eyes and teasing smirk immediately, and the beginnings of an anxiety attack threatened.

"Jesse? What's going on? This isn't funny. If your mother finds out we're together, she'll call the authorities."

"By the time she figures it out, you'll be safely on your way home. Besides, we didn't have a chance to get acquainted. Nice interview by the way. I loved how you caught Mom off-guard with the 'animal' thing. Jordan will catch hell for that. She's a control freak and would detest some stranger telling her something about him she didn't know."

"I don't think the animal issue was the deal breaker."

"Huh? Did I miss something?"

"Only my total flip-out for the grand finale. Jesse, please go back."

"What happened?"

"If you don't mind, I don't want to talk about it."

He flashed another sexy smile. "Fine. Keep your little secret." The car continued down the interstate, Jesse's eyes on me and not the highway. "Want to take a side trip with me?"

Given our first encounter made my knees weak, the thought of going anywhere alone with Jesse worried me.

"I don't think so, and I'm serious—turn this car around."

"Don't tell me you're afraid of me?"

"Of course I'm not afraid of you." Petrified would be a better description. "I don't want either of us to get into trouble."

"Where's the fun in that? Mommy will be occupied for the next couple hours, anyway. She's doing another interview."

My fingernails dug into the edges of the butter-soft upholstery. Jordan requested someone else to interview? *Selection A.* Did that mean I was his first choice or The Program's? Silly of me to think I could be the only candidate Jordan Mason asked to interview. Blue banded and five diamonds ensured he'd have his pick of top candidates and after my award winning performance, the decision would be easy. I hated feeling a twinge of jealousy over some boy I'd never met.

Jesse interrupted my thoughts. "I'll let you in on a secret. You don't have to worry about other candidates. I'm sure you're already chosen."

"Then you know zilch. Trust me. I messed up, royally."

"I don't think that's possible."

"Totally possible, and if your mother has any say, I'll be the last candidate considered."

"I'm telling you, Mars, Jordan's already made up his mind."

"Mars? Don't. That's my dad's nickname for me. And how would you know anything about what your brother wants?"

"Because he's been instant messaging constantly and I told him either he chose you, or I'd sway you my way." Another playful grin curled on Jesse's mouth. "And like it or not, *Mars* sticks because someone as pretty as you can't be from this planet."

"Beyond pathetic."

Peering out the front windshield, I noticed boats, not planes come into view, and the shimmer of water appeared on the horizon. "Where are we going?"

Jesse flashed a dangerous smile, one holding a secret. "I want to show you something."

I leaned over the seat. "What about my flight? The pilot is expecting me." *Breathe Marli.* "Dammit Jesse! I can't be late!"

"Calm down. You're with your pilot."

"What? You're joking, right?" His shoulders lifted slightly. I slid back into the seat, officially trapped. I clenched the hem of my skirt and snarled my frustration. "Great! I'm a hostage."

Jesse laughed. "You're cute when you're mad. I like how your mouth does that little corkscrew thing."

I pinned an infuriated glower to the eyes watching me from the rearview mirror. He blew a loud sigh and let me fume. A few minutes later, he braved jumping back into conversation.

"So your flight here. Awful?"

"You flew me to Miami, too?"

"Sure did."

Concentrating on smoothing the creases in my skirt, I kept my eyes down and attempted playing nice. "How long have you been a pilot?"

"We actually got our licenses before our driving permits."

I'd forgotten Jordan listed "flying" among his many accomplishments.

Casually, I slung my arm over the back of Jesse's seat. "Do you fly helicopters too?"

An unreadable expression covered his face. "Not exactly."

"How do you *not exactly* fly a helicopter?"

He kept his eyes trained on the traffic. "I never took the flight test. Aced the written exam, but something came up before I got a chance to pass the practical part."

"Why don't you do it now?"

"It's complicated. And personal," he replied, all humor gone.

"Personal, I get." I let it go and perched my chin on my arm. My nose was inches from his neck, the alluring scent of his spicy cologne mixed with citrus-fragranced shampoo emanating off his skin. "So where are you taking me?" the question sounding too husky to be innocent. I eased away, catching the hint of a smile on his mouth in the rearview mirror.

*Crap.*

His answer came out equally rough. "The harbor. I told you I have something to show you, but I need a boat."

"Let me guess. Not a canoe?"

"Slightly bigger," he replied inside a chuckle.

A few minutes later, we arrived at the marina. The faint smell of fish and motor oil clung to the humid afternoon air. Water spouted in small bursts between the joints of the pier, spraying the toes of my new patent leather shoes. At the end of the wharf, a massive white yacht, aptly named *HER MAJESTY,* bobbed in the water.

Definitely not a canoe.

Jesse took my hand and led me up the boarding ramp. Once aboard, I followed him down the gangway, gliding my fingers over the smooth fiberglass sides of the ship. He climbed a gleaming chrome spiral staircase to another deck. I twisted back and forth below, not knowing what to do—run, scream, or jump overboard. Given how unlucky the day had proven so far, I'd probably miss the water and hit the cement pier.

Jesse leaned over the railing from above. "You coming? We'll only be gone a couple hours, tops, and I swear I won't dump your bony ass overboard."

I chomped the corner of my lip, debating. *What harm can come from a boat ride?* I climbed the stairs, standing toe-to-toe with him.

"Two hours. And my ass isn't bony."

The cruiser slipped silently through the marina, sending ripples outward that gently rocked the vessels moored to the docks. Jesse caught my puzzled look when he slid a bright green flag into the post beside a glass panel.

"This saves us from having to stop for the border patrols."

"How do they know you're not stealing the yacht?"

"Because this ship requires special clearance before it can leave the marina."

"So you already assumed I'd come?"

"Let's say I hoped and wanted to be prepared."

After we cleared the border sentries, Jesse veered the yacht into open waters. He lifted a small radio from the control panel.

"Mike? Jess. Thanks for the clearance, but I need one more favor. Call Dr. Richard Davis in Maple Heights, Ohio, and inform him his daughter's flight is delayed. Tell him we'll arrange her transportation home to make up for the inconvenience."

"Jess, if I'd known—don't. Turn around," squawked a demand. "It's not worth the risk."

Jesse's gaze raked over me before he countered. "I beg to differ. Better scramble the frequency on the boat, too. I don't want to be tracked."

"You'll owe me for this one, Mason."

"Put it on my tab. And stop worrying." He disconnected and increased speed.

I fought to hide my sudden panic. "Scramble what frequency?"

Jesse gave my pink bracelet a spin. "You're on radar. I don't need the military out looking for you."

A surge of fear blossomed as I watched Miami's skyline quickly disappear at the end of a long, frothy wake.

*Great, Marli. If you're murdered, no one will ever find your body.*

The spring sun overhead burned bright, and sparkling ruffles resembling fine lace edged the curls of navy blue water splashing the yacht. A brisk breeze slapped my face, holding some of spring's coolness. Jesse touched my shoulder, startling me.

"Come, help me navigate."

I stood between him and the helm, the warmth of his body behind me, chasing off the chill. He placed my hands on the wheel, covering them with his own.

When he leaned over my shoulder, our cheeks brushed and my heart jumped. "See that large island in the distance?" I played along, spying several peaks rising out of the midnight blue horizon. "Beyond there is my family's private island. The water is unbelievably clear and the coral reefs beneath are awesome. That's what I want to show you."

He banked the yacht to the left and a few minutes later, floated into a small bay. After dropping anchor, we descended the stairs to the main deck. Jesse eased a hip on a barstool in the galley.

"Have you ever snorkeled?"

A surprise giggle blurted from my mouth. "No, Lake Erie isn't exactly known for scuba activities."

"It's easy. I'll teach you."

I tugged my skirt. "I'm not exactly dressed for water sports."

"My sister's about your size and she left several swimsuits in her cabin."

"Sister?" Nobody said anything in my interview about other siblings. Another missing puzzle piece surfaced.

Jesse towed me down a small corridor paneled in rich, cinnamon-colored wood. He opened the door to a small cabin and leaned against the frame, his expression sobering.

"My older sister, Kate, was in The Program and set up to interview with some law student in Manhattan, but she never showed. The police found her broken pink bracelet in her apartment on a note saying she'd run off with one of her college professors. She called my parents a few days later and said she was safe, but not returning. We think she's living somewhere in Canada."

"Oh my. Do you miss her?"

Jesse's toe scuffed at a wood plank. "Sometimes. I figure she's happy, or she'd have come home." A smile brightened his handsome face. "Check the overhead cubby and see if you can find something to wear. I'll get the gear and meet you on the rear deck in fifteen minutes."

The words Mrs. Mason spoke earlier made sense. *"Jordan is our first to proceed this far."* Now I wondered about Jesse's story.

A slow whistle pushed through Jesse's lips when I emerged from the galley. "You fill that bikini better than Kate ever did. Too bad you didn't post a bathing suit shot on your profile."

An embarrassing burn crept over me and I reached for a towel to cover up. When Jesse called my name, I whipped around just as his pen camera clicked, capturing an image of me in Kate's green polka-dot bikini.

"Jordan's search for perfection has ended. At the very least, he'll be jealous as hell." He tilted his chin. "Come on, sexy. Time to swim with the sharks."

"What?" I gasped.

"I'm joking. I promise to keep you safe."

All sorts of perils lurked in deep water, but I doubted any as dangerous as the one watching me with intense chocolate eyes. *Sharks* had to be safer than Jesse Mason.

Snorkeling along the surface, I watched fish of different sizes and brilliant colors play hide-and-seek among the coral. Jesse held my hand, keeping me from straying too far. However, when he curved his arm around my waist, an unexpected sensation, both delightful and terrifying skittered. When I rolled out of his reach, my snorkel tube dipped below the surface.

I attempted to cough up a lung as I climbed the ladder to the deck with legs wobbling like wet noodles. Jesse unsnapped my life vest and slapped between my shoulder blades.

"I think I swallowed half the ocean," I croaked when he asked if I was okay.

A shiver rolled over me when a cool gust of wind circled my wet body. Jesse wrapped a warm towel around my shoulders, holding me close. Water dripped from his long eyelashes like lingering raindrops. Chilled, pebbled skin rippled his arms and chest, making the droplets on his skin shimmer.

When his head tilted, I did nothing to stop the tentative kiss he placed on my lips. A delicate brush on my mouth, delivered with eyes open, awestruck...frightened. His eyes darkened to the color of bittersweet cocoa and a second, hungrier kiss captured my mouth, his tongue playful and sensual at the same time. I circled my arms around his neck and leaned into the deepening kiss, the towel dropping to my feet, leaving bare skin pressed to bare skin.

My toes *curled*. In two years of kissing Sam, my toes never curled.

A hard swallow rolled down Jesse's throat. "You should get dressed. I need to get you on that plane before Mike's tortured into telling where we are."

After changing, I found Jesse on the bridge readying the yacht for sailing. His eyes rolled a visual inspection over me. Not much to look at now. All makeup had washed away, the freckles I'd painstakingly hidden exposed, and my nose a rosy pink from the sun. I braided my wet hair to keep it from turning into a frizzy mess.

Jesse's hands framed my waist. "Check out the cute freckles dotting your nose."

"They make me look like I'm ten years old."

I stepped out of his arms, but he caught my wrists, tugging me back. His fingers tickled a heated trail down my arm. "Marli, trust me, you don't look ten years old. His arm slid around my waist, his breath hot against my cheek.

"Jesse, are you always this forward with girls?"

"Only the ones I like," he replied inside a gravelly whisper.

"You make me nervous."

His gaze dropped to my mouth and I knew what came next, but somewhere between the wet bikini and dry clothes, common sense found me. I pressed my hand to his chest to hold him back.

"About the kiss," I started.

"The one earlier or the one I'm about to give you now?"

"There isn't going to be a 'now.' The first one should never have happened."

Jesse's arms fell away and the chilled breeze wrapped me instead. He leaned against the railing to the side of me and I turned away, letting my thoughts swim with the waves lapping the sides of the ship.

"I wasn't trying to come on to you, if that's what you think. That kiss happened because it was meant to, Marli. The second I saw you—"

"Jesse stop! You and I...*this*," I gestured to our surroundings, "is wrong. I could get in serious trouble. Remember, you're not my assignee—your brother is."

He pushed off the railing. "Don't remind me. I know my place."

"That's not what I meant."

Jesse flipped a series of switches, ignoring me.

"Just take me back so I can catch a flight home before I do anything else stupid today."

"Like kissing me?" He slammed the throttle and the boat surged against the waves. I grabbed the railing to catch myself. "Sit down before you fall. I don't want to be accused of any other *stupid* acts."

"Now you're being a jerk. Sorry if I offended you. And, it's *me* who's acting irresponsible."

I waited for another snarky reply, but Jesse said nothing and concentrated on the vast carpet of aqua stretched before us. I stared at him—his toned body standing rigid against the wind, his hair fitfully brushing around the chiseled planes of his handsome face. My conscience chastised loudly when I licked my lips searching for a remnant of the forbidden kiss.

What was wrong with me? I'd let my hormonal heart take Jordan's twin brother for a test drive!

As if reading my thoughts, Jesse turned, a slight smirk tugging his mouth. "For the record, *Miss Davis*, I'm taking you home, so no arguing when we dock. The last thing you want is to draw attention to our sordid affair by taking a commercial flight."

"I don't think an innocent kiss qualifies as an affair.

"Innocent? What happened between our lips? Anything but and you know it."

Traffic congestion increased as we approached the airport. Some rock song played in the background, being the only sound inside the car since we left the marina.

"So now I get the silent treatment?"

Jesse didn't even glance sideways.

I twisted my thumbs, adjusted my skirt for the hundredth time. "O-*kaay*," I said to the window. After everything that had gone wrong today, I decided I'd probably never see Jesse again either, so I asked the ultimate question.

"Why do you wear a yellow band?"

Jesse didn't look at me when he answered, his tone cool. "What makes you think I haven't always worn one?"

"Your mother told me you were in The Program."

"She shouldn't have."

Patience didn't hold as my strongest virtue and my frustrated sigh filled the car. "Well…she did," I semi-whispered to my new friend "Window."

Jesse switched the satellite channel off, leaving a deafening quiet inside the car. I glanced over my shoulder. A mischievous grin twisted his mouth. "Candidate 2256 and five diamonds."

"Did you drop out?"

"More like kicked out and no, I'm not telling you why."

"You kind of owe me, don't you think? After all, you kidnapped me this afternoon."

"I didn't hold a gun to your head."

*No, you held you lips to mine instead,* but no need to resurrect that subject.

The car came to a stop and a robotic voice beeped in. "Toll booth malfunction. Approximate delay thirty minutes."

Jesse fisted a tuft of hair. "Damn. Wish this car hovered. We're running late."

"Isn't it illegal to hover?"

Cars still rolled on four tires, but government vehicles and designated commuter shuttles had the ability to air glide, using special lanes. The government banned private vehicles from being converted. The closest citizens could get were recreational hoverboards. I had an orange one buried somewhere in the back of my closet. Just as my thought closed, a couple of emergency units flew by.

Jesse's smirk dimpled his cheek. "I doubt anyone would notice if we flew down a side street."

"Right. A Mercedes lifting out of a traffic jam and flying over a bunch of cars would never catch anyone's attention. Give me a break."

His smile widened. "I guess it would have to be a really fast Mercedes. One the police couldn't catch."

"Do you always think like a criminal? Rules are in place for a reason."

Jesse took my hand, placing a light kiss on my wrist. "Rules can be broken, you know."

An unexpected stomach flutter made me pull my hand back. "Not all rules." The corner of his mouth tweaked and I quickly diverted my thoughts. I cleared my throat, drawing a cleansing breath.

"Is that what happened? You broke a rule big enough to get expelled from The Program?"

"Sort of."

I slipped my shoes off, turned in the seat and folded one leg beneath me. "Please tell me. We're stuck here anyway."

"Promise you won't freak out?"

"No. But, I'll try."

A couple of silent minutes passed uninterrupted. Jesse turned the car off and tipped his head toward the ceiling, closing his eyes. His tenor weighed heavy with regret, no…sadness.

"Last year I was arrested and entered into an agreement with The Program. If I voluntarily withdrew my candidacy, they'd make the charges disappear."

A sudden coldness slammed my core . "What did you do?"

"I didn't *do* anything. They found me innocent before the file sealed, only it was too late. My candidacy had terminated and my blue wrist shackle became bright yellow."

"If you were innocent, why didn't they automatically change everything back?

"Because I didn't want it reversed."

Traffic started moving again and Jesse faced forward, surely hoping I'd stop peppering him with questions. Not a chance.

"What were you arrested for?"

He did nothing to mask the irritation in his voice. "Marli, it doesn't matter. I said they proved me innocent."

I slapped the dash. "It matters to me! I spent the afternoon in the middle of the ocean with the frequency on my bracelet scrambled. I think I have a right to know *what* you were accused of. For all I know, you were charged with murder!"

"Rape!" he shouted back. "Satisfied?"

My heart jumped in my chest. *Rape?* The word formed on my lips but remained silent. I swallowed deep, searching for a quieter version of my voice.

"So…you're *not* a murderer."

Jesse chuckled with a heavy outgoing breath, and the tension squeezing the oxygen out of the car, eased. "Prepare yourself for one twisted story."

He wove a tale of how one night after doing a gig with his band in New Jersey, they snuck into a bar, hoping no one would check their ID. The bartender brought them bottles of beer, compliments of some girls. Jesse never remembered leaving the bar, but woke up the next morning surprised by a half-naked girl in his bed, accusing him of rape. Given his flirty behavior, I'd think a half-naked girl in his bed would be anything but surprising. However, the prick of jealousy I felt shocked me.

"How did you find out you didn't…um…*rape* her?"

Jesse didn't answer and took the exit to the airport. I remained quiet, waiting while he maneuvered the parking labyrinth. If by some miracle I came into this family, I wanted the skeletons out of the closet first. He parked the Mercedes in a slot marked RESERVED and angled toward me.

"So? What magic was performed to clear you?" I pressed.

"You sound like you don't believe me."

"You make it that way by avoiding my questions."

Jesse stared at the concrete wall ahead, tapped his knuckles against his lips. When he spoke, his voice rang with sincerity. "Being a candidate, I'd never been with a girl, you know…like that. I couldn't believe I did something so horrible.

When Jordan picked me up at the hotel, he grabbed my beer bottle off on the dresser to have anything left inside analyzed."

His next comment held a hint of caution. "Jordan's very smart, Marli. That's why The Program keeps their digs in him. Anyway, the test results came back showing the beer laced with some drug that alters memory. My DNA swab proved my innocence." Jesse's cheeks flushed. "I can't believe I'm telling you this. Sorry if I said anything to make you uncomfortable."

I swallowed loudly. "I asked, didn't I?"

"Yes, you did."

I touched Jesse's arm before he stepped out of the car. "Wait. Maybe I'm out of line asking, but your parents—"

He cut me off. "My father and Jordan decided I was a target. Something to keep in mind, Marli, before you choose to join our 'clan.'"

"What do you mean 'target?'"

We entered an underground tunnel and after a couple of turns. Jesse stopped. I could no longer see an entrance or an exit. He drew me close, his voice dropping to barely a whisper.

"Marli, I belong to a powerful family and there are people out there who don't like us."

My stomach dipped. "Okay, you're creeping me out. Who is your father, anyway?"

"Sorry, can't say." Jesse towed me around the corner to a waiting elevator. When I opened my mouth to ask more, he pointed to the security cameras. "Subject closed."

Lights on each side of the front door illuminated the front steps, welcoming me home. I lived in an older, two-story red brick home, nestled in a quiet neighborhood. A large porch spanned the front of the house with a wooden swing and a couple of rockers, their white paint chipped and faded.

Below each entry light, pots of wilted white petunias begged for a drink. Water from the sprinkler tube spattered against the pavement, splashing my bare legs and causing a shiver to pebble my skin. The front door squeaked and Rick stepped out, gathering me into a burly hug.

"Finally, you're home. Was that a limo I saw?"

Shuttles were the main mode of transportation. Some still owned private vehicles, but limousines were rare.

"Yeah. I think everyone in the neighborhood stared out their windows when we came down the street." I stretched out on the porch swing, kicking off my heels and dangling my bare feet over the side. Dad chose to sit in one of the rockers across from me.

"So? Tell me about the interview. I'm guessing by the private jet and limousine service, money isn't an issue for Mr. Mason," he noted with sarcasm.

"I hate that we can't meet. His mom did the interview, which felt more like I was applying for a job." *One I probably won't get.*" Their house is gorgeous with an awesome view of the ocean. Oh, and they own an island."

"An island? Figures."

I swiveled upright. "Jordan's twin brother, Jesse, was my pilot."

Rick stopped rocking. "Pilot? Like his brother? Remind me. How old is Jordan Mason?"

"Nineteen."

"*Nineteen?* You're not even out of high school, Marli. He's already got a year of college under his belt—"

"Almost three," I corrected. Rick's lips flattened and I explained before the lecture started. "Jordan graduated high school early."

His heavy sigh wavered between disapproval and skepticism. "I'm not sure I approve of you jetting around with this Jordan character, or his brother." He raised his hand when I opened my mouth. "I know, not my decision. Anything else? I got nervous when they called to say you'd be three hours late and while I'm not so good with details, I can't help noticing your hair is now braided, and the make-up you spent an hour on this morning is gone."

"Jesse took me snorkeling on their yacht after the interview. That's why I'm late."

Dad leaned forward. "Let me get this straight. You're not allowed to meet the boy you could be assigned to for *life*, but gallivanting off with his twin brother is okay?"

"Not exactly."

"That's what I thought. Pushing my limits is one thing, daughter, but messing with the government? You better watch your step." When I didn't reply, he released another loud sigh. "So, how was snorkeling?"

I gave a recap of my adventure, sticking to marine life, not Jesse, although my expression must have given something away. Rick relaxed into the rocker, a wide grin stretching across his face.

"What?"

"You tell me, Mars. Maybe you should switch brothers. You seem rather impressed with this Jesse fellow. Falling in love the old-fashioned way beats this arranged relationship crap any day."

Telling Dad why Jesse could never be an option didn't seem the best idea. I moved from the swing to the porch steps, the cold concrete matching my sudden somber mood.

"You only get hurt when you let emotions rule your choices."

"Lately, Pumpkin, your impulsive choices have been completely based on emotion."

"Maybe, but it still doesn't mean I'm not afraid of a committed relationship. There's no guarantee of a happily-ever-after with any guy, whether I pick him, or he's chosen for me."

"That's a rather cynical view. True, there are no assurances, but if you're referring to your mom and me, don't let what happened to us decide your actions. Once-upon-a-time I loved your mother very much."

Mom's leaving hurt Dad more than he let on and whenever we came close to discussing those feelings, he changed the subject.

"Speaking of 'lost loves,' Sam's called at least a dozen times. The kid is so damn annoying. Please call him before I lose my last thread of patience."

I brushed loose pebbles off the back of my skirt. "Dad? What should I do about Sam? I don't want to hurt him."

His rocker creaked when he rose. "Sorry, but nobody gets through life without being hurt some way. Sam will recover. It's you I worry about."

A hot shower and comfy clothes did nothing to settle the restlessness ticking through my body. I nestled into the window seat with my digital pad to work on homework, but Dad's comments about letting your heart decide your fate kept interrupting my concentration. Before today, I toyed with thoughts of dropping out of The Program, but my candidacy secured my family's future. Twisted blessings—even for my future children.

*Children?* Mrs. Mason's declaration flashed in my thoughts like a warning beacon. *"…you could be become pregnant right away, which would also serve the greater purpose…"* Whose "greater purpose?" Hers? Jordan's? Not mine.

The cell receptor buzzed against my hip—Jesse! I shut off the video feed before answering. Rick's Ohio State T-shirt and sweatpants didn't exactly scream "sexy," but then again, why did I care? Because I did—I was seventeen. Didn't all seventeen-year-olds obsess about their looks, or just the ones who sucked the lips off their assigned mate's brother?

"Jesse?"

"Good, you're still awake."

"How did you get my personal number?"

"I have my ways. I wanted to know you arrived home safely. My co-pilot is taking a break so I figured I'd call. Technically, I'm not supposed to talk to you. It's against the *rules*."

"Like you care," I teased, feeling brave with him thousands of miles away.

"Still holding a grudge, I see."

"Most hostages do."

"Brutal. If I'd formally asked you to spend the afternoon with me, would you have said yes?"

I paused a beat. "Probably not."

"Precisely my point. You would have missed out on a great learning experience, so technically, you should thank me."

"For kidnapping me?"

"Among other things."

"Jesse, don't go there, please," I warned, mostly because I'd been trying to avoid thinking about our kiss all night.

"I meant snorkeling."

My face flushed hot and I was glad the video was off. "Sorry. Guess I'm still worried."

"What if I told you didn't need to be? Got some info to share. Apparently, Mom hated the second candidate she interviewed. She told Jordan you made a much better impression."

"That's a shocker. The other candidate must have been a total loser."

Jesse laughed. "I was also right about the animal issue. She reamed Jordan for not saying anything and embarrassing her when you caught her off guard."

"How do you know all this?"

"I had a thirty minute delay before take-off, so I called Jordan. I wanted to make sure he got the bathing suit shot." Jesse's snicker bordered evil. "He did."

Air raced into my lungs so fast it hurt. "No one was supposed to know! Tell me you didn't say anything about the kiss."

"No! I'm not tired of living," he replied around a smile. "Jordan knows we went snorkeling, which he hated, but that's all. You can see other boys, Mars. Don't worry, our secret is safe."

*Until discovered.*

Jesse's co-pilot returned, ending our conversation with a generic "good-night," warding off any suspicion he flirted with his brother's prospective mate. Unlike Jesse, I couldn't believe what happened this afternoon qualified as "acceptable" by The Program.

The Program. Organized about ten years before my birth, the government matchmaking service culled girls and boys with exceptional genetic markers for candidates, aligning them into pre-arranged life relationships. Rick claimed it was set up to create some superior society—"genetic wonders" that supposedly would be smarter, healthier, and stronger than our international counterparts. I couldn't shake the feeling there might be something more…something darker.

I touched the tiny lump behind my right ear where a microchip had been implanted at birth to track my development for some government mega database. Everyone born after the year 2040 had them, but unlike the bands that would eventually be removed, the chip remained attached to your skull for life—*property of the U.S. government.*

Sam's instant message beeped me from my dark thoughts. *Hey babe, come outside.*

Afraid he'd wake Rick, I wrapped myself inside the lap quilt off my rocking chair and padded quietly down the stairs. Sam waited in the shadows in the corner of the yard, bouncing on the balls of his feet.

"Good, you brought a blanket." He gathered me into his arms and his lips sampled my neck. "I missed you, babe. Why didn't you call? "

"It's so late I thought I'd wait until morning."

Sam didn't care about my reasons. His lips pressed hard, his tongue pushing through my reluctant lips, smearing Jesse's kisses away. His hand moved behind my head, holding me tight to his mouth a second time, mashing my nose against his cheek. I shoved against his shoulders.

"Sam, I can't breathe!"

He threw his arms in the air. "What? I thought maybe you missed me."

"Shhh! Keep your voice down. And I've only been gone a day."

Sam fisted his hair. "I can't stand this damn Program. You act like they own you—dropping everything to fly off to some stranger's house. For what? A stupid interview?"

My teeth ground together. "You know it's more than an interview and in a sense, *yes*, The Program owns me."

"Drop out!"

"I can't!" I hissed back. Sam didn't know the truth behind my illegal enrollment, nor could I tell him to help explain my reasons for staying. Gingerly, I took his hands, dropping my voice. "It's complicated...especially now."

He yanked his hands free. "Oh, I get it. Why settle for the small town boy when you can have the rich brat. Tell me—is he better looking, too?"

"Sam, it's not like that. I told you, The Program paired me with Jordan."

"*Jordan*. First names now, huh? No more numbers." When I wouldn't answer, Sam pulled me close. I turned my head to avoid his kiss.

"I need to get back inside before Rick discovers I snuck out."

After a careful kiss at the front door, Sam said "I love you." I couldn't return the sentiment because it no longer felt right. He walked away defeated and pangs of guilt punched my gut. Dad was right. I couldn't do this without hurting Sam.

I tiptoed back to my room and burrowed beneath my quilt. Memories I kept buried deep stirred, bringing a clear recall of the day I entered The Program.

*...A woman with a wide-brimmed red hat perched on her head, walks around me while I stand in the center of the principal's office. She strokes my hair and pulls back my slouched shoulders. "Absolutely perfect. I agree, she should definitely be submitted. I'll notify her parents immediately..."*

The next day, a bright pink band holding four sparkling diamonds circled my wrist. I officially became a candidate in The Program. Later, my family ties unraveled. Mom and Dad had the worst fight ever. In the middle of the night, Mom placed Daniel and me in a taxi shuttle, and the three of us left for California. Without Dad.

# 4
# KISMET UNLEASHED

An endless chirping from the oak tree outside my window woke me long before the alarm. I wished for a cat—a hungry one. I blew a long, noisy breath and kicked my covers to the floor in frustration. Staring at the ceiling, I studied how the lavender and gray shadows gave the sponge-painted clouds a realistic appearance.

Mom loved to "express herself" by painting murals on our walls to make our bedrooms our own private world instead of just a room within the house. Daniel's room once resembled a pirate's ship with his bed beneath a huge mast sporting a skull and cross-bones that scared the crap out of me when I opened the door.

Considered "the princess," my room had been painted to resemble a castle, my bedroom door a drawbridge, my bathroom one centered in a turret. Painted stone balusters joined at the window seat to look like a balcony, and out my window, the view of my kingdom. The ceiling was my sky, complete with stars painted in glow-in-the-dark silver paint scattered between the clouds.

When I returned to Ohio after an incident caused an immediate change in custody, I no longer believed in fairytales. Dad and I painted my room a dusty purple, replaced the frilly bedspread with a dark plum and white polka-dot comforter, and tossed the satin accent pillows. Large hot pink, lime green, and black furry pillows took their place. The only thing I couldn't change was my "sky." Even after all these years, the stars still shone when the lights went out. I believed in wishing on the first star of the night and if I didn't get a chance to do so on a real one, I'd pick a fake one to hang my hopes on. The one directly over my head held last night's wish, the same one for the past several weeks. One that apparently wasn't coming true.

A wayward beam from the rising sun sliced across the opposite wall spotlighting the poster of a prima ballerina in a deep bow, my old ballet shoes draped off the corner of the frame. Mom started me in ballet lessons at age six and when I started loving animals more than pirouettes, she pushed my dance teacher to advance me to the pointe troupe in hopes I'd shed my tomboyish tendencies. The shoes killed my feet and the longer Saturday lessons stole the time I usually spent helping Dad at the clinic. When I cut ties from my mother and returned to Maple Heights, I left my shoes behind.

Of course she mailed them to me, along with the poster, instructing my father through one of many arguments to encourage me to continue. Dad asked me what *I* wanted. I hung the poster because it matched my room and draped the shoes in memoriam, but never laced them on my feet again. I enjoyed ballet and faithfully watched The Nutcracker every Christmas. Perfecting Tchaikovsky's piece from the famous ballet transitioned my love of music into a fitting epilogue to my short dance career.

Pushing away the memories and realizing sleep was no longer an option, I crawled out of bed. Sleep deprived and not paying attention to where I walked, I stumbled over a stray tennis shoe, accidently bumping the stack of study materials for my upcoming finals off the corner of my desk. A familiar red envelope slapped the floor.

Three weeks had passed since my interview and no word from Jordan Mason. Not even a standard rejection notice. His mother must have convinced him to seek other "respectable" choices—older, more mature candidates. After all, what bragging rights would you have to an assignee still in high school?

Maybe he changed his mind when he saw the stupid picture of me in his sister's bikini, thinking "too young," although Jesse didn't seem to mind. But then again, I might have been nothing more than an afternoon snack to "Mr. Rock Star." He hadn't called either, which in all likelihood meant he'd found someone whose kisses curled *his* toes.

My mental muse spoke up. *Stop obsessing about the Mason twins. You have finals to cram for and the last thing you need is boy drama.* I caught the reflection of a girl from the mirror in the corner. She appeared preoccupied, possibly with Jordan's eyes, or Jesse's lips. The poster child of a sappy teenage girl caught in a romantic delusion. Above the mirror I'd tacked a poster of my favorite rock band, "Hopeless," their title fitting the current chapter of my life.

I made my way to the kitchen in search of comfort food. The first rays of dawn peeked through the lace curtains and tiny dust particles swirled in the pale lemon shaft. Choosing to drown my self-pity in gallons of caffeine, I headed for the beverage maker. A message rolled over the digital display above.

*Mars—on emergency call—will be gone most of the morning—let Muffy out—love Dad.*

Rick belonged to a dying breed of veterinarians who still believed in making house calls. He also had a soft spot for strays, oftentimes keeping them until he found them homes. Muffy, a large, black and white spotted Great Dane abandoned on the doorstep of his clinic, was the latest rescue. Her home immediately became ours, and *letting Muffy out* qualified, by most standards, as an Olympic Event.

I didn't bother to change out of my boxer shorts and knit camisole. This early, no one was outside. Besides, the trees out front would hide me for the short duration of the morning chore. I removed the leash from its hook and inhaled deep before opening the laundry room door. Muffy lifted on two legs, draping her front paws over my shoulders. Her rambunctious tail knocked over the clothes hamper as she squirmed excitedly while I attached the leash to her collar.

I held tight to the railing on the back porch, the pressure of the leash cutting into my fingers. Muffy bolted for the nearest bush and I barely realigned my hands in the strap before she started for the stone steps at the end of the front walk.

Out the corner of my eye, I spied a white car approaching. I feared for both our lives if Muffy darted across the street for the cat napping on the trunk on Mr. Baxter's car. My pleas became lost in the morning air when the cat yowled and Muffy leaped over the steps. The leash snapped, setting Muffy free and launching me forward. One knee smacked the cold pavement of the sidewalk and my head, the hard ground—luckily covered with two week's worth of overgrown grass. Brakes screeched. I yelled Muffy's name seconds before my world went black.

The aroma of coffee curled in my senses and a cool dampness spread across my forehead. Impulsively I rose, immediately regretting the choice when a sudden wave of nausea attacked.

"Ugh, I'm going to puke!"

"Wait, don't move." Whoever belonged to the male voice pressed an alcohol doused cotton ball to my nose. "Lie back and breathe slowly until the queasiness passes." He took my hand and applied pressure to the fleshy web between my thumb and finger—two odd tricks, but together seemed to work.

I opened my eyes slower this time, discovering the kind voice belonged to some gorgeous boy. A different kind of unsettling warmed in my stomach with the gentle way he held my hand. Something about him felt...familiar.

"Better?"

I nodded, both confused and fascinated, but before I could ask his name, a sudden warm wetness splashed across my cheek. "Muffy! You're alive...and a very bad dog."

The cute stranger spoke at his watch, pretending to dictate to a recording device. "Note: The patient has identified the small horse seated on the floor next to me." I giggled and a smile ghosted on his lips. "You hit your head harder than I thought if you're laughing at my lame joke. Can you tell me your name?"

A sharp pain stabbed my brain when I sat up a second time. "Ouch."

Carefully, he lowered me into the cushions behind my head and when his neck came within inches of my face, I trapped the scent of his cologne in my lungs.

"Are you always this stubborn?" he asked. "Stay still. You've got a nasty bump on your head and half the skin on your knee is missing."

"What happened?"

"You took a nose dive in front of my car and scared the hell out of me." He draped the afghan from the back of the sofa over me. "While you might be comfortable in those little shorts and top, I'm not."

I forgot about my makeshift pajamas and gave him a wary glance. Something about the glint in his eyes made me want to sit up just to feel his hands on my bare shoulders again, breathe in his cologne…taste his neck.

*Marli Davis! Get a grip—he's a stranger!* One hot-looking stranger I swear I'd seen somewhere.

He regarded me, amused, and my cheeks flushed. "Trust me, you're safe."

*Great. He's not even remotely interested.*

He held up his index finger. "Can you at least follow my finger?" I crossed my eyes. "Girl, you're impossible." This time he batted his long lashes with dramatic overkill. "Please tell me your name."

I crossed my arms, attempting a serious expression. "Marli Davis. And you are?"

Eyes the color of a deep, mossy pond sparkled. "I hoped it was you. I'm Jordan Mason."

*Holy hell! How hard did I hit my head that I didn't recognize the guy whose picture used to be covered in drool until…I gave up hope….stopped dreaming.*

His bronze hair had been cropped short, but the sexy signature smile remained the same. Mortified, I wished for death. No makeup, morning breath, *not* my best boxers, and apparently, a lumpy head. I slid under the afghan.

"No way! I could die!"

Jordan pulled the blanket off my face. "I think you've already cheated death once today."

He rose and held out his hand. "Why don't you go change into something to stop my mind from wandering and I'll pour us some coffee. When you come back, we can get better acquainted."

When I stood, my leg buckled and Jordan lifted me in his arms. "Falling for me already?" The warmth of his arm under my thighs and the other holding me against him sent my head spinning and apparently stole my voice. "I could use a hint where to take you."

My cheeks flamed hot. "Sorry. Upstairs, second door on the right."

Jordan carried me as if I weighed nothing. We paused outside the door with "Marli's Room" painted inside a circle of hand-painted daisies. He fought back a snicker. "Cute."

A smile reaching his eyes played around the edges of his mouth. His intense stare felt so intimate, I dropped my eyes to avoid melting. The whirlwind of emotions I felt the day I watched his interview pod erupted.

"I can make it from here," I said.

After promising to yell if I needed help, he placed me on my feet, his hands framing my waist, hopefully to steady me, but the grip was too soft to be lifesaving. After an awkward moment, he retreated to the kitchen and I willed my heart to resume beating.

Not wanting to be away from him any longer than necessary, I wiggled into the closest items of clothing I could find. Quickly, I brushed my hair into a ponytail, scrubbed my face and teeth, and carefully applied some mascara, hoping to make my swollen eye less noticeable. I blew into my palm and popped a bubble gum-flavored mint in my mouth for extra measure.

My knight-in-shining-armor met me halfway, helping me down the last few steps. Playful eyes appraised my oversized Ohio State sweatshirt and denim shorts.

"Better. Although I think you could pull off wearing a garbage bag and look great."

"Yeah, right."

He held my chair—a gallant gesture not used by any of the boys I knew. We studied each other through the curling wisps of steam off our coffee until Muffy interrupted the spell when she sauntered in and plopped contently at Jordan's feet.

"You passed her trust test."

"What about yours?"

With my guard still high, I answered truthfully. "I haven't decided."

He sipped his coffee, never lowering his eyes from mine. "Fair and honest."

Muffy rested her head on Jordan's leg and when I reached to move her, his fingers wrapped my wrist. A surprise sizzle warmed my belly. He let go and started scratching behind Muffy's ears.

His voice squeaked a nervous pitch and a hint of a blush spread beneath his lashes. "I always wanted a dog, but penthouses barely accommodate children, let alone animals."

"Your mom acted surprised when I mentioned you liked animals."

He laughed and a piece of my guard chipped away. "Yes, I heard all about it. Sometimes she's overbearing, but she's just being protective."

"I doubt she could top Rick."

"Who's Rick?"

"My dad."

Jordan's brows pulled together then relaxed with recognition. "That's right. My mother told me you referred to him by his first name."

"I could tell she didn't approve. She probably thinks I'm weird."

"I think she called you 'unique,' which believe it or not, is a compliment. It's cool your dad's okay with it, though. You two must be close."

"I think so. We've been through a lot together." I swallowed the last gulp of my coffee, waiting for the inevitable subject of my mother or Daniel to be raised.

"My mom told me about your brother. I'm so sorry."

I muttered "thanks" and focused on the bottom of my empty mug, not wanting to break down in front of Jordan, although being around him already felt comfortable—safe. Like coming home.

A slow grin wandered over Jordan's lips. "You're easy to talk to. My life's so full of pretentious people it's nice to be around someone real for a change."

Aside from his fancy car, nothing about Jordan reflected an ostentatious lifestyle. Faded jeans covered his long legs, a well-worn navy-blue tee, snug enough to reveal he worked out, peeked from beneath his unzipped Cornell sweatshirt, and the toes of his sneakers were scuffed. He could easily blend in a crowd of teen boys, and yet, I knew I'd still pick him out.

"You do live a charmed life." I gestured aimlessly at the room. "This house is no oceanfront penthouse."

"You can live in this house. In mine, you *exist*."

Muffy reached her paw out for Jordan to shake and I laughed. "It's bizarre how she's taken to you. She doesn't act this way around most people."

"I can't believe I almost hit her. Can you imagine what a dog her size would do to a Porsche?"

The memory of the car coming down the street became clear. A white *Porsche*. "'Sweet Sally?'"

"You remembered. Impressive. Then you also know I meant what I said about road trips cleaning the cobwebs out of your head and helping you sort things out."

Jordan placed his hand next to mine, his pinky stretching a tentative stroke over my little finger. I sucked my bottom lip under my top teeth. He rolled his hand over in an open invitation and when I let my fingers glide in over his soft palm and braid into his, the air crackled between us.

"Marli, I have a confession to make. I knew it wasn't allowed, but I wanted to meet you when you came to interview. A last minute change in my soccer tournament schedule, however, landed me in Arizona—probably to make sure I didn't show up in Florida.

"You and your brother have a problem with rules."

"Jesse's doesn't believe they exist. But that's why he stuck around—to spy for me."

*He did a little more than spy.*

"I wanted to deliver your acceptance letter in person, except I haven't had a free weekend until now. My plan was to ask you out to dinner, but I arrived earlier than expected so I decided to find where you lived. Of course, I didn't count on a horse romping out of nowhere and a girl landing in front of my car."

He cradled my hand inside both of his. "I was so scared I'd hit her—*you.* Only I didn't know it was you, because I never checked house numbers. When you rolled on the grass moaning, I just wanted to get you some help."

"The last thing I remember is the screeching brakes. I thought the car hit Muffy. How did you get in the house?"

"Muffy. She ran back when I scooped you in my arms. I thought she might eat me, but instead, she led me to the back door. No one answered when I called out. She bolted to the living room and paced until I laid you on the sofa. I was paging an ambulance when your eyes opened."

"My dad's the only veterinarian in this area and he's on an emergency call. He usually takes Muffy out. I'm sorry I didn't thank you earlier. Maybe running me over was 'divine intervention?'"

"I did *not* run over you," he laughed. His eyes swept my face and settled in a serious gaze. "Do you believe in fate, Marli?"

For some reason, undoubtedly madness, I pulled my hand away. Confusion clouded Jordan's expression. He slid his arm on the back of my chair. Fingers lightly touched my shoulder creating a shiver and I tilted his direction.

"I used to believe in happily-ever-after, but then I grew up." Changing the subject, I continued. "Jordan? Your road tip. Am I something to be sorted out?"

He twisted the hair falling from my ponytail, tucking a stray strand. His fingertip brushed the shell of my ear and sent a ripple up my neck. He leaned on the table in front of me. My heavy gulp echoed.

"Yes," he replied. "I'm not a fan of this arranged setup."

"Me neither," I said, struggling not to stare at his mouth.

When he gave me an odd glance, I sat back, knocking off his arm.

*Crap! I insulted him.*

I tried to cover my blunder, hoping he'd offer his hand again as a gesture of good will. He didn't and I dropped my eyes to the tightly knitted fist in my lap.

"The Program scares me. I mean, you seem nice…*more* than nice, but I'm not ready to be permanently attached to someone."

Jordan eased his hand over my shoulder again, wrapping the wayward curl sweeping my neck around his finger. I held my breath, hoping the movement was purposely orchestrated and would continue, but his hand moved away and hung casually off the chair once more.

I lifted my eyes to his. He appeared contemplative, running his index finger slowly over his lower lip.

"How would you feel about dating?" he asked. "Taking things slow and deciding for ourselves if this is what we want?"

"But we're assigned to each other. We don't have a choice."

"Until I notify The Program I'm accepting you, we're not bound."

Without hesitating, he reclaimed my hand, his expression serious, "Marli, if we decide to make things permanent, I promise I'll never let anyone, especially The Program, treat you as property. You and I will always be equal."

For a second, I wondered if I imagined Jordan. Someone this good couldn't be real. "How will The Program handle us dating?"

His brow wrinkled. "They can't know. 'Committed or available' are the only options candidates have. I swear, though, if you don't want to be with me, I'll walk away. I won't put that kind of pressure on you."

We didn't even know each other, but the thought of a lifetime with Jordan Mason created a massive fluttering in my stomach. I loved his candidness and sincerity. Maybe I'd finally found someone I could trust again. I folded my legs into my arms and studied my wounded knee to avoid his intense eyes.

Jordan leaned forward, his arm sliding around my shoulders. "Does it hurt?" he asked, genuinely concerned. He blew across the scrape and my stomach tightened.

"A little," I lied, silently agonizing against the burning sting. But this was my protective position—the one I curled into whenever I felt insecure. "I don't know, Jordan. I'm still in high school. Then there's college—"

He eased back, a lazy grin curling his mouth. "Whoa, slow down. I'm not rushing you. I have things to work out, too. My second semester ends around Christmas. Let's see how we feel about things at that point."

Unable to handle another second under his penetrating stare, I hobbled to the sink, taking our empty cups. Too big of a coward to face him with my next question, I kept my back turned.

"What happens if we don't want to be together in six months?"

The warmth of his body standing close swamped me with an unexpected thrill. His hand smoothed over mine when he placed our stirring spoons in the warm water. "Having met you in person, I can honestly say I hope that never happens."

We shared corners of the dishtowel, drying our hands. I twirled the blue band circling his wrist until the five diamonds flashed.

"Of all the candidates you could choose from, why me?"

Jordan's fingers cautiously laced through mine. "This probably won't make sense, but I don't know *why*. I'm drawn to you. Something deep in those blue eyes of yours…a rare innocence. All I know, Marli, is you give me 'butterflies.'" He let go of my hands and stowed his in his back pockets. He glanced away, a telltale blush coloring his cheeks. "Okay, *that* sounded stupid."

I laughed lightly, my own cheeks glowing. "No, more like honest, which to me is wonderful. Personally, I love butterflies. I think they're amazing."

Jordan caged me against the counter, his eyes leveling to mine. He studied every laugh line, every freckle dotting my face. I stopped breathing when his head dipped and lips lingered close. He touched the corner of my mouth with his finger and I jumped.

"You, uh, have something right there."

Food dried in the corner of my mouth? Oh crap! I tasted my lip. Toothpaste? How horrifying…embarrassing…childlike! I would have slinked, no *ran* somewhere to hide, but Jordan didn't move. His body pressed close, his head still tipped and eyes so deep, intense…intoxicating, holding my own hostage. I licked my lips to ensure no other remnants lingered and those same eyes flashed dark. His thumb slowly wiped my damp bottom lip.

"I really want to kiss you," he whispered so softly I wondered if I'd heard a thought instead.

"Then why don't you?" *Did I say it out loud or were our minds communicating?* Our noses grazed and an eternity seemed to pass.

"You scare me," he uttered in a weightless breath over my waiting mouth.

Inside my chest my heart stilled; my lungs quieted and sealed just enough air to keep me from fainting. Jordan's fingertips tapped my skin delicately as they moved, almost bashful, along my jaw and wrapped the back of my neck. His lips barely brushed mine, but the spark in the kiss was undeniable—a witness to my soul that a crucial shift in my life just happened.

"Now I'm scared," I whispered, no longer feeling my legs.

His arm coasted around my waist, pulling me into him. A seductive smile appeared and my heart skipped another beat. "Can I kiss you again?"

My insides turned mushy, while my body obeyed the gentle command of Jordan's fingers splayed on the small of my back, nestling me against his warm, hulky frame. When I nodded my approval, his fingers braided into my hair, tilted my head back. My lips bloomed against his when they pressed with a second, more confident kiss. My arms circled his neck and held on while I rode an emotional wave of elation, fear, and something new I couldn't describe because I'd never felt it before.

When the kiss ended, our eyes locked and I worried what thoughts bounced in his brain. *Did I kiss okay? My breath?* He pecked the end of my nose and I flushed, embarrassed. *Crap! He's made a mistake and thinking of a way to escape.*

"Wow, what just happened?" He took a half step back, parked his hands on my hips. "I, uh…sorry, I shouldn't have—"

Another person suddenly possessed my body and I moved into the few inches separating us. I rose on my tiptoes, tugged his collar and settled my lips on his, hushing his apology. His tongue teased and my lips parted, welcoming the delicious taste of his mouth taking mine.

Jordan's arms wrapped tighter and I molded into his curves as if my body had done it a million times, familiar with every bend and angle. Heat ripped through my veins like fire chasing a stream of gasoline. No one had ever kissed me like Jordan. I never tingled all over before. It was as if I inhaled air for the first time and my lungs wanted more. Something clicked between us—bolts sliding effortlessly through locks. I never wanted our kiss to end, or Jordan to leave my arms.

His lips tickled the spot below my earlobe and my bones turned spongy. "Marli Davis—don't break my heart."

Through my lashes I studied his flushed face, eyes eclipsed to dark moons, his mouth swollen, moist, and I imagined it covering mine one more time. Leaning closer, I anticipated the heat of his lips, but before they touched…the back door slammed.

# 5
# BUSTED

"Marli? What the hell?"

*Company* appeared in the doorway, raging mad.

"Sam!" I pushed him into the laundry room to talk privately. "What are you doing here? Why didn't you knock?" I asked quietly, hoping to diffuse his anger. It didn't work.

"School? Remember? And I did knock, but you were too busy sucking face with some strange dude to hear." He punched the doorjamb. "How long has *this* been going on?"

"Sam, let me explain."

He shrugged away from my touch and wrenched the door open. "No! I don't need an explanation. I know what I saw."

I ran onto the back porch after him, but he'd already jumped in his jeep. The tires squealed backwards, leaving two indelible black streaks on the driveway. Rick would be livid.

Jordan's calm demeanor shifted when I marched into the kitchen, seething. Angry tears pooled in my eyes. I pushed my hand hard against my nose to stop the floodgates from opening, but it proved useless.

"I-I'm so embarrassed."

He pulled a white handkerchief from his pocket and blotted my cheeks. "Don't worry about it." He pressed a light kiss to my forehead. "Who was he, anyway?"

"Just my—" *My what?* Did I dare say "boyfriend?"

The sound of keys jingling in the lock of the front door rousted Muffy from her sunlit spot on the rug and saved me from answering. My father walked in not noticing Jordan or me, and yelled up the stairwell.

"Mars?" Is that a Porsche parked out front? And what's with Sam racing down the street?"

Dad's eyes narrowed when he spied me crying in Jordan's arms, crying. He moved with lightning speed across the dining room, his glare fixed on Jordan, whose arms fell away instantly. I stepped back, putting weight on my bad leg, and hissed against a jolt of pain.

Feeling a current of jagged heat race through my body when Jordan's arms wrapped me again, I ignored the tyrant marching our direction. Until the *tyrant* yanked me from Jordan's embrace and plunked me on the nearest chair, rather hard, I thought.

Rick knelt before me, clicked open his medical bag and proceeded to examine my wound. Jordan stood behind me, the gentle pressure of his fingertips on my shoulders keeping my mind off the stringent searing my scrape.

"Care to tell me what's going on, Marli? Let's start with the stranger intimately holding you when I walked in. Could *this*, by chance, be responsible for the permanent black marks on my driveway?"

"Muffy tore off for Mr. Baxter's stupid cat again. When I tried to reel her back, the leash broke and I crashed to the sidewalk. Jordan almost hit us both with his car."

"Jordan?" Dad glanced from me to the handsome hunk standing behind me. He rose to a guarded stance. "Let me guess—you're Jordan?"

Jordan extended his hand. "Jordan Mason, sir."

"*Mason?* Marli's Jordan Mason?" My father's brusqueness diminished somewhat. "The Porsche—yours?"

"Yes sir, guilty on both counts." Muffy nuzzled her head under Jordan's arm. "I'm just glad I didn't run over either of your girls, sir."

"Drop the 'sir.' It's Rick and I owe you an apology." He leaned into the kitchen counter, asking the inevitable. "So what happened with Sam?"

My face twisted in agony, but before I could confess, Jordan answered. "He walked in on me kissing your daughter, sir—I mean, *Rick*."

"What? Marli!" Rick morphed from friendly to warden status, giving Jordan a dark glower. "You were making out with my daughter? In my kitchen?"

"We weren't *making out*," I defended. "One kiss Sam saw and then he wouldn't even let me explain. He just stormed out."

"Do you blame him, Mars? Walking in on your girlfriend kissing someone else would push any boy over the edge."

"*Girlfriend?*" Jordan piped in, his brows pulling tight. "Sam's your *boyfriend?*"

Technically, dating outside of The Program was forbidden, even if Jesse thought differently. I checked my contract. However I hadn't officially been "activated" until I accepted the interview with Jordan. Up to this point, I considered myself a normal teenager, limiting my future to the day I currently lived and my destiny to the weekend.

I didn't need this argument with Dad, especially in front of Jordan. "I don't have time to explain Sam to either of you. I need to get ready for school."

"Marli?" Jordan hesitated, his accusing tone gone. "Can I wait and give you a ride?"

"No, I can drive myself, but thanks."

The voices in my head argued immediately. *Have you lost your mind? Of course you want him to take you to school.* However, if Sam saw me with Jordan again, things could worsen. I feared Jordan might already have second-guessed his decision to find me.

Dad placed a hand on my shoulder. "Your car is still in Andy's shop, remember? But I can take you, if you want."

I sighed partially in surrender, the other part secretly thrilled. "No, I'll let Jordan take me. I'd like one ride in his Porsche before he runs from this drama scene."

The inside of Jordan's Porsche smelled like his cologne—spicy, with a hint of citrus. *Sexy.* I wished I lived hundreds of miles from the school so I could breathe the sensuous scent for hours, not minutes.

Jordan's finger tapped my hand from the shifter knob. "Hey. Sorry I questioned your relationship with Sam. Your life before today isn't my business."

I tangled my fingers in his, helping him shift gears. "And, now it is?"

"Only if you say so."

A breath stalled in my throat, a debate ensued in my brain. If I said *yes*, I surrendered a little bit of the control I wanted to keep. If I said *no*, I ran the risk of pushing Jordan away—something I did not want right now.

"I think I say so."

When we pulled in front of the school, Jordan's Porsche summoned an immediate gathering of wide-eyed gawkers. I slumped in the passenger seat hoping the dark tinted windows hid me from faces I recognized—ones who knew Sam.

"Great," I scowled. "Guess I'm not slipping into school unnoticed."

Jordan's arm dropped around my shoulders, easing me closer. "Not a chance. You'll have to get used to this, I'm afraid. 'Fast and flashy' cars. Remember? "

I caressed the collar of his shirt, avoiding his eyes, but wondering if he could feel my pulse racing in my breath. "So you're a show-off? What are you covering for?

"At this moment, my obsession with wanting to kiss you again."

"I think that's an obsession I'd like to work on."

Jordan tipped my chin up and pressed a gentle kiss to my mouth. "You better go before you're late." One last kiss ended with a promise for a ride home.

Passing through the front entrance security barriers, I felt light as air with the taste of Jordan on my tongue. Heads whipped my direction and whispers followed me down the hall to the locker cubes where I found Sam. I recognized the faded blue jeans draped over worn sneakers, and the shiny mop of dark hair edging the open cubicle hatch. I nervously watched from behind as he angrily tossed his digital pad inside. Cautiously, I touched his arm.

"Sam?"

He turned, head tilted to the ceiling. His soft gray eyes were wet and my heart sank, realizing I caused his pain. He spoke so quiet only I could hear him.

"He's the one, isn't he? The guy you're assigned to."

"Yeah, he's Jordan Mason."

"Damn! I knew it!"

Sam's angry kick dented the metal wall below his cube. A group of his friends passed by, eyeing the two of us. I wondered how far the gossip train had already traveled, carrying the news of what happened this morning.

"Let's get out of here. First period's a bust anyway."

When we reached his jeep, Sam hugged me and I stiffened in his arms. "What?"

*I don't want you to touch me.* "Nothing," I lied.

As we pulled out of the parking lot, I caught a glimpse in the side mirror of a white Porsche sliding into traffic. I held my breath hoping Sam didn't notice. We usually went to the park on the edge of town, but Sam headed the opposite direction. Suddenly, he veered the jeep off the pavement and onto a gravel road.

"Let's see if he follows us in that fancy car now."

He noticed.

My head bounced against the back of the seat and the restraint scraped my neck. I yelled at Sam to slow down, seriously contemplating how to jump from the jumbling vehicle, when he brought the jeep to an abrupt stop. Clouds of dust covered us.

"Stop acting like this, Sam."

"I can't!" His knuckles turned white from gripping the steering wheel so tight. "Damn. So this is how it's going to be now? You, me and *him?* Not quite the threesome I've fantasized about."

"Knock it off." I leaned back into the seat. The bright sun beat hot on my head through the open roof and I covered my forehead with my hand to shade my eyes.

Sam's tone softened. "What happened to your knee?"

I inhaled a deep breath long enough to last through a recap. "Sam, Jordan thought he helped a stranger. He didn't know it was me."

His eyes narrowed, "Looked like he was getting to know you pretty fast, or at least your mouth."

"Shut up about the kiss! It just happened and I feel bad you saw us."

"But you don't regret it, do you? The kiss I mean."

My guilty reply slithered out. "No." *Not then, or the several times since.*

Both of us glanced elsewhere, unable to face each other. An uncomfortable silence settled between us. I shifted in my seat, trying to look around without being conspicuous.

"He's parked under the trees at the turn off."

"Oh," I muttered, searching the side mirror until I saw the Porsche tucked in the shadows.

"Do you want to get out of the sun and go sit under that tree over there?"

"I don't know, Sam."

"Ten minutes, Marli, is all I'm asking for. He can wait. Hell, you've been in my life for two years and he's been in yours what—maybe an hour?"

"It's not that simple."

"It *is* that simple. Give me some respect, would you? Don't walk away like I never mattered."

Sam's statement hurt, but my don't-tell-me-what-to-do attitude ruled the moment. I shoved the jeep door open and dropped onto the gravel. The jarring pain to my knee shot to my teeth.

"Fine. You want to talk? You got it. Ten minutes!"

I marched towards the tree in the middle of the field. Sam cursed and slammed the driver's door, running to catch up to me. He grabbed my hand, halting my angry steps. His arm hooked my neck and he nuzzled my hair.

"I'm sorry."

I wound my fingers through his and tugged his hand under my chin. "You matter, okay?"

We dropped at the base of a tree and I curled between his long legs, resting my head against his chest. His voice cracked.

"What happens now? Tell me how I'm supposed to let you go?"

"Sam, we knew this day would come."

"Did we? You've talked so much about dropping out of The Program I guess I hoped you'd follow *that* plan."

True, I'd thought about leaving, but when I read Jordan's portfolio after viewing the pod and realized I'd been matched with someone who shared my likes and dislikes on silly things like no lettuce on hamburgers, and strawberry shakes rocking over chocolate ones, my future suddenly didn't seem so grim. When I kissed him, I knew for sure.

Sam's calloused finger lifted my face and he lightly touched my mouth. "Your kisses taste different."

"That's ridiculous." *Could it be true?*

He kissed me again, long, easing me down in the deep grass. I'd wrapped myself in his Sam's arms almost every day over the past two years, but at this moment what once felt right, now felt wrong.

My head swirled with thoughts of how Jordan's lips felt on mine and how his arms felt around me. Then, as if a channel switched in my head, my thoughts flipped to *Jesse's* lips, *Jesse's* arms.

I shut my mouth tight against Sam's and pushed him back. "No more." He pulled away and my breath hitched when his purposely brushed over my breast. "Sam!"

He propped himself on his elbow, his other hand pressed to my stomach. "What?" A grin curled the edges of his lips, his hand sliding under the edge of my shirt. "It's not like we haven't played this teasing game before, Marli."

I pushed his hand away. "Don't."

Sam bent for another kiss, his fingers brushing up my thigh and snaking under my skirt.

"Stop it!"

His mouth stifled my protest, the kiss rough and territorial. And he didn't quit. He reached further, tugging at the sides of my panties. Panic-laced anger consumed me and I slapped Sam's face—*hard,* the sharp snap echoing across the field. I rolled out of reach, scrambled to my feet and smoothed my skirt down.

"Fuck! What's gotten into you?"

"Me? Where do you get off groping me?" I stomped toward the jeep, my knee throbbing from thrashing through the tall grass, the palm of my hand smarting and hot. Unshed tears tightened my throat.

Sam grabbed my elbow and whirled me to face him. "I know where the damn line is drawn.

"Do you? Is the *line* inside or outside my underwear?"

His answer came out in a low growl. "Lay off! I'd never damage the precious 'candidate.'"

He rubbed the side of his cheek where a definite red print of my hand glowed. My feet slid defiantly across the gravel when Sam yanked me closer. His jaw clenched tight and a bead of sweat glistened along the heavy ridge hooding his intense glare. I'd never seen Sam this angry.

"Sam, let go. You're hurting me."

His hands clamped my shoulders and he shook me. "You hit me!"

I cowered, waiting for the strike back, but the sound of a racing engine stopped anything from happening.

Gravel pinged metal fence rails sounding like machine gun bullets, and billows of blue smoke smelling of burned rubber snaked over the Porsche's tires. Sam released me when Jordan leaped over the fence. My stomach knotted with fear. This would end badly.

Jordan pushed me safely behind him, squaring to Sam. I clenched Jordan's shirt in my fists and pressed my face into his back, feeling the vibration of the hefty warning he leveled.

"Don't. *Ever.* Touch. Her. Again." Jordan's arm folded around me, keeping me tight against him. I gripped his forearm, peering around his shoulder.

Sam didn't budge, maintaining an arrogant stance.

"Or what 'Mister Blue-Band?' You'll hurt me?" He attached a menacing chuckle to his dare and raised his fists. "Come on, 'boy wonder,' let's see what you've got."

"Do *not* underestimate me. I don't want a fight, but—"

Sam swung his fist and I screamed, jumping back. Jordan blocked the blow, thrusting a balled hand into Sam's gut, dropping him to his knees. When Sam started coughing violently, the blue sky overhead swirled in my vision and white puffy clouds spiraled into each other.

My fingers spread over the gravel and in a very far distance, someone called my name.

The lamp beside my bed cast the only light in the dark room. Memories flashed sporadically until my mind centered on one—an instant playback where I watched Sam's body collapse to the ground after Jordan belted him. After several attempts, my eyes finally focused. Jordan sat next to me, a deep crease slicing his perfect brow.

I snickered so hard I snorted. "I can't believe you sucker-punched Sam."

Jordan expelled a loud sigh of relief. "What did they give you at the hospital? You're looped."

"Hospital? I don't remember going to any hospital." I scrunched my mouth. "Are you sure I went to the hospital?"

"Yes. I took you myself. Your dad isn't very happy with me."

"Does he know you're in here? He has rules, you know." I conjured up my best baritone imitation. "No boys in the bedroom."

"Trust me. I know. Why do you think your door is wide open? He's on the phone with his clinic. He's not about to leave me alone with you."

Another wave of silliness struck. "Why not? You're marrying me."

Jordan laughed. "Are you sure about that?"

My eyes closed and a silly grin plastered my face, "Oh yeah, because you're already hooked." I opened one eye, finding a shocked look on Jordan's face. "Poor guy. Now you'll have to walk Muffy."

Jordan bent, gently touched his mouth to my forehead. I could smell the rosewood scent of his aftershave clinging to his skin, and wrapped my hands around his neck.

"You smell yummy. I want to lick your skin."

A faint buzz stopped a possible steamy kiss. Jordan removed a silver receptor from his pocket. He pressed the speaker then claimed the kiss waiting on my dramatically puckered lips.

"Hey Jess, what's up?"

My eyes widened. *Jesse?*

"You've gone AWOL and the 'mothership' is going crazy. Where are you?" I giggled at Jesse's comical reference to their mother. "Bro, are you with a girl? Priceless! Mom will flip out."

"Actually, I think she'll be thrilled. I'm with Marli Davis." Silence. "Jess? You there?"

Jesse's teasing tone turned sullen. "Yeah, I'm here. Why are you there?"

"Uh, because I wanted to meet her. She *is* my assignee. By the way, you're right. She's beautiful, albeit slightly accident prone."

"Accident? Marli are you okay?"

"Hi Jesse," I replied in singsong.

Jordan kissed me again. "She's fine, or at least tastes fine." His lips pressed the sensitive spot below my ear and I moaned.

"More than fine," I hummed. Any common sense left in my fuzzy brain disappeared. "It's hard to tell which one of you kisses better. Jesse's make my toes curl, but yours—"

Jordan's lips froze halfway to meeting mine. His eyes narrowed. "Jesse kissed you?"

"Shit," Jesse hissed.

I forced a childish frown, sticking out my bottom lip. "You weren't supposed to find out. It's a secret."

Jordan snapped his phone shut. "I should go. I'll tell Rick you're awake."

"Wait!" I scrambled off the bed and my legs folded when the room twirled. Jordan caught me and I stood inches from his baffled eyes. My hand flared on the bare skin below the hollow of his throat and his pulse quickened under my fingertips.

At the moment, I felt coherent and intensely aware of the sensation Jordan's fingers evoked on the ribbon of exposed skin between my top and skirt.

"Don't be mad about the kiss."

Jordan's eyes remained hooded, his expression unreadable. A slight smirk twisted a corner of his mouth. "Tell me Marli, do *my* kisses curl your toes?"

"Let me check." I pulled his handsome face close, finding an invitation to compare waiting on his lips. Jordan's arms locked at my waist, crushing my body to him.

Dad walked in, catching us in an intense lip-lock, Jordan's tongue halfway down my throat. "Uh-hum!" Both brows rose over eyes burning my direction. "No wonder all hell broke loose today."

Jordan's face turned scarlet. He untangled from my arms and stepped back, putting a respectable distance between us.

"I should go. I've got a lecture tomorrow I'm required to attend."

I looked at the blackness beyond my window. "You're leaving now? But it's dark. It's not safe." Turning to my father, who already anticipated my question and scratched his scalp in frustration, I offered a solution. "Can Jordan stay the night? Please?"

"N-no, I'll get a hotel along the way," Jordan quickly offered.

Dad's resigned sigh confirmed I'd won. "Nonsense. Marli's right—about driving this late at night. You're welcome to sleep downstairs in the spare room." His finger tapped the top of my head. "But you, young lady, will remain upstairs."

I tried not to appear too joyful, but the wide smile on my face hurt. "Thanks Daddy." The endearment *daddy* I used when things needed to sway in my favor and worked like a charm. The sideways glower from Rick, however, informed me he also knew he'd been played.

A headache from Hell pounded my brain. Whatever made me slapstick silly last night left me feeling the total opposite once I woke. I rolled over and a piece of paper crinkled beneath my cheek. Rubbing my face hard to chase the last remnants of sleep away, I eased up against the headboard and unfolded the note.

*Marli—Sorry I didn't wake you to say goodbye, but your dad stood guard at the door. You looked so angelic sleeping and I desperately wanted to hold you one last time. I hope the kiss I left on your forehead will keep 'till I can put another one on your lips. —"Hooked."*

# 6
## GOSSIP TRAIN

My restored vintage pink Mustang spent more time in the shop waiting for special parts than in our garage. Running behind schedule and facing the probability of missing a shuttle to school, I conned Rick into letting me drive his twenty-year-old Volkswagen—a trip that turned out to be its last mission.

The "bug" sputtered and jerked when I pulled into a space in the parking lot and I worried it might never start again if I shut it off. When a poof of blue smoke exited the exhaust pipe with a bang sounding like a gunshot, I feared the junkyard was next. Everyone within earshot ducked. A few swore at me, but that wasn't what attracted their stares.

News traveled at alarming speed and yesterday's events followed me like a neon arrow, pointing to the girl who sucked the lips off some stranger in a fancy car, not to mention letting said stranger attempt to murder her jealous boyfriend. Correction—*ex*-boyfriend.

I walked down the hallway aware of the thousands of eyes burning into the back of my head. When I rounded the corner, Brit and Alex stood guard at my locker cube.

"Wonderful, locker stalkers."

Brittany appeared annoyed, her tone sharp. "You didn't return any of our messages and your father wouldn't let us talk to you."

I engaged my data pad in the docking unit and downloaded my assignments for today's classes before answering the onslaught of questions coming my way.

"I was busy being passed out. Jordan took me to the hospital and they gave me something to make me sleep. Dad's also royally ticked at the moment."

Alex's breath felt hot on my ear. "Jordan *Mason*?" Brittany moved closer, officially consuming the rest of the oxygen surrounding me.

"Yes," I whispered. "He came to see me."

"We need some major girl time. Let's go to that new doughnut shop."

"Are you nuts, Alex? I can't skip classes. I'm up for Valedictorian. Rick bribed Principal Anderson with a free checkup on her cat to excuse me yesterday."

"Lunch, then."

"Nope. English test to make up I also missed yesterday."

The bell rang and the hall became a sea of rushing bodies. I scanned my wristband to lock my cube. Brittany and Alex remained permanent fixtures in front of me. I couldn't talk about yesterday's events at school and risk someone hearing, nor could my friends come to my house with Rick watching my every move. Alex's house was the safest to share secrets.

"Can we do a girls night at your house? I'll buy pizza."

Asking Alex to wait until tonight for details would prove torturous. Her lips squiggled several times as she contemplated my proposal. "No ditching."

The late bell would ring any moment so I broke into a half jog toward my class and yelled over my shoulder. "I swear. Seven, K?"

"Pepperoni and mushrooms," Alex hollered back.

Yuck. She did that on purpose. I hated mushrooms, but sighed with relief that she didn't demand anchovies as her revenge topping."

Dad sounded crazed when I relayed the news his "baby" wouldn't start. Sometimes I wondered if given a choice between his old car and me, who'd win out. After yesterday, the car—hands down.

The wrecker driver anchored the Volkswagen, shaking his head at the river of dark liquid streaming from beneath the car. When he pulled away with my father's pride and joy, I faced an empty parking space...and Sam.

His rock hard body slumped with a hint of insecurity. One hand hid in a front pocket and he scrubbed the back of his neck with the other, his foot nervously scraping the pavement.

"Need a ride?" Most everyone had left so it was either him or a shuttle. Definitely not my first choice. "Face it, babe, we're going to have to talk about yesterday sooner or later."

I stopped at the open door of his jeep. "I'm not your 'babe.'"

"Whatever."

Sam parked in front of my house, angling to face me. I undid my seatbelt and mirrored his body posture. Offense versus Defense. He drew a long breath.

"I'm sorry, okay? Maybe I was an ass and deserved the slap. Probably the punch, too."

"*Maybe?* Am I the only one who remembers where your hands were?"

"Shit, cut me some slack, Marli. I said I'm sorry. I know what I did was wrong."

This was heading for a disaster. I checked my anger. "How's your stomach?"

"Hurts. But not as bad as my heart."

"Sam, don't start. You've known from day one I'd end up with a candidate. Thinking anything else was a fantasy." I reached for the handle, but he caught my hand.

"Wait. You're right. I pretended The Program didn't exist. I wanted to believe you'd never leave me, or at least nothing would happen until after summer. I wasn't prepared to walk in and find the future kissing you, and I lost it."

"Fighting wasn't smart. Both you and Jordan are built like brick walls. Someone could have gotten hurt."

Sam's eyes twinkled. "Brick wall, huh?" He flexed his arm and I laughed. The touch of his finger along the side of my face created a familiar tingle. "I love you. Always will. No government program can change that."

He leaned close and I knew he wanted to kiss. Common sense said "no," but it sounded like a foreign language in my head when his lips pressed. But when he leaned in again, I held him back.

"Sam, I can't do this."

He slumped back in his seat. "What about Prom? You said you'd go with me. Pretty sure it will be our last time together."

The sentence slid slowly like a dollop of honey off the lip of the dripper, pulling a golden thread to soften the landing. Upstairs on my closet door hung a midnight blue satin formal I'd spent an entire paycheck on. The dress looked amazing on me, but after what happened I wasn't sure Sam deserved to see me wearing it.

"*If* I go, I don't want a repeat of yesterday. Promise?"

He pulled me into a surprise hug, his lips sealing the deal on my mouth. "You got it."

Crap. I was going to Prom with Sam in a strapless gown that guaranteed my father a heart attack. If the gossip train reached him before the dance, Prom could be pre-empted by my funeral. I'd most likely be buried in the dress.

I stood on Alex's porch with a hot pizza container slowly blistering my fingers. What sounded like a herd of elephants thundered down the stairs to answer the door, the giggles and shushes hissed making me suspicious. Alex finally cracked the door and stomped her foot.

"Dang! You *brought* the pizza. I hoped that cute new boy who works behind the counter could have delivered it."

I pushed past her and into the spacious entryway. "What? You're on the outs with David again?" Brittany grabbed the pizza and started up the stairs.

Alex leaned on my shoulder. "Not me. Brit. She needs a date for Prom because Jason asked someone else."

Brittany's reply followed her into Alex's bedroom. "I don't need a date, Alexandra Nichols. I'm perfectly fine staying home."

Jason Curtis was Brittany's "Sam." They'd dated steady over the past six months, but apparently things had ended. Selfishly, I welcomed another topic to discuss besides me.

I placed a slice of cheesy pizza on a plate and proceeded to pick off the mushrooms. Brit sat quietly in a chair across the room, her gaze drifting over the bookcase to her side holding Alex's impressive collection of romance novels. I wandered over to her, precariously holding my plate of tomato based food as I crossed the carpet. Once I'd reached her, I sat my plate next to hers on the nightstand and pulled a book off the shelf feigning interest.

"Are you okay?" I asked, flipping the book over to read the back cover.

Alex emerged from her bathroom. "Not like she's got a lot of choices. She's a pinkie-slave like you." Alex flipped her head at me while looking at Brittany. "Did you tell her yet?"

"Tell me what?"

"I received a red envelope yesterday. I haven't opened it. Mom said I have to wait until Dad returns from his business trip, but insisted I stop dating Jason immediately."

The doughy cheese chunk in my mouth barely slid down my throat with my heavy swallow. "You've been eighteen for like what…a minute?" Only a week had passed since we celebrated Brittany's birthday. It felt like the government constantly watched us. "Are you going to open it?" The question hung in the air between us far too long awaiting an answer.

"I haven't decided. My parents—"

Alex's cell receptor buzzed merrily on the other nightstand, interrupting our conversation. A smile holding way too much knowledge spread over her lips. "Relax. I told you it would be okay." She sank deep into the pillows on her bed, nibbling a finger around a seductive giggle.

Brittany and I shared a wide-eyed glance and I mouthed *she thought she was pregnant again?* Brit bit into her pizza and bobbed her head slightly. I held up two fingers for the times I knew of that Alex thought she was pregnant. Brit held up three and mimed *Spring Break*.

No way could I live life so recklessly. We'd both scolded Alex about not using protection, especially considering prophylactics were practically handed out on street corners. But if we pushed the subject, she'd ultimately get angry and remind us her sex life was none of our business. Too bad she couldn't practice that same sentiment when it came to Brittany's and my relationships.

"Alex!" Brittany snapped loudly. "Tell David goodbye. We're not listening to you make disgusting sounds while you two have cyber sex."

I dropped the book.

"Gotta go, babe. The priestesses are here." Her sudden gravelly voice made me wish for a place to hide. "Don't you wish, but if that's the fantasy…sweet dreams." She shut the phone off. "David wants to know if you guys would be into 'group therapy.'"

"Disgusting on so many levels, Nichols," Brittany replied for both of us.

Alex laughed. "Speaking of group activities, what the hell happened yesterday, Davis? Word is your 'boy toys' got into a fight and the new kid on the block won."

"Crap. Does everyone know?" They both shook their heads. "For the record, it was Sam who started the whole thing. And he threw the first punch."

"Why were they fighting?" Brittany asked, handing me the book off the floor. "Did he catch you making-out in Jordan's car like you were in front of the school? My mom about had a come apart when she heard." My eyebrows lifted sharply. "What? You're shocked? Your candidate drives a *Porsche*, Marli. In this town, that's worth a ton a gossip on its own, not to mention the local veterinarian's daughter is locking lips with the driver in public."

My skin prickled with heat and I rubbed my arm to ease the sudden itch. A bead of sweat dribbled between my breasts.

"Sam caught Jordan kissing me in the kitchen when he stopped by to pick me up for school."

"Awesome!" Alex chortled. "How was it—Jordan's kiss, I mean. Mouth open or closed? Lips firm or mashed flat?" She fell back onto bed. "God, I'm jealous! I'll bet he tastes so sweet."

"Oh my gosh, Alex. Stop already." I pressed my finger to my left brow to end the twitching. "The kiss was good, okay?" They both stared at me. "All right...*epic*. Amazing. Beyond sexy!" I couldn't fight the smile creeping over my mouth. "And yes, Jordan tastes pretty sweet."

Alex did some fist-punch-kicking fest on top of her bed to match her squeals. Brittany dropped her head back to her shoulders and chewed me out for encouraging her.

"So that's what started the fight?" Alex finally breathed.

"Not exactly. Sam did something first...and I slapped him."

Their collective gasp could have pulled heavy furniture across a room. Both sets of eyes fixed on me. I couldn't hide the truth. An enhanced version would only be created to fill in the blanks.

"Fine, I'll tell you, but you have to *swear* this stays between us. If Rick finds out, he'll kill Sam."

I unraveled the story, cautiously revealing the part where Sam's anxious hands spun everything out of control. Again, I threatened a slow and painful death if the information leaked outside our threesome. Of course, I had no control over Sam's bragging rights.

# 7
# DEVIL'S ADVOCATE

A gentle stroke down the side of my face released tiny shivers in its wake. Lips brushed along my jaw and I fought against waking from the dream warming my body.

"Jordan," I whispered.

A firm kiss covered my murmur, but felt wrong—in a *good* way. The mouth fit perfectly over mine, but tasted different—the pressure more aggressive and the tongue, demanding. And yet, my body didn't question the source creating a hot tingle of excitement. Quite the opposite. I arched against a deeper kiss and arms circled my waist. The heart beating against my cheek thumped fast, the scent on the neck inviting.

The *scent*. The *lips*. The *taste*. Everything connected at once.

"Jesse!"

His hand clamped my mouth. "Shush! Do you want to get me shot?"

Rick did own a gun, but I was certain a bullet had never rested in the chamber, let alone burned through the barrel. However, I didn't think he'd hesitate testing his aim in this case.

I shoved Jesse hard when he leaned in for another kiss, causing him to lose his balance and topple off the side of the bed, dragging the quilt with him. I scrambled off the other side, reaching for my robe. The faint beep of Rick's alarm added panic to my anger.

"What the hell are you doing? How did you get in here, anyway?"

His grin disarmed me and my breath vanished. His head tipped toward the window. "You really should keep your window locked. You never know who might pop in."

When Jesse conducted an inch-by-inch inspection up my bare legs, I pulled the robe tight. The bikini on the yacht was out of my control, but Jesse stood on my turf—uninvited. If Jordan knew…

I pointed to the window. "Get out."

He kneeled on the window seat, evaluating his escape. "Are you nuts? If I fall, I'll be speared by that damn weather vane."

Cautiously, I moved closer. "I don't care. You can't be here—in my room. It's wrong and you know it."

"Whoa, you don't *care* if I'm gored to death? I have to say, I liked you better when you were sleeping—much more receptive. In fact, any more welcoming and we'd be doing a lot more than kissing."

Before I could stop him, Jesse unknotted the belt on my robe, exposing my cotton boxers and tight top. His gaze leisurely scrolled over me in appreciation, his unapologetic smirk making my cheeks burn.

Shocked by his brazenness, I bunched the fabric together, tied a double-knot, and glared angrily. "Dammit Jesse, put your eyes back in your head. And I'm serious, I want you to leave."

"Don't you want to know why I'm here?"

With every fiber of my being, but I knew Rick would check on me in less than five minutes and Jesse needed to disappear to save both our lives. Actually—one minute. The bedroom door across the hall squealed on its hinge.

"Why doesn't matter right now. Hide! My dad will kill you if he finds you in my bedroom."

Jesse barely made it under the bed, pulling his shoes beneath the eyelet bed ruffle just as the door cracked opened. Rick looked puzzled to see me standing by the bed instead of nestled under the covers—not as surprised as he'd be if he knew *why*.

"You're awake awfully early."

"I couldn't sleep. I'm thinking we should chop down that oak tree. Things keep waking me too early."

"Things?"

"Birds. I mean birds."

Dad walked over to my window, pulled it shut and locked the latch. "It might help if you kept the window closed. Your mother always wanted the window open while she slept, too."

"I'm nothing like Mom," I muttered, chancing a glance to make sure none of Jesse's limbs showed. Rick's eyes followed to where I let my mine linger a bit too long. I shifted the quilt slightly for insurance, causing a curious expression to cover his face.

"You have her good traits." He settled on the side of the bed, yanking the quilt up, watching my reaction. I didn't flinch. "Mars, we need to talk. Karen told me what really happened with Sam, not your edited version."

Karen? Dad's nurse? How would she know anything? The light bulb in my brain flicked on. David—her son and Alex's boyfriend, depending on the day.

"What exactly did she tell you?"

"Enough to know I want to break Sam's neck. I also didn't know about your public display of affection with Mr. Mason in front of the school." Dad rubbed his furrowed brow. "Daughter, I swear you're going to be the death of me, but I hate to think of what might have happened if Jordan hadn't been there."

Karen apparently didn't miss any details. Alex would definitely hear from me. I also swore I heard a growl from under my bed.

Dad looked at his watch. "We'll talk later. I know your dance is tonight, but you better meet Sam there. I don't want him around here anymore." He paused in the doorway, "Mars, I hate to ask, but could you put Muffy out for me? I'm running late. I bought a stronger cable leash."

"*Daaadd.*"

He ruffled my tangled nest of hair. "Thanks, Pumpkin—I'll owe you."

As soon as the front door shut, I dropped to my knees. "Okay, it's safe to come out."

Jesse dragged himself from under the bed. "I'm not so sure. What are you planning to do with me?"

I sat cross-legged on my bed, pondering the same question. Part of me felt unexpected excitement with Jesse being here, but another part of me—the one controlled by a shred of common sense, feared the consequences.

I had no idea what The Program would do about the situation and Rick would ground me for the rest of my life. But Jordan? His twin brother climbing in the window of his assigned candidate's bedroom—kissing her, well technically that already happened, but I was dressed and not lying on a bed—how would he react? We shared something, although I couldn't say exactly what the connection was, but it felt powerful enough to know he'd freak if he found out.

Jesse brushed lint off his shoulders and stretched an arm across me. "All right, who's Sam?"

"My soon-to-be-ex-boyfriend. His hands got a little carried away, but nothing to create an international incident over." Jesse *hmfed* a disapproving grunt. I picked a couple of stray dusty clumps from his hair. "Looks like I need to work on my housekeeping skills. If Jordan chooses me, maybe he'll invest in a maid?"

Jesse didn't smile back. "I don't want to think about you with Jordan." He glanced around my room, a teasing grin returning to his face. "I kind of like your domestic talents. It makes finding something to wear much easier when your entire wardrobe is spread across the floor." He caught my fist in midair, thwarting a playful punch. "Do you want to wrestle me? I warn you, I don't play fair." He kissed my neck below my ear, whispering, "And I *will* win."

"I don't doubt it." My hand on his chest stopped him from moving closer. "So? Why are you here?"

"Kiss me and I'll tell you."

"Stop playing games. This is serious, Jesse. If you don't want to chance falling to your death from that old tree, you better start explaining."

The bed groaned loudly when he dropped backward. "I had to see you, Mars. I can't stop thinking about you."

"Jess, you *can't* see me. It's against the rules."

He rested on his elbow. "You already know my thoughts about rules."

"What about Jordan? The kiss on the yacht is one thing, but you showing up here? You know it's wrong."

Jesse slid his fingers down mine from the hand dangling off my knee. "Then why does it feel so right?"

He pushed me against the headboard and when his mouth came close, I didn't block the kiss—I couldn't. His body stretched between my bent knees, his arms snaking around my waist. I knew I should stop him—stop myself, but the reckless moment filled a void left since Daniel's death. The need to please everyone, be the good daughter—the strong friend—the ideal candidate—the 'perfect everything,' disappeared. I was simply a teenage girl who desperately wanted to feel something besides sorrow, anger, and unbearable frustration knowing I could possibly fail.

Right now, I wanted to break the rules and lose myself in Jesse, but my dutiful conscience played dirty. She threw the memory of Jordan's eyes staring intensely into mine seconds before he placed that first sweet, tentative kiss on my lips. The kiss of a promise to care for me as a person, not just his genetic link. His second kiss I granted permission to, tasted of a future filled with hope and possibly the forever I'd dreamed about as a child.

I abruptly broke the heated connection between our mouths. "No more, Jess. I need to keep my head straight."

"Why?" he asked with a shallow breath.

"Because of Jordan. I don't want to mess things up. You understand, don't you?"

Jesse moved back, his brows scrunched. "Not really, but if I'm coming on too strong, I'll back off."

I struck a dramatic pose, finger pressed to my chin. "Let's see. Crawling through a bedroom window uninvited—trying to undress and seduce your brother's girlfriend—and you still need to ask? What do you think, Jesse?"

"So you two are officially boyfriend and girlfriend?"

We weren't officially anything, but that didn't change the situation.

"Titles aren't really the issue here, are they?" I moved off the bed and opened my bedroom door. "I need to get ready for school. You can see yourself out."

"Mars, wait. At least let me fix you breakfast."

I slapped down my conscience before she could object. "There's a catch. You take Muffy out first." I grinned wide, knowing this would be a true test of Jesse's strength and patience.

"Any doggy 'doo-doo' guidelines I should follow?"

"Just hold tight and enjoy your flight. There are pickup bags next to her leash in the laundry room." I almost felt remorseful, pushing him into the hallway.

"It's only a dog. How hard can it be?" Two seconds later, Muffy barked and Jesse yelped. "Leash hell! Where's her saddle?"

Still savoring the taste of my last piece of bacon, I gathered our dishes and placed them in the sink. "I better get going. I can't be late for my Calculus final." Jesse moved behind me, resting his chin on my shoulder.

"You sure I can't talk you into playing hooky?"

Holding me like this, he could talk me into anything without a problem. I turned and shook my pink bracelet.

"I wish. Only a couple more hours and I'm done with finals."

"Okay you win, but I'll take you and wait while until you're done. I've nothing to do today but spend time with you."

"What happened to coming on too strong? And what if someone finds out?"

Jesse's smile held its own warning. "I'm a work in progress. Don't worry. No one will find out. I move like smoke. Sneaky and silent."

"Smoke? Really? That's reaching, even for you." We stepped out into the warm morning sun blanketing the front porch. "Where's your car?"

"Around the corner. I didn't think it was a good idea for your dad to find a strange car parked in front of the house."

That gave me an idea. Pulling Jesse across the front lawn to the side of the house, I explained my father wouldn't know anything if I drove. He agreed until he saw my car.

"You're joking. *Pink*?" He stood planted on the grass, immoveable as granite. "No way. I'm not that comfortable with my feminine side." He grabbed my arm. "We're taking my car."

We rounded the corner and I tripped over my feet. Parked against the curb was a bright red Ferrari.

"Jesse, please tell me that's not yours."

He opened the passenger door. "Hurry up, or you're going to be late."

The car roared to life like a tiger waiting to pounce on its prey. To the side of the steering column I noticed a button marked "Hover."

"This *hovers*?"

Jesse glanced at me, a wicked wink eclipsing one eye. "I told you some rules are meant to be broken."

Déjà vu. Students froze into statues when we pulled in front of the school, necks straining to see inside the sleek, red rocket.

"I'll be back to get you in a couple of hours. Good luck on your test." Jesse took my face in his fingers, his mouth holding mine in a deep lip lock, curling my toes inside my shoes. When a second kiss loomed, I pressed my hand to his mouth.

"'Sneaky,' remember? I can't take the risk. Besides I've got to think about math, not you."

My Calculus test proved nothing but a mental strain. My thoughts weren't remotely close to anything academic. My brain and heart waged war. Why did Jesse show up? I was perfectly happy letting myself fall for Jordan before he waltzed, or climbed into my life and kissed me. Damn! Both Mason brothers' lips should be registered as lethal weapons. Once either of their mouths touched mine, I became an emotional, not to mention, hormonal mess.

The buzzer rang and I scanned my bracelet, saving my answers before sending to the teacher's computer for final grading. I'd barely stepped out of the classroom before Alex and Brittany dragged me into the nearest alcove. Alex's eyes were wild.

"Ferrari? Who the hell brought you to school?"

Brittany stood only remotely calmer. "Marli, what's going on? He's not Jordan."

"Would you two keep your voices down? You're right, he's not Jordan. He's his twin brother, Jesse."

Both sets of brows disappeared, eyes wide with shock—an appropriate response, given the bomb I'd dropped.

Alex's eyes shifted from side to side. "I saw him kiss you."

"Yes..." The corners of my mouth curled at the hot little memory flashback. I grabbed Brittany's arm when she teetered.

"No! Marli, you could get in serious trouble. What if someone demanded a DNA swab?"

"You mean a virgin popsicle?" Alex teased. "I'd like to see what color mine would turn."

The Program randomly tested candidates' DNA using special sticks that changed colors when sucked, should a candidate violate the chastity clause in their contract. The spit test also revealed *whose* DNA you shared.

"I can't get in trouble for kissing someone." Trouble, however, brewed inside me emotionally and I feared physically, if not checked. Still, this was my life and my so-called "love life" stayed my business. Not my friends'.

The anger rising surprised me. "You know what? Nobody owns me yet. I can do whatever I want." Breaking through their body fortress, I marched out the front doors. They both trotted behind and I turned a half step backward. "By the way, thanks a lot, Alex, for opening your big mouth. Worry about your own life and stay out of mine."

My mood lightened as soon as I spied the red chariot tucked under the trees at the end of the parking lot. I jumped into waiting arms, slamming our bodies against the side of the car. Jesse smiled wide at my reaction.

"Hello to you, too. I take it things went well?"

"Only missed one—a miracle considering you were all I could think about."

"I like the sound of that."

Surely an audience watched, but I didn't care. Jesse opened the car door for me and I slid inside, wanting nothing more than to disappear with him.

"We better go," he warned. "I'm sure that little performance didn't go unnoticed."

The Ferrari slowly made its way down my street. A serene scene, locked in a past time when life wasn't complicated and the government didn't intrude. Simple things like falling in love with the boy next door remained a choice you made for yourself, not one made for you.

"Mars? What are you thinking about?"

"How messed up my life is. I'm so confused. I've always known what's expected, but I used to know what I wanted. Now, I'm not sure I know the difference."

His voice quieted. "I know I should stay away. You're assigned to Jordan." He focused somewhere beyond the windshield. "As much as I want to be with you Marli, I won't hurt Jordan."

"Who says I'd choose you?"

He laughed. "Touché."

I squeezed his hand. "Can you stay a little longer? We could make sundaes."

Oddly, he pulled his hand from mine. "Oh now it's okay for me to stay? Don't you need to get ready for your date with the octopus?"

"Don't remind me, but there's still time."

Jesse's leather seat squeaked when he leaned closer and eased his arm behind my shoulders. "Do you have candy sprinkles? I like candy sprinkles."

I stilled when he twirled his fingers in my hair. "I wish you wouldn't do that."

He unraveled a long curl over my collarbone. "What? Touch your hair or make you feel like this?"

I swung the car door open. "Both."

We'd barely finished our ice cream when Dad's truck pulled into the driveway. Panic welled up as I imagined his reaction to the red sports car parked at the curb.

"Uh-oh, my dad's home early."

Jesse looked baffled. "So?"

I rolled my eyes. "*So?*" He doesn't know you're here. Crap—he doesn't know *you*."

"He will soon enough. Besides, I've something I want to ask him."

I whirled around, fear of the unknown taking the air out of my lungs. "What?"

No time for an answer because the front door slammed, rattling all the windows in the house.

"MARLI DAVIS! *FERRARI?*" Rick bellowed. "Now who's here? And girl, please tell me what I heard today is not true."

"Dad!" I rushed him when he walked into the kitchen, kissing his cheek with a big, guilty smile plastered on my face.

Jesse extended his hand, a gesture I might have thought twice about, but who was I to judge? "Jesse Mason, sir. I'm Jordan's brother."

Warily, my father shook Jesse's hand. "Why are you here, if I might ask?"

"My band is performing in Cleveland, so I thought I'd check in on Marli. For Jordan."

"Liar," Rick accused. Jesse's cheeks flushed immediately and he pushed his hands deep in his pockets, stepping back.

"Dad!"

Rick's cheeks puffed, his faced reddened. He placed his medical bag on the counter and moved between Jesse and me, his hands firmly pressed on his hips. His head dipped slightly, eyes sharp and locked on mine, the creases in his forehead rolled into deep furrows—all signs I walked a dangerous line.

Using great restraint to keep his anger subdued, Dad continued. "I said Sam couldn't come here anymore, but he's the least of my worries. I heard 'episode two' of your ever revolving love life, Mars." His eyes flashed between Jesse and me, his thumb hooking Jesse's direction. "Is it true? Were you two kissing in his car? Who's on your lip agenda tomorrow, Marli? Honestly, what's up with you?"

My eyes narrowed. All the suppressed frustrations pushed to the surface and I took a half step back. "For your information, Dad, and anyone else's for that matter," a pointed glance at Jesse, "whom I kiss is my business. If I want to kiss Jesse, I will. And I'll kiss Jordan if I want, too. In fact, I might march across the street and place a big wet one on Mr. Baxter."

Jesse's mouth tightened and Dad's flew open.

"Marli Elizabeth Davis!"

Dad shrilling my middle name, used rarely and generally not for positive reasons, meant I'd probably be grounded the rest of my life. Jesse's head lowered. Embarrassed at placing him in the middle of a domestic warzone, I pulled back my bubbling anger.

"I'll be fine with Sam. After tonight, I'm not seeing him anymore."

Dad's stance widened, his arms crossed. "You mean you're finally breaking it off with him?"

"Yes. It's only right with Jordan in the picture now." Jesse's face fell and I instantly regretted being so callous.

"Jordan? You're back to Jordan, now? Done with Jesse already? Make up your mind, Marli."

My nose burned and I knew tears would appear next, but I couldn't let Dad think he gained the upper hand in our argument, especially in front of Jesse. "Stop! *My* life, remember?"

I stormed upstairs, slammed the door to my room, and scrubbed my fists over my wet cheeks in frustration. A familiar melody chimed on my receptor and Jordan's handsome face appeared on the screen, a grin sliding up one corner of his mouth. My big fat cheating heart dropped to my shoes.

I slid to the floor against the door and answered in a small voice. "Hi."

"Hi yourself. Is everything all right? You sound kind of down for a Friday night. Hopefully it's because you miss me."

Jordan came the last three weekends to visit, but this weekend he stayed at Cornell to cram for finals. The only *studying* we managed was the human anatomy. It also made sense now why Jesse showed up today. He knew Jordan would be stuck in New York.

"Of course I miss you. I wish my dad would let me come there and spend a weekend."

"I think we both know why he doesn't; not to mention, I'd never get my homework done. So my lonely girl, what are your plans for the weekend?"

"Tonight is Senior Ball. Before we met, I promised Sam I'd go with him."

Jordan covered the phone, but I heard the explicit oath. He grew silent and I checked the video transmission. His thumb and forefinger pinched his nose.

"Jordan?"

"Give me a minute, Marli."

While his heart calmed, mine beat frantically. If he took the news about a date with Sam this badly, I couldn't fathom what his reaction would be if he knew Jesse waited downstairs.

"Marli, I don't have a good feeling about this. I worry about you being alone with Sam."

"I'll be okay. Brit and Alex will be there, along with practically the whole senior class. I already warned Sam to behave, and I'm sure Dad will enforce my midnight curfew. He's not happy I'm going with Sam, either."

"Why not?"

"He heard the rumors from his nurse about what happened. I'm surprised he's letting me out of the house."

"I wish I was there. I'd take you. Can you call when you get home, please?"

"Sure. And for the record, I wish you were my date instead of Sam, too."

"Marli, have fun, but be careful. I don't know what I'd do if something happened to you. Not now. I care too much."

Something in his statement stirred a funky ripple in my abdomen. I liked Jordan more than I wanted to admit, even with Jesse tugging on the other half of my heart.

I wiggled and tugged the corset-like contraption Alex talked me into buying, snapping and tucking everything into place. My breasts overflowed and I flushed red when I saw my reflection, quickly pulling on the dress to cover the black lace.

Dark blue satin hugged every curve and the deep slit up one side of the skirt, exposed my good leg clear to my hip. When I glanced in the mirror at all the skin the dress did *not* cover, I feared tonight might turn into another wrestling match with Sam.

I couldn't get the zipper up all the way and needed Dad's help. *May as well deal with the shock factor now.* Holding the dress against my chest, I cracked the door.

"Dad? Could you help me? I can't get—"

Jesse appeared at the top of the stairs, my breath catching when I saw the look in his eyes.

"Wow," he choked, averting his gaze to the floor. "Your dad took Muffy for a walk. I think he needed to vent some frustration."

The grandfather clock in the living room chimed the seven o'clock hour. "Great. Sam will be here any minute. Can you finish zipping my dress?"

Jesse followed me into my bedroom, leaving the door open in case anyone came upstairs. I gazed pensively at him in the mirror, standing behind me. He zipped the dress, placed a tender kiss on the back of my neck, and stared back at my reflection in the mirror.

"You're beautiful." Jesse turned me in his arms, his expression worrisome. "Marli, are you going to be safe with Sam?" His eyes dropped, unfortunately to my cleavage, *heaving* with my heavy breaths. "I mean, this dress..."

"Hey, eyes up here." I locked my arms around his waist. "Jesse, what I said earlier about Jordan, I'm sorry."

His thumb brushed my cheek. "Don't worry about it. I've a tendency to push limits, and you're definitely 'off limits.'" A mischievous grin curled the edges of his mouth. "Not that *that* could stop me."

I wanted to drown in his kisses like before, but the doorbell interrupted my steamy reverie. "I guess I better get this over with."

The back door slammed.

"MARLI!" Dad shouted up the stairwell then muttered a stream of profanities. Taking a deep breath and aware Rick salivated planning Sam's demise, I clutched Jesse's hand. However, seeing me come down the stairs in a strapless, body hugging dress with Jesse might take matters a treacherous direction.

"You better wait here," I whispered, feeling the gentle hug of his hand.

"Are you sure you'll be all right?"

"No, but I'm the only one that can do this. I have to break Sam's heart tonight. I just hope I can do it and come home dressed." His expression blackened and his grip tightened. "Jess, I'm joking." But I wasn't. Suddenly, I realized Jesse wouldn't be here when I returned. "You'll be gone when I get back. I don't know how I feel about that."

"Well, that's promising. You haven't ruled me out all together." He tapped my cell receptor. "I programmed in my number."

I gave him an unbelieving glower. "Jess…"

"What? I just want you to call when you get home so I know you survived. Delete it after if you're so worried."

We both knew I wouldn't, which meant delivering a sobering reminder of the boundary line we kept crossing. "Jordan asked me to call him, too."

It worked. Jesse let my hand fall. "Jordan? When did you talk to him?"

"He called while I was getting ready. He's not thrilled I'm going with Sam either."

"At least we agree on one thing. Did you tell him I'm here?"

My gaze dropped. "No."

Jesse tipped my face upward. A smug grin tugged his lips, undoubtedly pleased I kept this snippet from Jordan. "Why not?"

"I'm not sure, exactly." Dad's berating of Sam escalated. "I need to rescue Sam."

Rick caged poor Sam against the wall. "You have Marli back in this house by midnight Samuel Jenkins, or I'll have the police out looking for you! Understand? And keep your damn hands off—"

"Dad!" I moved between them. "Enough," I mouthed.

Jesse appeared around the corner from the dining room and Sam's brow furrowed. I explained he was Jordan's twin, hopefully deflecting any further reaction. When Dad evaluated my dress, I decided we needed to leave before he murdered one of us.

We paused on the porch and Sam's eyes roved the length of my body, his gaze fixed on my bulging chest. "You look *smokin'* babe."

# 8
# LAST DANCE

Sam guided me onto the dance floor, brushing through a wind of hushed whispers from the gossiping mouths we passed. His fingers splayed across my lower back, pressing me close.

"Marli, relax, please?"

*Relax?* My mind spun a million different directions. I'd left Jesse at Rick's mercy. Who knew what could happen once he had a Mason boy alone? And what if Jordan found out Jesse had come to Maple Heights to find me?

I checked off the faces of classmates dancing close by, some turning away when caught staring, others using the opportunity to pass judgment through steely glares.

*I wonder if any of them are spies for The Program.*

Rumors of "plants" paid to follow candidates my counselor dismissed to other paranoid applicants who'd broken the rules of conduct and ran scared. But what if the stories were true? What if one of these supposed friends passing judgment would, or already had, contacted The Program about my behavior?

Sam twisted a lock of my hair, forcing me from my obsessive thoughts. "Come on, can't tonight be like old times?" I cringed against the kiss to my neck, hating when his mouth covered the shell of my ear. "Everybody's figured out we're breaking up, Marli. They all saw you kissing both boys."

"Don't even go there," I quietly cautioned, not wanting to draw attention.

When the band took a break, I ducked outside under the pretense of going to the restroom. I checked my cell receptor, hoping for an instant message from Jordan. Instead, Jesse had left one only a few minutes earlier. *Be careful.* I tapped the reply *drive safe,* hoping he understood I wanted him gone from here and not waiting for me when I returned. Just the idea of Jesse's visit being considered forbidden made it more enticing. He existed behind a prohibited barrier and the want to crossover—to defy the rules or even break them, grew stronger each time I saw him. He had to stay away to keep me safe…from myself.

"There you are!" Alex called out. "We've been looking for you…" She blew a slow whistle. "You look *soooo* sexy. Sam will never let you go without a fight."

Brittany, who ended up coming with Jason after all, followed up Alex's comment with a harsh reminder. "Sam doesn't have a choice, and he certainly doesn't deserve Marli."

"'Sam bashing' now?" Alex debated. "Cut the guy some slack. He's obviously hurting."

"I doubt Sam's suffering too much," Brit replied under her breath, her expression twisted with regret when we locked eyes. She quickly explained. "I saw one of the sophomore girls hanging on him at the refreshment table."

Shoving past an unbidden ping of jealousy, I shrugged my shoulders. "She can have him. Tonight I'm breaking things off for good."

"It's probably for the best. I'd hate to see you get in trouble."

Alex giggled. "Marli's already *trouble* according to my mom. She called after her club meeting suggesting I reconsider my choice of friends."

We laughed at the outrageous assumption. Everyone considered Alex the "wild child." Her mother's observation, however, forced me to realize how reckless my behavior appeared. No wonder Rick always seemed riled.

I leaned over the railing, noting the clouds thickening and blocking the stars. A storm threatened, but in the atmosphere or my life? Alex climbed on the railing, holding the post for support and leaned out to look at the heavens.

"Rain, rain, go away..." she sang before pulling back under the eaves. A devilish grin brightened her face. "So what gives with Jordan's hunky brother?"

Head down, I picked at the sequins edging the slit on my dress. "The connection with Jordan is so strong, it scares me. Jesse's an escape. What I feel for him is pure lust."

Alex laughed but Brittany didn't. "Watch out. Things happen fast. You and Sam haven't gone too far, and if Jordan's in The Program you know he hasn't done anything either. But Jesse? Is he still a—"

"*Virgin?*" I gasped. Jesse never clarified one way or the other after he divulged his brush with the law. "I don't know and I'm not asking."

Alex slapped my shoulder. "Marli Davis, you're blushing. Mom's right. You are bad!" Out of the blue, she stopped giggling and stepped off the railing. "Uh-oh, speaking of *bad,* Sam's coming and he doesn't look happy."

Sam's angry footsteps echoed loudly on the planked porch. His gray eyes narrowed when he saw me. Flashbacks of the other day flickered. Being alone with Sam suddenly didn't seem the best idea.

"I better go. I'll call you tomorrow." I hurried to meet him, feeling an uncomfortable urgency knotting my insides.

Sam stared with an unnerving darkness set in his eyes. "Nice disappearing act, Marli. Let's go. This dance is lame and I'm tired of all the stares." His eyes checked off my body again and his hand lightly brushed my bare shoulder. My skin prickled. "What do you say we go someplace private?"

I pressed a fist to my queasy stomach. *Private* with Sam given his mood and the way I was dressed, screamed danger. For once, I decided to pay attention to the warning voices shouting in my head. Remaining at the country club kept me safe, but I needed to convince Sam to stay. I'd also call Rick for a ride home.

"What about the team party?"

His voice deepened, a finger tracing the edge of my bodice. "I don't care about the team. I want to be alone with you."

"But—"

I didn't get to finish my sentence. Sam pushed me against the clubhouse, the fabricated siding used to give a "log cabin" appearance, scraping against my naked shoulder blades. He pinned my arms to the rough surface, placing a hard, territorial kiss on my mouth. His tongue tasted of something bitter mixed with the lingering fruity punch flavor. I doubted any alcohol could be smuggled in under the security detail assigned to the dance, but chemical enhancements in small vials could easily be hidden inside a bra or an elaborate hair clip.

When Sam's knee pressed between my legs, the fabric at the top of the slit on my dress strained. "Samuel Jenkins, if you ruin this dress I'll kill you!"

His brow rose in a brash *like I care* arch. His mouth slowly grazed over the exposed skin on my chest and when he pressed his hips hard against mine, the satin finally surrendered with a small tear.

I fumbled with the receptor still in my hand, locating the "0" key. A message for help with my location would automatically dial the last number I used. Of course I thought that number would be Rick because he'd called to reinforce his concerns while Sam drove to the dance. Unbeknownst to me, however, my instant message to Jesse logged his number as the last one entered.

When Sam released my arms to indulge in a hand slide up my exposed thigh with one hand, while the other cupped a breast, I shoved him back.

"That's it, Sam! We're done. I'm calling Dad to come get me."

He scrubbed his hands through his hair, keeping his body close enough I couldn't move away. "No, don't. I'm sorry, really. I don't know what came over me. I'll be good, I swear."

"Is the punch spiked with something?" I asked, debating whether to give him another chance.

"Do you really think someone would be stupid enough to risk their graduation by pulling that stunt?"

"Yeah, I do. I tasted something metallic in your mouth when you tried to swallow my tongue."

He stepped back and drew a deep breath, his gaze turned to the golf course hidden in the black beyond. "You know me, Marli. I don't mess with that shit. I confess I had a couple of drinks from the decanter I carried into the party room because I was thirsty, but I swear I know nothing about it being laced with something." Gently, he stroked the side of my face. "Please stay."

He handed me the clutch bag I dropped when he caught me off guard with his groping fest, and begged for another chance. I hoped sincerity lie somewhere in the depth of his dark eyes and I wasn't making a mistake. I placed my cell receptor inside my purse and linked my arm through his. I'd forgotten, however, to cancel the distress call.

I stopped just outside the room Coach reserved for the team party. I never really fit in this part of Sam's world. We worked as a couple until Sam found himself in a situation where competition clouded his common sense—like the morning he caught me in Jordan's arms. His insecurities surfaced too fast for him to handle so he'd morph into the only skin he felt empowered within—a cocky smartass. I could almost see his body ripple with the transformation the minute he entered the room.

The second I stepped inside, I regretted my decision to stay. Athletes representing all the school's teams milled about, girls fused under their arms. A couple of cheerleaders sized me up from their perched positions on boyfriends' laps, and a lack of self-confidence swept through me. I fingered the slit in my dress hoping the glittery beads hid the inch-long tear.

Sam's team captain sauntered up to me, draping an arm around my neck. "Yo, Marli Davis, 'Princess of the Porsche,' or is it a Ferrari today?"

Loud mouth Craig Hansen had been a thorn in my side since elementary school and tonight proved no exception. When he planted an unexpected kiss on my mouth and tried to force my lips apart with his slimy tongue, the same medicinal taste I discovered in Sam's mouth seeped through, confirming my suspicions about the punch. I planted a knee firmly in Mr. Hansen's groin to force him back, but not before his hand grazed someplace off limits. I glared at Sam, who'd joined his group of foul-mouthed comrades huddled in the corner.

"Gotta watch my girl, Hansen," he shouted, summoning everyone's attention my direction.

"Shit Jenkins, she's not your girl," Hansen coughed. "She's everybody's lately. I'm just sampling the buffet."

I turned my back to the room, forcing down angry tears. Crying would only encourage the loathsome banter. Sam stole behind me and kissed the bend where my neck and shoulder met. I waited for the apology but instead, he accused me of being uptight and no fun. He gave my butt a playful swat, encouraging whistles and heckling.

"Jerk!" I snarled, which he followed up with his usual "whatever" and walked over to the refreshment table. A petite blonde in a short, tight skirt sidled close to Sam, holding out her glass for a refill. He hesitated before deciding which container of berry-colored liquid to pour from until Hansen gave him a thumbs-up. It appeared Sam also lied about his innocence on the spiked punch.

"You lying ass! Drop dead, Jenkins!"

I stormed out of the room, ignoring Sam's demand to stop. Wrenching my dress to my knees, I made a break for the exit, hearing Sam's footsteps gaining. I jumped the steps from the deck and ran down the gravel driveway, sliding sideways and landing in the dirt. The heel broke off my new shoe heightening my anger level.

A car skidded beneath the iron arch marking the entrance leading to the clubhouse and raced toward me with alarming speed. Dust plumes twisted in front of the headlights and the driver door flew open.

"Mars!"

"Jesse?"

He lifted me onto my feet and brushed the dust off the side of my gown. "What happened? I got your distress message and turned around at the first exit."

I didn't get a chance to answer before Sam caught up to us, following the oath he cursed when he saw the Ferrari. "Unbelievable!" he yelled, his echo swirling on the wind. "I can't even have one last night alone with you without one of the pretty boys showing up to swoop in and save you from 'big bad Sam.' Hell Marli. You promised."

Jesse's body stiffened and I pressed a hand to his chest. "Ignore him."

"Ignore me?" Sam raged and I cowered against Jesse. "That's all you've done tonight!" He pushed his fingers through his ebony locks, cocked his head and checked his tone. "Can I talk to you alone?"

"Like earlier?" I pointed to an old pickup across the parking lot. "Maybe you could throw me against the grill of that truck? That should leave some nice marks to match the scrapes on my back. Who knows? My whole dress could rip apart this time and you could finish what you started."

"What the hell?" Jesse drew me closer, his arms a warm shield of armor. "She's not moving an inch closer to you, jackass. I won't let you touch her again with your filthy hands."

"Going to keep your brother's mitts off her, too?" Sam smirked. "That's right, you can't. Marli's his 'government issued' property. He can do what he wants with her—things you can only dream about, loverboy."

Jess moved me behind him and took a stance I now recognized the Mason brothers did in preparation for battle. That's when Sam saw the band circling Jesse's wrist."

"Well, well. You're no better than I am with your piss-yellow bracelet. In fact, I'm guessing you're violating a shitload of regulations right now."

The gravel crunched beneath their shoes when they stepped closer to each other. I shuffled around Jesse, finding myself boxed in the middle.

"Not as many as you apparently have, asshole," Jesse answered. "Assaulting a candidate carries a hefty fine."

Sam's voice dropped, his tone menacing. "Nothing compared to 'stealing' one. I'll bet your brother would rip your head off if he knew what you were doing."

"I'd like to tear seven pounds of ugly fat from your shoulders just to shut you up!"

I pushed my arms out, keeping the two of them separated. "Jesse, stop," I begged. By now, an audience had formed along the deck overlooking the parking lot and my reputation received another blow. I watched for Coach to barrel through, or the police to arrive any second. "Guys, we're being watched."

Someone started yelling *"Fight! Fight!"*

Sam tossed his tuxedo jacket to the ground. "Bring it on."

"No!" I shrilled, wrapping my arms around Jesse's waist and pulling him back. "Get in the car before there's trouble." He wouldn't budge. "I'm leaving with you, okay? Please?"

Jesse's eyes shifted from Sam to me. He picked up the broken heel from my shoe and grabbed my hand, slowing his stride to match my awkward limp across the gravel.

Sam yelled after us. "Fuck you, Davis!"

Jesse immediately locked his arms around me, holding my flailing limbs tight and forcing me into the car. We sped off, leaving my memory of Senior Prom hidden behind a curtain of dust.

# 9
## GAME ON

Rain pounded the top of the Ferrari by the time we reached my house. I stared at the droplets trickling down the passenger window and absentmindedly traced their squiggly trails with my finger. Jesse pulled close to the back porch and turned the car off.

"Mars? You okay?"

"I don't know."

"Want to talk?" Jesse's fingers drew light circles on my bare shoulder. "Or anything else? These seats do recline."

I smiled against the glass. "And my father's bedroom window is right above us."

"Right." His hand dropped. "Marli, has Sam ever physically hurt you? You acted afraid of him tonight."

I jerked my head his direction. "Huh? *No.* Sam hasn't ever been mean. This whole thing with Jordan and me has him a little nuts, that's all."

"He's not the only one."

Jesse climbed out of the car and ran to my side, keeping his leather jacket over our heads until we reached the back door. A ribbon of light from the lamp in the upstairs hallway drifted across the kitchen floor. Jesse reached for me and I settled against him.

He rubbed my arms briskly. "Your skin feels cold. Have you got anything hot to drink?"

"There's some herbal tea in the cabinet above the beverage maker and cream in the refrigerator."

"Go tell your dad you're home and I'll brew a couple cups."

I paused at the top of the stairs, my heart beating two different rhythms; one for Jordan, the other for Jesse, both frightening me.

"Jess, thanks for being my hero."

"Anytime. It was the highlight of my day."

I tiptoed into Dad's room. The viewing screen played without sound. He lay asleep on his back, his mouth open and the beginning sounds of a snore rattling in the back of his throat. I kissed the rugged skin of his cheek.

"I'm home," I whispered.

"W-What?" He rose on one elbow, turning the clock to face him. "You're early. Is everything okay?" Something in my face told him *no*. He turned on the lamp, patted the edge of the bed for me to sit. "Things didn't go well with Sam, I take it."

"No. Tonight turned into a disaster."

He tucked my hair behind my ear, exposing my face. "Anything I should worry about? Do I need to have Sam arrested?"

Sam locked away sounded perfect. "No, nothing that serious." I stood and leaned against the corner of the wall, not sure how he'd handle my next revelation. "Um, Jesse brought me home."

Dad swung his legs off the side of the bed and put on an old pair of glasses. He pressed his palms on his thighs ready to pounce if necessary, and I straightened, ready to run if that happened.

"*Jesse*? What was he doing there?"

Telling Dad Jesse answered a distress signal I triggered meant subjecting myself to a relentless cross-examination, possibly landing Sam behind bars. As angry as I was at him, I didn't want to jeopardize his scholarship to Ohio State. The lame explanation I quickly invented, however, didn't go much better.

"Jesse said he had a hunch he should stick around. I think he had my phone tagged so he knew if I even went to the bathroom," I joked to lighten the situation, which had the opposite effect.

"*Stalking* is what I'd call it. Why did he bring you home?"

"I didn't want to stay with Sam. Someone spiked the punch and I didn't trust him to drive."

*Oops.* My revelation brought Rick to his feet.

"You're through with Samuel Jenkins, Marli, understand? Done! Over! Grounded forever if I hear you so much as talked to him, got that?"

"Fine with me. He's a total jackass, anyway."

Rick's finger shook dangerously close to my eye. "And another thing. You need to be on guard regarding Jordan's brother. He's got an agenda."

"Okay, we're not having this conversation. Jesse knows the boundaries." I lied through my teeth on that statement. Jesse only knew how to *cross* boundaries, not stay behind them.

"But do you? *Kissing* your assigned candidate's brother is a definite crossover. I'm sure Jordan wouldn't be thrilled if—"

"Enough already! You made your point. Go back to sleep. I'm going downstairs and sit with Jesse a while."

"He's not spending the night, Mars. I'm not running a hotel for the Mason brothers."

"I know! I know!" I marched across the hall to my room.

"And I'm keeping my door open!" Rick yelled before I slammed mine.

My cell receptor flashed on my bed. *Sam.* The guy had guts.

"Leave me alone!" I screeched and hung up, not waiting for a response. I deleted his number and muted my computer. I wasn't reliving my prom-night-from-hell with Alex or Brittany, either.

My satin dress hissed like a poisonous snake with my angry paces. I desperately needed someone to talk me down and only one person could do that. Jordan.

"Marli? What's wrong? It's barely eleven. Are you all right?"

"Yes," I answered, strangled by the word. "No, that's a lie." I bit my lip and the room rippled behind tears.

"Babe? What is it?"

"Things got ugly after I broke up with Sam tonight," I sniveled. "I left the dance early."

"Did he...hurt you?"

"Not like you're thinking. Things are a mess, that's all." I dropped onto the bed and kicked off my shoes. Mindlessly, I twisted a lock of hair around me finger.

"I wish I was there. From what I can see you look beautiful, but sad...like you could use a hug from a certain lonely guy I know real well." I blew him a kiss and he puckered one in return. "How's your heart?"

Jordan's question halted me.

"My heart?"

"Yes, your heart. You and Sam share a history. As much as I hate thinking about it, you must have feelings for Sam. "

"*Had*," I sniffed. "After tonight, all I feel is an urge to vomit when I think about him."

Jordan laughed. "That bad, huh? Care to enlighten me?"

"Pass. I'm wiped out." I'd only end up falling apart again. I also wanted to spend some time with Jesse before he left because Rick made it clear he couldn't stay.

"Can I call you tomorrow?"

"I'd be crushed if you didn't. 'Night, Jordan."

"Good night Marli. I, I—" his voice caught on a word having the power to suck my last breath, but he quickly recovered, "—miss you. Talk to you tomorrow."

A shadow flickered along the walls of the living room. Jesse had found a candle and placed it in the center of the coffee table, alongside two cups of steaming hot tea.

"Ambiance," he smiled, gesturing for me to sit beside him on the sofa. He took the afghan draped over the back and wrapped it around my shoulders. "You were gone a while. I almost came looking for you."

"Dad and I had a slight disagreement, and...I called Jordan."

He leaned into the corner of the sofa, tipping me against him. "How is my brother?"

"Worried, like you. I still didn't tell him you were here. I decided to save that piece of information for when I have the strength to argue. I also begged out of telling him about tonight."

"About tonight...what happened?" His jaw snapped sharply against my forehead. "Obviously, you were running away from Sam. What did he do?"

I gave Jesse an overview of what happened. A more enhanced version of the story would be all over town by tomorrow and I'd have to deal with Rick's overreaction. I tilted my head to see Jesse's reaction, receiving a quick tap from his mouth on mine.

"What happened after I left for the dance?" I asked.

"Rick tortured me." I punched his chest. "Ouch! He interrogated me regarding my intentions toward his young, impressionable baby girl. He warned me if I hurt you, there wouldn't be a planet in the universe where I could hide. He'd find me and shoot me. You're right. He owns a gun."

"*Baby girl?* Ugh! I can't wait until I'm eighteen so he'll stop treating me like one."

Jesse set his cup on the table, squaring my shoulders. "Your father worries about you, Marli, and turning eighteen won't change that." A mischievous grin curled his mouth. "I talked to him about your graduation present, but it will definitely have to wait until you're eighteen."

"Oh?" My curiosity piqued, especially when his grin grew into a taunting smile. "What is it?"

"Uh-uh. It's a surprise, but I wanted you to know he said okay."

"That's so unfair. At least give me a hint. Please?" I walked my fingers along the edge of his open shirt collar, undoing a couple more buttons and sliding my hands inside. "Pretty please?" I pushed him back into the sofa cushions and placed my lips at the hollow of his throat.

He held me back. "Has anyone ever told you if you play with fire, you'll get burned?"

I placed my hands on the sides of his face and captured his waiting mouth. Slowly, his tongue drew a wistful line across my bottom lip and I hesitated. What started as a flirty tease changed when I cracked my lips and Jesse became the center of focus. All thoughts of Jordan disappeared when Jesse's tongue slid a deliberate line along the top of my mouth and intense, tingling sensations danced through my body.

Jesse's arm slipped around my waist and pressed my body into his curves. His legs wrapped over me and my heart hammered behind the ribs his fingers counted. Heated blood raced in my veins and I eased my leg out of the slit in the dress, flattening my lower body against Jesse.

Suddenly, he jumped up and moved to the chair across the room, leaving me struggling to calm my jagged breaths.

"What did I do?" Stupid question. I knew exactly what I did.

Even in the muted shadows, I felt the intensity of Jesse's stare. "What *we* were doing—flirting with danger," he rebuked, equally breathless. "I won't cross that line with you, Marli. Not while Jordan's in the picture. You technically belong to him."

The statement smacked of dominance—something I feared. The need to prove my independence became urgent and the guilt building that I betrayed Jordan vanished.

"I *belong* to no one. In fact, Jordan wants to date until the end of the year and decide for ourselves what the next step should be."

Jesse slumped in the chair, his long legs almost reaching the sofa. A smile twisted inside his words. "Serious? No commitment?" He shook his head and scoffed. "Jordan's a fool. Leaving a life with you to chance is insane. If it were me, I'd make things permanent the second you turned eighteen."

The sudden spark of anger at his statement surprised me.

"Good thing my life's not in your hands then because I'm not getting trapped in anything permanent at eighteen, regardless of what The Program wants." I hugged a pillow nestled in the corner of the sofa. "Jess, I don't want a serious relationship with any one person right now. Not even Jordan."

He returned beside me, tossing the pillow to the floor. His fingers slowly combed through my hair and tangled in my curls, his lips brushing lightly across my collarbone. Slowly, he kissed a heated trail up my neck until his mouth touched my ear.

"Well, that changes everything."

I tilted my head, lengthening my neck to expose more bare skin for his lips to caress. His mouth settled at the nape of my neck, where he proceeded to check my blood supply. A niggle of something new, like a puppet string tugging from where he sucked to the private regions of my body stirred.

"Stop, Jess," I breathed.

His thumb stroked my bottom lip and he waited, as if knowing what caused my panic. I flushed at the thought and he smiled.

"You okay?" he whispered over my lips, his fingertips lightly brushing everywhere my skin was naked. His lips hovered teasingly over my mouth, waiting.

"Kiss me," I whimpered.

In one move, Jesse pulled me underneath him, his body molding intimately into mine. His breath blew hot on my chest where his lips nipped the soft flesh peeking out of the top edge of my dress. Molten heat trickled from the top of my head to the ends of my toes. My body became pliable, responding eagerly to every touch, every kiss, *everywhere*.

"You know what this means, Marli?"

Trembling, I shook my head in question.

A dangerous smile met eyes resembling pools of melted chocolate. "It means *game on.*"

# 10
# GRADUATION PRESENCE

A double homicide.

I blinked a hundred times, but Rick's red face remained—puffed and growing a deeper scarlet every second. Words spewed from his mouth, but nothing registered because I still wandered between reality and dreamland.

Jesse's bare skin felt warm against my cheek, his cologne lingering in the folds of his neck. My eyes drifted shut again and I returned to the fading dream where Jesse and I engaged in some serious body contact. I moved on top of him, settled into the angles of his body and sampled the soft skin on the chest pillowing my head. He tried to move me, but I claimed his mouth and he eagerly welcomed my morning "hello."

"I wasn't dreaming. Jess, last night was amaz—"

"*MARLI!*"

At that point, my skin plastered the ceiling and Jesse held my skeleton. My heart flat-lined.

"Dad!" *Damn.* I was beyond dead and no one would ever find Jesse's body.

We bolted upright and I hastily adjusted my skewed formal. Miraculously, everything remained covered, even though the dress had twisted almost backwards. When I followed Rick's murderous stare to Jesse's bare chest covered in smudged lipstick marks, I panicked, blurting out a preposterous excuse and sealing my fate.

"Dad, this isn't how it looks, honest. We fell asleep talking, that's all."

*Talking?* Even *I* wouldn't believe me based on the evidence.

His voice flattened to a dangerous calm. "Marli, go to your room."

"But, Dad…"

*"NOW!"* The verbal command shook the dishes in the china hutch.

I dashed upstairs, keeping my bedroom door cracked enough to watch. Someone had to witness Jesse's murder.

"Mr. Mason, it's time for you to leave." Rick's body filled the doorway leading to the stairs. "My daughter is only seventeen years old and until she's eighteen, young man, I don't want to see or hear from you, *or* your brother. Understood?" Jesse's reply was too low to hear, but as soon as the front door slammed, my father's bare feet padded heavily on the stairs. When he shoved my door open, the picture behind it fell off the wall.

"*Marli Elizabeth Davis.* I don't understand you and this…spending the night with a boy in that…" He was so flustered he simply pointed. "That damn dress—kissing his naked body!" He threw his hands in the air. "You're grounded until further notice!" He stomped across the hall to his room with me on his heels.

"Daddy, nothing happened last night, I swear."

He spun around and I nearly crashed into his body fortress. "Don't *Daddy* me."

My heart raced so fast I feared it would break through my ribcage any moment. When he slammed his bedroom door, I swear my nose twisted from being so close.

"You're not being fair! Please, can we talk rationally?"

The door flew open, Rick's demeanor rigid and unsympathetic. He stepped out of the doorway, silent, and I perched on the side of his bed.

"Dad, you have to believe me, we didn't do anything. Jesse never crossed the line and stopped me from doing anything stupid. And he wasn't *naked.*" He towered over me, arms folded firmly across his chest. The red slowly faded from his face, but his eyes offered no forgiveness. "We only kissed." A lot. In fact, my lips could be permanently swollen. "But Jesse didn't lay a hand on me." More like *two* hands, but nothing compared to what Rick imagined.

Dad dropped beside me, heaving a large sigh. "Marli, when I saw you wrapped in that kid's arms and legs, every nightmare I've ever had about you and boys raced into my head." He exhaled sharply. "I do believe you, Pumpkin, but it doesn't make what happened last night appropriate, by any means."

His hand lifted my face, his rough cheeks still rosy. "Mars, I know you're old enough to decide these things, and neither I nor the damn Program can stop you from having sex, but remember, you deserve to be loved for the right reasons, and by someone who'll stop at nothing to make you happy. And not just for a moment, Pumpkin, but for a lifetime."

"Dad, I'm not having sex with anyone."

"I'm glad, because life changes after you do. I'm an old prude, I know, but I still think waiting is a good idea."

"Until I'm eighty?"

"Eighty-five." Rick hugged me about the shoulders. "Young lady, I'm still forbidding contact from the Mason brothers until your eighteen, but I'll only ground you until graduation from your other friends. However, cell receptor and computer privileges are revoked for the weekend."

"But—"

"No 'buts,' Mars. This way, you get a few days to sort through your feelings without anyone's interference and I get some peace of mind."

The matter closed to further argument. While I could use some solitude to figure things out, not knowing if Jordan or Jesse called for the next two days would kill me. This would be the longest weekend of my life.

"Marli! We need to go before you're late to your own graduation!" Dad shouted as he had every five minutes for the past hour. The way he paced the floors, you'd think *he* was Valedictorian and delivering the farewell speech.

I fastened the single strand of pearls looped over the corner of my mirror around my neck—a graduation gift from my mother. It arrived earlier in the week with a letter wishing me luck. No apology for the part she played in the calamity I lived, however. She also managed to taint her "congratulations" with a reminder of my obligation to The Program.

Admittedly touched by her thoughtfulness given our distant relationship, part of me waxed melancholy, wishing she could be at my graduation. A bigger part of me, however, wanted Jordan or Jesse there also, only I couldn't decide which one.

After Senior Ball, I found myself in a sticky predicament where the Mason twins were concerned. I became the knot pulled taut in an emotional tug-o-war between brothers, only neither of them knew. So far, I'd kept my feelings to myself.

Dad's voice blared up the stairwell again, proving his final thread of patience snapped. I folded my graduation gown over my arm and grabbed the scribbled speech from the night table I finally finished last night. With all the distractions, namely Jordan and Jesse, I didn't have time to download it to the digital prompter for the podium.

"Great," he grumbled under his breath.

"What?" My eyes followed his gaze out the living room window, catching the glint off a white car pulling to the curb. There could only be one possibility and when I saw the Porsche, my heart jumped in my chest.

I squealed with unbridled excitement. "Jordan!" My breath caught. Oh, crap! *Jordan.*

"I thought I made it clear neither Mason brother was to contact you until your eighteenth birthday." He marched for the door, but I tugged the sleeve of his jacket.

"Dad, wait." My face twisted with a rush of guilt. "Jordan doesn't know about Jesse being here last week. I never told him and I'm positive Jesse didn't either."

His eyebrows vanished into his receding hairline. "What kind of game are you playing, Mars? You can't do this to those two boys. It's not right."

"I know, but please, don't say anything. I promise, I'll tell Jordan about Jesse, but not today."

He shook his index finger with a hefty warning. "Twenty-four hours. Either you tell him by then, or I will. Secrets are dangerous. You should know better." He reached into the lapel pocket of his suit jacket, handing me a lavender envelope. "I'm supposed to wait to give this to you after the ceremonies, but I'm guessing you'll be with Jordan and I may not see you."

I bounced on my toes at the probability of another gift. "Can I open it?"

"I strongly suggest you wait until you're alone. I'll take my car and meet you two there."

The doorbell rang and my heart climbed into my throat. I inhaled a deep breath and opened the door. "Jordan!"

He lifted me into his arms, swinging me in a circle. "Surprise! I couldn't stay away on such an important day." He kissed me hard, holding me so tight I thought I felt a rib crack.

"You're my best graduation present yet."

Our lips almost touched again, but the loud blare of Rick's horn killed the mood instantly.

Heads snapped and eyes gawked when I walked into the school on Jordan's arm. No one saw him the day he dropped me off, only his white steed. I watched the same two empty-headed cheerleaders from the dance give Jordan a once over and I glared back over my shoulder.

"Are we being watched?" An evil glimmer twinkled in Jordan's eyes when I shrugged. "Well, then…"

Jordan pressed me into every bend of his body, kissing me as if he needed my lips to keep him alive. Blood raced through my body, hot and icy at the same time. He pulled away, his eyes dark and beautiful.

"I've wanted to kiss you like that for weeks."

"I think you should check my pulse."

Before I could stop him, Jordan's lips pressed below my ear. "Still breathing?"

"Barely."

He placed a chaste kiss on my cheek and took my hand, feathering his lips across my knuckles while I fought to remember to move my feet.

The seniors assembled in the gymnasium to line up for our procession onto the football field. I stopped outside the gym doors and slipped into my gown. Rick handed me the flimsy square hat I dreaded putting on my head. Any breeze at all and the cap would be history.

Jordan draped a beautiful lei of fresh violet orchids around my neck, capturing my mouth in a deep kiss, ignoring Rick standing within strangling reach.

"Good luck, babe."

Leading the "D's," I almost made it out the door before hearing a formal, cold reminder.

"Candidate 5846?"

Ice filled my veins and my gut clenched unexpectedly.

"Yes?"

A man and woman stepped forward, followed by Principal Anderson. The man held a white plastic tube encased in a clear cylinder. A "virgin lollipop."

"We need a DNA sample," the woman stated in a softer, but firm voice.

"Why now?" My voice sounded too high. Guilty.

Principal Anderson spoke up. "Marli, there's been talk," she said delicately. "It's precautionary...you know, before we formally introduce you as Valedictorian."

"Wait? You think…" *Strangers kissing me in front of the school. The dance. Twisted lies created by malicious gossip.* Why wouldn't Principal Anderson suspect the obvious?

The Valedictorian had to be a Candidate. If my "dip-stick" changed colors, I no longer qualified. Another girl shuffled nervously near the exit doors. The "backup." I wavered between furious and mortally embarrassed.

"Fine," I snarled.

From the edge of my vision, I swore Jordan peeked in the glass panel of the gym door, but when I focused harder, I saw nothing. I'd die if he witnessed my moral standing questioned. Hopefully, Friday night's encounter with Jesse didn't *color* things. There were only so many days before DNA would be unreadable and I guessed five days probably wasn't enough to erase moral mishaps.

I held my breath when they inserted the stick into the tubing after collecting my saliva. Ten seconds and my life could change. Everyone sighed loudly when the tiny beep signaled the end of the test and the stick remained clear. Everyone except my so-called replacement who said something unladylike and joined the procession marching on the field.

The woman used a stylus to wand my bracelet's data chip and left. Principal Anderson apologized, explaining she had no choice, which I understood. Her burgundy-tinted lips curved in a relaxed smile. "I knew the rumors couldn't be true."

When we reached the platform for those speaking on the commencement program, I halted briefly on the top step. Next to my empty chair where Coach Smith should be, sat Sam. Having no choice and already noticeably late, I cautiously perched on the edge of my seat. Sam's arm casually slipped behind me and his fingers caressed my neck under my hair. My skin tried to crawl away from my bones.

"Stop. Touching. Me."

"Make me."

My elbow found Sam's ribcage and he swore loud enough, judging by the snickering crowd, to pass over the microphone through our vice-principal's opening remarks. Principal Anderson glowered. Sam and I smiled sheepishly like guilty children.

"Where's Coach?"

Sam cautiously leaned closer, guarding his side with his hand. "Had a family emergency."

"That still doesn't explain why you're here."

Sam's eyes darted to those nearby. "Second in command. Hansen's in jail—a downside to being eighteen." He leaned over, tucked a strand of hair behind my ear and quietly explained how a fight broke out after the dance, ending with a couple team members arrested.

"For once, my jealousy saved me. I followed you home and parked down the street, but fell asleep in my jeep. I guess I can thank 'Ferrari Boy' for showing up after all.

We stood for the presentation of the flag and sang the national anthem.

Sam angled closer. "By the way, I noticed he spent the night. Tell me, Marli, does your *Porsche Prince* know you're swapping spit with his brother?" My eyes bunched in a pained stare and a smug grin curled Sam's mouth. "Didn't think so."

Principal Anderson announced my name. Numbly, I walked to the microphone. My fist closed over my notes. It never dawned on me *Sam* could rat me out.

Clearing my throat a bit too loudly, I smoothed the crinkled paper. Two, maybe three paragraphs I recited reflecting on our high school experience, before a sudden gust of wind ripped through the stadium. Without thinking, I reached up to secure my flimsy graduation cap, letting go of my speech. The wind cradled the crumpled paper over my head and I watched in horror as my "words of wisdom" disappeared over the wall!

The stadium suddenly swayed, spots formed in front of my eyes, and my lips tingled. My mind became a blank page, unable to recall the words scrawled mindlessly on the paper floating away. I rambled something about making choices for our future, but ran out of thoughts halfway through a sentence, realizing *I* was the last person to counsel anyone about making correct choices.

Rick, poised below me with a camera, uttered the word "relax." I turned to Jordan, leaning against the railing not ten feet away. His handsome face rippled behind sudden tears. I was dying inside and coming apart on the outside.

Principal Anderson tugged the hem of my robe. "Are you all right, dear?"

I never answered, just dropped to the makeshift floor and knocked the microphone off the podium. A deafening screech echoed somewhere distant in my mind.

Escaping through a side door from the boy's locker room, we raced for Jordan's car, avoiding the crowd. After my enormous blunder of a farewell speech, nothing short of warp speed would be fast enough to remove me from the school grounds. The windows were tinted dark enough that nobody, under normal conditions, would know who sat inside. But alas, the only other time this glossy pallid of chrome and steel had rolled onto campus, I'd been one of its occupants.

Jordan slid into the driver's seat, about to close his door when Alex thrust her leg in between.

"Just a second *Dr. Dreamy*. We want a word with your illustrious passenger." Brittany wrenched the door open further, tucking her head sideways into the car.

Jordan turned to me for direction.

"These are my best friends, Brittany and Alex."

"I've heard a lot about you ladies." Alex crouched, micro-millimeters from his butt and he hugged the console with his other hip. "She scares me," he whispered.

"She should," I whispered back before shooting a pointed glare at my ogling girlfriend. "Did you want something, Alex?"

"Besides your sexy boyfriend?" she teased. "Yeah, what the hell happened? Talk about a memorable exit. You'll be the headliner for tomorrow's morning news." Her hands framed pretend headlines. "VALEDICTORIAN COLLAPSES INTO WAITING ARMS OF HANDSOME STRANGER AT GRADUATION CEREMONY—A TRUE ROMEO AND JULIET FINALE."

"I hit the stupid floor."

Alex and Brittany shared a glance. My eyes widened when a feeble grin eased over Jordan's mouth.

"Jordan? You didn't—"

"Catch you? I watched the color drain from your face and jumped onto the stage, right as you went limp."

Brittany laughed. "He almost fell in Principal Anderson's lap."

Jordan rescued me? The fleeting image of his chivalry in front of my classmates, not to mention Rick, created an overwhelming wave of horror. The grad party at the beach was officially out of the question. I couldn't handle a night's worth of humiliation, not to mention Sam would gladly tell Jordan about my public make-out session with Jesse, just for spite.

Jordan's arm slipped around my shoulders and his eyes twinkled. "She's right. Definitely one for the memory books."

"Is Jordan coming to the beach party?" Brittany asked.

His and my eyes remained locked. "I don't know."

"You wearing a bikini?"

"Guess you'll have to come to find out."

Ignoring Alex and Brittany completely, Jordan leaned in, his mouth close enough I could smell a recent breath mint. "Let's party."

# 11
## BEACH PARTY BREAKUP

We stopped at the department store for Jordan to buy some clothes for the beach. He walked out of the dressing room modeling swim shorts, the sight sending a drizzle of heat through my body. He hooked a finger for me to follow him into the dressing room.

"Are you crazy?"

Jordan yanked me inside. Something about possibly being caught in the act amped the sensual excitement between us and immediately, our bodies mashed against the mirror, mouths engaged in deep, dizzying kisses. His hands locked at the small of my back, fusing me to his body, and my hands pressed against his bare stomach, his muscles ripped so tight my fingers couldn't make an indentation.

I released a ragged breath. "Being with you all night may not be a good idea. My willpower has apparently vanished."

"Sounds promising, " he replied in a raspy whisper. "But I'll behave. I need to stay on your dad's good side if I want him to let you come to the island for the summer."

I checked for a heartbeat. "The island?" I squealed, immediately covering my mouth. "Are you serious? For the whole summer?"

Jordan drew me back into his arms and my hands wandered over his exposed chest

"Yes, if you want."

"I-I don't know what to say," I replied softly watching his eyes drift over my face as he leaned closer. He tightened his grip around my waist.

"*Yes, I'd love to go, Jordan,* would be a good start."

"Of course I want to go, but getting Dad to agree might be too much to expect."

Jordan's tongue drew a line up my neck, his breath hot on my ear. "We'll see. I can be pretty persuasive when I want something."

I locked my fingers behind his neck. "How well, I know." I slid my lips along his, but before I could seal the kiss, the sales clerk hammered on the dressing room door.

Hours passed and still no sign of Sam. The muscles in my core knotted so tight in anticipation of the worst they ached, and I skittered whenever a car pulled into the parking lot. Jordan's attentive touches irritated more than soothed and I snipped one-word replies when he asked why I was so jumpy. The lustful heat we shared in the dressing room fizzled the second we arrived and memories of the disastrous day washed through me.

Alex sucked the last of her water so hard, the plastic container popped and the muscles under my skin jittered. "Davis, relax. It's past midnight. Sam's not coming."

"I don't trust him. He wants revenge too badly to let this slide."

"Maybe he wised up to the fact you're with Jordan and is purposely avoiding the party," Brittany offered. Alex and I rolled our eyes at the incredulous statement. "Or not."

Alex tipped her head toward the beach where Jordan walked in the inky waves lapping at his ankles. "I think you need to stop obsessing over Sam and pay attention to what really matters."

"I've been a horrible date."

"You've been a bitch, but he's so knocked-on-his-ass whipped on you, he's put up with it. Go give him some serious lip sugar to make up for being so moody."

Brit leaned forward. "For once I agree with Alex. Forget Sam and concentrate on Jordan. One's your past, the other is your future and from what I see, a future worth keeping."

When I stared at Jordan's silhouette against the white ribbon rippling on the water from the full moon, I couldn't argue and my ribs squeezed tight. I rose, leaving them mid sentence and walked toward the shadowy heartthrob causing a nervous wiggle in my belly.

Quietly I approached from behind and flicked a spray of water over his back with my foot. He froze mid-step and I watched the muscles rope from his shoulders to his narrow waist. Before I could escape, he had me tucked under his arm like one of his surfboards and dangling head first over the water.

"I should dunk you for sneaking up on me."

I grabbed his thigh, my fingers accidently slipping inside a pant leg. A surprised squeal escaped Jordan's mouth and his leg muscle bucked. Quickly, he turned me right side up and put me on my feet.

"S-Sorry," I stuttered, embarrassed. "And not just about groping your leg. About everything tonight. I've been awful."

He smoothed my hair behind my ears, his palms settling at the nape of neck. A knowing grin curled his mouth and I watched his eyes slide shut before his lips tentatively touched mine.

"I'd say more like 'distracted,'" he whispered on my mouth before staking claim with a breathtaking kiss. "And you can grope my leg anytime."

The heated cravings in my body returned. I molded my body around his and the world disappeared in a rush of lust-filled adrenaline. Our lips barely parted to allow a breath.

"Think I could talk you into taking a walk farther down the beach with a handsome older man?"

"My dad's here?"

Jordan growled and nuzzled my neck. His stubbly chin tickled and I giggled with each nibble until his mouth settled on mine. His lips were warm with a hint of salt clinging to the edges and each time they pressed they remained longer, warming my insides. I tugged him to where our stuff lay spread out on the beach. We'd need the blanket for our impromptu "walk" someplace more secluded.

Suddenly, the beach washed with bright white light. I knew the sound of the motor, the way it raced between gears, the rusty squeal of worn brake pads, and the groan of the axles when the wheels were forced to stop moving. Clouds of dust swirled in the beams of light piercing the darkness. Car doors slammed and voices grew louder as they approached the party.

Time stopped moving and the pulse pounding in my ears drowned out Jordan's voice. When he touched my arm I flinched.

"What?"

"Sam's here."

"Is this why you've been on edge?" I tucked my chin to my chest and tipped against him. His arm came around my shoulders. "Let's ditch out on the other side of the bonfire and take the trail to the parking lot."

Sam's voice echoed loudly on the night air. "Marli! Where the hell are you? I know you're here because I saw lover boy's Porsche!" The party quieted and someone turned the music off. Sam's shadow stretched across the sand, moving closer to the gathering crowd.

"No escaping now. I better talk to him before things get ugly." Memories of the dance flashed behind my eyes, followed by ones of Jesse. I had to keep Jordan away from Sam. "Take our stuff and meet me at the car."

"Marli—"

"Jordan, I've got this, okay? Right now, I'm worried about one his dumbass friends damaging the Porsche," I lied, desperately needing Jordan gone before Sam found me. "I'll take Alex. Sam hates her."

Jordan bundled the beach blanket under his arm and grabbed our cooler of drinks. "Then I adore her." He kissed my cheek. "If you're not at the car in ten minutes, I'm coming back for you."

I watched him jog off into the shadows, puffs of sand blowing off each footstep. Sam yelled again and Alex stepped beside me.

"What a prick. Come on girl, let's do some ass-kicking."

I linked my arm through hers. "I always knew you had a soft spot for Sam."

"Oh there's a spot on Sam I'm sure is soft."

We tripped over each other laughing at our private joke until the crowd parted like the Red Sea and we stood illuminated in the headlights, facing Sam.

"Hello *sweetheart*," he sneered, his calling card of late. "Where's one of your 'knights in shining armor?' Should I worry about being ambushed?"

"Shut up, Sam. I'm the one ambushed here. Why can't you leave me alone?"

Alex stepped between us and snapped her spiky blonde head at Sam. "Jenkins, get the hell out of here. It's over and everybody's tired of the drama. Move on."

"Snarky little bitch. Still fighting Marli's battles, I see. She's going to dump your ass too, Nichols, now that she's got her fairytale life."

A low murmur rippled through the crowd.

I touched Alex's arm, tensed and ready to inflict pain. "Don't. This is my problem." My eyes drifted to Sam's face. A faint smell of beer surrounded him when I moved closer. "You've been drinking."

"Why do you give a shit?"

I tapped my foot on the gravel. "Because I care, okay? Is that what you need to hear?"

Sam spread his arms out. "Big whoop. You *care*. But not enough to want to be with me anymore." He stepped closer. "And your secret?"

I didn't have to turn my head to acknowledge Jordan owned the shadow reaching us from the embankment above. I sensed his presence at the edge before the dribble of pebbles started rolling.

"Look, Sam, I'm sorry I hurt you. It was never my intention, but I'm begging you, if you really love me, please don't say anything. Don't hurt me back."

His thumb brushed my cheek and I felt Jordan's dangerous glare cut through the darkness. "For you, not him." He turned to his sidekicks. "Fuck this. Let's go."

Jordan hummed some song playing on the media center in the kitchen and a spatula scraped against metal in time with the music. *So both Mason boys cooked.*

Before he figured out I'd awakened, I scrambled upstairs to my bathroom. My mouth felt like cotton and my breath could drop a fly in mid-flight. I nearly screamed when I caught my reflection in the mirror. A red indentation matched the button on the sofa pillow my cheek pressed all night. We fell asleep sometime around dawn, me on the sofa and Jordan on the floor, holding my hand.

I scrubbed my face, ran the ultrasonic wand over my teeth, and brushed the windswept tangles from my hair before bounding down the stairs. Jordan's back faced me and my gaze wandered over his broad shoulders, the muscles flexing against the fabric of his shirt with each whisk of the spatula; down long legs covered with a dusting of hair, to his manicured bare feet planted firmly in front of the stove. "Morning handsome" came out sounding too husky.

A smile reaching his eyes flashed. "Hey gorgeous. You're finally awake."

"Omelets? I may keep you after all." I pressed a quick smack on his cheek before gathering plates to set the table. When I folded back the tablecloth, a certain lavender envelope slipped to the floor. Jordan tucked it under his arm and moved away before I could grab it unnoticed.

The importance of Jesse's mystery card vanished, however, when I moved a couple of files Rick had brought home and uncovered a *red* envelope. Jordan's eyes followed mine when he moved behind me. He placed Jesse's lavender envelope to the side of his plate and reached for the red package.

I slapped the top. "I'll deal with it later." He opened his mouth and closed it. A thread of apprehension connected us. The red envelope meant another interview request—one that could result in a *choice.*

What if someone else wanted me? Jordan and I hadn't made anything official. As far as The Program knew, I remained available. Someone equal to Jordan had the right to choose me. The idea of dating suddenly wasn't so appealing. Unless Jordan exercised his right to choose me while he had priority, whoever came attached to this red envelope could. Jordan would be lost to me forever.

I moved my food around the plate, no longer hungry.

"Send it back," he suggested around a mouthful of eggs.

Not the reply I'd hoped for. Why didn't he declare his undying love and tell me we should make things permanent? Maybe trapped with high school kids for twenty-four hours, reminded him how young I really was.

Jordan pulled the lavender envelope from under his napkin. "I say we open something we know contains good news."

*Good news?* I didn't know whether to scream or laugh hysterically at the irony. Given a choice, the *red* envelope proved the safer option.

I jumped to my feet. "No!" Jordan froze, puzzled. I held out my hand. "Please, give me the envelope."

He pushed his chair back. "Why? What's inside?"

"I don't know what's in the envelope, but I know who it's from and we should probably talk."

"I'm listening."

My eyes fell to my pink painted toes. "It's from Jesse."

Jordan's lips disappeared and he ripped the envelope open. Three tickets drifted to the floor when he unfolded the enclosed letter.

"Hey! That's private!" I reached for the note, but he held it away. "Please, Jordan, at least hear me out first before passing judgment."

"Go ahead."

My chest tightened. "Jesse came to see me last week—the day of Senior Ball. I didn't know he was coming, I swear."

"When I called, Jesse was here, but you didn't tell me?"

"I was afraid."

"Thanks for the trust, Marli."

"Jordan, be honest. How do you think you'd have taken the news that Jesse was here?"

"Bad."

"Exactly. Besides, he was leaving when Sam came to pick me up, or so I thought."

Jordan's voice heightened, his jaw tight. "*What?*"

"Don't freak out. Sam turned into an ass around his teammates and I stormed out. Jesse came to get me and when I got home, I called you."

Jordan drummed his fingers on the table. I wished I could get inside his head, rearrange his thoughts so he'd see me in glowing white light—pure and innocent, not the total opposite, which he'd find once he forced the truth from my cheating lips.

A deep canyon set between his eyes. "And yet, you still didn't tell me about Jesse. Why?"

I scorched with burning guilt. Tendrils of smoke probably curled off my body. "I don't know."

*That's your answer?!*

Jordan pushed away from the table and marched into the living room, clenching the note. He dropped into the easy chair, filling the space and offering no invitation for me to join him. His body turned rigid, one knee shaking nervously.

"You. Don't. Know," each word enunciated hard. "Tell me what you *do* know, Marli. When did my brother finally leave my assigned candidate?"

Brutal. Jordan placed me beneath him. Put me in my *assigned* place.

He immediately recanted. "I'm sorry. I didn't mean that."

*Yes, you did, and worse, I deserved it.*

I looked away, the rims of my eyes stinging. Anger simmered with the hurt, but I couldn't hide the truth, or the consequence. "He didn't. Jesse spent the night."

"I don't think I like where this is headed." Jordan stared me down. "Where did *you* spend the night?"

"Are you accusing me of what I think you are?"

"Hey, you're the one keeping secrets. I know Jesse, and I watched you take a DNA test."

I didn't imagine Jordan's face in the window. "You *saw* that?"

"I thought they were running a random test, but now—"

"It *was* random!" I blared over him.

"Marli, you were singled out! Tested alone. And the timing is within the thirty day limit."

One question answered. Carnal sins were quarantined for a month.

Jordan jumped out of the chair when I hesitated. "That son-of-a-bitch! I'll kill him! You're *only* seventeen!"

The pain stabbed instantly—a sharp slice through me. The room seemed to vanish behind tiny dots and the air stilled, no longer coming in or out of me. Jordan's expression remained unreadable, but the way his jaw set, anger dominated.

I leveled a steely glare and forced words through clenched teeth. "Oh, I get it. *Seventeen* is old enough for you to claim me as your child bride, but too young for your brother to innocently kiss?"

"Marli, you're twisting things. For one, you can't be with me before you're eighteen and second, nothing with Jesse is innocent. He's a player, Marli—only after one thing. He'll hurt you and walk away."

We moved around each other—a power dance. I raised a brow. "So you think that's all I am to him? An easy *lay*."

He raked his fingers through his hair and I held my breath, hating that even though we were fighting, the simple action made me want to kiss him.

"Don't demean yourself, please. Jesse wants you because I have you."

My subconscious slipped on boxing gloves.

"Really? So it's all about *you*. And for the record you don't *have* me."

Jordan scrubbed his jaw, covered with enough stubble to tickle my neck. He didn't have a snarky comeback. His eyes grew intense and I wilted under his glower.

My voice all but disappeared. "I see. You haven't made a decision. All this talk about 'dating' isn't for my benefit—it's for yours. Well let me make it simple. You can leave. No strings. No 'commitment issues.' Just walk out the door."

*Please, before my heart shatters.*

"Apparently it's you, my dear, who's having trouble with *choices*." Jordan did some stupid prance in a childish jibber. "Oooh, do I want Jordan who's a control freak, but just wants the best for me, or Jesse—the irresponsible 'bad boy' who thinks life's a game, but turns me on."

"You're an ass! And stop blaming Jesse for what happened. He didn't do anything." I poked my chest. "*I* asked him to stay." Another poke. "*I* begged him to kiss me, and by the way, he's one hell of a kisser—"

"Enough!" Jordan roared.

A screaming silence filled the room. His gaze held mine hostage, the anger replaced by something I'd hoped I'd never see in his beautiful eyes. Hurt. I dropped onto the coffee table, unable to trust my legs to hold me.

Jordan's voice lowered, the tone still holding a curt bite. "All my life, I've competed with Jesse. In high school, he made my girlfriends his quest. Then he dropped them and broke their hearts. If Jesse hurt you like that, I couldn't forgive him."

"That explains 'game on,'" I mumbled.

Jordan's eyes narrowed as he read the note. The timbre of his voice sharpened. "What the hell happened between you?"

My stomach dipped to my toes and I reached for the fateful paper sheet. "If you don't mind, I'd like to see what I'm defending myself against."

He flung the paper at me in a disgusted gesture, turning his gaze out the window. Gingerly, I picked the letter off the carpet as if a grenade, minus the pin. My heart slammed my spine as I read Jesse's words.

*Congrats my beautiful angel! Wish I could be there to share your day, but I've been "banned from the kingdom." Enclosed are tickets for you and your girlfriends to attend my concert in Park City, Utah, on your birthday. Surprise!! Remember my sexy little vixen, 'daddy' said "yes," (before he caught us pawing each other, that is).*

*Can't wait to hold you and taste your sweet lips. Maybe all night again? My head's been full of naughty thoughts ever since. I didn't want to wash your lip prints off my chest. How's the "brand" on your neck? Bet you didn't know I was part vampire, but you didn't complain about my cold hands! Ha! See you soon, baby. —Jess*

Panic squeezed my chest. Jordan read these same words! What I did last Friday night went beyond playful flirting and a wave of fear surged. I could lose Jordan.

He flipped my hair back and exposed the bruised remnant. "Nice."

"It's just a hickey, Jordan. It's not like I haven't had one before."

"Oh, I'm sure Sam got his kicks off your neck, too."

*Ass times three!*

"I meant *you*."

Jordan's expression hardened, his eyes so cold I shivered when he stared through me. He started for the front door.

"So you're walking out on me?" I waited, hoping he'd take me in his arms and ravage my mouth with kisses full of need; tell me he'd never do such a thing.

He didn't.

"I think some time apart is needed for both of us." He opened the door. "Maybe you should check out the red envelope," he charged in an icy tone.

*Holy hell! How dare he be so pompous!*

"I might just do that."

Jordan's eyes flashed in surprise, but turned flat and unreadable a half-second later. "Enjoy Jesse's concert. His band is good—he's got that on me, and now, possibly you."

Standing in the doorway dumbfounded, I watched Jordan hop off the porch, his long legs carrying him down the walk. He dropped into the Porsche without so much as a glance my direction. With an ear-piercing screech, he disappeared, leaving fine wisps of blue smoke reeking of melted rubber floating on the air.

I collapsed onto the cement stairs, my gut folding tight. Unbidden tears rained onto my feet. I wished I could turn back the clock—had shoved Jesse out of my room that morning—no further...never opened the damn red envelope.

Brittany's solar car pulled to the curb. I figured she and Alex would show up sooner or later, wanting details about last night. I stood, my butt numb from sitting for so long, and waited by the front door.

They paused on the walk, taking in all the black stripes. Between the tire marks Sam left on the driveway and the ones Jordan's Porsche melted in the street, our place looked like "burn-out central."

Alex studied me, brows knitted. "What happened, Davis? You look like shit."

Spot on. I still wore my swim shorts and bikini top from the party last night, and my face had to be blotchy and swollen from crying.

"I feel like shit."

"Whoa, Davis said a bad word."

Brittany cautiously edged closer. "Alex, don't. Something's wrong. Marli?"

"Not out here."

They followed me inside, exchanging glances when they passed the plates of half-eaten omelets. The red package on the side of the table glowed. Jordan's terse words, "*Maybe you should check out the red envelope,*" remained suspended, not daring to fall.

Alex pulled in beside me, shaking the ominous package. "What's this?"

"Another stupid interview request. I'll return it tomorrow."

"Aren't you even a little bit curious?"

I swallowed down the pebble stuck in my throat. "No. I should never have opened the last one."

Brittany stared at me, confused. "But that was Jordan's."

A sob wrenched from my aching stomach. "I-I know."

She threw her arms around me. "Marli, what are you saying? That Jordan shouldn't have happened?"

"I-I screwed up. I-I told Jordan about Jesse...about everything. Because of my stupid choices, I left him none. He had to protect his own heart."

They both knew about my night with Jesse. Brittany warned me everything could blow up in my face, but I honestly thought I had everything under control. I hadn't planned on a graduation present sabotaging my future. I also didn't plan on falling in love.

I slumped to the floor, sagged against the cabinets. The pain in my chest crushed hard and I wiped my runny nose with the back of my hand. "It's over. Jordan left me."

# 12
## DOOR NUMBER "3"

The shower allowed me to have another melt down without anyone watching and get clean at the same time. I cried watching the sand Jordan and I kissed on for hours, circle the drain, knowing the scent of his cologne had rinsed from my skin.

I gasped when I walked into my bedroom where Brittany and Alex waited, finding the red envelope in Alex's hand—opened. Wrapped inside was the pod and if opened, added another twist to my already messy life.

"Do you know what you've done?" I glared at Brittany sitting across the room, "Why didn't you stop her?"

Both stammered "sorry," as if one word could erase events already in motion.

"Don't you want to know who's on the pod? "Alex asked. "I mean, if Jordan is gone, what could it hurt to peek?"

Brittany shrugged her shoulders. "You know, Marli, you interviewing with someone else might be what Jordan needs. The guy has to realize what he's losing."

"What about what I want? I don't need another complication in my life."

Alex's eyes twinkled. "You may like who's waiting behind *Door Number 3* better."

Impossible, but an intriguing thought. The curious part of me wanted to know and the other part, bruised and broken, wanted to punish Jordan. The smile creeping on my mouth felt foreign, but good. Maybe Alex had something. What damage could come from sneaking a peek?

I pointed to Brittany. "If he's a total loser *you* get to do the interview.

The chip stuck to my clammy palms when I tried inserting it into the computer. We sat mesmerized as the white dot in the center of the screen exploded into a million sparkles. The glittery background parted, revealing the perfect blend of Greek God and Archangel. Eyes the color of the deepest part of the ocean, wrapped in long, dark lashes, stared back from beneath loose waves of coffee colored hair. A hint of olive tint in his complexion suggested Mediterranean ancestry. When he spoke in a voice of deep, soft velvet...we melted.

"Hel-*lo*, Door Number 3," Alex whispered reverently.

Trouble sizzled—the worst kind. *Door Number 3's* name was Douglas Peterson and he lived in Juneau, Alaska. While my eyes remained on the talking hunk of hotness, I mentally rifled through my closet for a coat and boots. I booked a flight for Saturday morning.

I finished clearing the breakfast fiasco and put a pan of lasagna in the oven, avoiding eye contact after casually informing Rick about my weekend trip to Alaska.

"YOU'RE GOING WHERE? I thought you agreed to discuss matters relating to your candidacy and stop making impulsive decisions!" He slammed his bag on the kitchen table and slid a chair out, mumbling something about no longer able to handle a teenage daughter. "What happened from the time I left this morning to now?"

I leaned my hip against the counter. "I told Jordan about Jesse." A painful jolt tugged my heart at the mere mention of his name. "He exploded and left—probably for good.

"Did he say that?"

Unwanted tears chased over my cheeks, but I kept my voice steady. "'Space,'" I air quoted, "is what Mr. Mason wants."

*So 'space' he shall get.*

"He also hated Jesse's present, which, by the way, thanks for letting me go. At least you trust me."

"Don't give me too much credit there," Rick snorted. His demeanor changed when I didn't answer. He reprogrammed the oven. "Let's talk."

"Don't you want to eat first?"

"I think what's happening with you is more important than dinner. You have your old dad worried." He towed me into the living room—the place where all life altering events were discussed.

Like earlier today.

I curled into the corner of the sofa and he eased into the overstuffed chair across the room.

"So Pumpkin, do I need all the details? The last thing I want in my head when I go to sleep, is any romantic stuff involving you. The list grows daily on boys I want to kill."

At the moment, I welcomed his sarcastic humor. "A condensed version will work." Purposely avoiding any mention of Jesse's intimate note, I glazed over the fight scene, managing to keep the tears at a minimum, while inside I threatened to drown.

"I'm struggling not to spit out 'I told you so,' but on the other hand, if Mr. Mason can't handle the truth, it's best you end things now. Honesty is crucial in a relationship."

"Thanks for the restraint on the 'I told you so.' Don't judge Jordan too harshly, though. Remember, I only gave you the highlights."

Dad's chuckle echoed. "I'm certain there's a lot more to the story." He leaned forward. "So how did Alaska land on your weekend agenda?"

He didn't care too much for Alex, his opinion possibly tainted by Karen and earned by Alex's own actions, so I assumed the blame for the opened envelope. The rest he knew—I was obligated to interview.

He rose from the chair, stretching his back with a groan. Easing beside me on the sofa, he patted the knees tucked in my arms. "I hate to ask, but does Jordan know you're going to Alaska?"

"No."

He pulled my folded body into his arms, "Then I won't tell him, either."

*No worries there. He won't call to ask.*

The lights clicked off downstairs and a moment later, Rick leaned in my open doorway. Nestled in my window seat, I pretended to read a romance novel I'd borrowed from Alex's rare collection of paperbacks.

"If you actually turned a page, you might find out how the story ends." He stepped inside my room—a sure sign of another discussion. "Mars, if you still want out of The Program, I'll talk to Chuck. We'll find a way to make it happen."

"You'd like that, wouldn't you? Believe me I've thought about it, but things are better for everyone if I stay."

"What? Are you remaining a candidate for me?"

After Daniel died, I worried Dad would resent being stuck with a teenage girl. Daniel went to Ohio State football games with him, hockey tournaments, and even played on his bowling league. I never doubted Dad loved me. I just couldn't be his *son*.

Nor could I shake the fear I served as a reminder of Mom's betrayal and the guilt he shouldered for not protecting me from the consequence. If I stayed in The Program, Dad's future was secure. It was my way of making up for all the bad by trying to do something good.

"And Mom. She keeps her job if I stay."

"Marli! I don't need The Program's money. And your mother..." He stopped, pursed his lips. "Best not say what I'm thinking, but trust me, even she wouldn't want you suffering this heartache on our behalf."

"What about Grandma? If it wasn't for The Program, she'd be dead now. The government would never have let her to live this long."

"Your grandmother is my concern, not yours."

Dad joined me on the window seat. "Honey, forget everyone else. Do what makes *you* happy." He kissed my cheek. "Life's too short and you're too young...*waaayy* too young."

I waited until I heard the muffled sound of the viewing screen behind Rick's closed bedroom door, before sneaking outside to call Jesse...to thank him for his gift...and hear his voice.

He sounded sleepy and talked through a long, wide yawn. "Hi. How was graduation? Did you wow them with your speech?"

"I don't think it will be forgotten anytime soon."

After suffering through an embarrassing recount of my fainting in front of the entire assembly followed by Jesse's teasing, I thanked him for the tickets.

"I can't wait see you." His voice quieted. "I miss you, Mars." He yawned long again. "Forgive me, babe, but can we talk later? I just got in a couple hours ago and need to get some serious *ZZZ's* before heading to the island tomorrow."

The island? "You're going to the island?"

"I've got to take some supplies to the house for the summer and check the place out to see if anything needs to be fixed, you know—the usual maintenance stuff. I'm hoping I can get some help from my elusive brother. Speaking of which, have you seen Jordan lately?"

At that point, I tried to end our conversation, but Jesse became surprisingly alert and suspicious. Jordan wasn't the only intuitive one. I confessed about Jordan coming to my graduation, but quickly explained he didn't stay long. Why, I don't know. I didn't owe Jesse any explanations.

"Why didn't Jordan stay? Did something happen?"

I tugged a weed growing next to the steps. "Jordan despised your present." *And the note—the hickey, and presently...me.*

"He doesn't want you alone with me."

"No secret there. Jess, I've never seen Jordan so upset. He hates me."

"I don't believe that for a second." Jesse yawned again. "Sorry I caused so much trouble."

"You live to cause trouble."

"Not for you. I don't want you caught in the middle."

"Too late on all counts," I said. "I'm in the middle, I'm in trouble, and I'm coming to your concert."

After we said goodnight, I remained on the porch steps a while longer, listening to the crickets chirp their nighttime lullaby. I closed my eyes, imagining what night sounded like at the beach house. The way things ended with Jordan, I'd never know.

Didn't matter, I told myself. In two days I would be in Alaska with "tall-dark-and-handsome" from behind *Door Number 3.*

# 13
## HIDE AND SEEK

A pair of long, denim covered legs with expensive looking boots peeking beneath the hem, leaned against the taxi shuttle sign. My gaze traveled upward to a gray shirt, sleeves rolled to below the elbows, exposing well-defined forearms. A pair of large hands held a makeshift sign—"5846?" There, propped against the post, stood *Door Number 3,* Douglas Peterson, in the flesh. Toned. Tight. Flesh.

When I shrugged, he unfolded and sauntered toward me. "Number 5846, I presume?" he asked in the same low timbre I'd heard on the pod.

I extended my hand. "My friends call me Marli Davis for short."

He drew my hand to his lips in a gentleman's kiss. "A sense of humor. I like you already." A disarming grin appeared on his face. "Welcome to Alaska, Marli Davis. I'm Doug Peterson, your personal tour guide." He took my suitcase and led me a few short feet to where a little black sports car glistened in the sun.

"No way! A Lotus?"

"And she knows her cars. Impressive."

"Surprised. I pictured you driving some large mountain crawler with a snow plow on the front."

He slid behind the steering wheel. "You did not just use an ancient cliché of Alaska?"

I repressed a giggle at his attempt to appear offended. "I don't get out much."

Doug's laugh sounded melodic. I was in serious trouble. "Coming here from Ohio completely contradicts that statement, you know. Let's hope after this weekend, your opinion changes." He touched the ignition panel with his finger. A low, whirring sound replaced the powerful roar I expected and my eyes widened. "A hybrid," he explained.

"You're joking."

"I take it you were expecting something else…again?"

"I'm going with 'unexpected' from now on where you're concerned." *Hmm* purred in the back of his throat and my cheeks warmed in response.

Doug pulled onto Egan Drive and headed for downtown Juneau. Majestic mountains blanketed with pine trees formed a wall on one side of the highway, while indigo water edged the shoreline on the other. We passed under a canopy of gray clouds that settled over the city, winding our way through small streets lined with souvenir shops as we got closer to where the cruise ships were docked.

Doug touched my knee, sending a surprise jolt of electricity up my leg. "Hotel first? You probably want to get settled before I dazzle you at dinner?"

I pretended to be unaffected, brushing his hand away. "I doubt you can top the Lotus."

A penthouse suite at the new Marriott hotel was beyond my expectations. An infrared beam zipped across my eyes before the security lock released. The door opened automatically and once inside, I turned immediately to make sure a deadbolt existed. Doors magically opening in the middle of the night would freak me out.

Past the entry in a small sitting room, a low table with a hammered brass caldron full of fresh yellow long-stemmed tulips stole my attention. My finger caressed a velvet petal.

"Tulips?"

Doug handed me a bottle of water. "Your favorite, if I'm not mistaking. Sorry, I couldn't find pink ones, but I believe yellow is one of your favorite colors?"

"You know about pink tulips? And my favorite colors?"

"Favorite colors were easy, but the pink tulips took some serious investigating." He reached for my hand. "Come. I'll give you the VIP tour." He towed me through a set of double doors. "This is your bedroom and to the right is the bath, complete with a whirlpool tub and steam shower. There's also a laundry room off the kitchen."

I wandered into the bathroom. Exquisite tile work and marble covered the floors and a raised platform surrounding what could pass for a small swimming pool. A glass partition separated the tub from the steam shower. Large mirrors hung over the sinks and a wide full-length one covered the far wall.

"I may need a lifejacket to keep from drowning in the tub. This place is fantastic. Headquarters will love the bill."

Doug pressed me against the doorframe. His hands slipped inside my jacket and clamped my waist. "There isn't a bill."

I sidestepped, leaning against the opposite side of the doorjamb. *Too close, too fast.*

"Why not?"

He didn't move, his gaze moving a slow roll over my body. "My family owns the hotel. This penthouse is mine."

*Crap.*

"What do you mean *your* penthouse?"

In one step Doug caged me, pressing his hands on the woodwork to the side of my head. A sly smile crept on full lips—lips close enough to touch mine.

"Don't panic. I'm staying at our house on Douglas Island."

My loud gulp echoed. "Please tell me Douglas Island is not named after you."

"No, only a nephew." He pushed back, raising his arms as if an outlaw facing the barrel of a gun. "Now you've spoiled it. I have nothing left to talk about at dinner. I guess I'm forced to spend the time interviewing you."

"You?" I asked, surprised he even suggested it. "But I thought that wasn't allowed."

"I'm not letting someone else decide who's 'qualified' for me to spend my life with, and first impressions are too important." He stopped in the bedroom doorway. "I'll pick you up at eight for dinner. Dress casual. I'm taking you where they make the best fish and chips, and the atmosphere is always fun." He laid a key card on the dresser. "This is a security card so you don't have to do the eye thing. I'll let myself out."

I followed, catching him at the entry door. "Hang on. I want to know. My first impression? Good or bad?"

His arm reached around me, drawing me against him. "Your first impression? Scary as hell. I'm still trying to catch my breath." He kissed my surprised mouth and disappeared out the magic door.

I couldn't move, couldn't breathe...and I wanted to kill Alex.

Mango scented bubbles billowed around my body and each tiny pop against my skin stole a worry. Lulled into a slumbering haze, I slithered deeper into the warm water. When my cell receptor rang on the floor beside me, I jerked awake and snorted perfumed water up my nose. A wave of water cascaded down the tile step and carried the receptor away.

I stumbled from the tub and glided across the wet floor. Frantic, I wrapped the receptor in a towel and rubbed it dry. The face lit up and I checked the missed call. Jordan! I swiped the screen, but nothing worked.

Tears mixed with fruity snot dribble. I missed Jordan's call because I was in Alaska with some guy I didn't want to meet, standing naked in his bathroom. Wanting to kill Alex no longer remained a passing thought.

Black jeans, white button-up shirt, and burgundy faux leather jacket were as "casual" as I could get without wearing pajamas. After pulling on my boots, I walked out on the balcony, still bummed about missing Jordan's call.

Maybe he wanted to apologize—beg me to take him back. *Right*. He wasn't the one sucking the face off someone else. He probably called to permanently end things. Why deal with the drama? It was obvious I lacked self-control. I stood on a balcony in Alaska, for heaven's sake. Regret filled me. I'd accept my consequence with dignity and move on. Maybe the Fates had a hand in landing me in Alaska.

An odd buzzing vibration in my pocket startled me. My cell receptor came back to life, and a handsome face covered with a frantic expression stared back. Frightened to know the reason for Jordan's call, not to mention forced to divulge my latest impulsive decision, I purposely waited until the last ring to answer.

"Hello?"

"Marli! Where are you? Why haven't you answered my calls?" His sharp tone matched the expression on the screen.

I acted coy. "Jordan?"

His lips disappeared, but his voice softened. "Are you all right?"

"I'm fine. You're the one upset."

"I-I'm worried. Why won't anyone tell me where you are?"

The Program tracked me by my pink wrist shackle, but I deliberately set the GPS on my receptor to "private" so only Rick knew my whereabouts.

"Why do you care? You said you needed space. Besides, the last time I told you the truth about something, you ran away."

"Okay, I admit I handled things badly and wish I could take it all back, even though I had good reason. Please tell me where you are."

"You walked out on me, Jordan."

"And what you did with Jesse hurt. I thought we meant more to each other, but right now, I only care about where you are."

"I'm not ready to tell you, and my understanding is we're dating. To me, dating means I can see other people."

"I meant date each other. If you want to see other guys I guess I can't stop you. But not Jesse. I don't trust him. He's not even in The Program—a fact he seems to forget. Where are you?"

"Who said anything about trusting Jesse? I'm asking you to trust me. I trust you. You can't tell me you sit around alone all the time. So? Who else is in your life?"

Nail prints appeared in my palms from my clenched fists. I couldn't stand the thought of Jordan's mouth kissing another girl's, or his arms holding someone else. I wanted to take back my question, especially since Jordan took his sweet time answering.

"Will you tell me where you are if I answer your question?"

"Depends."

"Her name is Heather Sandberg."

*Is* as in *current* girlfriend.

"Oh." I should have stopped right there, but my seventeen-year-old brain groveled for more. "How long have you been with Heather?"

He pinched the bridge of his nose. "Don't do this."

"How long?"

"On and off for about two years. She studies abroad and the long distance relationship hasn't worked."

"I'm long distance," I pointed out.

"Yes, but the difference is I want you in my life. I'll make it work.

"Are you sure it's not just because we're 'matched?'"

Jordan sighed hard. "The Program doesn't control my feelings. The day I met you, I called Heather and broke things off. Please, tell me where you're at?"

"Is it really over?"

"Dammit Marli! Where the hell are you?"

He didn't answer my question, so I wouldn't answer his. "Not yet."

"Fine! Heather and I dated my senior year of high school. I think I held onto her because I liked having a girlfriend, not so much because I liked Heather. She isn't someone I could spend my life with—she's nothing like you. Yes, as far as I'm concerned, it's over. *Now?*"

My gnawed bottom lip felt raw. "Is she a candidate?"

The vein at his temple pulsed. I'd pushed too far. "Yes…and five diamonds, to answer your next question, but not compatible—and I'm not talking genetically." He exhaled an exasperated breath. "Please?"

I bit my lip harder, processing this new revelation. Jordan was involved in a relationship with a girl worthy of five diamonds, and possibly not "past tense."

*Bitch.*

"Not so easy, is it? Jealousy tastes nasty when it's served back to you," he said.

"I'm not jealous of your ex- girlfriend, if indeed she is out of your life," I lied, seething with envy. "It's a surprise, that's all. You've never mentioned any other girls. Are there more?"

"Is there anyone besides Sam? And no, nobody serious. Like I said, Heather never mattered that much, and *yes,* she's out of my life. Maybe that's why I've never said anything. She became ancient history the instant you became my present. Now can we be through with this conversation?"

"For now. And there wasn't anyone before Sam…unless you count Tommy Green. He was my second grade crush and the first boy who kissed me. I punched him and got sent home from school."

Jordan laughed. "That must have been some kiss. Next time I'll stand back and watch for your wicked right hook."

"Next time? Are you sure there'll be one?"

Jordan's cheeks puffed full, all humor gone. "I'd like one. Marli, I'm sorry I get jealous, but I can't help it. You're too important to me and it's hard to trust anyone around you."

The tiny flare of anger fizzled with his declaration. However, he had to understand where it came from. "I need your trust, Jordan, without exception."

"I get that, but I can't make promises where Jesse's concerned."

"You think I'm with him now, don't you?" At least with Jesse Jordan knew his competition.

He hesitated. "Sorry, yes. He's not answering his receptor either. I'm going crazy."

"Mine got wet and powered out." I paused, letting him squirm. "Breathe. I'm not with Jesse. He's at your family's beach house."

"How do you know that?"

"I called him the other night to thank him for the concert tickets. By the way, I *am* going."

"We'll talk about it later."

"No. I'm going."

"Maybe." The next sigh sounded rough. "This is hard for me, Marli. So, if you're not with Jesse, where are you? I'm a nervous wreck."

I pulled as much oxygen into my lungs as possible, bracing for the aftermath. "I'm...in Alaska."

"*Alaska?* What are you doing there?" Jordan grew quiet, his tone apprehensive. "You opened the red envelope, didn't you? You're in Alaska to interview."

"Yes—"

"Don't! Don't interview. Come home."

His voice held an edge of fear and suddenly, I wished things could be so easy...that I could simply call and say "I've changed my mind." The Program, however, never made anything easy.

"Jordan, you know the drill. I can't."

His expression showed the disquiet consuming him. "Why did you open it?"

I rolled my eyes. "*Someone* suggested I should."

"I didn't think you really would. I thought—"

"What? That I'd just patiently wait around until you decided to come back?" Which I'd have done if Alex hadn't opened the envelope.

"Something like that, I'm ashamed to admit."

We were headed into the same argument, both wanting control—both needing trust. He called me stubborn, but he didn't know about the betrayal I'd suffered, nor could I tell him. Because of what happened, I worried I'd never be able to totally trust in one person. The harder Jordan tried to keep me close, the more pieces of my guard fell away. The fear I'd lose myself entirely pushed me the opposite direction.

"Damn Program!"

"Jordan, stop. It doesn't matter."

"It does matter. I can't lose you. I love you!"

My voice cracked with the skipped heartbeat. "What?"

"Nothing."

I struggled to catch my breath. "Didn't sound like 'nothing.'" I waited, but no response. My heart pounded so hard, it hurt. "Jordan?"

"I think I'm falling in love with you."

"You *think*?"

"No. I'm positive. I can't quit thinking about you. I don't eat or sleep, and when I'm away from you and you don't answer my calls, my imagination goes wild."

"Oh my." The words tumbled from my mouth shaky and uncertain.

"Damn. This isn't how I intended to tell you and it's the last thing you need to hear right now. I apologize. I know you hate pressure and I keep doing it. Forget I said anything."

Seconds passed like hours before I could answer. I fingered the silky fabric of the drapes edging the balcony door.

"I can't forget something so huge and you're wrong, Jordan. I do want to hear it. I like the way I feel when you say it, but that's all I can give you right now.

"I didn't expect you to say it back." His video feed went dark and I chose to believe it happened because of water damage and not because he deliberately shut it off.

"Don't lie. Yes you did and I wish I could, but it's too soon. Everything's happened so fast and I'm confused. The only thing I'm sure about is that I don't want you to go away."

Jordan's handsome face filled the screen once more, his signature twisted smile crumbling another chunk of my guard away—the chink in my armor.

"Babe, I'm not going anywhere."

The clock in the living room chimed the magic hour. "I have to go."

"Tell me he's ugly, old and wrinkled."

A giggle burst forth. "You know three years age difference is the max, so unless you consider yourself 'old and wrinkly,' he's also nineteen."

"You didn't say he's ugly."

"Enough Jordan. I really need to go."

"What's his name?"

"Can't say. You know the rules."

"Damn! I hate this."

I leaned over the balcony. Doug waved from the parking lot below.

"I'm hanging up now. Good night."

The screen turned black without a reply and the awkward goodbye pinched. I remained glued to the terrace. Jordan loved me. I possibly loved him. The problem?

Door Number 3.

# 14
## MY ALASKA

"Fate" walked in donning blue jeans and a beige sweater. His tousled hair glistened with shine enhancer and his deep blue eyes sparkled. First date jitters hit and I wicked my sweaty palms along the sides of my jeans.

Doug's eyes skimmed the length of my body. "Wow. You look terrific."

"You don't look half bad yourself." I took the hand offered and walked beside him to the entrance. "Can't wait to see what you've got planned on your dazzle-meter."

The hotel doors opened to a glossy black jeep with enough gleaming chrome that sunglasses were required. Doug grinned when my tongue slammed the pavement.

"Is this more 'Alaska worthy' for you?"

"It's something all right." He opened the door and steps automatically extended below the shiny bumpers. "Hmm, for a minute I thought I'd need to be airlifted into the seat."

"Great, 'height' jokes. I can't win." He jumped into his seat, giving me a wink. "How's my dazzle so far?"

I gave him a playful once over with my eyes. "Are we talking about you or the jeep?"

The Red Dog Saloon pulsed with bodies dancing, eating, and lounging at the bar. Sawdust and peanut shells covered the timber plank floor and fishing nets crisscrossed each other overhead. Country music twanged from a small band in the corner, and servers balancing trays holding pitchers of beer, dodged the occasional enthusiastic patron.

The fish and chips lived up to their reputation and I inhaled my food as if I hadn't eaten for days. After dinner, we walked down by the water. Streetlights offered a faint glow along the boardwalk, more for effect than light, because the sun never completely disappeared this time of year.

We found a bench on the far end of the docks, near the water. In the distance, a cruise ship, lit up in carnival lights, headed for the open sea. I leaned into Doug's shoulder. "Is it weird to have it light all night?"

"You get used to it. It's not as bad as when it's dark all day."

Waves lapped against the side of the pier and a faint fishy odor lingered on the cool night air. A light breeze blew off the water and I welcomed the warmth of Doug's arms when he folded them around me.

"Marli, why did you accept my invitation? To be honest, it surprised me you were still available."

"I won't be eighteen for a few weeks, which is something my dad insists on. He thinks that's even too young. He wants me to go to college for a couple of years before deciding anything permanent in my life."

"Is that what you want?"

I began to think this conversation was my interview. "Yes. I mean, I'm not opposed to a relationship, but I'm not ready for anything permanent." I wasn't sure, however, how I'd answer this same question if Jordan asked.

"But if you wait, that makes you twenty."

"So? Twenty isn't ancient."

Doug pursed his lips and stared at the water. Something ghostly skittered through me. An unknown. He looked back at me, a forced smile on his lips. The haunting feeling remained, but I dismissed it when he drew a tender line along my face and my heart rate hitched for a different reason.

I turned sideways out of his embrace and took the conversation in a different direction. "What about you? What's your plan for the future?" *Besides me.*

"I'll probably stay in Alaska and finish my pharmaceutical training. I've even thought about pursuing medicine. If I do so through The Program, the pay proves to be worth the hassle of meeting all their requirements.

Jordan talked about the strict rules he worked under required by The Program so I understood what Doug meant.

We discussed Doug's family. His younger sister was also a candidate and he jokingly described her as "fifteen going on eighteen." I told him about Rick and Muffy. Guardedly, I touched on Daniel's death and the fact I was now an only child. When he asked about my mother, I rationalized her mysterious whereabouts as a matter of national security, avoiding anything personal.

Doug played with the fingers spread over my knee. "I'm sorry about your brother and the fact you and your mother aren't close. That must be hard for you."

"Thanks, but my dad's the one I've always been closest to. After the divorce, I wanted to live with him. Honestly, I'm content with my life."

*Or used to be.*

A cool gust of air caused an involuntary shudder. Doug opened his arms and I nestled within his embrace against my better judgment. His head dipped, his lips close and waiting acceptance.

An internal war erupted. I cared for Jordan…maybe loved him, but for whatever reason, he didn't want a permanent relationship. Jesse was off limits— forbidden. But Doug wasn't anything. Technically, I broke no rules by getting involved with Doug, even if just for the weekend.

Our lips pressed, my mouth giving passage to a deeper, spearmint-tasting kiss. After a few minutes of sensuous oblivion, we heard steps clomping toward us on the boardwalk.

"You two coming up for air anytime soon?"

A mischievous grin promising of more to come, eased onto Doug's mouth.

The docks' security guard loomed over us. "I hate to break up you lovebirds, but it's getting late and this isn't the best place for a young lady. I suggest you move it somewhere safer, and with the steam rising off the two of you, separate places might be best."

The jeep rumbled up the hotel driveway, stopping under the bright lights of the canopied entrance. All of a sudden, I became nervous. Should I invite him upstairs? I walked new territory here. I'd never stayed alone in a hotel, or been so far from home. And I didn't know Doug. What if—

Doug's voice startled me. "Sorry I kept you out so late. You must be tired."

I released a nervous breath. "A little. Mind if we call it a night?"

He leaned closer, twisting a lock of my hair around his finger. His eyes dropped to my mouth, parted and already releasing heavy anticipated breaths.

"Can I kiss you goodnight at least?"

I nodded and he placed a long, heady kiss on my lips. I sucked a deep breath, catching his sexy fragrance.

"Mmm, you smell good. Your whole penthouse smells like you."

Doug curled his fingers into my hair and pressed another kiss on my mouth "So my *scent* drives you wild? Guess I'll bathe in it before I see you tomorrow."

I pulled away. "Tomorrow?"

"My parents are hosting a barbeque for some friends and I want to bring you as my date, if you don't have other plans. My little sister is dying to meet you."

A knot coiled in my stomach. "Hmm, dinner with the family? What if they don't approve of me?"

"I'll adopt a new one."

The lights of the city and shadowy sun lent a soft glow to my room. The clock on the dresser said 11:30 PM. Back home it would be 3:30 AM—too late to call Jordan. I logged in a message for him to find when he woke. *Miss you.*

I slipped into the silky black and pink polka-dot pajamas Brittany talked me into buying, suggesting I needed something more appropriate than boxer shorts and a camisole. The tinkling sound of my phone ringing on the dresser pulled me away from the balcony doors.

"Doug?"

"Do you have everything you need before turning in?"

"Yes, thanks." I paused. "I had fun tonight."

"Me too. Can I ask a favor? Have breakfast with me in the morning? I'll have room service deliver say around ten o'clock?"

"A girl's got to eat. See you then." I disconnected and another call beeped in—Alex and Brittany?

"Why are you two up this late?" I knew why they'd called, but I drew out the anticipation, if for no other reason than to torture Alex.

"We have to know the details! Is he as gorgeous in person? Did you kiss him?"

"Slow down," I chuckled. "Yes, Doug's even more handsome in person and very nice. Sorry I haven't called, but I just got back to his penthouse."

"*His* penthouse?" Both picked up immediately on the little detail.

"Marli? You can't stay with him. That's against the rules." *Now* Brittany worried about rules. Where was her concern when Alex opened the red envelope?

"I'm not staying with him. His parents own the hotel. Doug's staying at their house outside of town."

"You didn't answer about the kiss, Marli. Did he kiss you?"

"Nichols, you're like a dog with a bone. Yes. Doug kissed me. Yes, it was amazing. Satisfied?"

"What about Jordan?" Brittany squashed my seductive fantasy and reinforced the guilt I struggled against.

"We're dating, remember? He called earlier. He knows where I am." They gasped, surprised. "You were right. This interview had to happen. Jordan wants to talk when I get back." I purposely left out his declaration of love. Some secrets belonged only to me.

"Be careful, Davis," Alex warned. "Don't blow it this time."

Light filtered through the slit in the heavy drapes drawn over the windows, and my mind slowly became conscious of a blaring alarm. On the ceiling overhead, 8:30 A.M. blinked in neon green. Breakfast would arrive shortly.

I showered and washed my hair, amazed at how I could pass through a wall of hot air and come away dry, with my hair flowing in shiny loose curls. If we had a drying halo at home, I could shave an hour off getting ready for school.

I squeezed into an ivory tube top, slipped a nutmeg colored sweater with the baggy neck pulled off one shoulder, over a short denim skirt. A wide leather belt, buckled loosely around my hips, finished my look.

My phone buzzed on the nightstand. *Miss you too. Come home. NOW!!*

A smile snapped on my lips. I rather enjoyed being in the power seat for a change. My fingers deftly entered a teasing response. *All in good time. –M.*

I purposely shut off the receptor, reminding myself Jordan shouldered part of the blame for my being in Alaska, and payback was due.

I'd barely finished making the bed when the doorbell rang. *Showtime.* Yanking the drapes open to let the morning light into the rooms, I made my way to the door as a second impatient buzz sounded.

"Coming!"

A muffled reply sounded from the other side. "Not fast enough."

I paused before disengaging the lock. "Did you bring breakfast? I'm only opening this door to handsome guys with food."

"Next to Pedro here, I'm very handsome and I have enough food for an army." I heard someone, I guessed Pedro, mumble something and Doug laughed.

I opened the door and Pedro pushed a cart of silver covered dishes into the dining area. Doug twirled me under his arm, "Unbelievable. You're more beautiful than yesterday."

My cheeks flushed. I wasn't used to compliments and since Jordan, Jesse, and now Doug were generous with spoken praise, my cheeks constantly burned.

"Do I look okay to meet your parents? I'm so nervous."

"You look perfect. Stop worrying. They're going to love you."

Doug sat across from me, dressed in jeans and a blue striped cotton shirt. Today however, the sleeves buttoned at his wrists and his hair, slicked back, gave him a polished, formidable look.

I popped a grape from the fruit bowl into my mouth. "You're right. You're better looking than Pedro, but it's a close call."

After breakfast, we set out in the Lotus for my next test. To say I felt anxious about meeting Doug's family would be a gross understatement. I worried how they'd judge me. Jordan's mother seemed indifferent, almost cold.

*Jordan.* Guilt blanketed me again. It shouldn't be like this. I shouldn't be having a good time and enjoying Doug's company. When Jordan blurted out he loved me, he sounded desperate, almost frightened—the shy, teenage boy I'd only seen glimpses of when his driven, restrained alter ego took a break. Jealousy seemed to be the trigger that flushed out his true character, and I couldn't help but feel a slight thrill knowing I caused his self-restraint to falter.

Doug took my hand, interrupting my thoughts. "Relax. Everything will be fine."

I wasn't so sure.

A few minutes passed after we crossed a bridge, before we stopped at a large ornamental gate. Once Doug passed the retina scan, it opened. A private lane stretched over the summit of a hill and opened into a large meadow. Beyond a wildflower blanket sat an exquisite log home—the entire south side a wall of glass, reflecting the majestic mountain range it faced.

My mouth gaped. "That's your house?"

Doug simply grinned, steering the jeep to an empty parking space among several expensive private vehicles. We stepped through ornate entry doors to an inside balcony overlooking the living room below. A massive stone fireplace stretched floor to ceiling, cutting through the center of a wall of windows.

He tugged me up a staircase to a small, sun-wrapped room with two telescopes poised on tripods, facing different directions. I closed an eye and gazed through one. The view filled with a large glacier pouring out between two mountains and dropping to the ocean, close enough I could see the dirt clinging to the edges.

"Awesome. You should see this."

Doug moved the telescope away. "I don't need a telescope." He tucked my hair behind my ear and pressed a kiss to my cheek. "I'm already looking at something amazing."

His lips brushed lightly over mine, his teeth playfully nipping my bottom lip. I slipped my fingers through his silky hair and welcomed the lustful kiss placed on my mouth.

"Well, well!"

Our teeth raked when we jumped and I checked my bottom lip for blood. A distinguished gentleman filled the doorway. Midnight black hair, threaded with wisps of silver at the temples, crowned his head. His eyes were the color of dangerous, deep water, and when he smiled his white teeth gleamed in contrast to his olive skin.

"Son, are you going to introduce me to the enchanting young lady you're nibbling?" The burn was instant on my cheeks. "My, that blush is powerful. He took my hand, the same way Doug had, curling it around his fingers and placing a delicate kiss on top.

Doug hugged my waist. "This is Marli Davis, the candidate I'm interviewing. Marli, this is my father, Antonio Peterson."

"Tony, please. Antonio sounds too formal."

Mr. Peterson's arm replaced Doug's around my waist. He guided me down the staircase and my brain pled with my feet to remain on the stairs and not stumble. A small, delicate woman met us at the bottom. Doug tucked her under his arm and placed a light kiss on her head.

"Mom, this is Marli."

She took my hand in both of hers. "Welcome. I'm so glad you could join us." She tugged me with her, "Come help us girls in the kitchen." I glanced at Doug for rescue.

"Uh, Mom?"

"Shoo!" his mother gestured to him. "She'll be fine. Go keep an eye on your father and find Doogie. He's been waiting all day for his Uncle Doug."

She draped an apron over my neck and tied it tight at my waist. Out the large window in the dining room, I watched Doug scoop a little curly-red-haired boy onto his shoulders, both giving me an enthusiastic wave. A young girl with features resembling Doug from her deep blue eyes to her dark hair, appeared at my side.

"So you're Marli. You're much prettier than your picture."

"You must be Marah."

"Marah and Marli. That should be fun to keep straight." Another young woman appeared out of nowhere, obviously Doogie's mother with her head of long, silky red hair. She wiped her hands on her apron and held one out to me. "Hi, I'm Andrea. Doug's told us everything about you we could drag out of him. We're hoping we can get more information while we have you all to ourselves."

A shuffle of snickers rustled through the kitchen. Great. *Interview, family style.*

The party moved indoors when the sun dropped lower in the western sky, cooling the air with its descent. I excused myself to locate the powder room on the second floor. Slowly, I walked the length of the hallway, admiring the pictures hung at various levels on the wall. A few were of Doug's father standing with prominent people—one with the President.

On my right, a door to an elaborate office rested open and as I passed by, a voice called out. "Miss Davis?"

The wood floor creaked against my weight when I stepped inside. Tony Peterson moved from behind an ornate desk and walked toward me, gesturing to a small table next to where I stood. On a mirrored tray sat a crystal carafe filled halfway with a rich, amber liquid. Mr. Peterson poured a small amount into what looked like an enormous goblet and placed it in my hands.

"Hold the snifter with both hands and gently swirl. It warms the brandy." Mr. Peterson covered my hands and moved the snifter in a circular motion. "Like this." He smiled differently and his eyes reflected something unrecognizable, lurking in the dark blue. He lifted the globe of tawny fluid to my face. "Close your eyes and describe the bouquet." I scrunched my nose in protest and attempted to pull back. Mr. Peterson's tone sharpened. "Miss Davis, you should acquaint yourself with these small, but important, social nuances."

To avoid a harsher admonishment, I did as instructed. A sweet, but strong nutty aroma wafted from the bowl reminding me of old, expensive wood, the kind that lined the walls of elegant restaurants with white linen tablecloths and fancy waiters.

When I opened my eyes, a pleased expression relaxed Mr. Peterson's sour grimace. A wry grin curved his mouth. "Go ahead, have a taste. I think you'll find the flavor mellow for a French cognac."

"No, thank you. I don't drink."

Another insistent nod suggested I not argue, but I still refused and handed him back the snifter. A gentleman I'd only seen twice all evening, stepped into the room. There was no mistaking the disapproval in his expression.

Tony Peterson's arm circled my waist. "Simon, you remember Miss Davis—Douglas's prospective assignee? She was about to sample my latest acquisition."

*No...I wasn't.*

His eyes carefully watched Tony Peterson, but he remained fixed in the doorway. "Sir, may I have a word with you in private?"

I slipped from Mr. Peterson's arm. "I should get back downstairs. Doug will be wondering what happened to me." They exchanged a curious glance as I walked between them.

The door clicked behind me and I stilled on the other side listening. I concluded that *Simon* was more than a butler and very brave when he immediately chastened Tony Peterson.

"Sir, what were you thinking offering alcohol to the girl? She's underage! We can't afford dangerous mistakes this early in the game."

Tony Peterson's timbre changed to almost a dangerous resonance. "Simon, Miss Davis is not your concern. I'm fully aware of the consequences, but I had to test my theory. She's strong, just as I'd hoped. You must understand, I will do everything in my power to ensure this transaction succeeds. I can't leave this matter to chance, nor can I trust my son to carry through on his own. This is business, Simon. Business."

What? My heart smacked my ribs and the sudden wave of adrenalin made me hot and light headed. I braced myself against the wall. *I was a business transaction? Some commodity to be wagered? Tested?*

Footsteps shuffled behind the door and I hurried down the hall. When I rounded the corner, I bumped into Doug coming the other way.

"Marli?" My legs wobbled and he grabbed my shoulders. "What's wrong?"

"I don't feel well."

"Must have been something you ate. Maybe you should lie down." He towed me by the hand down another hallway and into a room at the end.

I really just wanted him to take me back to the hotel, but when I suddenly did feel queasy, I was grateful for the edge of a bed I could sit on until it passed—not humiliate myself by vomiting on the light beige carpet.

Doug brought me a glass of water to sip and closed the door, silencing the room. He walked over to an elaborate bookcase and selected some soft alternative rock music to play over the speakers mounted in the ceiling. A pair of skis crossed each other in a corner, and various sized trophies and model cars nestled on shelves among real hardcover books. Pictures of Doug filled one wall.

When I realized we were in Doug's bedroom, a weight settled in my chest and icy threads crawled through me. I crossed to the other side of the room— away from the bed. Outside the double doors was a private patio, secluded inside a tall wall. No escape.

My voice trembled. "Doug, I don't think this is a good idea."

Gentle kisses skimmed my bare shoulder and Doug's lips grazed my neck before cradling the shell of my ear. "I disagree." He turned me, pressing a provocative kiss to my lips and hugging my body into his curves.

"Doug—"

"Shhh." He kissed the hollow of my throat, his hand wandering up my ribcage.

"Okay, stop, please."

His kisses became more demanding. "I promise not to cross any lines," but his thumb betrayed the promise, stroking across my breast

I shoved his hand away. "What the hell? I said knock it off!" I stepped away, angrily wiping any trace of his kiss from my lips. "I think you better take me back to the hotel. This so-called 'business transaction' is not happening."

Doug barely said ten words on the return trip, most used to cuss out a shuttle that cut him off in traffic. He parked the Lotus and angled to face me.

"Marli, I'm sorry about earlier. I was out of line."

"Slightly! Goodnight Doug." I shoved the passenger door open and escaped the metal cage.

Doug scrambled out of the car and shuffled on the pavement to stay in front of me, blocking my getaway. He put his hands up. "Please stop. I don't know how you got the impression this whole set-up was some kind of business deal, but it's not."

*Dare I tell him I overheard a private conversation to the contrary?*

I crossed my arms. "Oh really? Isn't that what this genetic match game is all about? The government buys our futures in exchange for special privileges? To The Program, candidates are merchandise; our arranged lives neatly packaged for trade."

Doug moved closer. "You make it sound cold, if not cruel. Marli, you're not some product to be marketed. You're a person—a very nice one it turns out and frankly, I'm glad I selected you for an interview." He lifted my chin. "In fact, I've decided I want you as my assignee."

I clamped his wrists. "You can't! I'm not eighteen!" I dragged in several deep breaths, pushing down the panic. "We've barely known each other twenty-four hours. That's not enough time to base a lifetime decision on. *My* lifetime. No! Got that? No!" I eased around him and marched toward the hotel.

"I don't have to ask your permission, you know," he yelled after me. "Please, just think about it."

I barreled through the entrance without looking back. I half expected him to chase after me, but the squeal of tires echoed behind me. I didn't think a hybrid could burn rubber.

After three attempts, I finally entered the penthouse. "Message Waiting" flashed in neon green against the ceiling and wall.

*Geesh! Why the techno show? What's wrong with a simple blinking light?*

I kicked off my shoes and crawled on the bed, hitting the message button. Several numbers scrolled, all from Rick. The fear of why he called eclipsed Doug's proposal.

*Why hadn't he called my receptor?* Because I'd shut it off to avoid Jordan.

The message storage on my receptor blinked "full" and I scrolled through the missed calls finding a rapid succession from Jordan that ended around noon. Rick's started after. The hair on my neck prickled. Rick answered on the first ring, his tone harsh.

"Marli! Why haven't you answered your receptor?"

*Because I'm torturing Jordan.*

"Dad, I'm sorry. I left early this morning and forgot my receptor." Great. Now I added lying to my impulsive actions. "I thought I'd be back before now, but the party lasted longer."

"Party? What kind of party?"

"Doug's family party." I knew my itinerary wasn't the reason he called. "Dad, what's wrong?"

His sigh sounded weighted. "Grandma's dying."

Grandma Davis was my last living extended family. According to my father, she'd suffered a massive stroke and not expected to survive.

"They want to disconnect her from life support and I have to be present when the procedure's done. I'm flying to Los Angeles in the morning. Mars, I hate to ask, but could you change your plans and meet me? I don't think I can handle this alone."

My dad asked very little of me, the one person who constantly turned his world upside down.

"I'll take the first flight I can get."

Making a mental list while listening to Dad's instructions, I realized my first task, and not a pleasant one, would be to call The Program's corporate headquarters. Only they could change my travel arrangements on such short notice. The last time I called, I needed an emergency grant to travel across the country without documentation...the night I left my mother.

The clock in the living room chimed half past eleven. Too late to call Chuck, my counselor and the one person who could talk me off the ledge I unexpectedly stood on. He put my world back on its axis when it tilted three years ago.

Rubbing my temples, I couldn't fight the flickering memory creeping forward. I remembered every horrid detail of the day things went sideways as if it just happened.

*…I'm meeting with my old counselor who's asking me questions about school, my friends—all the trivial things making my teenage world spin. His secretary buzzes him with some crisis and he leaves the room. While we talked I watched him doodle something on the side of his notes so when he leaves, I decide to check out his artistic talent. That's when I see it on his monitor.*

*A digital copy of a check for $100,000 signed by Grandma Davis and a note to the side from my mom—a "thank-you" for helping find someone to forge my dad's name on my enrollment forms.*

*Dad didn't give his permission. That's why he yelled at mom and we left in the middle of the night. She lied! I grasp my candidacy is fake. Maybe illegal. But why?*

*My counselor is doing something to his assistant's computer, so I quickly print a copy. I fold the paper into a tight square and tuck it in my jeans pocket.*

*Later, I'm working on my homework at the kitchen table waiting for Mom to get home from her job at the hospital. We live on the military base with her boyfriend, Jake, or I should say "Captain Jacob Randall." Mom calls to say she has to pull an extra shift—news that comes several beers too late and sends Jake into a rage.*

*He throws his bottle at the wall, sending shards of amber glass across the tile and narrowly missing my head as I duck into my bedroom to hide. I'm ordered back into the kitchen to fix dinner. Jake wobbles slightly and falls into his chair at the table. I feel his eyes on me as I nervously make grilled cheese sandwiches.*

*Cautiously, I walk through the broken glass in my bare feet with his dinner. His eyes are glazed half shut. I lean across him and place the plate on the table. A sick smile curls on his face and he snatches me, pulling my body against him. The jerk tries shoving his tongue between my lips while his hands paw my chest.*

*His fork is still in my hand and I manage to free one arm from his grasp long enough to thrust the prongs into his face, catching the corner of his eye. Blood instantly spatters my white T-shirt. Jake keels back in the chair, screeching, and releases me.*

*Two sharp chunks of glass slice the bottom of my foot on my retreat through my bedroom door, which I promptly shut and lock. I throw everything off the top of my small dresser and push it in front of the door.*

*While Jake screams threats and pounds on the door, I shove my mini-computer into my backpack and utter a silent prayer for help. I scoop my sweatshirt off the floor, push out the screen of my bedroom window, and escape into the darkness, hearing Jake's rants boom behind me.*

*Ducking around the side of the fuel station on the corner, I call Rick. After my horrifying recap through hysterical tears, he tells me to stay hidden until Daniel arrives. He forbids me to call my mother.*

*Maybe fifteen minutes pass before Daniel's car skids on the gravel to the side of the building. I jump on the seat next to him, locking the door, and we speed toward the interstate. Daniel peppers me with questions, but I'm too embarrassed to tell him what happened. He demands to know why I'm covered in blood and when I tell him about stabbing Jake with the fork and cutting my foot, he figures out the rest.*

*Two days later my shuttle arrives in Cleveland. I'm in a state of shock, but safe in Rick's arms. After I show him my discovery, still tucked in my pocket, he arranges for both Daniel and me to move to Ohio, without my mother's consent.*

*I'm assigned Chuck, my new counselor, who becomes Rick's ally and the force field buffering me from The Program...*

I wiped the tears washing my cheeks with the sleeve of my sweater. Several calming breaths returned my focus to where I was—sitting in the center of *Doug's* bed, in the middle of another fine mess, courtesy of The Program.

# 15
# BURYING THE PAST

I drifted weightless, the world above silent. Sunlight swirled overhead, the rays bent and jagged through the water. A cool blanket of aqua held my body hostage in a peaceful, suspended state. I closed my eyes.

*I could just let go, never surface. No more Program, betrayal, heartache. No more feeling torn, guilty...responsible. No Doug Peterson staking a claim on my future—me. No Jesse tempting me to break rules. No more Jordan...feeling his arms wrapped around me, lips kissing, tasting, torturing.*

"I love you" whispered through my mental reverie, the voice warm—beckoning, awakening sizzling tendrils of excitement in my body. A couple of bubbles rumbled through my lips, tickling my nose with the sudden smile. I opened my eyes, hoping I manifested a glorious image of Jordan floating next to me, but found only a powder blue emptiness surrounding me.

*Really Marli? Death by hotel swimming pool? You should have bought a new swimsuit for the news reports. Now you'll be hauled out of the water wearing last year's bikini.*

I kicked my pathetic ass to the surface, face-planted onto my lounge chair, defeated and grateful to be the only one poolside.

*What the heck was wrong with me?*

Jordan Mason, Jesse Mason, and Doug Peterson, in that order. My hormones soared, my body ached in new ways, and my mind never shut off. I never slept, barely ate, and tears hovered constantly.

I flipped onto my back and pulled the sunshade from the top of the chair forward. Maybe Grandma's death looming made me unsettled. Tomorrow morning marked the official "date of death" and an involuntary shiver raked through me with the thought.

I reached into the bag beside me, retrieving the handkerchief I always carried. Jordan's—the one he wiped my tears with that first morning in my kitchen. A sudden ache squeezed my heart. I wanted him here, holding me and kissing me until I became oblivious to my fears. He hadn't returned my calls or messages and I worried he changed his mind about his feelings…or his "ex" wasn't "abroad"—or an "ex."

Hiding inside my bright striped bubble, I dialed his number one more time. The sound of his voice soothed and the dimples set deep in his cheeks, made me want him with me even more.

"Hey baby. Poolside? Can you get a tan this far north—I mean in Alaska?"

*Huh?* "I'm not in Alaska."

"You're not *here*—er—wait. Did something happen? Did *he* do anything to you? If he did, I swear I'll—"

"Don't. Can you talk?" I struggled and failed to keep the sadness from my voice.

"Marli, what's wrong? Should I worry?"

"My Grandma Davis is dying and Rick's the one assigned to, um, 'pull the plug.'" Tears trickled over my cheeks. "Jordan, I'm scared. Dad begged me to come, but honestly, I don't want to be here."

Regret consumed me. My relationship with Grandma Davis held few warm fuzzy memories. I let my resentful feelings toward her, my mother, and The Program keep me from visiting. I justified my anger as the reason for staying away.

"Babe, please don't cry—not when I'm so far away and can't help. When are they on doing this?"

"Tomorrow morning."

"Which hospital?

"Cedars-Sinai. Why?"

"I want to know where you'll be, that's all. Marli, about Alaska—"

An urgent call from The Program broke in and I had no choice but to answer. I hated saying goodbye to the only solid piece of ground in the quicksand mire presently surrounding me, but relief swamped me when Chuck's face filled the screen.

"Marli, why is my favorite project in California? I received notification you unexpectedly left Alaska right after your interview with Douglas Peterson. What's going on?"

"Grandma Davis is dying and Rick asked me to come."

"Am I sorry to hear that?" He likely took some twisted pleasure in knowing someone who'd hurt me would no longer be an issue in my life.

"Be nice. Say, how did you know about Doug Peterson?"

"Whenever you're on an interview, you're tracked for safety reasons. I'd barely received notification before you vanished from my radar. Frankly, Marli, I'm surprised you accepted another interview."

"Long story."

"I figured as much. When will you return?"

"Friday."

"I want to see you in my office Monday morning, ten o'clock sharp. We need to get matters in place before you turn eighteen and discuss your interviews. I received Mr. Peterson's report. Glancing at the first page, he's quite impressed with you." Something in his tone made me guarded. "In fact," he continued, "Mr. Peterson filed a ninety-day hold for you."

Panic instantly consumed me. "What's a 'ninety-day hold?'"

"It means he's not exercising his option to choose you at this point, but wants priority in case someone else tries. You're basically off the grid for three months."

This couldn't happen. No way would I let Douglas Peterson keep me from Jordan. But…what if this wasn't Doug's doing? *"…It's just business…"*

"Can he really do that? Put my life on hold at a whim?"

"Afraid so. You interviewed, Marli. That sets protocol and with his status—"

"Five diamonds."

"Yes. Five diamonds, which—" Chuck's voice suddenly faded to a curious tone. "Wait a minute. Well, this is interesting."

A burning sensation started in my chest, either from skipping lunch or anxiety over new information Chuck would offer. The side of my face tingled and I worried a heart attack loomed. "What?" escaped on a tight breath.

"Jordan Mason apparently also instated a hold, only his registered first."

"Jordan? When?"

"According to the information I have, last Wednesday afternoon. I don't know why I didn't receive notification. Seems we have a dilemma."

"*We?* I'm pretty sure it's only me. You better have some answers when I see you Monday," I warned before disconnecting.

I stared in shock at the blinding shimmer of sunlight on the pool. Jordan stormed out Wednesday morning, ending our relationship, only to turn around later the same day and place some kind of invisible cage around me. Maybe it was the stupid red envelope and the fear someone else could claim me. Maybe he wanted to make sure no one separated us until we worked through the whole Jesse mess. While thrilled he cared about me that much, even after my confession, he used the same sneaky tactics my grandmother had. He froze my future without my knowledge.

Gathering my things, I marched into the hotel, grateful Rick had gone to the hospital so I could be alone with my thoughts. Maybe after taking one of the four timed ten minute showers allotted a standard room, I'd calm down. Fat chance. Once I stepped under the hot stream of water, I screamed.

"Dammit Jordan Mason! How could you? What gives you the right? What gives Douglas Peterson the right? My life! My. Freaking. Life! Doesn't anyone get that?"

My fingernails scraped my scalp hard enough to bleed. Shampoo suds drizzled over my face and I sputtered when they seeped in my mouth during my raging declaration. The water shut off before I'd rinsed completely and I slid to the shower floor, angrily slapping the puddles of soapy water. My whispered echo bounced inside the tiled box.

"Why Jordan? Don't you understand how scared I am? I need to protect myself from getting hurt. I'm afraid you'll break my heart, or…I'll break yours. That would kill me, either way. I can't lose you."

Clarity hit with the residual cold droplet from the showerhead. While it didn't change the fact I was mad as hell, I could no longer deny the truth. I'd fallen in love with Jordan Mason.

The shiny hospital floors mirrored the empty gurneys lining the hallway, waiting for their next passengers. Grandma's room was at the end of a long, dimly lit corridor. Dad and I halted in the doorway, afraid to enter.

Grandma's frail body lay propped on pillows, the pale blue white light above her bed illuminating her face, accentuated her sunken cheeks and the dark circles surrounding her eyes. Her gray hair, pulled taut off her face, matched the sallow hue of her skin and the expression on her face appeared more severe than I remembered.

The machine keeping her alive hissed and pumped. The monitor showed an erratic heart rate with sharp spikes and dips. A second line at the bottom stretched flat, no fluctuation in the neon green line measuring her brain activity. By all medical determinations, Grandma Davis was already dead. A part of me hoped we'd get here and she'd be awake and ready to go back to the care facility, or it would be over.

The doctor and two nurses arrived shortly after us, standing as sentries on each side of Grandma's deathbed. "Would either of you like to say anything before we start?"

The doctor's words shocked me and I became a stone statue next to my father.

Dad tugged my arm. "Marli? Do you want to say goodbye?"

*Hell no! If I touch her, death cooties will attach to me forever. It will be her ultimate revenge on me.* I prayed the terror I felt inside didn't show on my face.

My father's eyes glistened. Before him lay his mother, frail and unmoving, and he would be the one to end her existence. My superstitious fears seemed childish compared to his daunting task. I had no choice.

I stroked the top of her silver haired head, tucking back a couple of loose strands. Cautiously, I leaned in, pressing a light kiss to her cheek. "Bye Grandma."

Stepping back a few paces, I watched Dad cradle her in his burley arms, clenching her fragile body to his chest. A heart wrenching sound poured from him and uncontrollable tears drenched both our faces.

One by one, the tubes were removed. Monitors beeped once, twice, before the jagged red line smoothed straight, parallel to the green line beneath. The nurse turned the machines off and a tangible silence enveloped the room. Then I heard it—the gasping shudder of death officially consuming my grandmother. A surreal horror swamped me with the realization I'd witnessed the end of a human life.

Recoiling from the gruesome scene, I bolted out the door, my legs racing to catch up with the rest of me. I crashed through double metal doors and raced past a nurse's station until my legs crumpled. My face slapped the cold tile floor and I curled into ball and wept.

Blindly, I reached for the handrail, slowly pulling myself upright. A nurse who chased me, stopped when I rested my hand against the glass window and the diamonds in my pink bracelet sparkled under the lights. She silently backed away.

My breathing slowed and I focused on the scene before me. Without realizing, I'd ran into the maternity ward. Standing in front of the nursery window, I gazed at the newest members of the human population lined up in clear plastic boxes, tagged and marked for shipment into the world. I noticed the common link between them. A patch pasted behind each bitty right ear, covering the implanted chip. I wondered how many of these tiny bundles would be chosen as candidates for The Program?

I swept my moist cheeks with the back of my hand and stepped away from the window, fighting for air. My life spun out of control and I feared gravity alone could no longer keep my feet firmly planted on earth.

The sun's rays stretched through the windows at the end of the empty hall I aimlessly wandered, and the silhouette of a man walked in front of the shaft of light. I knew immediately who it was, even if I thought it totally impossible.

"Jordan!"

Sprinting down the hall and jumping into his arms, I nearly knocked him to the ground. Clinging to him as if he was the very oxygen I needed to breathe, I fisted his shirt collar and pressed my face against his neck. The soft locks of hair I fingered smelled of coconut-scented shampoo and the warm skin held a hint of his signature cologne.

Jordan carried me to a bench along the wall, safeguarding me within his arms. I raised my head to compassionate eyes staring back.

"It's okay. I'm here." He reached into his pocket and pulled out a dry handkerchief.

I wiped my cheeks and runny nose, mortified when I saw the huge wet spot on his shirt from my tears. "Sorry, I'm such a mess."

"Yes, but you're *my* mess and beautiful, in a swollen-red-snotty-nose sort of way."

A feeble smile eased on my face. It was true. I was his. At least for ninety days.

"Why aren't you with your dad?"

"I freaked and ran when that eerie sound..." My voice disappeared when the nightmare rushed forward.

"The 'death rattle.' I should have warned you."

I tipped against Jordan's shoulder, clenching his handkerchief. "I can't believe it's over—that Grandma is really dead." I inhaled a deep breath, holding it for a moment and closing my eyes. A soft kiss christened each eyelid.

"She's in a better place now."

I lifted my eyes to his. "Do you believe Heaven exists, Jordan?"

"I hope there's something better after this life." His thumb swiped over my damp cheek. "Although now that you're part of mine, life's pretty terrific the way it is."

The stress of the day took its toll on Rick and he returned to the hotel. Tomorrow would prove to be another grueling day. Jordan and I headed for the beach to watch the sunset. I needed to rinse my mind with ocean breezes and desperately wanted some time alone with him.

The sun faded on the horizon, its rays fanning outward in bright golden fingers against an amber sky. We found a private stretch of beach below the canopy of a cliff, kicking off our shoes and digging our toes into the cool, damp sand.

"I miss the ocean," I mused aloud. "Something about sitting on warm sand and having the sea kiss your toes is so romantic."

Jordan tugged me down beside him. "Speaking of romantic…" His teeth lightly nipped my jaw and his lips wandered the side of my neck. "We have this beach all to ourselves. It would be shame to waste the moment." His eyes reflected the final rays of the day, turning a dark topaz color.

"I love your eyes. They change color with the world around you—hypnotic."

His fingers wrapped my neck, gently bringing my lips to his. "Do I have you under my spell?"

I ran my tongue along his bottom lip, his eyes turning the color of dark whiskey.

"Definitely."

He cradled my head, holding me against his lips in a kiss filled with an intimacy we'd never shared before. He pulled back, tenderly stroking my cheek with his knuckles, his eyes soaking me in.

"I love how you feel on my lips."

"I kind of like being there."

Threading my hands into his thick hair, I pulled him back to me. Our bodies entangled, rolling together in the sand. Jordan moved on top of me and settled between my legs, key body parts pressed together. All the blood in my body heated and pooled deep. Despite my inexperience, I could tell by his body's reaction the wild craving to touch, and be touched, coursed through him with the same impatient heat flooding my own body.

He buried his face in my hair, kissing down my neck, until his tongue tasted the skin under the lace edge rimming my neckline. My breath caught in my throat and goose bumps rushed beneath the fingertips feathering across the bare skin between my shirt and jeans. Jordan lifted slightly, gazing at me without moving his hand from where it pressed my stomach, the heat searing my bare skin and everything inside me.

"Look at me," he beckoned.

I struggled to find enough oxygen to fill my lungs when dark, wanton eyes held my mine captive as I pushed each button on his shirt through the tiny holes until the fabric lay loose. The sight of his smooth chest turned my mouth dry. I pushed his shirt off and tasted the salty dew on his naked skin, feeling his moan rumble against my mouth.

Jordan flattened me into the sand, the kiss in response reckless and demanding. His hand snaked under my shirt and settled over my satin bra. I remained locked in his gaze, gripping his upper arms, unable to fight the dizzying thrill surging through me. He eased my top higher and a sharp breath burned my throat when his head dipped and he lightly sucked the skin along the edge of my bra. I purred low in my throat and small puffs of air warmed the damp skin when I felt his lips pull into smile.

"Am I pushing my luck?"

"I'm not sure." My eyes glossed over when he purposely shifted his hips and his fingers stroked my skin causing sweet, seductive shivers to build. "Maybe" sputtered on a quickening breath. I no longer heard the surf pounding the rocks, only the rush of blood in my ears, my focus centered on Jordan's touch.

His lips curled over the shell of my ear. "Want me to stop?"

I bit my lip against the delightful agony blooming. "I...*no*," the latter sliding into a sensuous slur. My subconscious folded her arms in disapproval.

"Jordan?"

"Hmm?" he mumbled, concentrating on torturing me more than forming words.

"What would happen if...if we went all the way?"

*Everything* came to a halt. I even wondered for a moment if Jordan actually stopped breathing, except I felt his heart hammer wildly against my palms.

He rolled to the side of me. "We'd be kicked out of The Program."

"Maybe it's worth it." I smoothed my shirt down and curled into the crook of his arm. "We could run away—"

"No!" He cut my sentence short, his tone sharp. "Damn! I shouldn't have let things go so far. I need to remain in control," he muttered with self-reproach. He sat up and leaned on his knees, his tone brittle. "Leaving The Program isn't an option, Marli."

I knelt beside him. "Jordan, there are always options."

He wouldn't look at me, eyes fixed forward watching the last remnants of the sunset kiss the horizon goodbye. "Not for me and definitely not for you." The stern declaration closed it to further discussion.

Anger flickered. "*You* don't choose my options, Jordan."

His fingers scraped the back of his neck and he granted me a fleeting look over his shoulder. Nothing more.

"You're right. Not *me*. But the answer is still 'no.'"

I should have left things alone, but I sensed something more. "Are you hiding something?"

He refused to look at me when he answered. "Nothing you need to worry about."

I scrambled to my feet and snatched my sandals. "I hate secrets."

Jordan grabbed his shirt, sending a cloud of sand into the air. "Dammit Marli, let this go, please." I brushed by him and he caught my arm. "Don't be like this." I jerked loose and marched toward the trail leading to the parking lot above. "Marli!" I didn't answer or slow my march. "Whatever. Run away!"

My teeth ground together. I whipped around, stopping him from coming closer. "I'm not the one running from something. Damn! You're so frustrating!"

Taking a shortcut straight up the hill, Jordan beat me to the car. When I reached for the handle, he pushed me up against the passenger side. "Stop this. You don't understand. There are forces at play here, Marli, and neither of us can afford to make mistakes right now."

I leveled an icy stare. "I'm not dumb. You're covering up something and lying about it."

"I've never thought of you as dumb and I'm sorry you don't trust me."

"Same here."

We drove back to the hotel in silence. It wasn't until we stood at the suite door that Jordan spoke, his voice distant as he announced he'd get another room. Exactly the opposite of what I wanted. I needed him here with me, but I could tell by his stiff posture that he still harbored some anger from the beach. Mine had waned in the forty-five minute drive.

I made a desperate plea, citing that if Rick didn't find him in our room in the morning, I'd undergo a grueling interrogation. I held out my hand and he left it dangling pathetically while he decided. When his fingers wove through mine and wrapped tight, a jolt of electricity seared my nerve endings. The simple touch proved the connection between us remained and I let go the breath trapped in my throat.

A stack of pillows and blankets piled on the sofa suggested Rick had already gone to bed. We tossed the cushions and snapped what looked to be an uncomfortable mattress into place. Jordan doubled one of the blankets and spread it on the floor. Judging by the hard lumps beneath my knees as I climbed on the sofa bed, Jordan had the softer place to sleep.

A question popped in my mind as I smoothed the sheet. "Jordan? Why did you come?" I wanted to ask earlier, but at the time, it didn't matter *why*, only that he had.

Suddenly a feathery weapon struck my head knocking me over.

"I didn't want you to go through this alone," my handsome assailant replied quietly.

He tucked one blanket under the corners of the mattress and I took advantage of the moment with his head down, to deliver a down-filled blow.

"Sure that's the only reason?"

Jordan grabbed the pillow and held it hostage. He sat on the edge of my makeshift bed and studied me with hooded eyes that still had a glint of mischief. "What are you really asking?"

Cautiously, I crawled closer. "I wondered if maybe you were curious about Alaska, enough that you couldn't wait until I returned." I desperately wanted to ask about the "ninety-day hold," but knew the topic could trigger another argument and spoil things.

When I tried to sneak the pillow, Jordan pounced and placed me in a headlock. When I raised my hands in surrender, he released me and patted the mattress for me to sit beside him.

"You are the sole reason I came." He tucked me under his arm. "But since you've brought it up, I have a confession regarding Alaska."

"*Now* you're sharing secrets."

His peaked brow matched mine. "More like my guilty conscience nagging." His fingers lightly stroked along my arm and my skin tingled. "When you called yesterday…I was in Juneau looking for you."

"*…tan this far north…you're not here…*"

"Juneau? You followed me to Alaska? Why?"

"You didn't answer my calls or messages. I got worried—something I don't handle well."

"Obviously. How did you know where I stayed?"

"I, uh, didn't."

I faced him, unable to stifle the giggle. "You flew all the way to Alaska because you were jealous—" I held up my hand when he started to object. "Admit it, *jealous*. But you had no idea where to find me so you were just going to 'hotel hop' until you did?"

"Something like that."

"So why tell me? I'd probably never have found out."

Jordan scrubbed his face against his palms. "I'm not so sure that's true. And after accusing me of keeping secrets, I need you to believe in me again."

After indulging me with a lusty, apologetic kiss, he launched into the Spanish Inquisition about the interview. When I revealed my proposed candidate was Doug Peterson, his brows screwed together.

"Do you know him?" I asked.

"How would I know him?"

He gathered me close again, asking about what we did and if I met Doug's family. I thought about all the things Doug and I did in the short time I spent there, but to preserve my life, I edited my reply.

"Doug took me to a barbeque where I met his family. They seemed nice. His dad even invited me into his private office and offered me a taste of some new brandy," I said, waving my hand in a dismissive gesture. However, I couldn't erase the memory of Tony Peterson's eyes, the feel of his hands, or his creepy sidekick, not to mention the topic of conversation where I became a bargaining chip.

Jordan nearly choked. "You were alone with T—Mr. Peterson?" The little vein below his cheek twitched and his tone reeked of disgust. "I can't believe he offered you liquor. You're a minor."

I hated reminders of my age, but when I tried to pull away, both arms wrapped tight. His voice turned small and fearful. "Hey, I didn't mean anything by it, I swear. I know you don't drink. It's just odd he'd do that."

"Mr. Peterson said something about me learning 'social graces.' It was all kind of weird. What I don't get is why you sound scared."

"Because I'm constantly afraid of losing you."

I placed a light kiss on his neck. "You're not going to lose me, Jordan."

"I wish I was as sure of that as you are. All the same, I'm glad you're not in Alaska anymore."

My thumb rubbed mindlessly across Jordan's palm. "I feel bad about disappearing and only leaving a note. I haven't had time to call and apologize."

A lie more than a truth. I had time, but chose not to call, fearing another rash decision from Doug.

"He'll understand." Jordan brushed the hair out of my eyes and kissed me softly. "I'm sorry about the beach."

"Same here, but I, uh, kind of liked what we did…before our fight."

Jordan brushed his lips over my knuckles, placing a tiny bite on my pinky. "Ditto."

I twisted the loose curl over his eye in my finger. "Someday, will you tell me what you're guarding from me?"

"Do you trust me Marli—I mean, *really* trust me?"

I thought about it for a second before answering. "Yes."

"Then please trust there's a good reason I can't say anything, right now. When I can, I'll tell you everything."

A mental "thank you" went to Brittany again for the pajama idea. When I came out of the bathroom, Jordan stood in front of the window in pajama bottoms that rode low on his hips. The moonlight found its way through a break in the clouds and the silver glow bounced off his body. Broad shoulder blades resembled stone wings guarding braided muscles, roped to a deep "V" at his lower back. I swallowed, unable to ignore the intense hot flutter that seemed to hover whenever I came within a mile of him. He shuffled a T-shirt over his head, covering my view.

*Damn.*

I folded into his open arms, laying my cheek against his warm chest. I felt safe in his embrace. Safe, from whatever unknown he felt he needed to protect me from. Safe from whatever unknown I left in Alaska, still haunting me.

He drew little circles over my back. "Hmm. Nothing underneath. I like." I gasped, hushing when his lips pressed and lingered, only for as long as he felt safe. "I'm glad you'll be eighteen soon."

"Is that the magic age when you'll seduce me?"

A wicked spark glinted in his dark eyes. "Is that an invitation?"

"What if I said I'm not sure I can wait that long."

Jordan growled, playfully biting my ear. I giggled and he silenced me with another kiss. And another. "We better stop. Our lives are over if your father catches us." I climbed into bed and Jordan settled on the floor.

A few minutes passed before I heard a muffled sound from the other side of the wall. I strained to listen. Rick was crying and my heart crumbled. Anger seemed to be the only emotion he openly showed, maintaining a tough image, especially since the testosterone levels rose in my ever revolving love life.

A sudden sob caught me by surprise and I held my breath, pushing down tears. The bed shifted and an arm wound around my waist. Jordan curled his legs under mine, scooping me close, but keeping the sheet between us. A soft kiss on the back of my neck caused a small shiver.

"Hey? Are you all right?"

Still holding my breath to keep from crying, I answered only by shaking my head. His embrace tightened and his nose nestled into the nape of my neck. A beautiful tune hummed against my skin between more gentle kisses.

"Your voice is beautiful," I whispered. The humming came to an abrupt end. "Please, don't stop. It's soothing. What is it?"

"A lullaby Mom used to sing to us whenever we became frightened. I can't remember the words, but the melody's burned in my memory."

The image of Jordan's mother cradling a bronze-haired little boy and singing him a lullaby after a nightmare seemed in direct contrast to the stern woman who interviewed me.

"More? Please?"

The melodic sound of Jordan's voice to the side of my ear encouraged a sleepy haze to tug my eyelids and I relaxed, molding to his curves. A perfect fit.

Bright light filtered behind my eyelids. Slowly, my senses became alert and I remembered Jordan lying next to me on the bed when I drifted to sleep. My arm reached over for him, feeling nothing. I jerked upright, looking around the room. Blankets folded neatly covered the chair, but no sign of Jordan.

"He went for a run."

Dad's voice startled me. He sat at the small table by the window, his head tucked in the morning newspaper. He remained stuck in the past and refused to read his news on anything digital. *"I like the smell of newsprint,"* he once told me.

"When we get home, Pumpkin, we need to have a serious talk about Jordan Mason."

"Why? Is something wrong?" *Did he find Jordan asleep next to me?* No. Jordan still lived.

"Not that I'm aware of. I'm more afraid there's something 'right' between the two of you. That's what I want to discuss."

"Great. Not you too," I muttered, gathering bedding and readjusting the sofa. The newspaper shuffled and Dad's eyes burned a hole in the back of my head. Keeping my back turned, I explained. "I'm meeting with Chuck next week."

"Oh? You'd tell me if there's something I need to worry about, right? You know how I hate surprises."

"Yes, I'd tell you, but no, nothing to worry about." *Only two ninety-day holds on your daughter. One by a boy you've never met.*

Rick rolled the paper and placed it to the side of his coffee mug. "Mars, Jordan asked me if he could take you to that fancy island of theirs for the summer. You'll be eighteen so I can't legally stop you, but I have my concerns, considering his twin will probably be there, too. Does Jordan know you're going to his brother's concert next week, or have you smartened up and decided against it?"

I straddled the chair across the table. "*Jesse.* He has a name. Yes, I'm still going and Jordan knows. He's not happy about it, but he trusts me."

"Or so you think. You're playing with fire, Mars."

"I like Jess, Dad. He's fun and only pretends to be the bad boy, but he's not in The Program. Nothing serious can happen between us and Jordan knows that."

He swallowed the last of his coffee. "Jordan believes nothing of the sort, I can assure you. Candidacy status won't prevent 'serious' from happening."

"Precisely why Jordan, and apparently you, too, will have to trust me."

"Sorry, but I'm siding with Jordan where his brother is concerned. He's trouble and has you in his cross-hairs. I'd give this summer vacation substantial consideration. In fact, I'd prefer you didn't give Jordan an answer until you've discussed it with Chuck *then* me." A demand—not a request. "Staying home may be best. They'll both be gone for a couple of months, giving you some time alone," he added.

Two months would also compromise Jordan's ninety-day hold and leave me vulnerable to Doug.

"But you won't stop me if I want to go?"

"This is your life to figure out, Pumpkin. I told Jordan I'd leave the decision up to you." Dad regarded me. "He wants to fly home with you this afternoon. I have a few more items to take care of, but I should be home Sunday night. I can trust the two of you alone, can't I?"

A flicker of last night's fight on the beach passed before my eyes. "Jordan's a stickler for obeying rules. Especially The Program's."

"It's your hormones I worry about, but I don't have a choice. Karen needs your help at the clinic Saturday."

Karen. Topic "A."

"Dad, are you dating Karen?"

Rick's cheeks turned three shades of pink, answering my question. "I'm too busy monitoring your love life to have one of my own." He kissed the top of my head." Right now, we're only close friends, which I wish was the case with you and Mr. Mason."

The thick marine layer cloaking the cemetery provided the perfect eerie setting. Through the mist, Dad stood over a gravesite, a small orb in his hands. Jordan's arms slipped around my waist.

"I'm waiting here. This private moment you need alone with your father." I didn't argue.

My spiked heels dug into the soft ground, pulling up small clumps of grass as I walked across the lawn. Slipping my arm through the crook of Dad's, I snuggled tight to his side. I focused on the words **LEAH MARTIN DAVIS** elegantly embossed on top of the brass globe and found it hard to believe an entire human fit in the cylinder he held in his shaking hands.

Due to land being at a premium, the government demanded cremation after death. Each family had a small plot assigned with their names engraved on a plaque in the center. A brass button marked where an individual urn lay beneath the grassy surface. As with everything else, the wealthy were the exception, still allowed their gaudy shrines. Whether underground or inside a marble crypt, however, the government-issued brass sphere remained the same.

Dad carefully placed the urn a small concrete box already in place in the ground. I dropped a single white rose on top before he sealed the box, and Grandma inside. Each of us took a handful of moist dirt, sprinkling it ceremoniously over the small grave.

I stepped back, feeling weirdly off-balance. Beneath the small mound of damp loam lay the remains of the person who'd been instrumental in altering my life. All the bottled up anger rushed like a bullet through me. Inside I vehemently screamed *I hate you!*

I clamped my hand over my mouth the keep the spiteful words from escaping. Another stronger emotion doused the flames of hatred. *Gratitude* muscled past the anger so powerful it dropped me to my knees. If my grandmother hadn't manipulated my life the direction it faced, I'd never have met Jordan.

"I love you, Grandma," burst through a sudden flood of tears, pushing the bubble in the back of my throat away. "I forgive you," came out on a mere whisper, but resounded like a cannon shot in the misty air. The wet grass pricked the skin of my cheek, the coldness of the ground I lay upon, seeping through my skin.

"Mars!" Rick cried out, falling on his knees at my side. I watched Jordan running across the lawn, the picture bent sideways. My dad's arm felt warm around my shoulders, but his voice stayed muted, disconnected. "Pumpkin?" drifted into my brain, registering zero. Jordan's hands framed my face and I wanted to smooth the worry line cutting his forehead.

"Marli? Baby talk to me." His voice drowned out Rick's, his gentle touch reconnecting my mind and body. I threw my arms around his neck, clinging fiercely.

"I love you," I whispered into his ear, feeling his arms tighten in response. "I really love you. I'm sorry it took me so long to say it."

A whispered response blew soft on my cheek. "I love you more. To the moon and back."

# 16
## COLLISION COURSE

A creepy silence filled the house in Rick's absence. I felt lonely the minute I closed the back door, until Jordan bounced on the landing from the basement.

"No monsters downstairs," he noted gleefully. He insisted on me staying put in the kitchen while he did some "manly" walkthrough, searching for predators that may have broken in during the week and taken up residency. He circled through the living room and ended in front of me, leaning against the kitchen sink.

"What about upstairs? The attic?" I tapped my finger against the cabinet door behind me. "I've been afraid to look under the sink. How many do you think could be hiding in there?"

"You're mocking me. I'm looking out for your safety—risking my life, and you dare to poke fun?" His hands traveled the well-used route above my hips, squeezing out any airspace between us. "And, I thought we'd check upstairs, together."

"You're so dramatic," I giggled when his lips skimmed my neck before pressing the sensitive spot below my ear—the trigger switch to my lust meter.

Our bodies, like magnets, cemented together. Jordan's kisses had changed. Instead of careful and hesitant, they had an eager, hungry feel to them, sending frightening thrills rippling throughout my body—thrills I no longer wished to ignore. Playing intimate contact sports on the beach moved our relationship to another phase, and keeping within required boundaries could prove challenging.

Jordan carried my bag to my room. An awkward silence pervaded the space. Both of us glanced at my bed and Jordan's Adam's apple rolled several times. "I'll sleep downstairs."

"No, stay with me," I begged. "I don't want to be alone. Not after everything..."

His lips took my thought, giving me his answer. I honestly feared shutting my eyes, worried the nightmare I witnessed yesterday would somehow find a corner of my mind to nest.

"Quilt stays between us," he declared.

While Jordan took his turn in the shower, I decided to call Doug, getting only voicemail again. *Could he be that upset with me?* I logged onto my computer to check my messages. A dozen from Alex and Brittany, one from Sam, but nothing from Doug.

I opened Sam's.

*Marli, sorry to hear about your grandma. Death sucks. Sorry I was an ass and messed things up. Forgive me someday? I heard you went to Alaska. What's that all about? Never mind. Not my business. Still love you. Probably always will. That sucks major too. —Sam.*

Jordan sneaked behind me, shuffling a towel over his head. "Hard to keep a secret in this town."

My heart ricocheted in my chest. "You scared the daylights out of me!"

"I hope not, I love your *daylights* almost as much as your *nightlights*." He kissed the top of my head. "Poor kid may never get over you."

I swiveled the chair and immediately forgot Sam. Jordan's hair stuck out in a wet, sexy mess. Beads of water clinging like final drops of rain fell onto his shoulders and wandered in tiny streams over his chest, moistening a thin line of hair that disappeared someplace I blushed hot thinking about. When he leaned forward to read Sam's message, I couldn't take it any longer and kissed his stomach.

"*Marli*..." In one move, Jordan lifted me off the chair onto the desk. I wrapped my legs around his hips and tugged the ends of the damp towel cradling his neck. His hands locked under my thighs holding me against him. His lips felt warm on mine, the inside of his mouth tasting minty. A slow burn grew low.

"You taste good," I rasped, letting my fingers slide through his damp locks of hair.

"And you're dangerous."

I returned to his eager mouth, our kisses taking on a feverish urgency. I crossed my ankles at the base of his spine, and warm, damp hands slipped under my tank top, sliding up my back to keep my body fused to his. His tongue invaded my mouth, demanding attention, darting deep, mine chasing back into his. I kissed his neck; he nibbled my ear. We switched actions, teasing each other, our hands exploring.

I wondered if Jordan tingled everywhere like me, his heartbeat loud in his ears. Did he want to shut out the world, ignore the inner voices screaming we crossed boundaries, and just give in to what our bodies wanted?

Still maintaining a leggy belt around his hips, I eased my arms around his neck, locking my wandering fingers into a safe hold. "It scares me, you know."

Jordan took the cue to slow down, moving his hands to bracket my waist. He pressed a breathy kiss to my forehead.

"What scares you?"

"The whole *sex* thing."

His body stiffened. He unlocked my hands from behind his neck and held them against his chest. His heart still bounced hard beneath the muscle I touched. He turned his gaze out the window for a second, taking a deep swallow before speaking. His voice cracked.

"Wh—why? Are you nervous about...I mean the first time..."

"I know the basics and Alex loves to fill in details, it's just—" I dropped my legs and tucked my head beneath Jordan's chin. "I don't know why I'm talking about this," I mumbled into his chest.

Jordan pushed me back a little, still keeping my hands prisoner in his grasp. "Because you're obviously worried and considering how fast things seem to be moving between us, maybe we should talk." He flicked the end of my nose with his thumb, a gentle smile stretching between his dimples. "Come on. Worst fear? That sex will hurt?"

"Ack!" I threw my head back and Jordan kissed my neck, nipping to below my ear.

"You just have to take it slow, be gentle, or so I'm told." I grabbed Jordan's face, a bright crimson color brightening the whites of his eyes. He laughed and kissed my palm. "I work with my own set of 'Alexes.'"

Unable to make eye contact, I played with his fingers. "What if I'm not...I mean, I don't even know if I'm a good kisser."

"Are you nuts?" Jordan tipped my face up with a finger. "Babe, your kisses are addicting. Why do you think I'm always trying to suck your lips off?" I tried to turn my head, mortified I'd said anything in the first place, but Jordan grabbed my shoulders. "Marli, don't." His knuckles gently brushed the side of my face. "Trust me, whoever is your 'first' will be one lucky guy."

A tender sentiment, but not the one I wished he said. "Whoever" left everything suspended and unattached. My "first time" still belonged to some stranger, apparently. No commitment voiced—no "*our* first time."

Jordan playfully bit my lip, following up with an uncertain light kiss. "Hey. Where are you?" His tongue slid between my lips, slow, deliberate "Come back to me." Unable to hold another thought, I took his mouth, meeting his demanding kisses with my own, awakening the hot tendrils stretching through my body. I broke away, breathless.

"Sometimes I'm scared I'm going to fall off the ledge. Like right now."

"I'll be falling with you," he promised on my lips before stepping back. "But not tonight. I made a promise to Rick—one I'm going to find damn hard to keep."

During the night, the quilt disappeared and Jordan slept "undercover," his body a warm vine around mine. I turned in his arms, nestled my face into the small patch of soft hair on his chest, winding my bare legs through his. Our bodies settled intimately against each other and I moaned, still suspended between sleep and awake.

"Damn! Marli, wake up." Jordan hissed, trying to untangle his legs from mine.

I reached around his waist, pulling myself tighter to his body and hooked my leg over his hip. "Five more minutes."

"NO!" The bed shifted and I suddenly reached for an empty pillow.

"Huh?" The cobwebs of sleep swiftly tore apart. I rose, trying to focus in the early morning shadows. Jordan stood with his back to me, pulling on his jeans.

"Jordan?" I turned and looked at the clock. "It's barely six o'clock. Where are you going?"

"Out of your room. Away from you." He picked my robe off the hook on the door and tossed it to me. "Cover up before I change my mind and climb back into bed with you, only *this* time, I won't be responsible for what happens. Jordan glanced over his shoulder. "You scared the crap out of me when your body shifted…where it should, but can't."

I pushed my arms through my robe sleeves. "What do you mean?"

Jordan looked at me in disbelief. "Seriously, Marli? I can barely zip my jeans." When he tugged his T-shirt over his head, I noticed the top button on his fly still undone. My naïve mind suddenly caught on.

"Oh!"

"Yeah. *Oh*," he laughed, his cheeks glowing. "My body is doing one hell of a job reminding me that sleeping next to you isn't a good idea."

"Whatever. I happen to think it's the best idea, but remember, I'm not the one who broke through the quilt fortress." I shouldn't have, but I started laughing. Jordan's face transformed through so many shades of red, I couldn't stop.

He pulled his shirt lower, over his body's obvious betrayal. "I'm taking my last shred of dignity and leaving this room before my lust-crazed demons take over. I'll scare up some breakfast while you get dressed."

Throughout breakfast, I fought the urge to giggle. Jordan's cheeks flared a rosy tint whenever our eyes met. He always remained in control and *my* lust-crazed demons enjoyed knowing I caused him to lose a little of that restraint. I placed the last of the dirty dishes into the dishwasher, feeling fingers lightly tickle my ribs and teeth rake my earlobe.

"Where did *Mr. Moral* go?" I teased, turning in his arms. Jordan leaned in, taking a long delicious taste off my mouth. "I lied. I loved waking with you in my arms, Marli."

I returned his kiss, lingering close enough to feel his breath on my cheek. "Not as much as I loved being there." A familiar warmth squiggled through my body. "Damn Program," I mumbled against his mouth after breaking from another intense lip lock.

The mere mention of The Program killed the mood immediately. Jordan pushed away to a respectable distance, "About that. We should be more careful."

"Ugh! Any more careful and shaking hands will be off limits. We can't be the only candidates The Program watches."

Jordan's eyes fell. Based on his body posture mirroring the day on the beach, this had something to do with his secret.

"What?" I pressed, feeling a touch of anger prick.

"Nothing."

The pat answer. The one that made me feel inferior, as if I couldn't handle whatever he kept hidden. Maybe he still didn't trust me. Whatever the reason, it awakened the untamed, immature monster I always shoved down.

"Right. Nothing. Again." I reached for my keys, only to have his hand wrap my wrist.

"Marli, don't be cross with me. I have to leave in a couple of hours and it's going to be weeks before we see each other again."

I didn't want to spend the time fighting either, but my obstinate alter ego wouldn't let go. "It's the same thing you couldn't tell me before, isn't it? Something to do with The Program?" A nod in acknowledgment. I tapped my foot nervously. "I told you I hate secrets, Jordan."

*Unless they're mine.*

"I know. I'm sorry, but you have to go with me on this." Jordan pulled me closer, kissing the wrist he held. "I will tell you when I can, okay?" He wiggled his nose against mine and I laughed, surrendering to his playfulness.

"Do you want to come with me to get Muffy?"

"Not even a little. I've got some calls to make, but you have fun." He kissed my pouty mouth. "Hurry back to me."

I'd barely opened the back door open when Jordan called out from the kitchen. "Marli? Some guy just pulled up in a black Lotus—one with Alaska license plates."

Peering over Jordan's shoulder, I watched Doug meander up the front walk. *Alaska* had dropped to the "lower 48" and the thought of facing Doug with Jordan in the same airspace triggered a major panic attack. Breakfast crawled into the back of my throat. I retreated to the laundry room with Jordan on my heels.

"Tell me that's *not* Douglas Peterson."

"I can't do that," I replied.

"You never described Douglas Peterson. I don't mind admitting locking you downstairs and not answering the door are the only rational thoughts in my jealous mind right now."

An idiotic smile suddenly twisted my mouth. "He's not *that* good looking."

"Dammit Marli, this isn't a game to me."

The teasing stopped when I realized how serious Jordan had become. "I never said it was. Calm down." He pressed my body to the wall and leaned in to kiss me, or I should say, mark his territory, when the doorbell chimed. "Jordan, knock it off." I headed for the door with him following close enough to qualify as my shadow.

I opened the front door and my lungs seized. Doug stood there, runway-model handsome and I understood why Jordan's jealous heart came close to having a fatal attack.

"Doug!"

Without hesitation, he gathered me in his arms, his luscious lips taking mine. The front door slammed behind us.

Jordan hooked a proprietary arm around my neck and extended his hand. "Jordan Mason, Marli's *assigned* match."

I swear a shift in atmospheric pressure occurred when Doug shook Jordan's hand and they exchanged a heated glare. The "testosterone box" surrounding me stole my air supply. I broke from Jordan's chokehold and Doug immediately claimed my hand.

His tone edged in an icy bitterness rivaling the glaciers he'd left behind. "I believe Marli's status remains 'unclaimed' as of this morning's posting."

Doug's hand slid up my cheek. "You worried me disappearing so suddenly, although I understand why. I tried to reach you, but you never returned my calls. Since I was already headed to Princeton to see my sister, I decided to stop by."

His thumb stroked the outside of my ear and I rolled my shoulder to knock his hand away. My stony gaze in disgust met with a tight-lipped smirk in return.

Jordan threw his arm roughly around my shoulder. "A trip to New Jersey within days of Marli leaving you? How convenient...and unbelievable. You drove thousands of miles to see if Marli survived her grandmother's funeral?"

Gently, I pushed Jordan's arm down, but he snagged my waist. Doug casually moved to my other side, his thumb drawing a line down my other arm, a hot trail following beneath my skin.

"She didn't *leave* me, and I don't expect anything from you."

Meanwhile, Jordan's fingers edged under the hem of my shirt and slid a torturous tickle along the small of my back, my body leaning into his deft touch.

"Well, as you can see, Marli's fine and I'm sure your sister is waiting. So. Leave."

Frustrated with Jordan's rudeness and irritated they both made my hormones scream, I stepped away. "No more touching, got it? None. Zip. From either of you."

Anger clouded Jordan's expression. "Hands off, friend. Marli doesn't belong to you."

Actually, I did—a thought becoming more annoying each time it flashed into my head. Ninety days. I belonged to both of them for what would prove to be three very long months.

A cocky smirk pulled Doug's mouth. "Nor is she yours...*friend.*"

"No more!" I shouted.

"Marli Davis?" Some stranger crept unaware into our presence, halting our argument.

"What!" I snapped, exasperated, immediately remorseful when the innocent bystander jumped back. "Sorry. I'm Marli Davis."

He reached his leather-gloved hand into the attaché slung across his chest, retrieving, almost in slow motion, the catalyst to either end the power war circling me, or start another catastrophic event. He handed me a *red* envelope.

"Have a nice day," he offered, a most oxymoronic statement given the situation.

Impermeable silence surrounded our threesome, all eyes obsessed with the shiny plastic dangling from my fingertips.

"I need to get Muffy." My legs were rubber by the time I climbed into Rick's truck. Once around the corner, I dialed Brittany. "Help. I'm in deep trouble."

When I arrived back at the house, I pulled close to the back door to prevent Muffy from escaping. She bounded through the back door, her tail whipping excitedly at the discovery of company.

Jordan and Doug sat at opposite ends of the table, with Brittany in between. Muffy headed straight for Jordan with all the force of a racehorse. She knocked one of the kitchen chairs off kilter, which Doug caught. He cowered in the corner trying, unsuccessfully, to look inconspicuous by holding the chair in front of him.

"Sorry guys. I have absolutely no control over her." I unhooked the leash and hung it back on the peg in the pantry. I handed a dog biscuit to Doug. "Place this on your palm and let her take it from your open hand. You'll be her friend for life."

Jordan glowered, but there wasn't time to react. Muffy saw the dog treat in Doug's hand. I remained close and Doug's arm slipped around my waist, holding me while Muffy eagerly devoured the biscuit.

"She's huge! You didn't give an accurate description of Muffy in Alaska."

"Marli's not very good with *descriptions*," Jordan snarled.

Moving to neutral territory across the room, I filled a bowl of water for Muffy and assessed the mood. Jordan's body remained folded in hard angles and he refused to look at me, his gaze fixed beyond the window. What seemed strange was how Doug assessed Jordan.

Brit cleared her throat, her eyes darting toward the stairs. I concocted a lame excuse about needing to return a sweater I borrowed and dragged her to my room. I'd barely shut the bedroom door when she clenched my shoulders in a death grip.

"I nearly died when I got here and found them arguing on your front porch. I'm glad I saw the pod, or I'd never known the other guy was Doug." Her eyes brightened, "Marli, he's so cute!"

"Trust me, the 'packaging' is misleading." She gave me a funny look, but I didn't have time for details and pulled her to the window seat, away from the door so no one could hear us talking. "Later. Right now I need to know what you heard."

"Something about Jordan messing with your phone? Oh! And some 'freeze'?"

"A ninety-day hold," I said, stiffly. Brittany looked puzzled. "Jordan and Doug both put a three month hold on me through The Program. Jordan has priority because he filed his claim first. Neither of them has told me. I found out from Chuck."

"What are you going to do?"

"I haven't decided—if I even have a choice. They both promised not to pressure me, but apparently, they lied. Well, actually Doug warned me he wanted to claim me in Alaska."

"You're joking."

"Wish I was. Brit, I'm so frustrated and I hate that Jordan keeps doing stuff behind my back."

"But if he hadn't done this, sounds like you might have ended up Doug's assigned mate. It's obvious Jordan doesn't want to lose you."

The muffled sound of raised voices sent both of us to the top of stairs, where we ducked in the shadows to eavesdrop. Doug's voice boomed and what he said caught me off guard.

"You think who you are entitles you to special privileges!"

Jordan yelled back in defense. "I do not! I did what I had to because I care about Marli and won't risk losing her to anyone, especially you, Peterson."

"*Care*? Is that what you call this? I think *control* better describes your actions. I wonder how Marli would feel about your idea of devotion if she knew how much you interfered in her life. The minute she said she tried to contact me, I knew you were the reason she couldn't."

"Peterson, Marli is my assignee. You and 'daddy' need to back off."

"Do you really want to drag *fathers* into this, Mason? I'd bet my life your match to Marli wasn't by random selection."

Fear wrapped my body in an icy tendril with Doug's statement. Another unknown. A big one.

Brit leaned close to whisper. "What are they talking about?"

There wasn't time to answer when Jordan's voice threatened to bring down the roof.

"At least my motives are legit. I doubt you can make the same claim. Do you honestly think I'd let Marli go without a fight? Never! My own brother's tried and failed!"

Doug got in Jordan's face. "Don't get too comfortable on that high horse. This is far from over and her lips tell me I'm still being considered."

"You're so damn arrogant, Peterson, and delusional if you think *you* have any chance. I outrank you genetically, remember?"

Doug shoved Jordan. "They're only numbers. Nothing's proven, yet. You're no expert, especially about Marli. It's not like it really matters."

Jordan pushed back. "Check again, *loser*. It matters. Besides, she's already said—"

Damn! Jordan had no right discussing my personal feelings with Doug. I stormed down the stairs, having no idea what to say, but needing to stop Jordan's rant.

"Stop this!" I screeched. "Sit." I commanded. Muffy immediately dropped her butt and I fought back the smile, not wanting to lose my edge. "I have some questions that need answering, although I'm not sure either of you is capable of being honest."

"Ouch," Brittany muttered, walking between them to a chair across the room.

Doug settled into the easy chair and Jordan perched on the arm of the sofa. I drew a couple of deep breaths, summoning bravery. My legs felt like strings blowing in the wind and I grabbed the edge of the credenza for support, then turned Jordan's direction.

"Jordan, is Doug right? Are you interfering?"

"Marli, whatever he's accused me of I did to protect you."

"Protect me? From *Doug?* Give me some credit. I think I can take care of myself where Doug or any boy is concerned." *Right*. If only I believed it myself.

Doug folded his arms, a smug grimace on his face. I immediately nodded his direction. "I'm also suspicious why you came all this way." When Doug started to object, Jordan let out a satirical huff. I threw both hands up. "That's it! Listen, I've discovered something neither of you apparently have the guts to tell me. I'm hurt and disgusted with both of you."

My eyes pricked with tears I didn't want anyone to see. I refused to break down before getting my answers. "Would one of you please explain the stupid hold you *both* put on me?" Silent tension choked the air surrounding us. Doug looked shocked. Jordan did not.

"Remember Jordan, it was your choice to date and not pressure me. But that's exactly what you're doing. The day you stomped out of here claiming 'betrayal' you put me in lockdown—before I even opened Doug's red envelope."

My body sold me out whenever I became nervous and my right foot tapped flat thuds against the tile floor. My bottom lip would have permanent bite marks, but it was the only way to fight back tears.

"You're a hypocrite, Jordan. You sat in judgment of me, making me feel horrible—even dared me to open Doug's envelope. You left me wondering if you'd disappeared from my life forever. Then you turn around and cage me until *you* decide to unlock the door? My freedom is not yours to decide."

Doug smirked and I shoved a finger his direction. "Nor is it yours!"

My throat closed and I swallowed the lump choking my airway, delivering my final wrath. "I'm only seventeen. My adult life hasn't even begun and I deserve to be treated better than a 'possession.'"

I turned to Doug, the chagrin of his choices reflected on his face. "Figuring out my favorite color or flower isn't enough to say you know me. How can you possibly make such a selfish decision about *my* life?"

Jordan's posture tightened. "You gave her pink tulips?"

"I gave her a lot of things."

"You—"

"Doug! Answer me! And they were yellow tulips, so calm down, Jordan." The adrenalin rush made me nauseated. I inhaled a cleansing breath. "Doug?"

"I wanted a fair chance at getting to know you before anyone claimed you."

Jordan approached me and I lowered my voice. "Why?"

"I was afraid."

"*You* were afraid. Did you stop to consider how I'd feel?" My gaze darted to Doug. "Did you?" Neither answered and a warm tear tumbled from the corner of my eye. "Apparently not."

I felt the color drain from my face and a sticky cold sweat prickle my hairline when my emotions and upset stomach collided. Jordan reached for me, but I dodged his hands and raced for the sanctuary of my bedroom. I locked the door and collapsed on the bed. Overhead, the make-believe clouds faded out of focus and I concentrated on deep breathing to calm down.

Seconds later, a rap sounded on my door. "Marli, let me in."

I wrapped a pillow around my face and screamed. "Go away Jordan!"

"I'm not leaving you like this." He paused, his feet shuffling on the other side of door. "Babe, please?"

When I unlocked the door, Jordan waited until I gestured for him to enter. His arms hung limp at his sides, his hands curling in and out. He sized me up with a measured glance before taking my hands. A deep, pained breath puffed his chest and he peered sheepishly at me through his lashes. The same boyish look that stole my heart nearly three months ago.

"Marli, I didn't mean to hurt you, believe me."

He cradled my face with quivering fingers and I stared into his eyes, searching for the truth behind the starburst of golden brown and green rays surrounding his widening irises. They turned shiny and bright as his steady gaze matched mine. His explanation came without hesitation, the tone soft but determined.

"I'm not apologizing for putting the hold on you. I knew when I walked out I couldn't live without you, but I was too damn stubborn to come back."

Unfortunately, a shield had raised around my heart. "This is exactly why I'm scared to stay in The Program. I hate to be manipulated. I don't think I can do this anymore, Jordan."

The corners of his eyes tightened, a glossy sheen appearing. "Marli, don't say that."

He wrapped his arms around my shoulders and I knotted the back of his shirt in my fists, pressing him close. "Then help me understand why?"

"Because I couldn't risk losing you before *you* were sure of your feelings. This way gave me an insurance policy." His lips brushed my damp cheek. "If you'd chosen someone else, I would have withdrawn my option and prayed you'd never find out. Marli, I told you I'd never force you into anything. I stand by my promise. The choice will always be yours. Program or not."

"Is Doug telling the truth about you interfering? Did you do something?"

His head dropped. "Yes. I called Mike and asked him to block the frequency on your receptor so no one bothered us. I wanted you all to myself in California. I know that's selfish and controlling, but I felt desperate."

"*Mike.* Who is he, anyway? Jesse had him tweak my bracelet frequencies on the yacht."

Jordan pulled back slightly, the vein in his jaw pulsing. "Jesse shouldn't have done a lot of things that day." He gave me an intense stare. "Mike works for my father. He's our techno wizard."

I stepped out of Jordan's arms in a flashback to the beach. "More secrets."

"One less," he corrected. "I told you; when I can, I'll share them all." His fingers tapped the bony knobs of my elbows. Slowly, each finger grabbed a little more of my arms, drawing me into him. "Forgive me? I really do love you."

"Don't do it again. I have to be able to trust you, Jordan, or we don't stand a chance." I couldn't explain to him the pain I suffered from those closest to me, or how that infidelity kept me from trusting people, relationships...life.

"You're right and I'm really, really, *really*...

"Okay, I get it. You're sorry." I lifted on my toes, accepted his apologetic kiss.

"Promise me you're not leaving The Program, Marli...or me." His hazel eyes held an intensity that wouldn't dissolve until I answered.

"I'm not leaving The Program." His brow tilted. "Or *you*."

His hands camped on my waist. "I have to go. Walk me out?"

"I don't know."

Jordan's lips swept across my mouth, taunting. "Sorry, did you think that was a request?" I knotted my hands in his hair, not allowing his mouth to move away.

"Give a reason why I should."

Sliding his hands over my hips, he locked my body to his, the sensuous kiss against my lips creating a freaky sizzle that raced through my body. When he released me, I feared I'd ebbed to a puddle at his feet. I also wondered how tight his pants were now.

Jordan led me back downstairs, but before stepping out the front door, he shared a warning with Doug. "I'm not your worst competition, Peterson. My brother is."

I stood beside the rental car while Jordan loaded his bags. There would be fallout from the bomb he dropped inside, but right now I only cared about saying goodbye to him. He drew me into his arms, onto his lips, eagerly taking from me without regard for who watched.

"Marli, lie to me right now and tell me I have nothing to worry about next weekend."

"I don't have to lie. I made the decision in California to end things with Jesse."

Jordan nodded toward the house. "Will you be all right alone with Peterson?"

"Yes," I replied, hoping I'd masked my fear of the opposite. "I'll make Brittany stick around. I stole another small kiss. "Go, before you miss your flight."

Shoving my hands into the pockets of my shorts, I marched back to the house. Time to deal with the Alaskan iceberg melting in my living room.

When Rick called to check in, he wasn't thrilled to find out I had unexpected company, especially when I told him Jordan had left. The shrillness of his voice suggested if he could, he'd crawl through cyberspace and strangle me.

"So why's this Doug kid in Ohio, Mars? I thought things ended after the interview in Alaska."

"Doug's on his way to see his sister at Princeton. I'm a side trip."

"Pumpkin, you're anything but. Like it or not, I'm sending Karen over."

He hung up before I could argue. Given Doug's behavior in Alaska, this was one time I'd welcome a chaperone.

Brittany's dad called and she had to leave. I waved her off from the porch, promising a full report later. When I walked inside, I caught the end of an intense phone conversation. I inched closer, staying tucked in the shadows of the entryway.

Doug scratched his head, his voice low and tone contrite. Whoever bent his ear on the other end sounded angry.

"Mason beat me here. Yes, she found out. His came in first." He clamped the back of his neck in a tense vise. "I understand how important this is. Quit pressuring me!" He tucked his chin to his chest. "I'll try, that's the best I can do." He caught a glimpse of me and abruptly ended the call.

"Who were you talking to?" I asked, stepping into the kitchen.

"My father."

"You said Jordan's name."

Doug's jaw tightened. "We were discussing the ninety-day hold I missed."

Confusion swirled with caution. *Mr. Peterson knew?*

"Is that what he's pressuring you about?"

Doug trapped me against the wall, arms wrapping my waist. "It's family stuff, okay?"

"But—" Before I could utter another word, his lips covered my mouth in a hot kiss edged with territorial intensity.

I bounced my hands off his chest and shoved him back. "Don't!" I crossed the kitchen and picked up the frying pan Jordan scrambled eggs in earlier. *If he comes at me again, this is going up the side of his head.*

Doug regarded me from the doorway. "I get it. *Hands off.* So, why is Mason's brother someone I should worry about?"

*Because Jesse's kisses curl my toes.*

"Jesse gave me tickets for graduation to come see his band play at a resort in Utah. I don't get what the big deal is. He's not even someone I can consider."

Doug grabbed my wrist and took the pan I subconsciously twirled. "You're flinging what I presume are eggs, everywhere." He kept my arm in his grasp and dropped the pan in the sink. "What's wrong with Jesse?" He kissed my wrist and I yanked my hand away,

"He's not in The Program." I thought by saying it aloud, I'd believe the possibility of a relationship with Jesse could never happen because of his yellow band. My heart, however, was colorblind.

"Mason's brother isn't in The Program? They're *twins.*"

"How do you know that?"

"Doesn't matter. And you didn't answer my question."

"Nor did you answer mine." I proceeded to vigorously scrub the pan. "Jesse's story isn't mine to tell."

Doug dried the pan after I finished. "If he's not someone worth considering, then why go?"

"The tickets were a gift. Besides, Jesse's my escape. He's not worried about band colors or diamonds. Our friendship worries Jordan."

Doug boxed me against the counter, his hips pressing me in place. "If I didn't know better, Marli, I'd say a part of you wants Mason's brother to be more than a 'friend'."

I tried to move and Doug's eyes darkened alerting me to stand still. *Very* still. "Okay the 'Jesse subject' is officially closed," I announced, struggling to keep the panic out of my voice.

"You got it. No more talking period."

Doug fastened his lips to mine in a demanding kiss. I raised my knee *hard,* buckling his body.

"Shit!" he coughed. "What was that for?" He gingerly lowered onto a kitchen chair.

I tossed him a package of frozen peas. He pressed the bag of vegetables to his crotch and I turned away, my cheeks flaming hot. "I warned you to stop kissing me."

"Why? Because you're afraid I'll convince you to cross enemy lines? Make you a traitor?"

I slammed the freezer door and whirled around, my eyes immediately locking on the shiny white plastic between Doug's legs. I closed my eyes and quickly conjured up the picture of Jordan kissing me goodbye before opening them again. It wasn't easy training my focus on Doug's face, especially when he smiled and purposely crushed the package. *Ass.*

"You couldn't even if you wanted to."

He rose, reaching me in two long steps, arms folded and hands tucked in his armpits.

"Trust me, I could."

Something about the way he said it, made me nervous he may be right. I rubbed my forehead as if to erase the thought. "Doug, I think you should leave."

He moved closer, backing me against the cool appliance. "Don't worry. I'm not going to kiss you." He lifted my chin with a finger. "I'll leave if you promise me something in return."

"What?" A nervous quiver circled the word.

He stepped back, but grabbed my hands. "Come to Italy with me. Our family has a villa outside of Florence where we go each summer to visit my grandparents and I want to take you there."

"*Italy*?" Anxiety gripped as I tried to wrap my mind around his request and the reaction I'd get from Rick, not to mention Jordan. "Wow! I didn't see that coming. I-I 'm pretty sure my dad won't let me," I answered, trying to reclaim the hands Doug now held to his chest.

"He doesn't have a say if I request it through The Program."

"Sounds like I don't either."

"Marli, the last thing I want is to force you to spend time with me. I was wrong for being pushy in Alaska. Please consider coming? Italy's beautiful and in all fairness, you haven't given me a chance in this fight."

"I'm not a battleground."

"You most certainly are, but I intend to level the playing field it so it's a fair war. Two weeks is all I'm asking."

*Then what? A six-month hold?*

Doug placed a gentle kiss on my cheek. "Please?"

Before his lips could travel to my mouth, the back door opened with a lazy whine. "Marli?"

The Calvary had arrived.

# 17
## MY MISSION IMPOSSIBLE

Unable to sit a second longer, I sprang to my feet and marched the length of the reception area. On my tenth turn, the door opened and one of my favorite men appeared, his toothy grin softening the edges of his rugged face. Chuck Wilson.

"You're wearing out my carpet."

"I almost ordered 'take-out' you were taking so long."

He draped his arm loosely around my neck, lugged me into his office. "I've missed you, too."

Chuck rolled his chair close to the desk, which served as a computer. The top appeared clear, but when turned on, became a screen. Rows of small drawers holding the pods of the candidates he sponsored, filled the bottom shelf of the credenza behind him. He pressed a code in the center and my drawer, sixth down on the left side, popped open.

I slipped my feet out of my shoes and curled my legs under me. I watched him slide my pod into a slot and an uneasiness bucked in my stomach.

He pushed back, crossing one leg over a knee. "So, how are things, starting with your love life?"

"Straight to business," I answered in a gruff, mocking voice. His brow curled into a heavy no-nonsense ridge. "Hmm…my *love life*. A mess—no, more of a disaster."

A mischievous grin returned his casual demeanor. "How so? I've nothing but glowing reports on you from two very smitten young men."

I'd sell my soul to see those reports.

"That's the problem, isn't it? They both want me. How does The Program feel about bigamy? I could live the summers in Alaska and the winters in Florida."

"You should be flattered, my dear. Let's get the preliminaries out of the way and I'll see what I can do to help. Lend me your arm so I can get your records updated. Anything new you want to warn me about?"

I laid my arm across the glass desktop, now illuminated in soft sky blue. "Not unless there's some limit on hormones. I think mine have gone berserk."

He laughed, turning my pink band until the tiny gold chip lined up over a flashing black bar on the corner of the desk. "Oh what I'd give to be young again. Sorry, but hormonal overload is normal for your age."

Three small beeps sounded and the bar changed to neon green. Blue changed to opal gray and my record instantly appeared. Numbers cascaded over the desktop. No new information highlighted in lemon yellow, or flashing red alerts. After the report downloaded, he scanned my bracelet a second time to restart my data field for future entries.

"Chuck, is there any way besides the DNA sticks The Program could find out if someone, um…"

I struggled to find some way to explain without having to blurt out the obvious. I needed to know if my wristband could sell me out. Things with Jordan had heated up and I felt my guard weaken each time we were alone. Luckily, Doug topped my list of things to avoid like poison ivy and black widows. But then there was Jesse.

He tapped the screen and it returned to a glass desktop. He leaned on his elbows, resting his stubbly chin on folded fists. "Exactly what are you asking?" I ducked my face in my arms and he patted my head. "Remember, what you tell me doesn't leave this room."

I left my face hidden, forced to say the word. "Sex. Would my bracelet register if I've had *sex*?"

The caring hands lifted immediately. Chuck sucked all the air in the room into his lungs and held it. His tone took on a steely edge.

"Marli, please tell me you haven't. I know this is personal, but have you been intimate with someone?"

"*No*," I answered, mortified. His forehead crinkled, his eyes hooded. "What?"

A frustrated sigh ruffled his upper lip. He buzzed his receptionist. "Carol, please reschedule my next appointment and hold my calls." My eyes widened. "We need to talk, Marli. Bring your chair around here. I have something to show you, but I warn you, I could get fired for this, not to mention it's going to upset you."

The pit of my stomach lurched.

Chuck pulled a small remote from his desk drawer, clicked a button, and opaque shades covered the windows to his office. Another click projected a wall-size viewing screen. His hands flew over a small illuminated keyboard until a graph appeared on the screen—*my* name in the first block.

"When deciding candidates' commissions, The Program speculates what purpose would be the most beneficial for you and them. See these columns?" A little green arrow blinked *look here*.

"They each represent an area you're rated on starting at birth, and each year an assessment is made—a 'grade' of sorts. A 5.0 is the highest-ranking number, with fractional allowances for anything falling below. You were chosen as a candidate based on your genetic code, but the final assessment reached at age fifteen determined your commissioned assignment in The Program."

"My destiny?"

"Yes, basically. That's why we meet every few months, to see if anything has happened that might alter 'destiny.'" He tapped my knee. "I'm happy to report that in spite of everything you've been through, nothing has affected you adversely. In fact, each evaluation reflects an increase."

He entered another graph to the side of mine. Candidate 2255: JORDAN MASON. Numbly, I watched him overlay Jordan's graph to mine, pointing out the similarities we had in almost every category. The only area where Jordan surpassed me was academically. Throughout his education, his grades were flawless.

Then I saw it. The "final score"—our genetic markers. Candidate 2255: 4.99. Candidate 5846: 4.98. A nearly perfect match. The room wobbled and I folded, my arms wrapping my head.

"I worried this might happen. There's more, but maybe you're not ready."

I eased upright again. "I don't care. Tell me everything." I waited for him to gather his thoughts, undoubtedly struggling with ethical issues.

"Some things may be classified, which means I can't tell you. Understood?" I nodded. "And, if I feel something is too disturbing, *I* get to decide whether or not to tell you."

Proceeding cautiously, Chuck opened another file, pulling yet another graph to the other side of mine. The bold words DOUGLAS PETERSON jumped at me. At that moment, I noticed something identical on both Doug's and Jordan's graph, but not on mine. Under each of their surnames was a bold, black box with a small gold "lock" icon.

I pointed to the black bars. "What are those?"

"Information neither of us has access to."

*Jordan's secret.*

Chuck rolled my band. "Back to your earlier question. See the diamond in the middle, how it's slightly larger than the others? It's a reminder of your commitment to abstinence. If this rule is broken and, how can I say this delicately, *virtue* compromised, but between committed assignees, they're allowed to remain with The Program.

"*Committed* assignees?"

"Those who have accepted each other in some form as sole life partners. If Jordan claims you and it's accepted, you'd be considered 'committed.'"

"What if I don't want to be claimed?"

"Marli, we've been through this. The last page of your contract clearly spells out the obligations you've agreed to. If Jordan had four diamonds, it would be a mutual decision, but he doesn't. He has five. The choice is his."

*And Doug's.* The queasiness returned.

He poured me a cup of water from the dispenser next to his desk. "Shall I continue?"

"I'm fine."

His brows tweaked. "Sure?" I nodded. "Okay, back to our discussion. If a candidate becomes physically involved with someone else, they're expelled and lose everything. Purity is essential because of the risk for contamination of the gene pool. Now, do you understand why I'm so concerned?"

"Jesse." His name slipped from my mouth on an outgoing breath.

"*Jesse Mason?* Chuck jumped up and planted his hands squarely on the arms of my chair, his face close enough I could see *my* fearful expression in *his* eyes. "Swear to me you haven't been intimate with Jesse Mason."

Every seductive memory of Jesse flashed behind my eyes, ending with the morning I woke in his arms. "I haven't had sex with Jesse, if that's what you're asking." *Fantasizing doesn't count.*

He dropped into his chair, rubbed his mouth hard. "I hate to pry, but I need to know. How involved have you been with *any* guy?"

"I haven't crossed any lines." *Tiptoed to the edge, perhaps dangled a foot, but not crossed.* The sudden feeling of intrusion into my personal life irked me. "I don't like what you're implying. I can pass your damn 'virgin dip-stick' test."

Chuck laughed so hard he snorted. "I'll remember that one."

"Why is Jesse such a big deal? Technically, he's 'blue banded.'"

"Not anymore, and any involvement with him could compromise your standing with The Program." Chuck tapped a couple more keys and Jesse's chart appeared with only one entry. Candidate 2256: 4.98. Exactly like me.

"Jesse was an unfortunate loss to The Program, but nonetheless, he's forbidden from getting involved with candidates. That means *you.*"

"But his numbers…"

"Are irrelevant!" Chuck blared over me. "Marli, just because the numbers are the same, there are other factors that make Jordan the best candidate selection."

"Hey!" I charged back, "for your information, the only thing I'm guilty of with Jesse, Jordan, and even Doug, in a momentary lapse of judgment, is having an overactive imagination."

Chuck's palms rose defensively. "All right, I get it. But would you clarify the momentary lapse in judgment?"

"A moment of weakness, that's all. Nothing to get excited about." He looked at me with eyes full of skepticism. "I said, it was nothing. Can we drop it now?"

"I'm worried, Marli. To what extent are your feelings for these boys?"

"I'm not sure. I know Jesse is supposed to be off limits and I don't know *what* I feel toward Doug, but Jordan? I think I'm in love with him. Is that possible so fast?"

Chuck's posture changed, his doe-brown eyes softening. He pointed to a smooth gold band on his left finger. "I fell for my wife on our second date and have enjoyed every moment of the past twelve years with her."

A wistful sadness snaked through me, wishing my parents' relationship had such an ending. I desperately wanted a "happy-ever-after," but worried my future would turn out as bleak as theirs.

"Marli? Do you want to go on?"

I shook my head, not sure of anything, but desperate to know everything. He referred back to the screen, closing Jesse's one-liner chart, leaving Doug's graph—his accumulative marker: 4.97.

"Wow. I'm stuck in the middle. Is Doug equal to Jordan as a match? He seems to think so, and threatened to claim me in Alaska."

"Doug can't do anything until the ninety days expire, and then only if Jordan chooses not to, or something else happens." I opened my mouth to object, but he caught himself. "I'm not implying anything, just stating facts. But that's why you received Doug's request. He's the next likely choice."

"After Jesse."

Chuck heaved a loud sigh. "Yes, *after* Jesse, but…"

"I know. Just doing the math."

My mind instantly recalled the envelope still sitting on the credenza in the entry. "Chuck, are there other boys compatible with me? I received another red envelope."

"Did you open it?"

"No, I'm sending it back." *I didn't want to open the last one.*

He opened another screen and his boisterous laugh startled me. "My, girl, you are popular! I show *ten*. No wonder Jordan Mason panicked."

Oops. Major slip.

"Jordan knows this? I thought it's confidential. Did he also know about Doug?"

Chuck's face twisted, his lips pressed flat. A heavy breath blew from his flared nostrils.

"There's a reason Jordan and Douglas' bands contain an extra diamond, however, this information is for 'your ears only.' The fifth diamond represents power. While I can't divulge details, Jordan comes from a very influential family and being involved with the government through his research, I'm sure he has access to someone who cheats for him…like I do for you."

*Wizard.*

"Jordan and Jesse won't talk about their dad. I have no idea who he is, but I met Doug's family when I was in Alaska. They seemed normal. Rich—but normal."

*Other than the creepy feeling attached to the memory of Mr. Peterson in his private study.*

Chuck winced. "I'm not sure Doug is aware of how powerful his family is. Jordan does and yes, there's a very good reason he hasn't told you." My mouth opened to ask, but he silenced me before the words formed. "*No*, I can't tell you, in either case."

"The fifth diamond I'm missing is because I don't come from a wealthy family?"

"I suspect your middle class standing may have factored in, but it isn't applicable where you're concerned." He took my hands, spiking my anxiety. "Marli, you saw the numbers. Jordan was almost seventeen before someone entered the system with a genetic code even close to his. *You*. Your other markers cemented the selection."

I pulled my knees to my chest. "I'm so confused I don't know what to think."

"There isn't anything to think about." Chuck steepled his fingers under his chin. "Can you handle one last shock?"

"Probably not, but tell me anyway."

"I told you each candidate has a specific purpose assigned and their numbers helped decide their assignment. Well, *you* are one of the few chosen exclusively for reproduction."

"Reproduction! I'm commissioned to be a *breeder?*" I leapt to my feet and pressed against the wall, away from the screen showing more about me than I knew. "I know kids are expected at some point, but to make that my sole assignment? It's not fair." The world bubbled under water filling my eyes. My voice quieted, the words feeling small against the vast room.

"I want out."

The chair whirled without Chuck's body holding it still. He clamped my shoulders. "You can't mean that, Marli. Too much is at stake. And what about Jordan? He'll be assigned someone else if you leave. He won't sever his ties with The Program." Chuck backed away. "But you already know that, don't you?" His accusation stung.

"Maybe."

His voice turned concrete hard. "There's no 'maybe.' Jordan *will* stay. Now do you want move ahead, or should I start the process for withdrawal."

Robotically, I returned to my chair. "For the record, I want to be something besides a baby machine."

"Duly noted." A dim smile returned on his lips.

"Does Jordan know *this* too? It would explain his sudden 'ice man' routine when things heat up between us. Reproduction? Crap!"

"All right, maybe the term is too clinical." Chuck gave a guilty sigh, "Yes, I suspect Jordan knows, especially given his cloning research."

"Why? I don't understand."

"Your gene code and high markers if paired with Jordan's *or* possibly Doug's," he held his finger up to silence me, "*not* Jesse's, has the potential to create a child with a perfect '5.0' genetic code—something that's never happened, but everyone is hoping you'll change."

"Who's *everyone*? Jordan? At least he gets to keep living his life. I'll spend life as a test rat."

"Marli, you know that's not true."

"Do I? I find it hard to believe Jordan and I are the only ones with high scores."

Chuck leaned back in his chair, his silhouette black against the screen. "The nation is divided into East and West sectors under The Program. You and Jordan are the only ones in this sector, and as far as I know, fractionally higher than any other matches. Marli, you have no idea how valuable you are, but if things stay on track, you will."

The room spun for a fracture of a moment. *On track—for what?* Did I really want to know? At least I knew I'd get to have sex. Chuck laughed when I said it, but went ballistic when I pushed the joke further.

"Maybe I should rethink the 'Jesse option' this weekend and end this craziness. Life on the outside may be better."

"*WHAT?*" The alarm in Chuck's tone resounded off all four walls. "I thought we decided Jesse Mason was not an option."

"Before you go 'psycho' on me, I already decided to tell him I can't see him anymore. But I'm going to his band concert."

"Rick agreed to this? What does Jordan think?"

"Dad's allowing it because it's my birthday. Jordan? He's not thrilled, but he understands. It's Doug's proposal I'm worried about."

Chuck pinched his nose and groaned. "I know I'm going to regret this, but what proposal has Mr. Peterson presented?"

I gave him the rundown on Doug's invitation to go to Italy for two weeks, followed by a threat to take me against my will by formally making the request through The Program. I added that Jordan had asked me to come to their family beach house for the summer, even clearing it through Rick. When I told Chuck I hadn't given either of them an answer, he wanted to know why not.

"Because I'm afraid I might give them the impression that I want more from them. Chuck, I'm not even eighteen. I'm not ready to be somebody's life partner, let alone have a kid."

"You may only be seventeen, Marli, but you're wiser than most your age. I agree, though, far too young for the whole family package."

Chuck closed down the viewing screen and expanded the desk monitor, touching colorful circles and opening screen over screen. He shook his head, his lips tightening in a worrisome knot. My stomach dipped and I swiped a shaky hand over my forehead.

"Unfortunately, under the terms of the ninety-day hold, you don't have a choice. You're required to give Douglas Peterson equal time with you."

"No!" I cried. "I don't want to go! Jordan will flip out. What if I lose him over this?"

Chuck held my trembling hands, allowing me a minute to regain composure. "Marli, you're not going to lose Jordan."

"Why, because we're assigned to each other?"

"No, because you care for each other. Trust me, if your heart is set on Jordan, there isn't anything Douglas Peterson can do to sway you, here or in Italy."

He walked me toward the door, gave my shoulders a squeeze and reassured me everything would work out.

*Easy for him to say.*

Chuck offered to have Rick call if he had reservations regarding my trip to Italy. I stopped moving and Chuck leaned around my shoulder.

"Something tells me he knows nothing about Italy?"

"Or the ninety-day hold, but he will soon enough." I held up my cell receptor showing an anxious Rick calling.

# 18
## NO CHOICE

Nothing short of a tranquilizer dart could calm Rick by the time I finished explaining the "ninety-day hold" and my unexpected trip to Italy. Luckily, he remained trapped in California, but he responded exactly as I suspected, which frightened me. Jordan's reaction would be equally, if not more so, intense.

Mentally, I'd played out worst-case scenarios all day, my muscles twitched to the point of pain, nerves raw and senses on overload. When my cell rang at precisely ten o'clock, I feared my heart exploded. We set the time, knowing our day would finally be over and we could concentrate on each other before going to sleep. I took a measured breath before answering, my chest still pounding with fear.

"Hi."

"What's wrong?"

All my self-confidence slithered away. "Why?"

"Because you're munching your thumbnail, which means your bottom lip is already raw."

Damn! I forgot to turn the video feed off before answering.

"So what's going on? You look worried, which scares me."

"What? Do you have a 'mega screen' receptor?"

"At the moment I'm linked to my viewing screen, so basically, *yes*. You're transmitting on sixty inches of digital quality, wearing my favorite blue plaid boxers."

"I'll make sure these boxers are in my suitcase so I can wear them on the island." I decided to start with good news in hopes of diverting any natural disasters when I released one, of many bombs.

"You're coming? Awesome!" Jordan freaked when I shut off the video feed. "What happened to your transmission?"

"Relax, I'm still here. Promise to hold onto your good mood? Think of me on the beach alone with you in a skimpy bikini as I tell you I have to take a trip before I can come to the island, and...I have to leave my receptor behind."

I swear he sucked air through *my* cell.

"Oh? Where, and do I want to know with *whom?*" His sixth sense proved my greatest enemy.

"Are you picturing me in an itty-bitty bikini?" Maybe I should have chosen naked.

"Damn. I'm not going to like this, am I?"

"Pretty sure you're not. I'm going to Italy with Doug Peterson."

Silence—the deafening kind after a blinding bolt of lightning leaves the air white hot, milliseconds before the shattering crack of thunder. I heard his labored breathing building.

"*I-t-a-l-y?* With. Douglas. Peterson," each word pronounced with the precision sharpness of a straight edged razor. "You and Peterson alone in Italy?" The last calm phrase spoken. Rick's reaction paled miserably.

"No way! I won't allow it!"

"Excuse me? What do you mean 'you won't allow it?' You don't own me."

"I do..." he stopped short. A smart move. His breaths deepened and the volume turned considerably lower.

"I'll go insane thinking about you there with him. How did this happen?"

"Apparently, I don't have a choice. Because of this stupid ninety-day hold, I'm required to give Doug equal time. I *have* to go." Tears trickled over my cheeks. "Don't be mad at me. I'm only following the rules."

Jordan's voice quieted. "Don't cry. I'm sorry. This isn't your fault, it's mine. If I'd left things alone, you wouldn't be in this mess."

"But if you hadn't, I could be planning something more permanent with Doug than a two week trip to Italy."

"*Two weeks?* Shit!*"

The breaking point.

"Stop!" I shouted. "I can't take being micro-managed by everyone. The constant monitoring is draining and I'm too young for what's expected of me. I want something more from life than to breed perfect little babies!"

"Babies? Where the hell is *this* coming from?"

There went my unfiltered "brainwave to mouth." I couldn't let Jordan know what Chuck told me. Getting him in trouble and me transferred to another counselor wasn't an option.

I answered flatly, trying to cover-up my emotional breakdown. "It's nothing."

"*Babies* aren't exactly nothing. Don't tell me Peterson is pressuring you about sex."

"No more than anyone else."

"That's not fair. I've never pressured you."

"I know. Sorry." I took a big breath, about to open a door I'd hoped would remain closed and locked. "Jordan, do you want kids?"

"Someday, sure. Marli, if we're having this discussion, turn on your video feed. I need to see you."

"Warning, you're entering a disaster zone."

"I told before, I like disasters, especially cute ones...please?"

I pressed the button. A blood-curdling scream, followed by wicked laughter vibrated over the tiny speaker.

"Oh, you're *so* not funny Mason and in serious trouble!"

"I live to be in trouble with you." His brow furrowed and he pressed his finger to the screen. "I wish I was holding you."

I did the same as if could magically feel the touch of his skin. "Me too. I hate this long distance stuff."

"You're killing me, Marli. I haven't been whole since the day you landed in front of my car. Now tell me, what's up with the 'baby' talk?"

"I talked to Chuck today. He pulled out The Program's crystal ball and told me my future."

Jordan stayed silent for what constituted an eternity. His expression changed with his thoughts, frightening me. He knew what Chuck revealed.

"What do you want for the future, Marli?"

"A normal life where I have you, *and* I can be a veterinarian. I want to raise puppies…for a while anyway."

"Any particular breed? I mean if we're having a canine family, I should get a say."

"Labradors."

"What? No Great Danes? How about a fluffy Newfoundland? I thought you loved a challenge?"

"That's you, not me. Besides, making you happy is the only challenge I want."

"You make me happy, babe." Our fingers reached out again. "A normal life and puppies before babies. I think we can manage that. You do realize, though, when you become a veterinarian there'll be two 'Dr. Masons' in our household. Someone requiring emergency brain surgery could get us confused."

"I think where we place a thermometer will keep us separated."

We laughed hard and I forgot about the bleak future Chuck painted. As long as Jordan shared it with me, I knew he'd keep me safe from The Program's tentacles.

A major case of the hiccups replaced my giggles.

Jordan quieted again. "I'm still don't like the idea of you alone with Peterson in Italy. Tell me again why you can't take your receptor?"

"In all f-airness to Doug, you can't have c-ontact with me until I return. Sorry. Another idiotic r-ule."

"Marli, close your eyes and concentrate on my voice."

I lay back on the pillows and did as instructed. "K-ay."

"*One*, breathe in and hold. *Two*, release it slow. *Three* inhale and hold. *Four*, release." He repeated the counting exercise in a low timbre until he reached ten.

Then he screamed.

"Damn you, Jordan!"

Blood pounded in my ears. Jordan folded over his desk, laughing so hard, tears rolled from the corner of his eyes.

"Don't you *ever* do that to me again!"

"Sorry, babe, really. But your hiccups are gone, aren't they?" I waited, trying to force one just to prove him wrong. "See. All better." I scrunched my nose and huffed. "Come on. Don't be mad. I *heeealed* you," he said in some contrived spooky accent and I couldn't stop the smile pulling my mouth.

Jordan's voice deepened. "I'm crazy about you, girl."

"I kind of like you too."

"Marli, when you get back, can you come straight to the island? In fact, pack a suitcase and I'll have a courier pick it up while you're gone."

"What about my luggage from Europe?"

"We have a storage locker at the hangar. I'll leave instructions with Mike. He'll be flying you to the island in the helicopter."

"*Helicopter?* I've never flown in one! What if—"

"You'll be fine. You *are* fine and I miss you so much it hurts."

"Jordan? You trust me, don't you? I haven't changed my mind about Jesse. I'll end things with him this weekend and after Italy, I'm through with Doug."

"Yes, I trust you. Enjoy Italy. It really is beautiful and you deserve a vacation. I'll have you the rest of the summer."

"Sure you can handle me for a whole summer?"

"I'm sure I can *handle* you just fine." My cheeks warmed instantly, putting a smile on Jordan's handsome face. "You look exhausted. I should let you go."

"Stay on the phone until I fall asleep? Please? It will feel like you're here. Dad's gone one more night and I'm kind of nervous."

"You'll hold me close to your heart?"

"I'll put you inside my shirt if you say 'yes,'" I teased.

"You don't play fair, and when it comes to peeking *inside* your shirt, Miss Davis, I want to be there in person."

No hint of regret mingled in his sinful chuckle. I placed my cell receptor in the docking station on my night table, so I could watch him. He flipped pages in a large book, entering notes on his digital pad.

"What are you working on?"

"An essay on my latest research is due by the end of the week." He glanced at me, his eyes following a path through cyber space from New York to Maple Heights, "You look soft and sleepy. I wish I lay beside you."

"I wish so, too." I yawned wide. "Hum to me, Jordan. Like the other night. I want your voice in my head when I fall asleep."

He smiled sheepishly. "*Hum* to you? What have I started?

*"Pleeease..."*

"Fine, but eyes closed. No more talking."

I watched him for a few minutes as he continued studying, while humming in his pitch perfect tenor voice. Every now and then a phrase to a chorus actually escaped his heart shaped lips.

I longed to taste those lips…to hold him and feel him holding me. Drifting into a lazy dream state where the mind reaches out to pick the last thoughts for your dreams and the last noises for a soundtrack, my eyes sealed shut.

I pictured myself in the middle of a meadow holding a daisy with one last petal. I plucked it.

*He loves me.*

# 19
# PARK CITY

We rolled between the rows of private planes to the hangar where a familiar Lear jet waited to depart. I hadn't seen Jesse since the day Rick kicked him out of the house, and butterflies tickled inside my stomach. I checked my breath against my palm.

*Are you crazy? You're not kissing him.*

My heart stopped for half a beat when I spied Jesse walking from a door at the far corner of the hangar. He had the same build as Jordan, with a gait that also held a confident, sexy sway.

*I'm so going to kiss him.*

Jesse paused midway, his eyes locking on mine as he tugged the lapels of his jacket. He smiled wide and held out his arms, "Marli!" We collided at a halfway point, locking lips.

"I've missed you." A slower, gentler kiss found my mouth. "Thanks for coming," he whispered.

"I feel guilty for missing you, too," I confessed.

"Let's hope you feel guilty for a lot more reasons after this weekend."

Another hangar awaited our arrival. As we claimed our baggage, the sound of a horn bounced off the corrugated metal walls. A custom painted motor coach with the band's name "No Regrets" spread the length of the hangar opening. Three guys bounded from various doors, one larger than the others.

"Who's the giant?" Alex asked.

Jesse motioned *giant* over. "Alex this is Hank, or as we call him, *Moose*."

*Moose* lifted Alex a good foot off the ground until her wide eyes leveled with his. "Nice to meet you Alex." He dropped her, gently, and Brittany and I doubled over in laughter.

"I hate you both," she snarled, stomping away.

Brittany took off after her, but Jesse curled his arm around my waist. "Brittany can handle Alex. We need to board."

Inside existed a mini luxury home on wheels. Jesse led me to a back bedroom, closing the door behind us. He climbed onto the bed, pulling me to his side.

"Jess, I don't think so."

"Relax, Mars. You're wound up tight enough to break in half. I'm not going to try anything, *yet*."

I wrapped both hands around a taut bicep. "I may not be able to fight you off. So tell me 'Mr. Muscle,' where did you get these arms? *Rock stars* aren't known for being buff."

A playful grin tugged the corners of Jesse's mouth. "Weights and running. I need to be prepared. Never know when I'm going to have to rescue a beautiful damsel in blue satin. Jesse eased me underneath him, stroking a finger down my throat and across my collarbone. "If memory serves me right, this position worked well for us."

He seared my lips with a long kiss. My toes *twitched*. How could I follow through with my plan? How could I not? I loved Jordan and with that love came with a price. Break Jesse's heart.

Alex and Brittany decided to check the gift shops downtown while the band set up. I bowed out, claiming a headache and welcoming some time alone.

Nervous energy crackled around me, knowing what I faced before moving forward with Jordan. However, the *want* for Jesse played the stronger demon. I called Jordan to regain my focus.

"Hey there. How was your flight?" Jordan sounded suspiciously chipper.

"Good, and I miss you already. In fact, I keep looking around to see if you're lurking around some corner."

"My life was threatened if I came within a hundred miles."

"Sorry, but you can't follow me everywhere I go."

"Watch me."

"This is Jesse's weekend. We agreed you'd let me do this my way."

"*We* didn't agree to anything. In fact, I'm thinking of taking the first flight I can get and ignore your demands."

A small part of me wished the same thing, but I promised Jess—no, Jordan.

"So, has he kissed you?"

At least he asked if Jesse kissed me—not the other way around.

"Subtle, Mason." I blew a rushed breath, knowing my answer wouldn't be what he wanted. "Not that I need to tell you, but *yes*. Jesse kissed me."

*Sucked my lips off.*

"I knew it! Did you tell him his brother will kill him if touches you again?"

Twenty-four hours hadn't passed and Jordan could already spit rusty nails. I couldn't imagine how foul his mood would be after two weeks of me being in Italy.

"Stop the jealous tirade. I'll take care of things after the concert."

Jordan said nothing. The bridge of his nose would be bruised by the end of the weekend from endless pinching.

"I miss you." Still nothing. A sliver of loneliness tugged at my heart and I wished I had a signal for video feed. "What are you doing right now?"

"Lying on my bed and wishing you were here next to me. I miss you too."

"What if I told you your wish may come true? I've been accepted to Cornell."

Welcome laughter sounded in my ear. "Right when I think I'm on the verge of losing you, I get a glimmer of hope."

"Why would you think you might lose me?"

"I know my brother, Marli."

"So do I. Dust off your 'trust button.' I can handle Jesse."

*Yeah right. Whom was I kidding?*

"For your information, Miss Davis, I'm wearing my 'trust button' and the damn pin keeps sticking me in the heart."

Our call was suddenly interrupted when Brittany and Alex burst through the door, followed by the band and Jesse.

"Mars!" Jesse called out. Jordan cursed in my ear. Jesse grabbed the receptor out of my hand, "Hey bro, don't you worry. I'll keep Marli safely tucked in my arms and give her lots of *personal* attention."

He snapped the cell shut and dropped it in my outstretched palm. "You promised this weekend would be about us. If I'm going to do a 'threesome,' it certainly won't be with my brother."

I conceded to a soak in the hot tub with Brit and Alex when the band left to practice. Soothing hot bubbles boiled across my shoulders. Whiffs of thick steam coiled in the crisp air, framing a full moon—a haunting backdrop against the black sky.

"I could live someplace like this," Brittany wished aloud. "It's so peaceful. I'll bet its spectacular in the winter. I can think of only one other place that might possibly be prettier—*Alaska*." She leaned forward in the swirling caldron. "Speaking of which, Marli, are you ready for your trip to Italy with 'tall, dark, and unbelievably handsome?'"

Alex had been on a family vacation until yesterday. She knew nothing of my commitment issues. "Italy? You're going to Italy with 'Door Number 3?' How's 'Dr. Dreamy' handling that?"

"Bad. I think he's trying to find a way to stow away in my luggage. I found out I can't take my cell receptor, either. I'm not allowed *any* contact with Jordan when I'm with Doug."

"Marli, it's only fair. Don't you think Doug suspects you're not excited to go? Give the guy a break."

My suspicions about Brittany crushing on Doug were officially confirmed.

"I *am* excited to see Italy." Just not with Doug. "When Jordan got upset, I reminded him it was his and Doug's actions that put me in this predicament."

"What are you talking about?" Alex chimed in. Again, she'd been out of the loop and Brittany quickly filled her in on the details of the ninety-day hold.

"And I thought my love life was complicated."

"Complicated doesn't begin to describe your love life, Nichols," Brittany chided.

I couldn't shake the feeling *I* was out of the loop this time.

The eleven o'clock hour left the resort lobby quiet and peaceful. I sank sideways in an overstuffed chair and closed my eyes, humming the melody Jordan sang to me. I could endure the next few weeks because at the end, I'd be with him—making out on warm white sand under blue skies or a blanket of shimmering stars.

My sultry thoughts took me back to our infamous afternoon on the beach in California, and the rush of feelings accompanying those thoughts, made my body tingle.

"I'll pay a million bucks for whatever thought created that sexy smile."

I smacked my chest. "You scared me! And you're early."

Jesse towered over me, his fingers playing with my damp curls. "And you went for a swim without me." He bent his knees, bringing his handsome face within inches of mine, his lips brushing across my cheek. He pushed away a wet, curly strand falling over my face and slowly stroked the length of my nose. "Love those freckles."

Before I could argue, he slid his arms beneath me, lifting me in his arms.

"Where are you taking me?"

"Somewhere we can be alone." The elevator doors opened and Jesse swung me inside, pushing *penthouse.*

I wiggled out of his arms and moved to the opposite side. "This isn't a good idea. I promised Jordan—"

"Jordan isn't here. *I* am. Hopefully it's late enough he won't call, but if he does, I'll bust your damn receptor."

The elevator doors opened and we faced the door to the penthouse. I parked against the wall, refusing to exit. Jesse punched the lock button, freezing the doors open. His arms pressed the frame, his body filing the space and blocking my escape.

"Give me one damn night, Marli. Nothing will happen that you don't want, I swear. At sunrise, you can walk into whosever arms you want." He held out his hand and I tangled my fingers through his, following his lead.

Avoiding any furniture accommodating a horizontal position, I wandered to the wall of windows. The lights of Salt Lake City sharpened the edges of the mountains silhouetted against the silver glow. Gold dots speckled the black hills where many houses, twice the size of mine in Maple Heights, sat nestled among the pines and aspens. I wondered if behind a window stood another girl facing me, who also suffered from the bittersweet sting of love. Maybe one caught in a triangle between two boys, both loving her, but her heart only loving one of them.

Jesse's arms circled me from behind and his chin rested on my shoulder. "Beautiful, isn't it?"

"The view is incredible from here."

"I'm talking about the reflection in the window—me holding *you.*"

I turned, my heart hammering in my chest. "Jess, we need to talk." My mind raced for the right words. He held my waist, guiding me toward the sofa. I didn't need a seductive diversion, having finally got the nerve to discuss the inevitable.

"About us—"

He crushed his lips to mine before I could finish my sentence. I gasped and he took the kiss deeper, his tongue invading my mouth and enticing mine in seductive play. His hands caressed my throat to my shoulders, where he tugged at the collar of my jacket, pushing the sleeves down my arms. My coat dropped to floor, taking my self-control with it.

I wrapped his neck, slid my fingers deep into his sun-kissed locks. Jesse's hand at the small of my back pushed my body intimately against a deliberately placed knee. He tore out the clip holding my curls in place and fingers threaded through the damp strands. His touch pricked every nerve ending on a downward quest, until his hand splayed across one of my *other* cheeks. Common sense slapped me fast, but when I tried to push away, he gripped tighter, grinding against me. His hand snaked inside my shirt and plucked my bra strap open with practiced finesse.

A hot fervor hummed through my blood, but the memory of Jordan's words *I love you* wouldn't allow my body to respond. Jesse's touch felt foreign— invasive, and I tried to break free, but he clenched tighter, ground harder. A tear dripped, pooled between our lips, and I cinched my eyelids shut to force the others back, sensing my slow surrender.

"Shit!" Jesse cursed, releasing me so fast I fell backward onto the sofa. "I can't do this!"

After refastening my bra, I crawled on the floor beside him. Gingerly, I fingered the loose locks of hair draping over his hands. "Jesse? I know you wouldn't purposely hurt me. I-I'm sorry."

His face scrunched. "You know nothing, then, because thoughts of taking you raced faster than the ones telling me not to. And don't apologize. I'm an ass, or at least *tried* to be."

"That was an *act?*"

Jesse's grin was too sly to be innocent. "Started that way—but..."

The puzzle pieces fell neatly into place, "You wanted to make me mad so I'd dump you without feeling guilty."

"*Dumping* is kind of harsh, don't you think? But that was the intent, only you didn't take the hint or I stopped listening for one."

"You scared me and...I wanted you to stop, but my body started to think differently."

Jesse picked my jacket off the floor and pulled me onto my feet. "Let's get some fresh cold air." He grabbed something from a backpack on the chair and shoved it in the back of his jeans.

"What did you put in your waistband?"

"You don't want to know. Let's just say one can't be too careful."

"Jess, do you have a gun?"

"Shhh! Yes," he whispered when the elevator doors closed. "I have a gun and a permit to carry it, but that knowledge stays between us, understand?"

"Does Jordan *pack heat* too?"

Jesse looked surprised. "Yes, Jordan 'packs heat' when necessary. Any more questions, or can we close this topic before someone overhears?"

Owning weapons violated the Security Agreement all citizens were required to enter into at age eighteen. If caught with a gun, jail became your new home. Before graduating high school, however, seniors were required pass a weapons safety course as part of a self-defense curriculum. I surpassed my friends...and Sam.

The government issued special permits to those who qualified, such as law enforcement. For a private citizen to obtain a permit almost took an act of Congress. So how did Jesse and Jordan get one? Another mystery...or secret.

When the elevator doors opened, we faced three disgusting drunks. One stepped too close for comfort and I latched onto Jesse's arm.

"Well, well. Look what we have here, looking all soft and sexy in a tight pink shirt."

I smelled alcohol on the spit exiting his vulgar mouth. Every muscle in Jesse's body tensed. His arm came around my shoulder, pulling me into his guard. We muscled through the drunken trio, but when their ugly spokesperson tugged the back of my shirt, my elbow went full force into his gut, folding him in half. He coughed up what sounded like his last drink. Once outside, I let go the breath I held.

"Nice move, Mars! I'll have to remember to watch your elbows."

"You almost got a knee earlier."

His arm hooked loosely around my neck. "Ouch. Just the thought hurts."

"Keep that thought in mind next time you reach for something that doesn't belong to you."

Jesse came to halt, the gravel shifting under his feet. "That's the bitter truth isn't it? You belong to someone else."

A light breeze blew around us and he gathered me close when sudden shudder shook me. His chin found a spot on the top of my head to rest and his arms wrapped like a favorite blanket. A kiss lingered in my hair and fingers gently stroked the back of my neck.

"You stole my heart, you know," he quietly offered.

"You left mine a little bruised, too."

Somewhere, a clock chimed the midnight hour, each stroke taking a piece of my childhood and ringing in my adulthood.

"Happy Birthday, Mars." His voice cracked. "I won't say it, but you know how I feel. From now on, I promise to respect your relationship with my brother and leave you alone."

The twang of a steel guitar strumming a lonely melody echoed up the canyon from the little bar at the end of the road. I hugged Jesse's waist. "Dance with me?"

He laughed when I balanced on tiptoes and finally lifted me on top of his feet so my head could rest on his shoulder. He brushed my hair aside and kissed the back of my neck as we swayed to the music. I'd spend one last night loving Jesse Mason before setting him free at dawn's first light.

A twig snapped and Jesse immediately moved me behind him, holding my arm with one hand; the other poised over the lump at the base of his back. An uneasy feeling slithered over me.

"No, Jess," I begged on a whisper.

Slowly we circled, stopping short when we faced the drunken threesome from the elevator. The man I'd gouged appeared fully recovered, and the flash of moonlight against the shiny steel shaft in his hand left a light trail in my vision.

*Knife.*

The demon's eyes lowered to mine, filled with an evil flicker of revenge. I withered against Jesse's back, bunching his shirt to my chest, my knees violently shaking. Nausea gurgled in my stomach and the taste of bile licked the back of my throat.

"What do you want?" Jesse snarled.

"This doesn't involve you 'twinkle toes.' Step aside. We're taking the little lady."

"The hell you are! You'll have to go through me first."

"Fine. Have it your way."

Suddenly, Jesse folded, gagging for air.

"Jesse!" I shrilled.

*"Grab her, you idiot!"*

One of the disgusting creeps saw Jesse's hand move to his back, "*He's got a gun!*"

The knife blade danced on the gravel when the assailant dropped it, but when Jesse's body collapsed over it, the pinging stopped.

A haunting sound rippled in the air. Half cry, half scream—the shrill resonating through the stillness before falling silent. It took a few seconds for me to connect the wailing with my screaming, as my mind and eyes tied back together, staring at my trembling hands covered in blood—*Jesse's blood.*

## 20
## COMPLICATED GOODBYES

"You killed him!" The assailant stumbled backward, the horror of Jesse lifeless body lying in the grass mirrored in his charcoal eyes.

"What about the girl? She can identify us." All three looked at me, but only one understood an important factor—the one possibly saving my life.

"No! Stay away from her. See her bracelet? She's one of *them*. This place will be crawling with cops any second. Let's get the hell out of here!" They bolted, leaving Jesse bleeding on the ground.

Rage flared within me. I reached under Jesse and pulled out his gun. Another flash of unrecognizable time as I scrambled to my feet, clicked the safety and leveled the barrel toward the dark figures, tripping over rocks and logs in their attempt to flee.

"NO! MARLI!" Someone grabbed my ankle and I fell forward, landing hard on my elbow. The report from the discharge of the gun reverberated into the carbon-colored night. Another scream howled, fading over the ridge after its own echo.

"JESSE!" I shrieked, realizing *he* held my ankle and was alive. I crawled to his side.

"Give me that." He wrenched the gun from my hand and wiped it across his chest. Suddenly, he hissed and his face contorted. "Damn! Marli, you could have killed someone!"

"You mean I didn't?"

"I doubt it, maybe caught a foot, but more than likely, just scared the shit out of them." Jesse fumbled under the bloody hem of his shirt until he found something resembling a button on his belt. He sucked in a sharp breath and held it. A tear dropped from his eye.

"Jesse? Where's your cell receptor?"

"My right front pocket," he winced, his eyes disappearing in folds of skin. When I reached in the pocket, his fingers pinched the back of my neck. "I can't believe I have the perfect opportunity to embarrass the hell out of you, and— *shit!* Marli, hurry!"

My face warmed at his innuendo. "You're disgusting and I know you're going to live, so I can hurt you later."

"You've already hurt me far worse than any stab wound, now hand me the damn cell before I pass out." His fingers clenched my arm, signaling another wave of pain.

I flipped it open prepared to dial for emergency services, but the screen was unlike any receptor I'd seen. There were five squares, each containing only a name, no number. *Dad, Jordan, Wizard, Home,* and *me.*

"Jess?" I asked confused.

"Wizard," he demanded through gritted teeth. "Press *Wizard.*"

I obeyed without question, tears spreading over my cheeks as I watched Jesse writhe on the gravel. He swallowed a deep breath and took the phone.

"Mike, we've got a problem. I've been stabbed. Send someone, *fast.* No, likely a flesh wound, but between Marli's screams and the gunshot, someone's surely called the police."

He rolled his eyes. "No, not me. *Marli.* Yes, she's right here. I know! I know! Moose should be here any second and I'll have him get her out of here. NO! Don't even think about making *that* call. He's...*fuck*...the last person I want to deal with."

Jesse dropped the cell receptor, his hand crushing mine before he lost consciousness. Fresh, bright red blood oozed onto the ground, and my stomach lurched when the metallic smell hit. I crawled away and threw up in the grass. Mike shrilled from the phone and I quickly retrieved it from where it lay next to Jesse.

"Mike, it-it's Marli. What should I do? Jesse's drifting in and out of consciousness. He's lost a *lot* of blood," I sobbed, trying to hold the phone in my slippery, bloody hand.

Mike's voice sounded stern and commanding. "Marli, listen. This is very important and there is absolutely no room for argument. Where's the gun?"

"In Jesse's hand."

"Give it to Moose. He'll know what to do. You must go with Moose, do you understand? *You* cannot be involved in this. We'll take care of Jesse. Do what Moose tells you and everything will be all right, but if you don't, Marli, you'll put everyone in jeopardy, including Jordan."

He disconnected and I collapsed onto Jesse's chest, his breathing labored and heartbeat slow. "Jess, I'm so scared. Please don't die."

A black van raced up the hill and skidded within inches of where we lay. Two men I didn't recognize jumped from the van, just as Moose rounded the side of the building, out of breath. The two unknown men leaned over Jesse, one holding a medical bag. Moose lifted me and I twisted inside his locked arms calling for Jesse, until someone held a cloth over my mouth.

Muffled voices rambled in the background, the cool, damp rag across my forehead drifting a memory forward.

"Jordan," I mumbled.

"She's coming around. Get me some water. Miss Davis?"

The face belonged to one of the strangers from the van. My eyes finally opened wide enough for me to recognize my surroundings. I lay on the sofa in Jesse's penthouse. In the corner sat a man in a black T-shirt with the word SECURITY stretched over a massive chest. No expression existed on his face, but when I rose, he immediately shifted in his chair ready to lunge in my direction. The man talking, wearing a black jacket with a medic patch, tried to push me back into the pillows. I eased into the bend of the sofa, dragged my knees to my chest and raised my hand in defense.

"You need to stay still until the anesthesia wears off." My brows touched. "Necessary measures," he answered my unasked question.

I rubbed my temples, willing the fogginess in my head to go away. "What's going on? Where's Brittany and Alex?"

"Asleep in your suite," answered Milo.

The baritone voice boomed from the corner chair. "Anyone watching them?"

"Brody's there. He'll keep us informed."

Moose walked into the room dismissing everyone and sending Milo in search of a pop machine I knew didn't exist. I said nothing, sensing a reason he needed to talk to me alone. My stomach did its usual calisthenics routine preparing for bad news and I wrapped my arms tighter around my folded legs.

He sat precariously on the coffee table across from me, and I worried the cheap furniture wouldn't support his massive body. As if reading my thoughts, he jiggled the table slightly and smiled.

"Sturdier than I thought."

"How's Jesse?"

"He's fine. A few stitches, but no major damage. He'll be sore and grouchy for a few days, but otherwise all right. We found the creeps who attacked you and things are taken care of."

Slowly, I twisted and perched on the edge of the sofa cushions. "I shot at them. Did anyone get hurt?"

"Only Jesse, but we have a bigger problem." He slapped an envelope on the table. "I don't know if these are directed to Jesse or you. We're scrambling to stop them from posting to cyber news sites before morning."

I tipped the envelope up and six color digital prints fanned across the table: Jesse and I eating dinner on the roof café at Flannigan's on Main Street...only we weren't eating. My hand pressed Jesse's cheek, his lips fastened tightly to mine, his hand at the base of my throat. Another shot showed Jesse holding me in the air—a playful catch after he snuck up behind me just outside the parking terrace. His mouth on my neck? Not so playful.

Two pictures taken through the penthouse window burned my cheeks hot, knowing Moose had already seen them. Jesse's hand up my back, my shirt in his fist, blue-checkered bra exposed. The second, his hand cupped my butt, held me against his knee—both with undeniable positioning of mouths locked together.

The next picture was eerie and both Moose and I exchanged a fearful look—me walking the edge of the hot tub behind a misty curtain. If my bright orange bikini didn't appear to glow, I would have appeared a ghostly apparition against a black backdrop.

The last picture showed Jesse and me dancing on the grass wrapped in each other's arms, right before the stabbing. I gulped down the panic squeezing my throat shut.

"Who took these?"

"We're not sure. At first, we thought a fan groupie followed the two of you, but the picture of you by the spa—"

"Brittany and Alex were there. Why aren't they in the picture?"

"Precisely. It appears *you*, not Jesse, may be whom the photographer targeted."

"Why?"

Moose tapped one of the digital prints taken through the penthouse window. "Your pink band—his yellow. I'm guessing taboo?" Each picture clearly identified the "taboo" around our wrists in vivid color.

*Spies?* Chuck would freak if he saw these. I picked up the one exposing my bra. Rick would kill me, hunt down Jesse and dismember him—or at least a *part* of him. But worse? Jordan would magnify "ballistic."

"You don't think the guys who stabbed Jesse could be responsible?"

"No. It appears the scumbags you encountered were only stupid drunks. We figure this is personal." Moose looked at ornamental clock on the wall, ticking away one disaster and bringing us closer to the next one.

"Marli, here's how this will play out. Pay attention because I only have a few minutes to fill you in, after which we can never discuss this again. *First*, there was no shooting. *Second*, no gun exists. And *third*, you were asleep here in the penthouse, waiting for Jesse to return from band practice. Nothing happened, nor can you say anything about this to whomever asks, including your friends and family…not only this weekend, but forever."

"What about the pictures?"

"Managed. If asked, deny being Jesse's date, but if at all possible, say nothing and avoid the press junkets."

*Managed.* Who would "manage" Jordan when he found out?

Moose leaned closer. "Marli, you're going to have to trust me." The phrase had been said so much the past few months I found myself repeating it before he spoke the words.

"Jordan's going to be beyond angry." But with whom…Jess? Or *me*.

He shrugged his shoulders sympathetically. "Sorry, wish there was a way to control that fallout."

"I have to tell him before this explodes." I stared out the window at the blackness, considering. Another complication surfaced in my mind. "What about the concert?"

"Jesse's insisting we go ahead with the performance."

"What? Is he insane? Stupid question."

Moose's mouth curled with a light chuckle. "He wants to fulfill our contract with the resort to avoid any unwanted attention. We're booked with three other bands, but we have first billing. We'll leave after our set, so make sure you girls are packed. The sooner we're out of here, the better."

I questioned my friends monitoring and he explained that due to Brittany's involvement with The Program, they decided to take precautions, just in case something else developed. I couldn't handle any more *developments*. Moose also informed me that tonight I couldn't leave Jesse's suite.

When I quizzed him about the men in the van and the personality challenged "bulldog," another slight smile stretched his mouth. They were the security team Jesse's family paid to keep him out of the limelight as much as possible. I guessed if these pictures hit the cyber world, there would be a new security team.

"They only know what they're told. Tonight, Mike handled things."

"*Wizard.* Milo and Brody don't know the real story either, do they? That's why you sent Milo on an impossible errand. There's no pop machine on the second floor." Moose regarded me carefully, lips pushing to a straight line, confirming my suspicions.

"They think Jess got mugged on his way to check the equipment trailer."

"Who knows about the photos?"

"The security team, Mike, and the two of us. Jesse hasn't seen them."

"And Jordan?"

He blew a heavy sigh. Damn!

The door clicked when the security code cleared. Moose gave me a look and I understood. This conversation officially ended. I tucked the pictures under my arm and raced for Jesse's bedroom.

"Find me a receptor, Moose. I have to do my own damage control."

I gasped when I passed in front of the dresser mirror and my hands shook as I slowly opened my jacket, revealing the rusty color of old blood, soaked into the middle of my pink top. If someone saw the size of the stain across my chest, they'd think *I'd* been shot. Dried blood matted in my hair and crusted between my fingers. The palm of my left hand and over my wrist sported a gnarly case of "road rash." A gross purply-green bruise formed on the side of my right hand and my right elbow stung.

All of a sudden, I felt every ache, every sting as if it just happened. My visual recognition showed my brain exactly where to hurt and underneath, panic surfaced. What kind of mysterious world had I fallen into? Fresh tears heaved from reserves somewhere in my body and I slumped to the floor.

The door squeaked open. Moose towered over me, a look of horror in his eyes. "Marli? What can I do?"

My neck cranked backward to see his face. "I need to talk to Jordan. Now."

He lifted me by my forearms—new bruises I feared, helping me to the foot of the bed. He handed me Jesse's cell receptor—the one I talked to Mike on when the universe fell.

"Call Jordan from this one. Mike keeps the frequencies scrambled so no one can trace the calls. It's for special situations like tonight."

"Figures," I whispered. I studied the large belt buckle close enough to see the *button*. The same one Jesse had on his belt—the one he made sure he pushed before doing anything else.

"Moose? What's that?"

He sucked a breath. "It's a 'panic button' of sorts. When pushed, it sends a signal to whomever is closest. It also works as a homing device with coordinates, in case one of us—"

*"Disappears?* Anything else? Cars with wings?" I rode in both Jordan's Porsche and Jesse's Ferrari. There could have been a switch labeled "wings."

Moose shook his head. "Let me know if you need anything. In one of the cabinets in the bathroom is a first aid kit for your arm, and you'll find clean T-shirts in the top drawer. Oh, and if you push #1 on the receptor on the nightstand, it will buzz in the living room. Otherwise, I'll leave you alone until morning."

I followed him to the door, locking it after he walked out. No more surprises. I was done.

I inched myself into a hot shower, every muscle ache yielding to the warmth. The sting from the spray hitting the raw skin on my hands and knees stole my breath. Rust-colored water circled the drain, the coppery smell of blood overpowering in the steam, and I fought back a wave of nausea. Several scrubbings later, I emerged clean—black and blue, but clean.

Jesse's T-shirts almost reached my knees, giving me some modesty, but two layers were necessary to hide the parts of me illegal for public display. I tugged the collars to my nose. The scent from the bottle of cologne tucked in the drawer, the same fragrance Jordan used, lingered in the cotton. At the moment, I couldn't say who the sensuous scent made me long for more; Jordan or Jesse.

Easing between the cool sheets, I sank into the downy pillows. My lungs filled deeply and exhaled slowly. The bright light of the receptor illuminated the red rash on my arm. I crumpled the cologne-laced shirt against my nose and touched the tiny square on the cell labeled "Jordan."

His voice sounded thick and sleepy. I'd have given my soul to be asleep in his arms. Again, I wished for video transmission, but there were no other buttons on the *spy* phone.

"*Jesse!*" I'd startled him awake using the "secret cell."

"No, it's me," I whispered. "Sorry I scared you, but I need to talk to you."

"Marli! How, why—"

"Why am I using Jesse's 'secret decoder' receptor?" Silence ensued and I worried my inside joke wasn't well received.

"To be honest—yes." Another moment of silence. "What's going on? Where's Jesse? *You* wouldn't be calling from this receptor if something hasn't happened. Spill it—now!"

I wielded an equally snarky reply. "I'm fine, thanks for asking. Oh, and yes, I miss you too. What's that? Happy Birthday? I love you, Marli? Or is that only for regular calls?"

"Marli, of course I love you, but I'm scared to death of what you're about to tell me. I've been calling you all night to wish you 'happy birthday,' however someone's not answering *her* receptor."

"I left it in my room." I held my breath, realizing what I said.

"Where are you, Marli? It's four o'clock in the morning in *New York*." Stated, not questioned. I heard his jaw clamp. He knew where I was.

"Jesse's penthouse." Stated quick—like ripping off a band-aid.

"Tell me you're joking. You said you ended things, Marli."

"Nothing about tonight is a joke, believe me. But before I say anything else, Jordan, I need you to swear you'll stay calm."

"Don't ask the impossible."

When my silence demanded the promise, he said he'd try, but nothing more. I, in turn, guaranteed him I'd ended things with Jess. I pulled a deep breath and held it a moment wishing its release would cushion my next revelation. I squeezed my damp lashes tight, wringing out the tears bubbled in the corners of my eyes, and let out a long, shaky breath.

"Jordan...Jesse and I were attacked tonight. Jesse got stabbed, but he's okay."

*"WHAT?* Stabbed! What about you? Damn!"

The infamous "f-bomb" Jordan seldom used preceded the *shit, shit, shit,* and punctuated the end of one rant, which emptied into another about how he'd warned Jesse to not let anything happen to me.

I folded my knees so tight against my chest I could barely breathe and my thumb throbbed from my teeth clamped in a vice around the knuckle. Water poured from my eyes and nose as I listened, hearing the unmistakable fear in Jordan's tone wrap the angry words until his voice disappeared behind the heavy heartbeat thrumming in my ears.

"Stop! Please listen to me for a second." I could hear his forced breaths, but he remained silent. "Jesse did protect me, twice. Once in an award-winning performance as an 'ass' trying to get me to storm out on him, and again when the drunks came at us."

"So he did try to force you to leave. He said something about that the other day, but I knew he couldn't pull it off. He cares too much. Please tell me he didn't do anything inappropriate?"

The pictures would answer that question and my lack of response forced an another ugly oath from Jordan. Cautiously moving to my side, I hissed against a sudden jab of pain.

"Babe? Are *you* all right?" His jaw crunched in my ear. "You never did answer my question. Did you get hurt?"

"My hip is sore where I fell, but it's the bruises on my hand and elbow that kill. I must have been holding the gun too tight when I fell."

"*GUN?* What on earth were you doing with a gun?"

"Trying to shoot the guy who stabbed Jesse."

"It was *LOADED?* Hell Marli, you could have killed someone! I can't believe Jesse was so careless! Carrying a loaded gun while with you? You could have been—"

Wizard broke in on the call, placing me in a holding pattern of uncertainty. I started a mental countdown. Around sixty-three, a voice, strained, speaking through measured breaths hissed in my ear.

"I'm booking the next flight to get you the hell out of there and away from Jesse before you do anything else stupid."

"Did you just call me 'stupid?'"

"No, I said what you *did* was and I'll add reckless, selfish, and deceitful. Tell me *love*, is Jesse's hearing gone? Can he only read lips? From what I'm seeing on this digital file Mike forwarded, you have a peculiar way of ending relationships. *Kiss off* is something you take literally. I can see how heart wrenching this was for you. Cute bra, by the way. Don't think I've seen that particular one. Maybe you bought it especially for Jesse?"

"That's enough, Mason."

"Why, *Davis?* Too uncomfortable for you? Imagine how I must feel—no wait. Imagine how I *will* feel when these go public in a few hours." His voice dropped to a quiet calm. "How could you do this to me, Marli?"

The cell receptor went dead. He'd hung up on me!

Emotions rose too fast to evade with Jordan's declaration. Him being angry I understood and even his fear I could handle, but hurt? I was totally unprepared for the assault of guilt that crumbled my defenses. I swallowed down the painful burn in the back of my throat, forbidding the floodgates to open.

When the cell rang seconds later announcing "Jordan," I jumped, losing the breath I desperately needed to sound remotely normal. I didn't give him a chance to speak.

"None of those pictures are what they seem, Jordan. Even the hot tub one is wrong. Brit and Alex were there—no boys."

His response came fast, his voice tight. "That's the only picture you're not latched onto Jesse's mouth, or his hands attached to your body. You've no idea what you've done."

"I didn't *do* anything! I told you, I'm through with Jess, although you don't seem to care that your twin brother could have died defending my honor! I think you should point your accusing finger into *your* chest. You're the epitome of selfish!"

"Don't even try and put this on me, Marli. I've made a decision, one you won't like, but right now, I don't give a fuck."

"Whoa!" The little hair on the back of my neck that coiled into a tight spring right before bad things happen, pinched. "What do you mean?"

Jordan's tone remained brusque, unforgiving. "You're officially eighteen. I'm making this setup permanent and if you need "tradition," we'll fly straight to Vegas and be married by morning. Anything to keep from losing my mind constantly worrying about you."

Immediately I recognized the dangerous, powerful feeling swelling inside. Not joy…far from it. *Anger* boiled to rage with frightening speed. I propped myself against the headboard, stunned.

"Pardon? Is that your pathetic excuse of a marriage proposal? A 'marry me or else' load of garbage! Well, someone catch me, please—I'm swooning in all the hearts and roses!"

I tried to temper the seething emotions bouncing inside, but it proved useless. "*Setup?* So that's all we are? A 'set up?' Forget this, Jordan. Forget *you*! I wouldn't marry you if my life depended on it."

"It probably does! I can hardly wait to see what kind of trouble you get into when you go to Italy with the *Italian Stallion,* although judging by past performances, he's in for one hell of a send-off!"

I gasped and all the guilt overwhelming me mere seconds ago, disappeared.

"*You're such an ass!* A control-freaking ass! *You* have no right deciding anything for me—ever! I've had enough. I'm through with this craziness—all of it! To hell with The Program...*and* you! We're done, Jordan Mason. Done! Done! Done! Never call me again!"

I slammed the receptor shut and threw it across the room. A numbing tingle framed the edges of my body. The pompous jerk actually thought *marriage* was the only way to keep me safe. He didn't even let me explain the pictures. The nerve! I could take care of myself. A familiar prickling sensation surrounded my lips.

*Breathe Marli...breathe..*

All four walls crashed in at once. Jordan asked me to marry him, and basically I told him to go to Hell. In only a few short hours, I managed to remove both Jesse *and* Jordan from my life. The "S.S. Destroyer of Love's" next port? Italy.

Brittany and Alex believed the lie about Jesse's mugging. Luckily I'd brought a long sleeved shirt which covered the bruises. When the questions started, I told them an abbreviated version of my break-up with Jesse. I said nothing about the pictures, however, or my horrific argument with Jordan. The hurtful memory, coupled with my aches, caused unbearable pain. I refused to check my cell for messages.

The photos would be public now and Rick would be plotting Jesse's murder. I also didn't want to deal with Jordan's accusations or *commands*, not that I expected he'd ever call again after last night.

After packing for our trip home, I returned to Jesse's suite. The security tag team lingered together in the kitchen and their conversation ceased when I walked in. Jesse's bedroom door opened and he hobbled in on Brody's arm. He eyed everyone crowding in.

"Guys, mind clearing out? I want to talk to Marli alone." One by one they left. "Bolt the door, Marli. We need to talk and I don't want any interruptions."

*Another demanding Mason brother.*

I did as asked and curled on the sofa facing him. Jesse twirled a lock of my hair around his finger.

"Are you okay, babe? Moose said you were banged up pretty bad."

"I've been through worse," I lied. My heart hadn't felt such pain since Daniel's death, and yet, this seemed more unbearable. I looked away and pushed down the lump choking me.

Carefully, Jesse leaned forward, lifted my chin. "What is it?

"Jordan and I broke up for good this time."

"Why do you say that?"

I dropped the envelope in his lap. "Because of these."

Jesse's eyes, brows and lips changed positions with each picture. "Holy shit! I better talk to him."

"I wouldn't suggest it. He's not listening to reason about the pictures. Honestly, I'm so tired of being in the middle of your insane competition with each other." I bounced off the sofa, pacing in step with my rant. "And Jordan's possessiveness...I mean, he thinks he has to constantly protect me, like I can't survive without him. He actually *demanded* we go to Vegas and get married so he can quit worrying about me. Can you believe that?"

Jesse put his hands up. "What? Jordan asked you to *marry* him? What did you tell him?"

"*No*, of course. There's no way I'm marrying him...right now. Not like this. Probably never. Gripes! You're *both* a pain in the ass! I'm out of here. I'll see you at the concert."

"NO REGRETS" kept the crowd on their feet clapping and dancing the entire hour. I noticed Jesse wince occasionally when reaching over his guitar. After their set closed, Milo and Brody took Alex and Brittany in the motorcoach, leading away the throng of groupies, mixed with Press posing as fans, from the exit. Moose and the "silent hulk" drove Jess and me to the airport in a separate car.

Holding the side with the stab wound, Jesse eased his arm on the back of the seat in an attempt to pull me closer, but I moved against the door.

"I can't."

Jesse raised the glass partition between the front and back seat to give us privacy. He angled toward me, keeping his distance, but his fingers played with my hair...and I let him.

"Jordan does love you, Mars. He's just not good with situations he can't control, which is, essentially, where he's been since he met you."

"I don't want him to control me."

"His fear of losing you blinds him to where the line is on control and protecting you. He's so worried if he lets down his guard, someone will take you from him, or worse, that you'll fall for someone else."

Jesse's phone buzzed and he checked the number. "Speaking of the devil, I just received his billionth death threat. Think I'll crash with Moose in Buffalo a few days and give Jordan time to cool off. I can't talk to him when he's like this."

"He didn't believe me when I tried to explain the pictures." Jesse's thumb traced down my arm. I clamped his hand. "Please, don't." He dragged his arm back to his side of the backseat.

"I'd like to know who took those. Wiz said nothing hit the news sites. It appears to be personal and you probably received the only hard prints."

My twitchy neck hair pulled. "Weird."

We discussed all the reasons for the pictures and the list was long, but not the suspects. I threw out Heather Sandberg's name and while Jesse scoffed at the idea, he didn't dismiss it entirely. I wondered about Doug, but said nothing. The idea he'd follow me thousands of miles and just take pictures didn't make sense, especially when we'd be leaving for Italy in a week. Jordan would be another likely suspect; however, his reaction and wanting his twin brother to suffer a painful death ruled out the possibility. The "spy theory" seemed the most logical. I'd be home in a few hours and although it would be around two in the morning, if The Program wanted retribution, I felt certain someone would be waiting.

"So now what? If Jordan's gone and I'm out of the picture, do you think you'll be reassigned to Doug Peterson?"

I'd pushed the frightening thought far back in my brain, but the possibility, unfortunately, was likely, and I hated Jordan all over again.

"I'm committed to going to Italy, but I don't want to think beyond that. All I know is I'm vulnerable right now, so I've got to be careful not to repeat the past."

"Personally I don't like the guy, but I may be biased." We chuckled but stopped, allowing an awkward quiet to fill the space. "What about Cornell? Aren't you already registered?"

The ping of regret hurt worse than I expected. "There's still time to change things. Maybe I'll spend a semester at Ohio State and stick closer to home."

"Won't Sam try to weasel his way back into your life?"

My laugh sounded too loud. "No. Last I heard, he'd already moved on— found someone new to mend his broken heart. Guess I didn't mean that much to him after all."

Jesse took my hand and kissed it. "You know that's not true. Sometimes it's easier to guard an aching heart by pretending to give it someone else."

I said nothing, listening to the sound of the road beneath the tires hum a sad whine and feeling the gentle stroke of Jesse's thumb on top of my hand. The car slowed and took the exit to the airport. Ten minutes and the final chapter of my life with the Mason brothers would close.

Jesse tugged my hand. "Do you love him?" I didn't answer. "Mars? Between you and me only, I swear. Do you love Jordan?"

The lump in my throat barely moved when I swallowed and a hot tear dripped off my cheek.

"With every piece of my broken heart."

## 21
## TUSCANY ROMANCE

The in-flight movie thankfully captured Doug's attention. I, on the other hand, stared aimlessly around the first-class cabin, listening to the plot ramble through my earphones. I was on my way to Italy, one of the world's most romantic places on earth, with a handsome, sexy boy…and miserable.

Unable to stop them, my thoughts drifted to Jordan. We hadn't spoken since our fight the night of Jesse's stabbing. He didn't even try to talk to me about the pictures, just assumed the worst, which hurt. His insinuation that I couldn't survive without constant rescuing, followed by a chauvinistic demand for marriage to alleviate *his* worries, brought all communications, in fact our entire relationship, to a screaming finish.

Jesse called a few times, leaving messages, ironically asking me to give Jordan another chance, or return to him, but warned he wouldn't let me go this time. I'd already been offered a state of permanency with one Mason brother and in such a non-romantic way; "live organ donation" sounded more appealing.

The problem? I wanted something permanent with Jordan. Taking back my refusal to his off-handed proposal would have been easy. Stubborn, I refused to budge and held onto the fairytale fantasy. He called and instant messaged me constantly over the week, but I ignored him, choosing to cry myself to sleep listening to his messages, instead. Two days ago, everything stopped.

I did break one rule. The day after I returned from Jesse's concert, a small package arrived, which I opened before realizing it, too, came from Jordan. Besides a custom designed computer with installed features not available to the general public, he'd sent me an additional birthday present—my own *pink* "secret decoder" receptor. I hid the tiny device inside a box of feminine hygiene products no boy would dare touch.

Peterson's villa, an old restored farmhouse perched on a grassy knoll in the town of Siena, had been in their family over a century. Doug's grandparents were the present residents. Exquisite, leaded-glass entry doors sparkled in the midday sun, dotting the portico in colorful glitter. Inside, the mouthwatering smell of something seasoned heavily with garlic drifted to where we stood on a floor of natural stones laid in an intricate circle beneath our feet. Across the foyer, double doors led to a kitchen where the sound of voices chattering excitedly in Italian and clanging pans competed for attention.

"Ciao!" Doug called out.

A little lady, wide as she was tall, burst through the doors, waving her arms in the air. She grabbed Doug, pulled him from his great height to her level and smothered him with kisses. Doug latched tightly to my hand when several people surrounded us, hugging, kissing, and pinching our cheeks.

"There's our beautiful Marli!" *English* and a voice I recognized.

"Mr. Peterson." I acknowledged guardedly.

"Tony, please," he grinned, his expression light, unlike in our last encounter. Here, he definitely appeared more casual, donning a pair of khaki shorts and a bright red shirt, with bare toes wiggling in sandals. "We're more relaxed here. No timetables. We just indulge in fun." He winked, patting Doug's cheek, "And lots of 'amore.'"

*That* word I knew.

"Marli? You came!" Marah rushed from the kitchen and pulled me out of Doug's guarded embrace. She towed me up a narrow staircase. "I hope you don't mind sharing a room with me. We have our own bathroom and a view of the pool." She darted a teasing look to Doug who lagged behind, dragging our suitcases up the stairs. "Anyway, it's not fair if he gets you all to himself."

Marah continued jabbering to our room at the end of the hall. Doug caught my arm, holding me outside the door. "I'll come for you in twenty minutes. You'll need a break from 'chatter-box.' I'm thinking of taking a cool swim before lunch. Care to join me?"

"Make it thirty and I'll be the girl in the beach towel waiting in the hall." I stretched on my tired toes and kissed him lightly. "Where's your room?" I asked with a playful lilt.

"At the other end of the hall. Grammy will probably sleep on the floor between our rooms to keep things proper." He kissed my forehead. "See you in thirty."

Walls covered in pale blue and peach floral wallpaper surrounded the twin brass beds. Arched glass doors encased in heavy wooden moulding, opened to a balcony overlooking the pool. The sound of laughter drifted from the yard below. I stopped my unpacking and walked out on the private terrace. Below, a large rectangular swimming pool carved out the center of a manicured lawn. A rambunctious water fight ensued, drenching anyone nearby.

"It must be fun to be part of a large family."

Marah joined me. "Maybe someday you will find out. I see the way Doug looks at you. He's never brought anyone to Italy before." She gave me a formidable look, protective of her brother. "He adores you, Marli."

"I know. I like him, too."

I put the last of my things in the top drawer, pausing before placing the small blue box on top. I slipped the receptor from its hiding place and turned it on, halfway hoping for a missed call, but discovered nothing. Disgusted, I turned it off and tucked the box under a stack of panties.

Midnight tolled on the antique clock downstairs, the deep chime echoing throughout the house. I lay awake, my mind unable to shut down from either the day's excitement, or the time difference. More likely though, because thoughts of Jordan haunted me.

The sultry night air whispered over my bare legs. Outside, a nighttime lullaby echoed as crickets sang to each other and frogs called from the pond at the end of the property. Slipping from bed, I walked onto the balcony. The full moon cloaked the grounds below in a silvery glow. The hem of Jordan's Cornell University T-shirt ruffled against my thighs and I closed my eyes, letting my thoughts scatter on the Tuscan night air. I nearly fainted when two arms circled my waist and a pair of lips nibbled my earlobe.

"Doug you scared me!" I hissed, glancing through the open door to make sure I hadn't awakened Marah. She flipped over, but settled deep into her pillow again.

"Sorry," he muttered, his lips softly caressing my neck. "I couldn't sleep, so I came to check on you. The sight of you silhouetted in the moonlight forced me to your side."

He turned me in his arms and a flicker of disappointment scrunched his mouth when he eyed the carnelian bear—Cornell's mascot, spread across my chest. As if suddenly remembering the thousands of miles of ocean keeping me from Jordan, Doug's expression changed and he pressed my mouth with an unabandoned kiss, pulling my body into his. Only a thin layer of cotton separated my skin from his hands, slowly gliding down my back and over the curve of my hips, bunching the fabric upward.

I pushed away his hands. "No." Even in the dark shadows, I could see the unapologetic grin. A nervous gulp barely cleared my throat. "You should go."

He brought my hands to his mouth. "You don't honestly think I could sleep, *now*." Fingers lightly stoked my arms. "Let's go down to the kitchen where no one will hear us."

*Hear us do what?*

He tugged me past his sleeping sister, out of the bedroom and down the stairs. Doug poured us cups of herbal tea, placing a plate of cheese and a loaf of bread on the wooden trestle table. Dark eyes evaluated me and I crossed my arms over my chest, wishing I wore more than panties under the oversized shirt.

He settled on the bench across from me. "You're sexy even in Mason's T-shirt. I damn near swallowed my tongue when I saw you upstairs standing under the halo of the moon."

"Looking is one thing. *Touching* is another. Neither of us needs to jeopardize our status in The Program."

"You know, Marli, if we're officially committed, they really don't care how far we take things. The diamond in the bracelet remains intact once the diamond goes on the finger."

"Well I don't see myself wearing any diamonds in the near future. The one in my bracelet isn't falling out because of a reckless choice." I already suffered from one of those. Doug's expression showed I bruised him with my blunt statement. I quickly amended my harsh words, "Doug, trust me, you're not ready for a 'drama queen' like me."

My gentle tease brought an easy grin on his lips. "You underestimate what I can handle. I think it's *you* who's not ready, but I can be patient, knowing what the prize will be in the end." He reached across the table, taking my hand. His fingers lightly traced up the inside of my arm and under the edge of my sleeve. "*Very* patient."

His sensual tone sounded more like a warning and I mentally wrapped caution tape around my heart.

An older, more portly version of Tony Peterson with thick waves of silver hair, appeared from the dark hallway, startling us. Doug released my hand immediately.

"Gramps? Why are you up so late?" he choked.

*Gramps* gave us a long appraising stare. I felt my T-shirt shrink under his scrutinizing eyes. I crossed my legs, pulled by bed-head locks over my shoulder to hide my chest, and hugged myself tight. My parental conscience, cursed to me whenever I left home, waved an "I told you so" finger for not wearing pajamas. I thought about wearing my silky polka-dot pajamas, but the air felt too hot, and…well, I just wanted to wear Jordan's shirt.

Doug surely also felt his grandfather's judgmental glower, wearing only loose gym shorts. I didn't even want to think what he wore…or *didn't* underneath.

"Needed some milk to settle my stomach. Too much garlic in the sauce tonight." He poured a glass and settled next to his grandson.

"So, tell me about yourself, young lady. All I know is you and Douglas are in some government program in the States, and that my grandson is quite smitten with you."

My cheeks blazed hot. "Um, I'm from Ohio…my parents are divorced and I live with my dad, and, uh, I'm also fond of your grandson."

He smiled, giving Doug's shoulder a squeeze. "I like her. You need someone to keep you reined in." He rubbed the milk moustache from his upper lip with a paper napkin. "I best be getting back upstairs before your grandmother misses me. You wouldn't want her to come looking for me and find the two of you 'undressed' like this." He ruffled Doug's hair and mumbled "goodnight."

Doug's brow arched, "So you're 'fond' of me? Hmm, can't get more platonic than *fond of.*"

I nibbled a chunk of cheese remembering that my association with Doug represented a business merger in his father's eyes. "I think friendship is a good place for us right now. I am curious why your sister and grandfather think you're 'smitten' with me? What exactly have you told people?"

Doug moved and straddled the bench next to me. I gulped my cheese chunk, feeling the warmth of his breath below my ear.

"That I can't stop thinking about you, worrying and wondering what you're doing every minute of every day."

"Shhh!" I interrupted, covering his mouth with my hand. Doug sat back, stunned. I lowered my voice. "Doug, we both know why I'm really here. Please don't make more out it." I took his hand loosely in mine, playing with his fingers. "I need you to understand I'm going to college and pursuing what *I* want before committing to anyone. In fact, I've already registered at Cornell University."

In a surprise move, Doug tugged at the fabric against my chest, his touch waking sleeping hormones I didn't want disturbed.

"Figures," he snorted, slowly drawing a line between my breasts. "Next you're going to tell me enrolling at Cornell has nothing to do with Jordan Mason. After all, he'll only be graduating from there next year."

I clamped his hand before it settled elsewhere and the corner of his mouth curled. "How do you know that?" I wanted to keep the subject on Jordan and off whatever thoughts played in Doug's head.

"I did my homework. I wasn't going to let him have the upper hand again."

"I'm not a contest prize and I wish everyone would stop treating me like one."

When Doug took our empty mugs to the sink, I swear I heard "that's what you think," muttered under his breath.

"Jordan isn't an issue." The pit of my stomach lurched with the declaration. "He isn't speaking to me at the moment."

Doug returned next to me. "Why not? Did something happen at the concert?" Doug's brow creased. "Did his brother do something?"

"No, and the subject is closed." I leaned over and took the liberty of planting a kiss on lips parted in surprise at my news. "I agreed to this arrangement so I could get to know you better, but I want to take things slow, please?"

"Sounds good to me," he whispered before kissing me back. His hand crawled up my thigh and I brushed it away.

"Much slower." I pinched off a chunk of bread from the loaf and stood. "We better get back to our rooms. I'm sure Gramps is listening to make sure *two* doors shut."

After five days of eating the most wonderful Italian food, I worried my dress wouldn't fit for tonight's party. Doug's grandparents' fiftieth wedding anniversary had been touted around town as *the* event to attend.

I slipped a sundress over my swimsuit and bounced downstairs, humming a favorite tune. We'd walked all over the open market this morning, so when the invitation for a cool splash in the pool with a handsome young man presented, I didn't hesitate.

Doogie came barreling into the kitchen from the yard, his wet feet smacking loudly against the bright blue tile floor. He ran into my legs, squealing for help when "Uncle Doug" chased in after him. I scooped the wet toddler up, twirling him back and forth. He wrapped his arms around my neck and kissed my cheek.

"I wike you Marwi."

Doug placed a modest kiss on my mouth in front of the kitchen full of witnesses. "I wike you too, *Marwi*."

I flashed my eyes at Doogie. "Yum! Uncle Doug tastes like chocolate chip cookies. I wonder if Doogie tastes like cookies, too?" I nuzzled his chubby cheeks and his playful giggles turned to squeals, getting us ejected from the kitchen.

The doorbell chimed and Doogie squirmed out of my arms, running for the door. Doug followed to greet the visitor whose shape appeared distorted through the faceted glass.

"Jan!" Doug pulled his sister into a big hug. Doogie jumped up and down, clapping his hands until she gathered him in her arms.

Jan rivaled any fashion model. Tall and willowy, with long wavy tresses the same rich dark brown color as Doug's. When she saw me, eyes the color of strong coffee leveled a cold stare. I smiled, waiting for one in return, but her expression remained reserved.

"So, you must be Marli. I've heard all about you."

Her icy tone unsettled me and my voice cracked with nervousness. "Doug? Why don't you introduce us?"

"Oh! I forget you two haven't met. Sis, this is Marli Davis, and Marli, this is Jan—the sister I told you attends Princeton."

I held my hand out. "It's nice to finally meet you." She kept her hands around Doogie's legs and nodded, giving me a stiff smile. She brushed past me, cooing to Doogie as she walked into the kitchen. The room erupted in jubilation at her arrival and I was left standing alone in the entry trying to figure out what just happened. For the first time since my arrival, I felt like an outsider.

Andrea's husband, Brandt, a stout, bearded gent whose smile reminded me of the Cowardly Lion in the Wizard of Oz, wielded a humorless laugh from the landing above. "Let me guess. *The Ice Queen cometh.* I can see by the look on your face she treated you as warmly as she does me."

"It's that obvious?" I could feel the chagrin inside, but thought I hid it on the outside.

He lowered onto a stair. "Sit with me, Marli. We outcasts should stick together." I dropped next to him, listening to the boisterous voices drifting out the kitchen doors. His fingers twisted my pink band. "She's jealous of you."

"Of *me?* Why?"

Brandt's clipped response surprised me. "The Program rejected Jan's application for some minor genetic abnormality. Mr. P. considered the refusal a personal insult. Now she works part-time in a satellite office for The Program, but it's not as prestigious as being a candidate."

He gave my band another spin. "Be careful, Marli. Much is expected of Doug and consequently, *you,* if your relationship becomes serious." He paused, as if he debating his next comment. "Tony Peterson is a powerful man. If he wants something, he'll stop at nothing to get it."

A chill scraped over me, but before I could ask more, Doogie came searching for his dad and the two disappeared through the kitchen. I continued up the stairs, my head swirling with cautionary thoughts. Brandt's warning rang true with the uneasy feelings I experienced in Alaska. Something dark and forbidden exuded from beneath Tony Peterson's charming exterior.

A peaceful solace filled me when I closed the bedroom door. I went straightaway to the dresser and pulled my secret cell from its hiding place. I wished, *hoped* for a missed call—*anything* giving me a hint Jordan still cared. Nothing!

Frustration swirled with anger. I hated Jordan for hurting me—for coming into my life and turning it upside down, then taking his arrogant, gorgeous self away from me. I shut the phone off and shoved it back in its hiding place. Damn me for caring. Damn him for *not*.

I decided to stop checking for calls and, in fact, to quit giving Jordan any thought whatsoever. Tonight was the party. I'd brought my strapless blue prom gown and resolved to be nothing short of damn sexy for Douglas Peterson. Business arrangement or not, I needed to feel like someone cared. If he wanted to take things to the next level, so be it. I wandered onto the private veranda, watching the Peterson clan. Why wouldn't I want to be a part of this? Surely over time, I'd come to love Doug. Forget Jordan.

Familiar arms wrapped around me and the spicy cologne I'd become addicted to over the past week surrounded me.

"Hey beautiful. I wondered where you'd disappeared. It's a good thing my sidekick saw you come upstairs."

I turned in Doug's arms, kissing his lips with a sudden, fervent passion. "You were busy," I answered in a lustful rasp.

His eyes turned to bottomless black pools, his voice deep and husky. "My schedule just cleared."

Doug guided me back into the bedroom, closing the balcony doors. His dark, dreamy eyes studied me carefully. He kissed my waiting mouth tenderly, anticipating. Our kisses grew rough, carnal, and the same exciting warming sensation Jordan could trigger, started to build between my thighs.

But I didn't want to think about Jordan or *feel* anything. Jordan only cared about being in control. At least Doug didn't lie about his intentions. I knew what he wanted, and at the moment, it was me.

Doug plucked the buttons open on my sundress and it dropped around my ankles, leaving me in only my bikini. This should be the point where I pulled away, but instead, I fisted the sides of his T-shirt and pushed it up, tasting a hint of salt flavoring the warm skin I sampled. His shirt joined my dress on the floor.

We tumbled onto the bed, lips locked and legs braided. My heart slammed my spine, my breaths short and fast. Doug's lips moved down my neck and across my collarbone. His fingers stroked my inner thighs and I curled my fingernails into his shoulder blades when his hand deliberately brushed between my legs the same time his tongue dipped inside the edge of my swimsuit top. He nipped his way back to my lips, waiting—*wanting.*

"Marli?" he whispered, his lips so close I could feel his pulse in his breath. "Are you sure?"

I could barely breathe, let alone talk. All I could do was nod permission. He kissed me hard and pinned my legs with his as he sank against mine. His teeth tugged the straps of my swimsuit top off my shoulders and a hand moved around my back and loosened the ties.

A loud pound on the door brought Doug off the bed and onto his feet in one move. I snatched my swim top from his fingers and turned away from his penetrating eyes.

"What!" Doug yelled.

"Dad's looking for you, *that's* what," commanded the voice of disapproval on the other side of the door. Jan.

"Shit!" he hissed. "Tell him I'll be right there." His answer sounded as contemptuous as his sister's, but resigned. "I need cold water fast," he growled, disappearing into the bathroom.

I shimmied into my sundress, still holding my swimsuit top. When Doug came out of the bathroom, face wet, I threw him his T-shirt. He stared at me, still puffing heavy. Embarrassed, I bunched the front of my unbuttoned dress closed, and retreated to the bathroom. Doug swore a loud oath and an argument ensued between him and Jan before he closed the bedroom door.

I turned the shower on and stepped under the cold spray.

Thankfully, the kitchen had emptied when I came downstairs, dressed in a modest white button-up blouse and khaki shorts, my wet hair wrapped in a towel. I retrieved a pitcher of cold lemonade from the refrigerator and poured a glass. The sound of elevated voices echoed from the long hallway off the dining room and when I realized one of those elevated voices was Doug's, I ventured closer to listen.

"We did nothing, I swear! Jan's imagination has blown this out of proportion. Don't worry, Pops, I know what's expected. I'm just so sick of all the stupid rules. Who gives a shit about the color of the bands, or some asinine numbers game?"

Tony Peterson's tone reeked with disgust and anger. "Don't ever talk to me that way! I have every right to expect more from you than your sisters. You're my namesake, Douglas—my only son. You'll be head of this family someday, and it's imperative you achieve such prominence with honor and dignity. Bedding Miss Davis early will not get that for you.

"And for your information, the band color does matter, more than you know. It will determine things far beyond today's lust. Also, those asinine numbers you crudely refer to are what will create the world's greatest generation."

I felt my face grow hot with anger and readied myself to burst into the room to defend Doug, when Mr. Peterson's voice lowered and I became the topic of conversation, freezing me in place.

"Marli Davis is the girl who could secure you a prestigious station. Smarten up, Douglas. The boy who gets Miss Davis will someday hold the *power*."

"It's *you*, Pappa, who needs me to be powerful. Your vendetta with Banks is your war, not mine."

*Who was Banks?* A rush of air filled my lungs when recognition slapped. President Banks?

Mr. Peterson continued his tirade. "Douglas, you're smack in the middle of that war, and you know it."

"Trust me, every time I look in her eyes, *his* face is a constant reminder."

"Maybe I could do something more to ensure—"

"Don't!" Doug interrupted loudly. "You've caused enough damage. I'll get Marli on my terms, so back off. I've got this."

*Damage?* What—oh no! The pictures! Did Mr. Peterson purposely cause my break-up with Jordan? *...Tony Peterson is a powerful man. If he wants something, he'll stop at nothing to get it...* Brandt's statement hit with sudden clarity. Mr. Peterson wanted me with Doug. I pressed my ear against the door again.

"Time is running out, Douglas. Any contact?"

"Nothing penetrates your 'force field,' not even family."

"Enough! You tire me with your disrespect. Grow up and take matters under control, or I will—on *my* terms."

Footsteps sounded toward the closed door and I quickly retreated to the kitchen. The heavy wooden door slammed and hurried steps marched down the hall. I barely made it to the corner of the bench before Doug appeared.

"Marli?" he questioned, surprise covering his face when he rounded the corner. "I was just coming to find you." He kissed my cheek. "You smell wonderful, and taste, um..." licking his lips, *"clean?"* He lightly brushed my cheek, whispering, "Sorry about this afternoon. Maybe we can pick up from where we left off later?"

"About earlier," I began, "we should probably talk."

Doug moved to the bench across from me. "Marli, if Jan hadn't knocked on the door, do you think—"

"I don't know. I don't know about anything anymore." Doug looked confused. I pushed away from the table and he grabbed my arm. "I need to get ready. Please let go."

*Let me go.*

Once behind the closed bedroom door, I slid to the floor and dropped my head onto my bent knees. This afternoon I came close to giving in to another reckless impulse—one with dangerous consequences. Maybe that's what I wanted. A consequence big enough to alter the course I presently walked. The problem being if my course changed, Jordan's did too, not to mention Doug Peterson now believed I wanted a more permanent relationship. With Jordan out of the picture, when the ninety-days expired I'd surely be slotted as Doug's life partner.

Suddenly I felt trapped. Tears bubbled against the rims of my eyes. All I wanted was to go home; have dinner with my dad, and spend the summer hanging out with my friends. Life before Jordan Mason seemed so simple…uncomplicated. But now? Terrifying.

But the ominous unknown The Program presented didn't frighten me. It was the thought of Jordan gone from my life. Regardless of everything that had happened, I still wanted him.

# 22
## JORDAN

Stale smoke swirled near the ceiling in a filmy haze. I sidled up to the counter catching Mick's attention. *Miguel's,* the tavern bearing his father's name, was a short walk off campus and sometimes I tagged with the guys from the lab for a beer. Didn't seem to matter that I wasn't legal age. Mick never asked and I never told.

"Mason? To what do I owe the honor?" He finished polishing a glass and threw the bar cloth over his shoulder when I didn't answer. "Silent and brooding. I'm guessing girl trouble?'"

*Girl trouble* hardly defined my predicament. "You wouldn't happen to have an Adams Utopias in your private stock?"

"Dude, a bit 'high brow' for a college pub. Besides, it's banned in this state."

I'd been informed Mick kept expensive spirits stashed for his more *affluent* customers. I pushed a hundred dollar bill across the counter. "I didn't ask if it was legal, just if you had some."

Mick raised a brow, his gaze sliding over the room at the few patrons scattered in the smoky darkness. He unlocked a cabinet under the bar and pulled out the glossy gold decanter. He flipped a glass over, poured it half full and treated himself to a separate shot. When I gave him a questioning glance, he leaned close. "Jordan, it's 27 proof. You seldom drink. You'll be lucky to finish this and walk out of here knowing your name." He took my hundred dollars and didn't give me change.

The nutty flavor, rich with notes of vanilla, lingered on my tongue long after I swallowed. I threw back the rest, a dribble worth twenty dollars slipping from the corner of my mouth. I pulled my handkerchief out and wiped my chin, rubbing my thumb over the blue silk threads monogramming my initial in the corner. Once I owned a set of six. Now I had five. Marli had one.

I tapped the glass for more, this time a full glass. The second sample of ale swallowed smoother than the first. I reached for the decanter with my slowed reflexes, but Mick grabbed it first. "I don't think so friend. Why don't you tell me what's wrong instead?"

My words slurred as they tumbled over my thick tongue. "Mick, have you ever said something so stupid you knew the minute the words left your mouth, the consequences would be huge? Life altering?"

"Life altering, huh? That must have been one hell of statement. Were you drunk?"

"Nope," I replied, punctuating the *p*. "Stone cold sober. Just ape-shit jealous. I'm an ass and a stupid control-freakin' idiot!" I pounded the bar, upsetting the peanut dish.

"Easy friend." Mick moved the dish out my reach. He replaced my beer with a tall glass of ice water. "If you screwed things up so badly sober, I'd hate to see what you'd do drunk."

I opened my cell receptor. Like a fool, I dialed Marli's number. Nothing. Did she really not take her receptor? She wouldn't purposely ignore me…would she? No way did she really mean we were *over*. We couldn't be "over." She was my assignee. I had priority…unless *she* wanted Peterson. Damn! I squeezed my cell so hard it should have exploded.

I stared at the number pad, trying to bring the numbers into focus. Why not? Miss Davis probably hooked up with Doug Peterson by now, so why should I suffer? Heather Sandberg—Number 7? My finger trembled over the call key, my gut twisting into an aching knot. I didn't want Heather. I wanted Marli. The hurt boiled inside, then something worse. Fear I'd really lost her.

Gentle fingers curled over mine, closing the receptor. The voice sounded whisper soft with breath smelling of peppermint. "Why call someone who isn't here, when I am."

My head tilted sideways, or maybe the room did. Her golden mane fell over her bare shoulders, the ends tickling my arm. She looked pretty—I think. Big blue eyes and full, cherry gloss lips. Sexy as hell. She leaned into me, her perfume permeating my fuzzy brain. Something floral, mixed with enough pheromones to make me feel surprisingly lonely...and needy.

I liked the way her fingers played around the edges of my ears, softly rubbing my lobes. Damn. I swallowed a baseball-size lump. She shifted, allowing me a full view down her shirt. No bra. Everything turned warm and hazy. My pants tightened. She had a fantastic chest. So did Marli. Got close enough to know her assets were real, not manufactured like the angel melting her lips to mine.

Shit, she tasted good, but not like Marli. Marli was French silk pie where this girl resembled imitation chocolate ice cream at best. However, when you're craving *chocolate*, you'll take what you can find.

I wasn't real clear how we got from the bar to the inside of my car; however, at this moment I didn't care about details. Fingers made fast work of the buttons on my shirt and I hissed when her cold hands pressed my chest, but her hot lips warmed the spots to a blistering heat.

My hands? Not where they should be. Marli would have had slapped me several times by now.

Marli. *My* Marli.

The seductress was good. *Too* good. She straddled me, pushing the seat back, her tongue searching for my internal organs.

*Marli.*

My brain wanted Marli. My body desired whatever "flavor" I currently sampled, especially when she stroked over the swelling in the front of my jeans.

Even through denim, the touch seared and my will-power slipped dangerously fast.

*You love Marli!* The voice in my head screamed louder, catching my attention when my belt buckle tugged apart and the top snap of my jeans clicked open.

*She'll never be with you if you do this…and you know she'll find out.*

I clutched the siren's fingers tugging down the zipper on my jeans, and forced her into the passenger seat.

"No." One word. Two letters, wielding a lot of power. She reached for me again and I caught her arm. "I said 'no.' Game's over…I'm taken."

"You're sure don't act like you're *taken*," she spat, readjusting her top. I felt sick to my stomach knowing my hands had trespassed under there. I zipped my pants, cursing my lack of self-control.

"I'm also a fucking jackass. Doesn't change anything." I reached across her and opened the door. "Get out." I ordered. She called me a vile name and slammed the door. I wish she had hit me. Punched me hard. Better yet, slit my throat and left me to die.

I opened my door and puked fifty bucks of ale into the gutter. Disgust laced with a heavy dose of guilt churned my stomach. I felt woozy and angry. No way could I drive, so I locked the Porsche and walked home.

By the time I reached my apartment my senses semi-returned. I dropped into the chair by the fireplace and flipped the switch, igniting a small flame. July. Who burned fires in July? Marli. She liked them all year. I stared at the deep, furry black rug spread at the hearth and imagined myself lying there making out with her until every inch of my body ached.

What had I done?

I closed my eyes, willing the room to stop moving while I synchronized my breathing. *One Mississippi…Two…*

My cell receptor buzzed and I pressed the speaker without looking.

"Jordan Mason." *Three Mississippi…*

"You sound pissed."

Jesse.

"What's it to you?"

"You tell me. Your buddy from the bar called and said you left your car. I'm checking to make sure you aren't lying dead in some ditch. Get a bit ripped tonight? Does this have anything to do with a certain blue-eyed beauty in Italy?"

I pounded the armrest, my knuckle catching a decorative rivet. "Shut up," I snarled, sucking the torn skin to ease the sting.

"That's what I thought." Jesse grew quiet. "Talk to me, bro."

"Why should I? If you hadn't taken her to your damn concert, none of this would have happened. And we're still not square on the photos." For payback, I belched into the phone.

"Nice one. And I already explained the pictures. Marli was innocent and we both know who took them…and *why*. Accept that you won and let the rest go."

Bolting from the chair too quickly, I grabbed the fireplace mantel for support. "I've won nothing! I blew it and now I've lost her." My knees folded and I dropped to the rug holding my earlier daydream. The squishy surface gave under my weight and I half-flopped, half-rolled onto my back. "Jess," I sighed, "she won't even take my calls."

"Sounds like you're giving up. Guess Peterson gets her by default." He tsked-tsked in my ear and I wished I could rip out his tongue to stop the annoying hiss. "Hardly worth all the trouble his dad put into getting you out of the way."

True. All Tony Peterson needed to do was wait for my self-loathing pity party. If he offered enough bribes, Marli could possibly be reassigned to Doug before her plane touched down in New York. I doubted even my "ace in the hole" could save her.

I pinched the tender skin between my eyes in a futile effort to halt the pressure building. "She doesn't want me. My hands are tied."

"So that's it? You're not even going to try?"

My jaw screwed tight. "Dammit Jess! What do you expect me to do? Go to Italy and drag Marli back by her hair?"

"If that's what it takes, hell yeah!"

It would be a repeat of Alaska. Me, crashing through airport security waving my dumbass band to bump me to the front, something I didn't believe in, but then I'd never been in love before and out of my mind with jealousy. When I found out Marli would interview with another guy who could claim her, I went bat-shit crazy. I had all the hotels in Juneau mapped out, but no plan. When she called to tell me she'd flown to California, I walked right back through the doors I'd exited and bought a ticket to Los Angeles.

"I couldn't find Peterson's place in Alaska with the security blocks he had set up, so I know Italy will be impossible. Plus we have no access rights internationally."

"Alaska? You hunted Mars down in Alaska?" I shuddered when Jesse trilled a familiar chuckle. "Man, you're *whipped*."

"Right now, I'm broken hearted, drunk, and queasy. Even if Wizard could figure out where Peterson has Marli, I'd never get within a hundred miles of her." I turned off the fireplace, fearing my toes would combust any second. Tears swirled the edges of my eyes. "God, I love her, Jess, but she won't even talk to me. Maybe I've got to let her find her own way instead of pushing all the time."

Jesse's patience wore thin and I could hear the tension in his tone, which seemed beyond loud when he yelled in my ear. I held the receptor away, still able to hear every chastising word.

"Are you listening to yourself? Try this on. Marli *Peterson*. Has a certain ring to it, don't you think? Where do you think Doug will take her for their honeymoon? Someplace special. You know how Mars is. Now picture this…she'll want her 'first time' to be like a fairytale. I guess Doug could pull it off, or at least her clothes. Wonder if she'll wear black lace…*sheer* lace—"

"Shut. Up. One more word and I'll kill you!"

"About time you got in the game! You love Marli, so fight for her! *Make* her talk to you. Fix this, Jordan, before it is too late. She loves you. Don't let Peterson change her mind."

Sunlight burned my eyelids. My throat felt rough as sandpaper and my back ached from trying to cram my six foot three inch body onto a five foot span of wood, not to mention fighting to keep from falling onto concrete.

The screen door squeaked. "Jordan?"

The image of Rick Davis standing over me wearing a bathrobe open enough to answer the question "boxers or briefs," left an indelible picture in my brain. He rubbed his stubbly chin and ran his fingers through hair poking every direction.

I groaned, straightening out my painfully folded body from the porch swing.

"Rick, I need your help."

## 23
## PUPPY LOVE

While I beat myself up for my part in the disaster called "my life" and blamed Jordan for the rest—*most* of it, time ticked away. The shadows in the room had changed from bright to soft gold with the afternoon sun slipping away.

I washed my face with cold water and poured a gallon of eye drops into my eyes to shrink the swelling. Marah jumped into the chaos, styling her hair and wriggling into a champagne colored formal that made her appear ten years older. It wouldn't surprise me if her father sent her back to change into something more age appropriate.

I ran around in my black lace corset trying to find one of my shoes, which somehow became separated from the other.

"Doug would love to see you in that," Marah teased.

"If I don't hurry, that's precisely what's going to happen."

Voices echoed from the patio below, announcing the first guests. I slithered into my dress, checking to make sure the mended tear blended into the sequined trim. Taking a gander in the mirror, I adjusted the corset, trying to hide my accentuated cleavage. Damn! Doug's father would send me back to the room, if Doug didn't ravage me first. Correction. If I didn't *let* Doug ravage me.

*Prom night from hell all over again.*

Tugging at the zipper, I remembered I could only close it so far on my own. Marah was momentarily indisposed so I explored under the bed for my lost shoe. Bingo! One silver stiletto looking for a mate. When I reached under the bed, Marah slipped out, leaving the door open.

"Marah!" I called out, but she was already out of earshot. I strapped on the stray heel and attempted to finish zipping the dress myself. My arms were in a position a contortionist would envy, but I still couldn't get the last couple of inches.

"Damn dress," I snarled.

"May I?"

The voice that made my knees quiver came attached to two warm hands, replacing mine, now cold and numb from lack of blood flow. Doug's fingers lightly brushed the length of my naked back.

"Doug," I whimpered. "Please...don't." *Stop.*

He zipped my dress, pressing his lips to my neck. "You're breathtaking, Marli." His eyes dropped to my *enhancements*. "Actually, you're indescribable."

"Douglas Peterson," I warned, feeling the blush on my chest under his gaze.

"Sorry, but it's kind of hard not to stare."

I pushed Doug to arm's length, taking him into full view for the first time. He looked deliciously handsome in his black tuxedo, his hair slicked back, emphasizing his dark, indigo blue eyes. My insides melted when his gaze slowly traveled over my body, and my voice sounded way too breathy when I commented on how dangerously sexy he looked. He leaned in to kiss me, but a rap against the door frame kept our lips from touching.

Jan stood in the doorway dressed in an amazing teal green formal that shimmered from tiny matching sequins that covered every square inch.

"Marli, may I talk with you privately?" Doug drew me close. "Don't worry baby brother, I'm not going to bite her."

I brushed his arm. "It's okay."

Doug paused in the doorway and flashed a warning look at his sister. Jan returned a wry smirk.

"She'll be fine. If she's not out in fifteen minutes, you can come in and search for her body."

Doug snorted and walked out, shutting the door hard enough to rattle the window panes.

Jan gracefully sat in the rocker, watching me nervously fuss with the strand of pearls my mother gave me.

"Marli, I need to know what your intentions are where Doug's concerned. He's very important to this family and I don't want someone taking advantage of him."

"Why do you think I'd do something so cold and calculated? All I want from Doug is his friendship." The minute I said it I wished I could take it back. "Oh my. I didn't mean for it to come out like that." I moved to the edge of Marah's bed and faced Jan.

"I don't want to hurt him, but what Doug wants from this relationship I can't give him." I had no clue why I felt compelled to confess to her and the shock on her face made me feel horrible. Shock turned to bewilderment.

"You honestly don't know, do you?" Her whisper sounded more like a thought than a statement. "My gosh, you're sincerely genuine." She parked beside me on the bed. "Marli, forgive me, please. I misjudged you. The only thing you could be guilty of is, like you said, innocently breaking my brother's heart. I can't believe I was so wrong."

"Wrong about what? What are you talking about?"

"Nothing. Nothing at all."

Jan sighed, considering. "Marli, if your feelings aren't what Doug believes them to be, you need to tell him, regardless if it hurts. Do it for both your sakes. You can't be true to anyone, if you can't be honest with yourself." She opened the door to Doug leaning against the railing across the way.

"That was close, sis. You had two minutes left."

"Quit being a brute. Focus some of that testosterone positively and be a gentleman to your date. She really is lovely. I'll see you both downstairs."

Doug's gaze locked on me as he edged closer. After spending a week with him, I could read him pretty well and knew his focus centered on what happened earlier. I also had a sense his feelings had deepened beyond some obligation to honor his father. But mine had not and after my confession to Jan I realized things with Doug couldn't go further.

Then he kissed me. A slow, soft kiss, that built with intensity and my body leaned into his curves, now etched in my memory, welcoming the feel of his fingers twisting into the hair at the nape of my neck, his hand spread wide at the base of my spine to ensure an intimate hold. The edges of my sanity started fraying when his cell receptor rang, startling me.

"Sorry!" I quickly examined his lip to see if I'd drawn blood. He seductively sucked my finger into his mouth and winked. My lust meter shifted into overdrive.

His arm slid around my waist, but immediately fell limp when he answered. He stepped back as if I'd turned radioactive. "Mr. Davis?"

*Rick?* We agreed to check-in calls on Sunday nights. Today was Friday. My irritation instantly turned to worry, recalling the last time Dad called unexpectedly.

"I'm fine, thank you. No, no problem, we're on our way to my grandparents' fiftieth wedding anniversary celebration. Thank you. I'll convey your wishes. Yes, she's right here."

Doug handed me the phone, the expression on his face difficult to read. He pushed my hair to the side and pressed his lips to my bare shoulder.

"Dad? Is everything all right?"

"I'm not sure. Are you where you can talk? It's important."

Hair follicles stretched on the neck Doug currently nibbled, anticipating bad news. I also heard the seriousness of Rick's tone. Doug wasn't thrilled at my suggestion he go downstairs where his family waited. I explained the urgency of my father's tone meant the call was important and I needed a moment of privacy, promising it wouldn't be long before I'd join the party. I lowered my voice just in case he eavesdropped after closing the bedroom door.

"Okay, I'm alone. What's going on? Is everything all right?"

"Well, I'm not sure. You see, this morning when I let Muffy out, I found a stray sleeping on our front porch. I need your opinion on whether we should keep him or not."

"Seriously? You've called me in *Italy* to discuss a lost mutt?"

"I know it sounds strange, but hear me out, please. I said it was important."

"Okay, I'm listening."

"Like I said, your input matters. Now, how to describe him? First, you should know Muffy's already likes him. In fact, he can hardly move about without her on his heels. Mars, he's got the saddest eyes—the kind that tug your heart. He's looking for someone to love him."

"You're such a sap, Dad. What breed is he? If he's going to grow close to Muffy's size, you should think twice. Remember I'll be away at college and two large dogs will tear your house apart."

Dad chuckled lightly in response. "I can tell he's been obedience trained. He only barks if he feels protective. He's a bit spooked by me, but I think with the right person, he'd probably share a few wet kisses."

Oddly, I found myself intrigued, wanting to know more. "What does he look like? Is he furry? Stocky or lean?"

He laughed, my nerves calming with the lighthearted sound.

"Definitely lean—long legs for his breed. His *fur?* Thick, a little wavy, and sort of a caramel color. Shiny. He's been taken care of. I hope he's pretty much full grown because believe it or not, he's taller than Muffy. He stands way over six feet on his hind legs."

*What?* All the giant breeds ran through my head: Great Pyrenees, Mastiff, Russian Terrier, possibly a Scottish Deerhound, although none of them had fur the color Rick described. Still, any dog, even a tiny Chihuahua loose in the house with Muffy spelled disaster. I was about to paint the destructive picture in

Rick's mind, when he brought me up short and sent a shock wave rippling through my universe.

"Interesting thing is when I discovered him, he wore those fancy jeans you kids like so much. Apparently, he comes with a fine white Porsche, too."

Tears pooled along the edges of my eyes and dripped silently from the corners. "Jordan," I whispered.

"Yes, Pumpkin. Jordan. I found him asleep on the porch swing this morning. I think he's had a rough go of it and desperately needs to talk to someone, and it isn't me. What do you say?"

I looked around. The party had moved onto the lawn by the pool and Doug appeared engaged in an intense conversation with his grandfather.

"Yes! Please! Thank you Daddy!"

"I thought that would be your answer. You can't fool your old man...for very long, anyway."

I slipped into the shadows of the doorway where I could keep watch. My heart raced and my lungs felt like they'd burst any second.

"Marli?" Jordan's usual smooth, confident voice sounded small and pensive.

"Jordan!" I said in a rush. My voice cracked and tears strangled in my throat.

"Please don't cry. We don't have long and there's so much I need to say."

"You drove all the way to Ohio to call me?"

"You weren't exactly returning my calls and I knew you'd talk to your dad, so I took a chance. Besides, I needed to apologize to him, too. I know I made a mess of things, Marli, but I'm lost without you. Believe me, the last thing I want is to control your life. I just want to share it. Tell me I'm not too late? I don't want another assignee. I want you. I love you, Marli. Only you. Please give me another chance and let me back in your heart?"

I clenched my fist to my chest, unable to stop one tear chasing another. "You never left it." I swiped my cheeks with the back of my hand. "I thought

I'd lost you," I quietly confessed. "Jordan, you're the only one I want to be with. I love you so much it hurts."

Jordan sniffed. "Damn, I can't believe I'm crying. You have absolute power over me."

"Then I command you to stay in my life."

"Yes, Master," he replied around a gentle laugh.

My voice steadied. "So what now? I'm in Italy and you're in Ohio. Neither of us is where we should be—together."

"How is Italy?" he asked, the apprehension in his tone unmistakable.

"You were right. Italy is beautiful and don't worry…nothing's happened." I swore I *felt* the sigh on the other side of my ear. "I'm okay, especially now I have you back."

"You've always had me, babe.—'butterflies,' remember? You hooked me the moment you fell into my life and our first kiss cinched it."

More people moved out onto the lawn and Doug glanced at his watch. "Jordan, I don't have much time. Doug will come looking for me soon."

His breath blew heavy against the receiver. "Damn. Sorry. I promised myself I wouldn't make the same mistakes, but this is hard. Just promise you'll come home to me."

"I want to come home right now. I don't want to stay another week."

"We both know it's not that easy and I can't risk jeopardizing the ninety-day hold, making you….*his*."

Doug waved to me from the yard and started for the house. I had to calm down or he'd get suspicious if he saw me upset.

"Shoot! He's coming. I better say goodbye and pull myself together."

"Call me the minute you leave Italy and I'll meet you in New York. We'll shop for whatever you need before heading for the island."

"There's a suitcase already packed upstairs in my closet. A part of me hoped things would work out and I could still come."

"And the other part?"

"Very warm and tingly at the moment."

Jordan laughed—a sound I wished I could record and play back every private second between now and next weekend.

Doug's footsteps echoed on the wood planked hallway. I dropped my voice to a whisper. "I'll see you in a week. Meanwhile, take care of my heart. Love you."

Most of the candles had burnt out inside the lanterns. Music played softly from the patio speakers. Cloaked in darkness, Doug and I swayed to the melody in our bare feet on the lawn.

"Marli? Where have you gone?" Doug quietly asked. "You've become distant. Did I do something?"

I pulled my head from where it lay on his chest and stared into his worried eyes, "No. You've been the perfect gentleman."

"I don't want to be the *perfect gentleman* in your life, Marli. I want to be more."

We stood completely still in the damp grass next to the black water of the pool. The echo of dishes clinking caught my attention. Jan paused on the patio, holding a stack of plates, peering into the darkness as if she could see my eyes. What she said earlier struck a chord inside me, loud enough it finally got my attention. Time for the truth.

Taking his hand, I led him to a stone bench beside the pool.

"Oh this can't be good," he half-laughed.

I kept his hand tucked tightly in mine, taking one of many big breaths before meeting his anxious eyes. "Doug, this afternoon I wanted you with every beat of my heart, but for all the wrong reasons. I wanted to punish Jordan and surrendering my virginity to you, not him, seemed the cruelest way."

I couldn't have been colder.

"It always comes back to Jordan, doesn't it? Was it really him on *my* cell receptor tonight? Not your dad? Please, don't stop with the brutal honesty now, Marli."

"Okay, I deserved that. But you need to know something. When I came to Italy, I was only with you, no one else. I've been committed to you this whole time."

"Because you had no choice."

"That's not true! Jordan and I *did* break up. Tonight's call surprised me. I had no idea he was at my house. And honestly, if my dad had told me, I'd probably have hung up, which is why he concocted some story."

"I think you know how I feel about you, Marli, and this afternoon in your arms, I thought you felt the same way."

Pangs of guilt needled. "I'm really sorry. Don't hate me," I begged quietly.

"I could never hate you. You're being honest—something I haven't been."

A shiver of anxiousness crept up my spine. "What do you mean?"

"Marli…" he hesitated, "I pushed things today for a reason. I hoped we'd have sex and you'd stay with me, even if only to keep what we did secret. I thought, in time, you'd forget Mason. I realize now, that's never happening."

"Wow. Talk about manipulation." I decided I had to ask about the pictures, even if it exposed my eavesdropping escapade.

"Doug, can I ask you something?"

"Anything."

"Did your dad have someone take pictures of me and Jordan's brother?" Doug's brow twisted tight and he pulled his hand away. "I overheard part of your conversation this afternoon. When I came downstairs, I heard yelling and went searching for you."

"How much did you hear?"

"Enough to know you're under a lot of pressure…and your dad wants me as your assignee."

Doug stared out at the pool stretched into a black ribbon across the grass. No one lingered on the patio, the speakers off, leaving us in a sudden, screaming silence. After a couple of audible gulps offering stiff competition with the frogs, he spoke, his voice soft, but the tone edged in steel.

"I didn't know about the pictures until this afternoon. I hate that my father's obsession caused you heartache. In fact, I'm disgusted with myself for hoping it worked—you and Mason finally over, and you free…for me."

"The pictures aren't what broke Jordan and me apart. It was his need to control me, which is exactly what you and your father are trying to do. I know when I made the decision to stay in The Program I'd surrender some freedom, but I won't tolerate deception. Trust is too important to me, and I can't be with someone who isn't honest.

"I don't understand or want to know why your father is involved in my personal life, but you need to give him a message for me. *Love* can't be controlled. Regardless of who becomes my life partner, Jordan will own my heart. I'm always going to love him."

Doug turned his palm up on his knee and after a second of hesitation, I laid mine over the top, braiding my fingers into his. A deep sigh eased out and he covered our folded hands with his other one in a protective cocoon.

"I told you in Alaska I wanted to claim you, but after spending this week with you, I could never force you into a loveless relationship. I respect you too much." Doug lifted my chin, "I feel sorry for Mason's brother. He'll live every day knowing you're with Jordan in every way he can't be. I can't imagine *that* kind of pain."

Doug pulled me to my feet. He asked if I wanted to stay and I confessed I wanted to go home. I knew I'd only be thinking about Jordan and that wasn't fair to him. He agreed to take me to Florence in the morning so I could catch a flight to Rome. To avoid any embarrassing moments with his family, we made a plan to sneak away under the pretext of going somewhere to watch the sunrise. He made some major points on the chivalry scale because I knew the fallout he'd face alone would be gruesome. What I didn't notice, however, was how he'd moved me slightly until I teetered at the edge of the pool.

He grinned mischievously. "One more thing, Miss Davis."

"Yes, Mr. Peterson?" I asked, welcoming the playful tone in his voice.

He kissed me hard then pulled away enough for me to catch the wink—before the *splash*.

## 24
# THE SCAVENGER HUNT

The pilot announced our descent and excitement consumed me. In a few short hours, I'd finally be wrapped in Jordan's arms. Italy would officially become the past, the bittersweet memories locked away forever.

I had to check through The Program's database, proving I'd returned to the United States. Because "impulse" seemed to the mode I functioned in lately, I changed my flight in Rome and landed at Miami International, not JFK in New York. I needed to let Rick know before law enforcement became involved.

When I passed through the security door after scanning my pink band, I found a private waiting room. A telecom machine sat in the corner and I paid for a ten minute rental of a communication device. I didn't dare use my "spy phone" for fear of alerting Jordan to my whereabouts and spoiling my plan.

"Hi Dad. Guess what? I'm back!"

"Mars? Why are you home a week early and calling me from *Miami International?*" Even on the small video screen I saw his brows linked with suspicion.

"Long or short version?"

"I'm sure the long version would answer several questions, but since this call is probably monitored, I've no choice but a condensed version."

Hmm. Something I hadn't considered.

"Doug figured out your call had something to do with Jordan. I couldn't lie to him and after we talked, probably for the last time, he offered to send me home."

Dad inhaled several deep breaths, his eyes hooded beneath the familiar furrowed brow I'd seen a lot lately. His gaze finally lifted, but the deep-seated concern in his expression alarmed me. "Mars, are you serious enough about Jordan to cut every other possibility out of your life? Pumpkin, you're barely eighteen."

"Daddy...I think I really love Jordan. That's why I flew to Florida. I want to surprise him at the beach house."

He scrubbed the thinning hair on his head hard enough to create a bald spot. "Mars, I'm not ready for this change in your life. Damn Program."

"The government doesn't control my heart. Falling in love is part of growing up, you said so yourself. Please say you understand?"

A moment of silence preceded the sound of surrender. "Just promise me, Mars, you won't do anything rash before I see you again—like elope."

"No way! *I'm* not ready for that kind of permanent." My candidate number paged. "Dad, I have to go. I'll call you later. By the way, give Karen my best. We'll talk about *your* love life when I get home."

I smacked a loud kiss in the receiver and rushed to get my final clearance so I could begin the next journey.

Once settled into my hotel room, I recalled my cyber account and checked for missed calls to my personal receptor. I'd asked Jordan to grab it from my nightstand in Ohio, but only because I knew it was password locked. Who knew what surprises lurked in my Inbox. Of course he could have his trusty I.T. man unscramble it, but *he* played on my team right now.

I loved the thrill of seeing all the missed calls from Jordan before we made up, reinforcing he did want me back. One new call flashed and my heart sank. Doug. Not wanting to, but feeling guilty for the way things ended, I punched in the hotel's security code and returned the call. He answered on the second ring, his voice barely above a whisper.

"Hi," I said, nervous and suddenly doing the math on time zones in my head.

"Marli? Good, you're home safe." I knew the ID showed Ohio and video reception didn't work internationally on my private receptor, so he'd never be the wiser.

"How did things go after I left?"

His huffed a caustic laugh. "My father is furious with me; Marah won't speak to me; Doogie keeps asking for you, which results in dagger eyes from both Andrea and Brandt. Gramps cursed me in Italian and I think Grammy spit in my spaghetti tonight. My mother's the only one who's consoled me and even her expression shows discontent. You are completely blameless in their eyes."

"Doug, they need to know this wasn't your fault."

"You don't understand, Marli. I can handle their disappointment, but I don't want their memory of you tainted. Besides 'Daddy Dear' deserved justice served up to him for a change. I'll pass on your message when we return to the states."

"Doug, I'm sorry how things went down."

"You can't help who you love, Marli. I wish The Program had placed you with me first so I'd at least have had a fighting chance at winning your heart."

I lifted the swimsuit top from the pile of folded laundry on the bed. The strings that so easily slipped apart in Doug's fingers dangled from my own, reminding me how close I came to crossing a dangerous line. I dropped the swimsuit top as if it burned my flesh.

"No more guilt trips, Doug. I'm struggling to find balance in my life and as much as you wish you could be the one to create it, you're not."

A thought struck me like a lightning bolt. Doug became suspicious when I asked him to write down the number "4233" and request an interview. After begging for his trust one last time, he tentatively agreed and we said what I hoped to be our final goodbye. I prayed he followed through because "4233" was Brittany.

Wizard delighted at being my partner in crime with planning my surprise. He set my plan in motion by arranging a call to Jordan on a special frequency so he'd believe I remained in Italy. Apparently, Jordan also waged a bet with Mike that I'd come home early, which made my deceit more amusing by deflating his ego a tad in the process. Mike had fifty bucks riding on the bet.

The next morning I arrived at the Masons' private hangar at ten o'clock sharp as instructed. My favorite airplane was missing, but a certain white Porsche in the corner gave me a dizzy rush. Jordan would find my first surprise when he picked up his car.

Mike jogged across the hangar, jiggling a set of car keys. He looked to be a couple years older than Jordan and Jesse; built lean and shorter, his shiny hair the color of obsidian and cut to hang at a harsh angle across blackberry-hued eyes.

"This is so dangerous, girl. Jordan's going to flip out."

"Where's the fun if you can't flirt with danger once in a while?" Crap. I sounded like Jesse.

"So, did the call work?" he asked.

I almost had to run to keep up with him as he headed for the car. "Like a charm. Jordan thinks Doug's still in hot pursuit of my bones."

"Doug probably still is. Be careful, Marli. Petersons don't give up easily."

"Oh, I pretty much destroyed any chance of a future, trust me." We stopped in front of Jordan's Porsche and I immediately felt a zing of excitement. "I've got to ask. Can you make it snow in Miami, too? I mean you seem to be able to perform all this techno magic, surely a little thing like controlling the weather couldn't be that difficult."

Mike tossed me the keys, a wide smile pushing his cheeks. "I'm only god of my computer, not the universe. Wouldn't want that job."

Two beeps and the security system disengaged. I laid my blue plaid boxer shorts on the driver's seat with a note on top simply stating *Find Me.*

Mike returned the keys to Jordan's locker while I waited in the infamous silver Mercedes. Something bleeped on the dash panel *Call from Jordan.* I stiffened watching the digital display scroll the three words four times before disappearing. The car wasn't running so I felt certain the call couldn't patch through, although my heart beat somewhere besides in my chest with the thought. When Mike slid behind the steering wheel, I told him about the attempted call. He quickly hit some button that disabled any the video feed in case Jordan called again, then shook his head.

"I'm sure glad Jordan will be arriving after I'm gone tonight because he's going to kill me for not telling him you're here."

I wiggled my brows and gave him a sly smile. "I'll do my best to help him forgive you."

"Girl, you're going to have to do better than a smile to save my ass."

Our next stop—the marina. Mike included the dock patrol supervisor in our plan and while they talked, I quickly boarded *Her Majesty* with my bag of tricks. Mike told me the security paperwork already filed with Border Patrol placed Jordan at the helm. I draped my powder blue camisole over the captain's chair, tucking Jordan's monogrammed handkerchief into the neck in such a way the corner with the embroidered *"J"* lapped over the edge. I left my second note *You're getting warmer.*

Carefully, I descended the ladder on the back of the yacht into the suspended sport boat. On the driver's seat, I laid out clue Number 3—the top to my new black bikini, which I fastened through the safety belt so it wouldn't blow out to sea. The miniscule amount of shimmering fabric trimmed with silver metallic ribbons, guaranteed me sun exposure with minimal tan lines, not to mention a certain someone's complete attention. The third note I pinned to a strap read *You're getting hotter,* the double entendre purposely intended.

The butterflies in my stomach increased to epic proportions when we returned to the airport. Strapped to the pavement on the other side of the Mason's hangar sat a bright red and white helicopter.

Mike loaded my bags and walked the perimeter, making a preflight safety check and releasing the clamps from the rails. My dry throat burned. A familiar voice boomed from inside the hangar and he stalled in his enormous shadow when he spied me.

"Marli? Holy shit! No wonder this is hush-hush."

"Moose? I thought you were in Chicago with the band."

He offered his hand to help me climb into the chopper. "I flew home after the concert last night. Singing isn't my strongest talent. I recorded the instrument track yesterday morning." He heaved himself into the seat in front of me and turned to give me a teasing grin. "Maybe the guys will stop going for each other's throat now that you've returned."

"Are they still fighting about the pictures? I found out Mr. Peterson was responsible, hoping he'd break Jordan and me up for good."

I looked at the myriad of buckles that were supposedly to wrap me safely to the seat. No simple "insert A into B." I fumbled with the harness while Mike secured the luggage and some big bag with a medical insignia on the other side of me.

Without making eye contact, he concurred with my revelation. "That's kind of what Jordan figured and after some investigating, we, uh, removed the source." He jumped into the pilot seat and started switching toggle bolts.

My radar pinged. "Say what?"

"We're burning daylight. Better get airborne," Moose warned, ending the conversation.

Mike leaned around Moose's brawny shoulder and reached for the tangled mess I created with the safety harness. With a couple of twists, he had everything snapped in place. He fastened the headset over my ears so I could hear them talk over the noise. Grinning too wide, he gave me a quick lesson on what to do in the event of a crash.

I clenched my flotation device so tight he laughed. "Your fingers will go numb if you don't soften your grip. Relax, Marli. We haven't dumped a chopper yet—don't want to be 'shark bait.'"

"That's not funny." A nervous sweat beaded on my forehead. "I think I'm going to be sick. Tell me again why we can't take the yacht?"

"Neither of us have clearance to sail *Her Majesty*." Mike handed me a dark green plastic bag. "Here, just in case, but stop worrying. We've flown this island hopper many times, and we'd rather face sharks than Jordan if we let anything happen to you."

Moose interrupted with a message from the control tower. "Uh, Wiz? We don't have clearance to land on the island yet." Their eyes darted back and forth and I knew they held back something because of me.

"What's going on? I thought you already had permission. In fact, I watched you download the flight plan in the car computer on the way back from the marina."

Mike looked to Moose, who merely shrugged his shoulders. "It seems Jordan's father hasn't left. His chopper is still on the helipad."

*His* chopper?

Ahead of us on the runway, a gentleman wearing a fluorescent orange vest quickly approached the helicopter. "Now what?" growled Mike under his breath.

"Mr. Reynolds, we have about a thirty minute delay on take-off. The eagle is still on the nest and we haven't received a security clearance on air space. The tower will notify you when everything's clear."

Mike shut down the blades and I blew a loud sigh.

"Sooo…anyone care to explain 'the eagle' or 'the nest?'"

Moose chuckled and Mike cleared his throat. "Jordan's dad's helicopter is 'The Eagle,' and 'the nest' would be the beach house. This chopper is 'Baby Bird.'"

My stomach floated. "Two helicopters," I muttered. "Great. Just great."

I gathered Jordan's family had wealth, but private planes and multiple helicopters, not to mention a ship the size of a small house sent my head spinning. I'd never been around such opulence and the pressure to prove myself worthy hit ten-fold all over again.

The mention of high security preventing us from even taking off triggered the same unanswered question. "Who is Jordan's father? No one will tell me."

The cockpit became silent with the exception of the soft whirring sound of the blades overhead winding down. Mike turned his gaze out the window and I couldn't help notice his thumb flipping nervously against his thigh.

"Sorry, but that information is—"

"Let me guess. *Confidential*," I clipped. "You'd think with all the secrecy, Jordan was part of a royal family." Mike's eyes darted sideways to Moose.

A muffled buzzing sound stole Mike's attention and ended my inquisition. He pushed a button overhead, identifying the caller.

"Damn. It's Jordan."

"Is it on video feed?" I shrieked.

"No, just speaker, but be quiet, or he'll hear you in the background." He pressed the answer key. "What's up Mason-1? You headed out with Mason-2 yet?"

"We're in the pilots' lounge at O'Hare. Jesse's downing some major caffeine and getting an oxygen treatment. Between the concert last night and being stuck in a recording studio all day, he's beat."

"Precisely why all paperwork shows you the designated operator. Your itinerary is loaded in both the jet's and ship's computers, and the keys to your car are in your locker."

"Thanks *Mom*. Hey, have you heard anything from Marli? She called late last night and said she was staying the week, which worries me. Peterson's a snake. I only wish she knew the truth—"

"Uh-hum, Jordan," Mike blared over him. "Sorry, but it looks like I'm getting paged. I swear I haven't *heard* from her, but if I do, you'll be the first to know."

"I better be, or you'll pay."

"I believe it's *you* who's paying. Fifty bucks better be in my desk drawer."

"Fine. Can't believe I lost this one. Oh, I almost forgot. Has my dad left yet?"

I lifted my head watching Mike, whose gaze fixed on the instrument panel.

"Yep. Your mom should be in a good mood when you get home," he laughed along with Jordan. "Fly safe and don't forget to leave me a flight report this time."

Mike hung up and Moose playfully punched his shoulder.

<*Baby Bird - this is the tower - do you read?*> The squawk from the speaker on the instrument panel startled me. Mike confirmed we had clearance for takeoff and my heart raced in anticipation.

I re-attached the harness and took a quick inventory of my floating cushion and little green bag. Several men clad in glowing orange vests made another quick assessment of the helicopter before giving the "thumbs up." I grabbed the steel bar to the side of me and felt the ground fall away and my stomach swirl to my toes when the chopper turned heavenward.

We flew along the shoreline and below, police shuttles were in pursuit of a little black sports car.

"*Hold on!*" came Mike's abrupt warning in my ear as we launched upward and practically sideways before sharply dipping. "Sorry! The news chopper buzzed me and I had to clear air space." He reached back and gave my knee an apologetic squeeze. I'd made use of my little green bag.

We rounded a group of islands I recognized as the ones Jesse sailed to the day he taught me to snorkel. The rainbow reef under the surface of the crystal water looked even more spectacular from the air. We passed over a row of small cliffs encircling the bay and headed into open waters again, confusing me. I thought the beach surrounding the lagoon was part of the island the Masons owned. Apparently, I'd been duped...again.

Ten minutes later, the chopper's speed decreased as we inched closer to a small tropical desert island. White sand edged all sides, almost glowing against the transparent deep blue-green waters. A bay shaped like a crescent moon appeared beyond a protective wall of rock topped with dense trees. Below, a dock stretched into the water with a few small personal watercraft moored against it. On the hill rising above the pristine beach, a gray clapboard two-story house blazed bright orange in the late afternoon sun.

The weather vane on the pitched roof shifted at our passing and the palm trees bowed at our arrival when the chopper lowered onto a concrete pad. The blades slowed, their shadowy movement giving the appearance of a strobe light against the white sand. Mike lifted me to the ground, keeping a wary eye on the bag clutched in my hand. I was mortified I'd puked, but he'd left me no choice.

He placed my bags at my feet. "It's all right, Marli. You're not the first person to barf on one of my flights. Just focus on Jordan. I wish I could be there to see his face when he finds those sexy little boxers on the seat of his car."

My body stiffened when I caught sight of two figures standing at the edge of the lawn, under the trees. Eva Mason stepped out of the shade and walked toward us with open arms.

"Mike! Marli! I see you made it in one piece." She gave me a formal hug and kiss, barely touching my cheek, and moved to Mike.

When planning my surprise with Mike, I discovered nothing went on in the Mason realm without Eva's approval. I gathered very few were allowed beyond the walls guarding the family's personal life. It was as if they all lived in some ultra-secret world and only a select few were privy to be included. I hadn't reached that point with any of the Masons. Not even Jordan.

Tonight, I'd stay alone with Eva Mason—a thought I'd pushed to far corners of my mind. The way her eyes swept over me in the mere seconds before her "air kiss" brought home the realization I still auditioned for her acceptance.

She gestured toward the house. "Mike, will you and Hank come in for a moment? Meg made fresh lemonade."

"Thanks for the offer, but we need to get the chopper back before Jordan and Jesse arrive. We don't want to risk spoiling the surprise after all this work." He gave her a polite hug and returned to the chopper.

Mrs. Mason pulled me quickly toward the grassy area as the blades increased in speed, sending sand flying everywhere. *Baby Bird* swooped overhead and disappeared.

Eva Mason linked her arm through the petite woman standing next to her. "Marli, this is my best friend, Meg. She helped raise my children and has kept our household in line since before Jordan was born. She's a dear member of our family." She turned to Meg. "And this lovely young lady is Marli, the candidate selected for Jordan."

I bristled at the cold reminder of my status.

Meg gave me an impish smile, "Ah yes, Marli. You've reached celebrity status around our house. I hear your name mentioned more than anyone else's, and you're definitely the topic of most conversations."

She air quoted "conversations" and both she and Mrs. Mason giggled at their inside joke. It would prove to be a long night.

Mrs. Mason hooked her other arm through mine and the three of us walked toward the house. "Well, I guess it's only us girls." She tugged me closer. "Marli dear, you still look a little green. You need something in your stomach. Meg made some delicious ginger cookies this morning."

I stopped inside the entry, dropping my bags onto a hardwood floor glistening against the sunlight pouring through double glass doors leading to the kitchen. This house was the complete opposite of the penthouse.

The room before me felt comfortable and inviting. A deeply tufted sofa, covered in bright floral fabric, edged the entry. On each side of a stone fireplace, two overstuffed chairs, large enough for two, beckoned you to sit. Bookcases filled with board games, rare magazines, and actual books, lined the walls behind them.

I closed my eyes and took in the musty scent of the wood-paneled walls blending with the salty smell of the ocean. All the anxiety overwhelming me moments ago disappeared. My body relaxed in the serenity of the world I'd stepped into.

Eva placed a hand on my shoulder. "Marli, dear, there's a powder room around the corner if you'd like to freshen up."

My eyes followed hers to the bag still clutched in my hand. "Oh! I-*yes*. I'm so embarrassed."

Her smile put me at ease. "Don't be silly. I've ridden in that toy helicopter. The thing bounces around like it's on a giant spring. Trust me, you are not the only person whose stomach couldn't handle the horrid experience. Personally, I prefer the yacht."

She tucked a strand of hair behind my ear. "Do you think your queasiness will ease by dinner? Meg planned on grilling salmon, but I can have her prepare something more bland."

"I should be okay, and grilled salmon sounds great. Thank you."

After using the facilities and splashing some cool water on my face, I felt renewed. My cheeks actually looked pink again. I walked out to find Mrs. Mason perched nonchalantly on the arm of the sofa. She looked so different from the last time I saw her, all prim and proper for the interview. Here, she seemed casual and carefree dressed in white pants rolled half way up her leg, and a green floral halter tied in a knot behind her neck.

"Marli, your room is upstairs at the end of the hall. You have a perfect view of the lagoon from your window and the softest bed in the house." She pulled away the scarf wrapping her head and draped it over the back of the sofa. "Leave your bags here in the hall and come join us for some refreshments. Afterward, we'll help you get your things upstairs where you can rest before dinner."

"Mrs. Mason? Thanks again for letting me come."

"Eva, please. Mrs. Mason sounds far too formal. And thank you for including me in your surprise. I'm excited to see my son's reaction at finding you here. Your presence is already a breath of fresh air and I look forward to getting to know you better. The interview could hardly qualify as a proper introduction."

Her arm curved around my shoulder and she led me into the kitchen. A small round table covered with a lace cloth sat nestled in the cozy glassed nook. Bright blue plates and tall frosted glasses waited on each side of a tiered crystal dish. Ginger cookies artistically fanned around the bottom and fresh green grapes cascaded from the top. Meg nibbled on a cookie, her arm resting on the back of her chair as her daydreams carried her beyond the window panes.

I sat across from Jordan's mother and helped myself to a cookie while she poured me a glass of lemonade. She pinched a lemon wedge into her ice tea and raised a brow.

"Now Marli, let's talk about you and my boys."

## 25
## TROPICAL BLISS

From my bedroom window, I marveled at the dreamy full moon hanging lazily on the horizon, its radiant reflection rippling on the water. Jordan would be in Miami now and have found my first clue. By the time that big moon disappeared with the brightness of the morning sun, Jordan would be here and I hoped, in my arms.

After indulging in a sumptuous bubble bath, I slipped between the silky sheets wondering if the buzz of excitement would ever settle. The scent of lavender lingered on my dewy skin—skin satiny smooth and ready for Jordan's touch. My racy thoughts battled the weariness caused from zipping through different time zones the last couple of days. A cool breeze whispered over my bare legs and tendrils of hair tickled my cheek as sleep finally won out.

*...Jordan crawls onto my bed, his fingers lightly stroking my arms, his lips kissing a path from just below my ear, down my neck, and across my chest. Even in my slumber, I delight in the fullness of his lips resting against mine. I giggle when he kisses my toes, his touch tracing slowly up my legs. Fingers tease, counting my ribs under my shirt...*

When I felt a purposeful touch in a place I *wasn't* imagining, I woke to find lips pressing my stomach and *my* hands braided into locks of hair, colored copper in the pink morning light.

"Jordan!" I yelped, only to have my startled cry squelched by the crush of his lips. He lowered me into the pillows and his body molded intimately to my every curve.

"You're here," I whispered only loud enough for his ears.

"I'm here and want to strangle you!" he hissed in my ear. "Knowing you'd already arrived made the trip the longest ever!"

Jordan slithered down my body, lifting my shirt and letting his tongue circle my navel. His hot breath on my stomach—ironically caused chills to scurry over me. I whimpered, halfway protesting when his lips nipped away fabric to reveal more skin to sample. He eased back over me and his mouth grazed my jaw line.

"Kiss me," I begged.

"Uh-uh. Not yet. I think you deserve some payback." He kissed my eyelids, the apples of my cheeks, moving to my chin after a gentle nip of my bottom lip, fueling my frustration.

My fingers outlined the defined muscles on his naked back, feeling the flesh pebble under my touch. I walked my fingers from his neck to the base of his spine, sliding my finger around the waistband of his boxers. He moaned softly in my ear, shifting his body.

I'd missed the way Jordan's body felt against mine; the soft hair on his legs tickling when our legs slid side-by-side; the weight of his torso pressed to my stomach; his chest brushing mine with his deep breaths, making my breasts tingle and sending a wave of heat to seat between my thighs.

Folding my legs over his hips, I held him tight to me—the fervor building with each hot, moist kiss to my neck, my jaw; his lips pecking the edges of mine without landing on my mouth in a sensuous tease, all while slowly rocking his pelvis against mine in the familiar rhythm my body had craved for weeks. No other boy fit so perfectly to my body. Only Jordan. It was as if our bodies came off the same assembly line and then split apart.

I slid my legs slowly down his, my heels digging into his calves as my body arched to meet his. Something felt different…a need for more; my body urging his to comply—his obeying the command. Maybe it was being away from him, the fear I'd never hold him in my arms again, or the comfort of knowing he wanted me in his life as much as I did him that made the moment so intense, but I definitely had never reached this pinnacle before.

Jordan lifted slightly, studying me with eyes darkened to eclipsed moons. "Look at me, babe."

His body stilled, but mine couldn't. He pressed a light kiss to my mouth, parted and gasping. When his mouth moved to the sensitive spot below my ear, his stubble chafing the skin where my nerves splayed open, and his thumbs lightly rubbing over the knit fabric covering my breasts, I lost it. *It.*

Literal waves of sensations I'd never experienced rolled through me, ripping me apart. My toes curled, my legs trembled, and the blood in my veins sang with the molten heat flooding my senses and rippling under my skin.

Jordan's mouth crashed against mine, his tongue plunging deep with each mew straining from the back of my throat. My fingers clenched his hard as he held my hands pressed to the mattress at the side of my head. I gasped with each agonizing, delightful, wave of raw passion, barely getting air between our lips; tasting, biting, and searching.

My reckless breaths mixed with his, suddenly fast and equally urgent. I stroked my tongue slowly across the top of his mouth, encouraging his deep moans to rumble against my chest. He released my hands, leaving a wet trail down my arms as he wrapped his arms beneath me, clamping my body to his. He fell limp, his head heavy to the side of mine. I tangled my fingers in his silken curls feeling the dampness at the roots.

We lay silent, no longer moving and the only sound in the room being our laden breaths slowing. I closed my eyes, squeezing lingering tears I was totally unaware had dampened my cheeks. I burrowed my nose into Jordan's hair, inhaling the musky scent mixed with the coconut essence of his shampoo.

I was mortally embarrassed. He couldn't know I'd totally lost control. I wished he'd roll off me so I could close my legs and hide any evidence, not to mention every time he moved, another tiny bubble of ecstasy slithered up my spine.

Jordan's head eased onto my chest, nestling under my chin. I traced the planes of his face, stroking the long lashes brushing his cheeks. He took my hand and kissed my palm, pecking his mouth to the inside of my wrist and slowly working the length of my arm. Every nerve ending in my body was frayed so when his mouth kissed the inside of my elbow, a shiver washed over my skin.

"You should leave," I whispered.

"I can't," he replied, never raising his head and still pinned against me. "I need a sec."

When he finally rolled, he pulled me on top of him. My hair brushed his bare chest, which rose and fell as fast as my own. I laid my head there, unable make eye contact, relishing the delightful caresses on my back under my top.

"Babe, you okay?"

"I'm fine." *More than fine.*

A few long silent minutes passed

"Do you still want me to go?"

I circled his body with my arms and hugged him. "No. Never."

He hugged me back. "Good because you feel perfect on me."

I didn't say anything for fear he'd stop playing with my hair and rubbing my back, which felt amazing now that my sensory overload had fizzled.

"Marli, I've been so lost without you. I'm sorry I hurt you."

I pillowed my chin on my arm, daring to face him again. "I was so afraid I'd destroyed us. I shouldn't have overreacted."

He brushed the hair away from my face and held it. *Could he tell?* My cheeks burned with the humiliating notion and his dreamy eyes sweeping my face didn't help. A wide grin spread over lips still wet and swollen.

*He knows.*

Jordan smoothed his knuckles down the side of my face. "I think this time, *overreacting* was justified. I pushed all the wrong buttons."

Apparently he'd learned to push all the right buttons because although my body still ached in private places, my want for him returned the second his kisses turned greedy and the touching...well...hell.

Outside in the hall, the door to the next bedroom—Jordan's *mother's* bedroom door, squeaked.

Jordan moved away, much to my dismay. "This time I better go. I'll see you downstairs for breakfast." He picked up his red T-shirt top off the floor and yanked it over his head, grinning wickedly. "You're lucky this is all I took off." He leaned down and took another quick taste off my mouth. "Especially when I witnessed the hottest damn thing *ever* happen. Girl, just so you know, you were *my* complete undoing."

He tossed my black swimsuit top onto the bed before slipping out the door. "We're going for a private swim later."

I flopped back into the pillows. Did Jordan experience the same thing? If so, we were in serious trouble. I picked up the swimsuit top. Only two hours had passed in my eight week stay and we were already over our heads in deep water.

"Yum, ham and cheese omelets," I noted, joining Jordan at the stove.

He gathered me into the crook of his arm and kissed the side of my hair. "I've got a raging appetite for what I nibbled on earlier. *Eggs* aren't going to satisfy my hunger." He moved the pan off the heat and his lips possessively covered mine.

"Great. I just lost my appetite," Jesse snarled. He grabbed his cup of coffee and stormed out the back door, slamming the screen door against the house.

Jordan's mother walked in, witnessing Jesse's exit and Jordan sampling my mouth. "Son, try and curb your enthusiasm for Marli a bit, please? At least in front of your brother."

Jordan held me close despite her presence. "Mom, Jesse and I talked on the way here. It's going to take some adjustment, but everything will work out."

"Easy for you to say. You're standing in the winner's circle," she clarified.

Meg slid the omelets onto plates. "I'd throw you two into the freezer, but the steam pouring off you would melt everything."

I stepped out of Jordan's arms, taking the plate she purposely held between us. "I think your mom's right. We should be a little less—"

"No way!" Jordan punctuated. He held the chair for me, giving his mother a stern look. "I'm not letting anyone, including Jesse, make us feel uncomfortable. I messed up twice trying to be *correct* and damn near lost Marli. Jesse will have to find a way to come to terms with our relationship."

Breakfast conversation turned to less emotionally charged subjects like the weather and the possibility of war somewhere besides on this island.

I rocked lazily on the porch watching Jordan and Jesse unload the last of the supplies from the boat. Jesse remained cold toward me and Jordan's constant touching didn't help matters.

The screen door squeaked and Eva Mason appeared, holding a cup of tea. "Care for some company?" she asked, easing into the rocker next to me. She took a long sip, her gaze fixed somewhere in the distance. "Marli, I saw Jordan slip out of your room this morning. I hope you two are being responsible. I know how fast the passion of young love can take over common sense."

A burning heat crawled out of my yellow T-shirt up to my forehead. "He surprised me this morning. I hope you don't think—"

"Please! I trust you both. I do worry about Jesse, though. He fell so hard for you I think it caught him off guard. He's never cared about anyone enough to give his heart away. I saw trouble that first day when I walked in on him teasing you. Something about the way he looked at you. Well, I don't need to tell you."

Feelings of guilt and an overwhelming need to confess took over. "I never meant to hurt Jesse. With everything happening so fast, I think I encouraged him. My feelings for Jordan surprised me because I've never felt this way before and it scared me. Jesse became an easy distraction and it broke my heart when I ended things."

She sipped her tea, processing. "The heart chooses who it will love and no matter how wonderful someone may be, if you don't feel that burning passion you'll never be able to love them completely. Sometimes we're on the receiving end of that pain and sometimes we're the one inflicting it on someone else. Either way constitutes heartbreak—an unfortunate casualty of love."

She stood, leaving the rocker in a ghostly movement. "As for you and Jordan, trust your heart. A mother knows not only when her child is hurting, but also when he's happy, and Marli, Jordan's never been happier."

"Hey, there are my two favorite girls!"Jordan yelled as he carried a bin up the stone path.

Jesse mumbled something behind him, keeping his eyes trained on me.

Meg appeared behind the screen and called back. "So what am I? Chopped liver? Do you ever want to taste my triple chocolate cake again?"

"Okay, my bad. My *three* favorite girls." Jordan jumped onto the porch and bent to kiss me before walking inside. "Dad swears Meg's triple chocolate cake is almost better than sex."

"Jordan!" his mother huffed, slapping his shoulder. "Watch your manners. I'm sorry, Marli. I thought I raised him better." She followed Jordan into the house, chastising him until their voices disappeared.

Jesse put his box down and leaned on the railing. I rested against the post opposite him.

"Mars, I'm sorry for being an ass. I thought I could handle seeing you with Jordan, but the truth is I can't. When I saw your shorts on the seat in the Porsche, the same ones you wore the morning I snuck in your bedroom window, the pain shot straight to my heart." He stared at me intently. "Marli, promise me one thing. Don't let me see you in that black bikini. If I see you in that skimpy swimsuit and Jordan's hands on you, I'll kill him."

"Don't say that, Jess. And you need to get a grip on your feelings, because if I end up with Jordan, I'm going to have you in my life, too. We have to find a way to exist around each other. I shouldn't have to constantly worry about your reaction to everything."

He clamped my shoulders. "I'm trying, but when Jordan kisses you, *I* kiss you. When he touches you, *I* feel your soft skin and know the smell of your hair because it's burned in *my* memory. I get that you're with Jordan. And if you marry him, I'll die all over again, knowing how he'll be with you in a way I never can. Don't ask me not to *feel*."

A couple of gulls landed close by and Jesse's stare veered to them and off me. "Accepting you and Jordan together isn't going to happen instantly. I need time." He picked up the box and turned to the house. "I meant what I said. Don't wear that bikini in front of me. I have enough painful memories of you to erase without adding more." He threw the screen door open and disappeared inside.

"Getting over you is going to be impossible for him."

I whirled around, finding Jordan standing on the lawn a few feet away.

"How long have you been standing there?"

"Long enough," he replied, taking me in his arms and placing a light kiss on my mouth. "Mom's right. I should be more sensitive."

His mentioning his mother brought up something we needed to discuss about this morning, and his second kiss confirmed I couldn't put off telling him why ground rules had to be put in place.

"Speaking of your mother, she saw you sneak out of my bedroom."

Jordan grinned wide with no hint of remorse. "She better get used to it because I plan on sneaking into your room every chance I get."

"Don't you think that's something for me to decide?" He looked stunned. I put my hand on his cheek. "Hey, I'm not saying I don't want you to, I just don't want any one getting the wrong impression."

His hands skimmed my hips and settled at the base of my spine. "I've been away from you too long and want you near me," he paused, kissing my cheek, "to hold you," his lips pecking the sensitive skin below my ear, "kiss you all night," ending with another feverish kiss on my lips, leaving me totally breathless.

A flashback of what else happened this morning returned with the warming tingles taking over. "Hmm, there's something else."

"Something else?" he smiled, his cheeks coloring too much to be innocent.

"Yeah…I-I think you overestimate my willpower. When we get into it—"

"*Into it?*"

"You know what I mean. Kissing…and touching…and—"

"And?"

"Okay, you're not helping! Things start to get out of control and you know what I'm talking about. You *know* what happened to me and while I can't deny I didn't like it…" *loved it…*

I pinched my eyes shut and lowered my head. "Jordan, I've never experienced that before and it scared me because I did like the feeling. I worry it will happen all the time, or…I'll want to…maybe do more." I pushed my knuckles against my cheeks. "Ugh! Alex would love this moment!" To add to my humiliation, tears started behind my eyes. "I'm sorry," I mumbled. "I shouldn't have said anything."

Jordan slid a finger under my chin and lifted my face. "You've seriously never felt that before?" I shook my head and tried to step away, but he held my arms. "Hey. Don't pull away and get all embarrassed. Talk to me." He gathered a little more of me. "Marli?"

I lifted my eyes, the burn on my cheeks strong when his gaze locked on me.

"Babe, while my ego would love it if I could make it happen every time, trust me, it doesn't work that way."

"How would you know? Has it happened to you?"

This time he backed away, head down and hand clamped on the back of his neck. I couldn't stop the giggles bubbling from my throat and kept my hand over my mouth, but it didn't help. Jordan turned so red I wondered if he'd self combust.

"Oh my gosh! Just this morning?" He shook his head side-to-side. "No! How often? Mason?"

Jordan chased after me as I continued taunting and I squealed when he caught me. He kept me suspended, pressed backward and against his chest, his mouth at my ear.

"You are so going to pay, girl. I'm a weakling, okay? You turn me on. Hell, you make me ape-shit horny and push me over the damn edge practically every time we make-out. Happy now?" He slowly lowered me to the ground. "But I love what you do to me." His mouth hovered over mine. "I love you. And I never want to stop loving you or experiencing all the crazy emotions you create." The end of his nose pressed mine, his pants still breathy. "We'll take things slower, I promise. Just don't lock your door—keep me out. I need to be with you."

I brushed the side of his face, leaving our noses engaged. "I love you, too. I want you with me…always." Another tiny giggle escaped. "Ape-shit horny? Really?"

His cheeks flushed bright again. "Yes. Really."

Our lips pressed, the kiss gentle, but filled with a knowing we didn't have before this moment. A new connection…another wall crumbling away.

Jordan hugged me tight enough I thought my ribs cracked. "Let's go for that swim. I can't quit thinking of you in that bitty black bikini." He laughed as if the Devil himself. "Actually, more like you *out* of that bikini." His grin widened when I scowled. "We'll take it slower *after* our swim."

I tugged him by the hand toward the beach. "I've got a better idea. How about we stay dressed and you take me on a tour of this beautiful place."

He groaned, his steps flat and heavy on the sand. "Fine. Walk and talk. Can I at least picture you in my mind wearing the bikini?" He stopped and closed his eyes, a crooked smirk tugging a corner of his mouth. I punched his shoulder and he stumbled over his foot. "Ouch! Stop reading my mind."

I took off running when he started a low growl in the back of his throat. He scooped me up and swung me around, but didn't put me down. Instead, he carried me in his arms, which I found delightful.

I twirled the messy curl on his brow while he explained how his father inherited the island after his grandparents were killed in some horrific accident when Jordan was a baby. He told me how it took three years to build the house because they had to bring everything by water and could only work on it so many months out of the year.

Of course when I asked about his father's identity, he clammed up and gave me the same excuse he used in California. "When," I decided, had an indefinite timetable in Jordan's world.

He asked me how I felt about my parents' divorce and my decision to live with Rick. I told the version of the story where my mother chose a military career over parenting, taking her some unknown place overseas.

I deflected any questions that could lead to my illegal candidacy by divulging the details of Daniel's death; a subject I'd never discussed with anyone besides Rick and Chuck. Not even Brittany or Alex.

We ended up on a secluded stretch of beach on the opposite side of the island. The sand looked like snow; brilliant white against the ultramarine ocean. The water appeared darker and the waves bending to the sea almost translucent. Sea Hibiscus, Bougainvillea bushes covered in vivid pinks, purples, and oranges, and shrubs spotting bright yellow trumpet-like flowers, added color patches beneath and around the several trees surrounding this sliver of paradise.

I sat cross-legged on the sand watching Jordan venture closer to the water. In the distance, waves crashed against a rocky point sounding like a cannon. When Jordan noticed I hadn't followed him, he turned my direction and dropped next to me. Another wave…another boom.

"The water is different here," I noted. "The color is even bluer."

"This is the windward side of the island. It takes the brunt of the wind and there's no cliffs to shelter the bay, so the waves travel farther and are stronger.

The water is deeper so the color is more intense. This is where Jess and I surf. The swells can get impressive."

"And noisy."

Jordan laughed, swinging his arm around my shoulder and pulling me close. "And hypnotic. I can sit here for hours and watch the ocean literally change with the day. One day I recorded the sound of the waves breaking over the rocks. I listen to the playback when I'm stressed or can't sleep. It's my favorite lullaby."

He kissed my hair and continued to stare out at the sea. I still couldn't wrap my head around this world he lived in and a part of me felt excited to possibly share in it someday. Another part of me, however, worried about the price paid to live in luxury. Because we'd unlocked the door to our personal lives somewhat during our walk to this heavenly place, I chanced asking another question...one on a deeper level.

"Jordan, can I ask you something really personal?"

He smiled down at me, his eyes glittering with mischief. "I don't think you can get more personal than earlier. That pretty much defined 'personal.'"

I blushed immediately, not wanting to relive my embarrassing confession. "Okay, let's not go there."

"Damn. I was so hoping luring you to my secret hideaway would change your mind *back* to letting me practice."

I smacked his chest. "Jordan! Stop it already!"

He kissed my hand before I could use it as an assault weapon again. "Okay, I'll stop...for the moment. So what do you want to ask me?"

"How do *you* make your money? I understand your parents are wealthy, but do you—"

"Live off their money?" He scooted away from me and returned his gaze to the horizon. I'd offended him. "No, Marli, I'm not a trust-fund sucker, if that's what you mean."

"No! I didn't mean that at all!" I waited for him to look at me, but when he didn't, I crawled in front of him and took one of the hands draped off his folded knees. "Don't be mad. It's just that I've never been around anyone so well off and if we end up together, I don't want you to think I only like you because you're rich. I don't care about money."

I wrapped my pinky tight around his and kissed his knuckle. "I still don't get why The Program aligned me with you. Seeing all this just makes me think they made a mistake. You need somebody—"

"You. I need you," Jordan stated forcefully. His eyes flashed at me. "Stop talking yourself down and trust me, no 'mistake' was made." As fast as they settled, his eyes lifted away. A couple large swallows rolled down his throat.

I knelt so I could rest my chin on his knee, and served up a pout worthy some attention. "I love you?" I questioned, hoping to bring back his playful mood.

His eyes dipped to my face, a ghost of a smile resurrecting his dimples. He tucked a strand of hair blowing in my face behind my ear, but when he spoke, his voice stayed quiet. "I love you, too, babe. You're my everything."

He opened his legs and I moved between them, resting against his chest and admiring a scene worthy a magazine cover. Jordan's chin settled on a favorite spot on top of my head.

"Our cars," he began, "were graduation gifts from my Grandpa Mason. He said if we got flawless grades from middle school through high school, we could have any car we wanted. We put him to the ultimate test, much to my mother's disapproval, but he came through and told Mom if bribery helped get us into elite colleges because of our grade point average, it was money well spent.

"When we turned eighteen, we received the inheritance our other grandparents left to us. One-half was a cash lump sum, which Jesse used to start up his band. Mine is still in the bank. When I figure out where I want to live, I hope to buy a house." He took a deep breath. "The other half is held in stock shares with SpringCor, the business my grandfather started. Jesse's and my inheritance is in the part of the company that has real estate holdings. The quarterly dividends are what I live off of. Our trust fund does pay a monthly allowance, but it gets eaten up by fuel costs for the jet and insurance premiums, which our parents make us pay. The chopper belongs to SpringCor and we're only allowed to use it for commuting to the island. Anything left over, I use to take trips to see this really hot girl I'm madly in love with so I can make-out with her. I'm trying to convince her I'm worthy of having her in my life."

He pulled my hair to one side and kissed my neck. "Satisfied? Now my turn. How did you end up with a pink car?"

"On the morning of my sixteenth birthday, this huge box truck backs up our driveway and the driver and unloads this old, rusted out Mustang. I got so excited I started jumping up and down, yelling for Rick to come see. He already knew, of course. I think he thought the two of us restoring the car, which the original color was 'lipstick pink,' would distract me from the divorce."

"You were thrilled to receive an old junker?"

I straddled his lap and locked my hands behind his neck. "Not just any old junker. My Grandma Adams's first car and also Mom's. When I was little and we'd go to my grandparents' farm in Pennsylvania, I'd sneak out to the barn where Grandpa stored the car. The doors were rusted shut and the window was broken out, so I had to crawl inside to sit behind the steering wheel. I'd pretend I was driving to get an ice cream cone before heading to faraway places."

"Like where?"

My thumb swept over the shell of Jordan's ear and he drew his knees up to snug me against him. Inky circles slowly consumed the olive green irises of his eyes and his breaths sounded heavy.

"Any place besides where you live sounds exotic to a ten-year-old."

"We can go anywhere you want, you know."

"Well *my* 'trust fund' has barely seven thousand dollars, which will more than likely get eaten up in rent if I stay all four years at Cornell. I'll have to work my butt off at the clinic on the weekends I go home, or find me a part time job that will work with my school schedule if I want to eat."

Jordan's expression clouded. "The Program starts paying you monthly once you're eighteen." He groaned when I shifted off his lap and sat next to him.

Automatically, I folded my knees to my chest, but tipped my head against his shoulder. "I want to pay my own way as much as I can. I don't have a choice but to let The Program foot the bill for college, otherwise, there's no way I could attend someplace like Cornell. But I don't want to rely on them anymore than I have to. I won't sell my soul to pay back the debt."

Jordan slid his arm around my waist. "Even if *I* am the debt?"

I left my head on his shoulder, but turned my face to his. "You'd never take my soul."

His thumb glided over my cheek. "You're right, I wouldn't. I'd much rather have your heart."

I pressed my hand to his chest. "It's already there, next to yours."

"I'll take good care of it, I promise." He kissed my nose. "And you, if you let me."

"I told you, I don't want your money."

Jordan lowered me onto the sand, moving his body over mine. "I'm not talking about money. I'm talking about Marli Davis, the person. You're strong, stubborn, and I get that you want your independence. All I want to do is stand next to you, not in front of you. But you've got to understand that I have this overwhelming need to protect you." He gently stroked his fingers through my hair. "If something happened to you that I could have prevented, I'd never forgive myself. I'm not good at staying in the shadows, Marli, although I'll try to not be controlling."

I rose enough to steal a kiss off his mouth; a risky move resulting with his hand smoothing up my thigh and his finger drawing a lazy line under the hem of my shorts.

"I like it sometimes when you're my superhero, but I want to share 'the cape' once in a while, okay?" I pulled his hand away and laced my fingers through his. "And take things slow."

He shook my hand in a businesslike manner. "Hi, I'm Jordan Mason." He winked. "Slow enough?"

I pulled his head so his lips rested on mine. "Faster."

# 26
# THINGS THAT GO "BUMP" IN THE NIGHT

Thunder rolled through the heavens stirring me awake. We'd experienced almost a month's worth of perfect weather, but things changed over the past few days. Swells rolled larger and the water turned murky from the higher tides. Air usually feeling light and smelling of summer, became muggy, the salty smell earthy from the blowing dust and dirt.

The scent of rain filtered into the breeze growing stronger as the storm approached. The usual nighttime lullaby sounding of soft waves sizzling over warm sand, transformed into something almost frightening when the angry surf pounded against the shore. I winced with a flash of lightning and braced for the crack of thunder.

Jordan whispered sleepily through my hair. "Marli, what is it?"

"Thunderstorms scare me."

He climbed off the bed and pulled the glass panels shut. "Good thing we fastened the rain covers on the boats. Looks like a bad one heading our way."

He slipped under the covers, breaking his own rule, and drew me close. Lightning flashed again and he cupped one hand over my ear, the other one gently rubbing my back as the next wave of thunder rocked.

Tonight I was grateful I agreed when Jordan asked to stay. Ever since our talk on the beach the first day, he respected my wishes and left my room at midnight, unless I made the suggestion he linger longer—meaning all night. I liked sleeping in his arms, although Jordan insisted on sleeping on top of the quilted coverlet with me under, keeping a fabric shield between our bodies.

I snuggled against his bare chest, feeling his arms wrap tighter in response. A simultaneous flash and ground shattering rumble made me jump, bumping his chin.

"Ouch, girl. You're going to knock my teeth out."

"Sorry for being such a baby."

Jordan turned on the light next to the bed and propped my pillow behind him. "Don't apologize for being afraid of something." He placed a tender kiss on my lips and gave me a rough hug. "Try to sleep. You're safe tucked in these arms."

We spent the next morning cleaning up broken tree limbs and scattered palm fronds. Jesse re-attached a couple of loose shutters and Meg swept up glass from a shattered window in the laundry room. Eva rode in the sport boat with Jordan to check the yacht for damages and reposition the anchor. I found a stray cushion in the bushes at the edge of the front lawn. Jesse met me on the porch, turning a tipped rocker over for me.

"Mars, are you sleeping with Jordan?"

His question halted me. "Define *sleeping with Jordan*," I replied, annoyed at the insinuation and defensive of his prying into my private business.

Jesse's hands slapped the side of the house, pinning me between his arms. "You know exactly what I mean. He goes into your room every night and sneaks out at the break of dawn. What the hell is going on?"

I ducked under his arm and opened the screen door. "I'm not having this conversation with you."

He remained on my heels as I traipsed upstairs to my room, grabbing my elbow and whirling me to face him. "Marli, I'm not just anyone. I know how close to the edge you'll go. I've been there, remember?" When I tried to shake my arm free, his grip grew stronger.

"I haven't forgotten that night, Jesse, but it's in the past. What I do with Jordan is none of your business."

I yanked my arm hard, upsetting my balance and I stumbled backward onto the bed. Jesse landed on top of me and my body tensed under his weight. My heart raced, but not the way it used to when Jesse was this close. I tried to push him off, but he held my wrists against the mattress.

"The hell it's not!" he snarled. "The thought of anyone crossing a line with you, even my own brother, makes me insane."

I tried to wiggle out from underneath him, but he was too strong. "Jordan doesn't cross any line I don't invite him to, but again, not your concern." I sighed when he wouldn't budge. "What do you want from me?"

"The truth. Are you having sex with Jordan?"

Jordan raced into the room. "*No*, she's not! Now get off of her!" He grabbed the back of Jesse's shirt and shoved him into the wall, knocking a picture off and sending shattered glass across the floor.

Jesse punched Jordan in the stomach and I screamed, leaping off the bed and throwing myself between them. A piercing pain in the arch of my foot pulled another shriek from my lungs. Jordan grabbed me just as Jesse's fist hit Jordan's jaw and consequently the side of my head, sending us both crashing to the floor.

"Jesse stop! Jordan! Marli!" The shrill of Eva's voice bounced off all four walls, bringing immediate silence. "What on earth is wrong with you!" Suddenly, she dropped to the floor and lifted my leg. "Marli! Lord have mercy, you're bleeding!" She slapped away Jordan's hands. "Don't touch her!"

Jesse sank to floor, "Shit! Marli I'm so sorry!"

"You two should be ashamed, acting like a couple of immature jackasses." Eva pushed my hair away from my face. "Marli, where else are you hurt?"

"My head," I cried. "I think I-I got a punch meant for Jordan."

"No!" Jesse wailed.

I tried to reassure him that I was okay, but it was too late. He ran down the hall to his room, slamming the door hard enough to shake the entire house.

Jordan crawled to me, taking my cut foot in his hand. Blood dripped from his lip where Jesse's fist made contact.

"Let me see your foot."

"Ouch!" I screeched when he pulled a chunk of glass out.

"You need stitches."

"No!" I cried. Eva cradled me, smoothing my hair to soothe me.

"I'll get the medical bag. I can do it." Jordan's voice sounded flat and void of emotion. "Mom, do we have any whiskey or vodka?"

"I think we have both downstairs in the liquor cabinet, but there's alcohol in the bathroom you can use for sterilization."

Jordan paused in the doorway. "It's not for sterilizing. I don't have anything to numb Marli's foot. I need to get her drunk so she doesn't notice the pain."

The rest of the day I heaved remnants of alcohol, which I'd never drank before. Jordan sat on my bed, a pillow in his lap where my head rested. His mother applied cold compresses to my face and Jordan's jaw, in between emptying soiled basins.

I tried to lift my head, but the room turned sideways and Jordan forced me back into the pillow. If I didn't puke, I giggled obnoxiously. I tried talking, but my speech slurred and drool came out of my mouth easier than words.

Eva placed a cold rag across the back of my neck. "How much vodka did you put in her orange juice? I'm afraid her hangover is going to hurt far worse than her foot or head." She wiped my numb mouth, then looked at Jordan. "Let me see your lip, son."

"Mom, don't. My lip's fine and my jaw's sore, but nothing's dislocated. Just let me sit here and hold Marli. Damn, what was Jesse thinking?"

"What were *you* thinking, Jordan?" Eva scolded in return. "Both of you share the blame here. And I expect that hole in the wall fixed before we close up the house, mister."

"Sorry about the wall, Mom, but when I walked in on Jesse holding Marli down on the bed, I lost it. He had no right treating her like that." I felt his hand flex on my arm, fighting against the resurfacing anger.

"True, but I don't believe he'd ever physically harm Marli. He loves her too, Jordan. Keep that in mind. Might not hurt for you to take a moment and put yourself in his place. Maybe you'd have a bit more compassion. Remember, he is your brother—your *twin*." Eva's cool hand brushed my cheek. "All I know is that your father is going to have both of your hides for this."

"Jordan, who's your dad?" I attempted to enunciate, but the grin on Eva's face told me it didn't sound the same as it did inside my head.

"Not now, Marli. Be quiet. You need to sleep off the booze," Jordan replied in a sullen tone.

"Be quiet, be quiet. Later, later, alligator. In a while, crocodile. Oooh! Jordan can we make out? You haven't kissed me for hours. I think I forgot how." I tried to make a smacking sound, but I couldn't feel my lips pucker.

Jordan laughed and his mother fought to hide her amusement, but her small shoulders shook too hard to be discreet.

"Oh my, you have your hands full." She set an empty basin on the table next to the bed. "She hasn't thrown up in a while, so hopefully her stomach is empty, but just in case. How's her foot?"

"It's a clean slice and not deep enough to cause any damage. Strange thing, it parallels an old scar." Jordan's fingers lightly stroked the side of my face and I closed my eyes. "I guess we both have secrets."

I fought to stay awake, a battle I slowly lost. My eyelids closed, but I held on to my conscious state enough to listen to the continuing conversation.

"Jordan, are you sure? If things don't work out between the two of you, can you trust her? Our lives could depend on her discretion."

"She handled Jesse's stabbing okay, and I have no intention of letting her out of my life unless she asks to leave. I want to marry her, Mom, but I'm not sure she's ready." Jordan kissed my shoulder and even in my sleepy state, I hugged his waist tighter in response. "She's so young. I don't want to take any of her life away."

"Son, you're not exactly old. Marli may be young in years, but she's what Meg calls an 'old soul,' and the way she looks at you, I don't think she'll turn you down whether you ask her today or ten years from now. As far as telling her our secret, you may not have a choice," Eva cautioned.

"Why? What's going on?"

"Your father's on his way. I don't know how to handle this situation. He's always been better with you boys. Kate was my challenge."

The bed moved and a soft kiss pressed my cheek. "Sweet dreams, Marli. Hope you feel better tomorrow. Good night, son. If you need anything, find me. Otherwise, I'll see you two at breakfast."

Darkness cloaked the room when I finally became coherent. I sat up, holding my throbbing head. I looked around to see if I'd been part of an unreal nightmare. The hole in the wall next to the door glared at me and the stabbing pain on the bottom of my foot told me otherwise.

Jordan left, which made my heart ache and somehow, I now wore my boxers and tank top. Not sure I wanted to know the answer to that mystery. My tongue felt covered in fur and my throat, painfully scratchy. I decided to venture to the kitchen for a drink and hopefully some type of pain reliever to dull my assorted aches.

Gingerly, I made my way to the bathroom, closing the door to keep from disturbing anyone. The light nearly blinded me and I gasped when I saw my reflection in the mirror. Eyes blackened by smeared mascara competed with a tangled hair nest. I scrubbed my face, brushed my teeth, and dragged a comb through my matted locks. A small bruise colored my left cheekbone and my eye appeared slightly swollen compared to the other.

The medicine cabinet yielded nothing for pain, but I remembered my purse on the entry table downstairs had some aspirin tucked inside. All I had to do was get downstairs gracefully and quietly.

The pain in my foot rocketed to my teeth by the time I descended the last stair. Fumbling in the dark, I finally located my bottle of pills and pondered on how many I could take before death would come for me, a welcome choice at the moment. I clenched a couple of the tiny capsules in my fist and hopped to the kitchen for water.

The brilliant light in the refrigerator made me blink a couple of times to focus before reaching for a cold bottle of water.

"You must be the reason for all the commotion around here."

The voice, smooth like Jordan's but deeper, scared me near death. I screamed, tossing the water bottle to the floor. It rolled toward the table, leading my eyes to the silhouette of someone sitting in the dark against the silver glow of the moonlit window.

"Well that should bring everyone running." *He* stood; his shadowy figure large and ominous as he retrieved my bottle from the floor. Whoever he was made a correct assumption. Jordan clambered down the stairs and ran into the kitchen, scooping me into his arms.

"Marli! Why are you down here? Is it your foot? Your head?

I remained speechless, trembling, and pointed in the darkness toward the intruder.

"Sorry, son. I didn't mean to frighten her."

The stranger handed the bottle of water to me, his face now faintly illuminated by the light from the refrigerator. His features were familiar. I'd seen him somewhere before, but in the shadows I wasn't sure. Tall, like Jordan, having the same chiseled facial features, and from what I could see, matching caramel colored hair, but eyes darker, more like Jesse's.

Jordan's hushed voice heightened with surprise. "Dad! When did you get in? I didn't hear your chopper."

"I came by water. Luckily, I was at the penthouse when your mother called, so Mike brought me in his private boat. My sudden absence will have everyone scrambling in the morning, but your mother said it was urgent and I answer to her first."

He eyed Jordan standing in the middle of the kitchen holding me in his arms. "Tell me son, do you always run around half naked when there's a pretty lady in the house? No wonder your brother's gone half crazy."

I hadn't noticed until that second that Jordan only wore black, *form-fitting* boxers. His arms under my thighs suddenly felt intimate, and a burning flush traveled the length of my body. I turned my face into his shoulder and he hugged me close to his body—his gorgeous, sexy, underwear-only-clad body.

"Marli scared the hell out of me when she screamed. I thought she'd injured herself and all I cared about was finding her." Jordan carefully placed me on a stool. "Let me see your foot, babe. How's the pain?"

"It throbs. I came down for some aspirin and your father startled me." I touched the side of Jordan's cheek. "I'm sorry I've caused all this trouble. Maybe I should go home so you and Jesse can work through this without me here complicating things."

His father took my foot in his hands and pulled the bandage back. I winced when he turned my foot toward the light from the refrigerator. "The sutures look good, Jordan. You did a fine job. They should heal quickly if she'll stay off her foot and keep it elevated." He shot me a sideways glance, but I still couldn't figure out his identity with the shadows hiding most of his face.

Jordan placed his hand on his dad's shoulder. "It's easy when you've been taught by the best. I only wished you hadn't given up medicine. I would have liked to work beside you in an operating room."

His father grinned, exposing dimples like Jordan's. "My son flatters me. But you, young lady, are going nowhere. My sons will have to learn to sort through this with you here. No one is sending you home, understand? You're our guest and I'm hoping much more than that, someday.

"I guess now is as good a time as any to decide if you want to be a part of this insanity we call a family." He stood and faced Jordan. "Turn on the light, son. It's time Miss Davis met the source of her near-fatal heart attack and the reason why we've kept her in the dark for so long. No pun intended, Marli."

Jordan touched a panel on the wall, flooding the kitchen in fluorescent light. I did indeed know the man standing before me. His prominent, well-respected persona plastered billboards and numerous media transmissions. He commanded the respect of anyone in his presence, and in my late brother Daniel's eyes, he was a hero.

The similarities in his two sons were obvious, but not having known until now, I'd never have made the connection. There was no mistaking the handsome man to be Jordan and Jesse's father. I smiled inside knowing Jordan would be every bit as good looking when he grew older. I also fully understood the necessity for all the secrecy. The thousands of questions I had were answered, as well as a couple of new ones coming to mind.

Jordan walked behind me, resting his hands on my shoulders. "Um, Marli, this is my father—John *Banks*."

I stared into the chocolate brown eyes of the legendary man standing in front of me, and my hand shook when I held it out to him. "Nice to meet you, *Mr. President*."

## 27
## REVELATIONS

The water crept closer, capturing a little more of me in its foamy edges with each wave. I watched the gulls circling overhead playfully duck from the warm summer sky into the sparkling peaks of the waves, their webbed feet skimming the surface until their downy bellies rested on the water.

I'd grabbed an apple and a couple of towels, slipping out of the house when Jordan and Jesse were loudly summoned for a private meeting with their father. With all the confusion inside, I welcomed the solitude of my private spot on the beach.

Most of the night, Eva, Jordan, and I sat in the living room with Jordan's father politely answering my barrage of questions. Before the morning sun fully ascended on the eastern horizon, however, nature's morning chatter was interrupted by the loud pounding of an ominous black helicopter. The 'Eagle' returned to the *nest*.

Immediately dismissed to our rooms when four large men walked through the door, President Banks's private entourage of bodyguards and Secret Service detail had a few questions of their own. They were less than happy to wake and find the President of the United States missing. I wondered what security protected Mike for participating in the covert abduction.

A wave smacked a nearby rock, sprinkling me. I adjusted the rolled up towel under my injured foot, moving farther back from the teasing fingers of water. The gulls swarmed to make breakfast off the apple core I threw their direction. I closed my eyelids, concentrated on the sound of the waves breaking in the distance and not my tumultuous thoughts.

"There you are. I've been looking all over for you." Jordan plopped onto the sand next to me, leaning on a raised knee. "I see you're obeying doctor's orders and keeping the foot up, but why all the way down here?" He raised the bill of the baseball cap shading my face from the bright sun. "Marli?"

I remained hidden under my hat, while Jordan played with my fingers. "It's a lot to absorb," I answered. "Your father is the President of the United States, but no one can know. You go by a different last name and your father can't publicly acknowledge you. I'm having a hard time understanding, that's all."

"Babe, take off the hat and look at me, please?"

"No. I like hiding from a world that's very confusing right now."

"Fine have it your way." Jordan stretched out beside me on the beach towel, taking my hand. "Marli, you don't need to hide to feel safe. Nothing's changed."

"*Are you serious?*" I yelled through my fabric mask. "Everything's changed! I don't even know if you're Jordan Mason or *Banks?* I can no longer 'fly under the radar.' From now on, I have a personal bodyguard. How am I going to explain that little detail to Rick? Oh, that's right. I *can't* tell him. He's just going to believe I'm being stalked!"

Jordan yanked the hat off my face and threw it into the ocean before I could blink. He held my face so I couldn't look away. "I'm still Jordan *Mason* and for your information, you've had a bodyguard since you returned from California. My father insisted on it when he found out you interviewed for Douglas Peterson. You've just never seen the guy. The only time he couldn't watch you was when you were in Italy. We don't have jurisdiction internationally."

"Even when you weren't speaking to me?"

Jordan's brow arched. "It was *you* not speaking to me, if I remember correctly, and yes, even then."

I pried his hand from my face before a permanent mark formed. "Why? What's the big dark secret about Doug? I deserve to know everything."

"Actually, the less you know, Marli, the safer you are. I'll tell you this much. Doug Peterson's father is a powerful man, but not in a good way. I don't think Doug even knows much about his father's life. He's the one who had the pictures taken. They were meant to tear us apart so he could have you re-assigned to Doug."

"I know." Jordan looked surprised. "I overheard a conversation in Italy."

"Damn, I wish you hadn't. If Peterson knew…he's dangerous, babe. If there's such a thing as an 'arch enemy,' Tony Peterson qualifies in my dad's eyes."

I leaned up on my elbow. "Tony Peterson knows about your family? What if he told someone?"

Jordan twisted a lock of my hair around his finger. "If our family secret gets out, so does his—something Tony Peterson doesn't want. There are several skeletons hidden in the Peterson closet. Doug himself is harmless. He's like me—the son of a prominent man. The difference is I know most of my father's business dealings. I'm pretty sure Doug can't make the same claim."

"So that's why you're obsessed with Doug? I thought you were just worried I'd be taken in by his dashing good looks and smoldering kisses." Jordan's jaded expression proved I'd pushed the limit. I feathered the side of his handsome face. "Hey, I'm joking."

His ran his thumb across my bottom lip, "The thought of him kissing you, holding you…" A bubble rolled down his throat. "The nightmare kept me awake every night you were gone. It drove me nuts." He suddenly pulled away. "Well there's an epiphany I didn't expect. It must be the same for Jess when I'm with you."

I gently touched the swollen corner of his lip. "Your lip looks sore. I don't dare kiss you for fear it will hurt."

"I don't care if it hurts like hell." Without warning, he hovered over me. "Not kissing you is *never* an option." He leaned down softly touching his lips to mine. "Have I told you I love you today?"

"No, as a matter of fact, but it's been a little crazy." I raised my head up enough to plant another tender kiss on his mouth, catching a slight flinch when I did so. "But you can tell me now."

Jordan eased his body over mine, settling a leg between my thighs. A harder, eager kiss met my lips, followed by a soft moan, either mine or his...or both.

Without warning, cold water enveloped our legs. I gasped, my open mouth only inviting a deeper kiss. I folded my arms around Jordan's neck, his hands sliding under me and clenching me tighter to him when a second wave rolled in. He lifted me in his arms before the third wave wrapped his knees, sucking both towels away.

"The towels!" I rolled sideways in his arms, but only retrieved one before Jordan lost his balance, sending both of us crashing into the ocean.

Jordan hauled me onto the lawn and fell beside me, both of us struggling to catch our breath from laughing. He took the towel I managed to grab and twisted it, wringing cold water across my chest and down my neck.

"Aack! Jordan!

His gaze slowly moved over my drenched body. "Purple. Very sexy."

"Huh?"

He knelt to my side, his arm stretched across my hips. "Your soaked sundress is delightfully revealing," he answered brazenly.

I smacked his chest. "You're unbelievable."

"I'm a guy. I can't help myself." He scooped me up before I could put any weight on my bad foot, indulging in another shameless glance. "Nor do I want to."

Jordan carried me to my room, placing me on the edge of my bed and carefully removing the wet bandage. He gathered the bedspread around me and leaned me back onto the bed. "I like the purple almost as much as the pink," he grinned, pecking my nose.

"Pink?" A fuzzy recollection answered my own question. "*You* dressed me in my pajamas last night?" Heat instantly wrapped my face.

"You'd puked on your clothes and I didn't want you sleeping in them. Mom was in the shower and Meg had already gone to bed. I had no choice." His cheeks burned scarlet. "I kept my eyes closed as much as possible, I promise."

I scrunched my eyes shut. "I can't believe you saw me in my underwear. I'm so embarrassed."

"Trust me, you have nothing to be embarrassed about. Plus, I now have a sweet memory that will probably keep me awake at night the rest of my life."

"Good."

Jordan kissed me. "No, *fantastic.*" His mouth pushed on mine to stifle any more snarky replies. He wrapped my foot while I remained in my fabric cocoon. "Marli, tell me about this other gnarly scar."

Jesse appeared in the doorway, saving me from answering. "Sorry to interrupt, but Dad needs you downstairs."

Jordan kissed my big toe. "We'll pick this up later."

*Not if I can help it.* The skeletons in my closet needed to remain locked away.

President Banks decided to stay the night, along with his security detail. Resting my foot on a chair, I sat at the kitchen table putting together a tossed salad, watching the men grill steaks on the back patio. Eva Mason never left her husband's side. Their loving glances and tender kisses warmed my heart.

"It's hard on her having him gone so much." Jesse's voice shocked me. He pulled out the chair across from me, taking a handful of snap peas.

"Are you okay?" I asked carefully. "I'm sorry for causing all this trouble."

He shook his head, "Marli, *you're* not responsible for any of this."

"I could have answered your question and avoided this whole mess. Just so you know, Jordan doesn't spend every night with me, and if *I* ask him to stay, we sleep. That's all. Sleep, okay?"

"You don't owe me any explanations. I should keep my nose in my own damn business, so when it comes to being stubborn, you have competition. Jordan and I were doomed to fight over you at some point." He reached over and gingerly touched my bandaged foot. "Does it hurt?"

"Not as much tonight." I playfully threw a crouton at him, hitting his forehead. "*So*...you and Jordan?"

He tossed the crunchy morsel into the air and caught it in his open mouth. "Like I said, this isn't easy for me."

I took his hand. "Jesse, I need you guys to fix this."

His hand slithered away. "I'm working on it, Mars." He glanced out the window. "I should get away from you before there's more trouble."

Following his gaze I saw Jordan glowering, his father's hand on his shoulder holding him back. "You're not the only one having trouble, Jess. Jordan's struggling too."

"Pardon me if I don't exactly feel compassion for my brother. After all, he has you, doesn't he?

"Nobody *has* me. I'm assigned to Jordan, remember?"

"The only memory I have is of one steamy night. Now I can spend the rest of my life knowing my brother is creating more of them with you. Shit! I can't do this." He pushed away from the table and disappeared out the front door.

Jordan marched in from the patio. "What's going on?"

"Jesse's still upset." He opened his mouth to speak. "Uh-uh. Don't say a word unless it's to apologize to *him*."

"Why? What did I do?"

"You 'got the girl,' Jordan."

"What am I supposed to do, Marli? *Share* you?" Jordan looked so intense, fists pushing his hips, his cowlick twisting a curl forward over his scrunched brow.

"We could alternate weekends."

His head cocked sideways, an expression of disbelief covering his face. I couldn't hold back the laugh.

"You're impossible, girl, you know that?" Scratching at the back of his neck, he exhaled a large breath. "So where is he?"

"Somewhere out front."

Jordan kissed my head. "Finish the salad, I'll be right back."

No way. The salad could wait. I quietly hobbled to the front door, spying Jordan leaning against the porch post and Jesse on the step, shredding a long blade of grass. I tucked out of sight and listened.

"Jess, I get it and I'm sorry. What can I do to make things right?"

"Guess you wouldn't consider giving Mars up?"

"Sorry, can't do that one."

"Didn't think so. Just don't hurt her, Jordan. Watching you love her is one thing, but watching you hurt her isn't something I'll stand by and let happen."

"I hope I never do," Jordan replied. "Who knew, huh? The government decided who I'd share my life with, but they never factored in my heart. How lucky am I to have been assigned Marli?"

"Jordan, could you really have spent your life with some girl you didn't care for? Maybe that's why I didn't fight to get my blue band back. I couldn't live with someone I didn't love."

Jordan's knee knocked Jesse's shoulder. "Even if she was drop-dead gorgeous and her body rocked?"

"Like Mars?"

"Yeah...like Marli."

Heat instantly leaped onto my cheeks.

"Meaningless sex for a night is one thing, but for a lifetime? And for what? *Kids* the government can turn into mindless minions? How do you teach a kid about love if you don't feel it yourself?"

"Whoa, going deep, Jess. I guess I assumed the relationship would eventually turn into more. Don't ever tell Dad, but that's why I delved into my medical studies. Deep down, I hoped he let me be and not push it. Then Mom announced she'd be interviewing *two* candidates and I blew up."

"I remember that night. I heard you guys arguing and thought 'geesh, Jordan's got a set' if he's threatening to cause a worse scandal than my fiasco did."

"You were set-up, Jess. You didn't do anything wrong."

"Would you really have dropped out?"

My lungs seized. *Jordan* threatened to drop out of The Program?

"You know I couldn't. Not after Kate. And when I think about who Marli would have been assigned to, I get sick."

"For what it's worth, I'm glad you didn't. She deserves someone like you, seeing how she can't have *me*." Jesse chuckled, glancing toward the door. I shrunk tighter to the wall.

"Are we good, Jess?"

"Better, but this isn't going away overnight."

"I know." Feet shuffled closer. "So tell me about this meaningless sex."

Jesse laughed. "Dude, what are we? *Girls*?" Feet stopped again. "But I suggest we can the sex talk. I smell someone burning she's blushing so hard."

"Marli? She's in the kitchen."

"Seriously, Jordan? You have so much to learn about your little 'assignee.'" Jesse pressed his face to the screen, bending the mesh. "Doesn't he, Mars?"

He pulled the door open and Jordan poked his head around the corner. Our noses touched.

One by one, everyone drifted indoors, leaving Jordan and me alone by the fire. He added another log to the burning blaze, sending a cloud of fiery embers into the black sky. In the distance, the hollow sound of waves lapping against the wooden pylons of the pier echoed.

Jordan straddled the lounge behind me, his long legs crossing over and holding mine. "Are you warm enough?"

I patted his arms crossed over my chest, "I'm perfect. It's a beautiful night and I'm with the most sexy boy I know. What could be more perfect?"

"I can think of a couple of things." When his lips moved below my ear, I lengthened my neck for him to nibble. "We're back to pink, I see. I feel a restless night coming on."

"Are you looking down my shirt?"

Tiny puffs of air exited his nose with his quiet laugh, tickling my collarbone. "Possibly."

I twisted, capturing his smirk with my mouth. "You're hopeless."

"Hopelessly in love with you." He pulled me back against him, his head resting to the side of mine. After a couple of quiet seconds passed, he brought up his earlier question, dissolving my peaceful world. "Marli, how did you hurt your foot before? That's a gnarly scar."

"Nothing much to tell."

"Uh-huh. Try again." His teeth grazed my ear releasing a heated ripple to race through me. "Come on. It's only fair. You know my secret."

Jordan's intent on solving my puzzle scared me. What if he hated me for keeping the truth from him? He'd never trust me again. Worst of all, what if…he wouldn't want me anymore?

There were also new reasons to proceed with caution in unveiling my guarded past. Up to this point, Jordan's father remained a mystery. But with the truth revealed, I knew anything remotely questionable in Jordan's life could cause a scandal. His father held a position of power—one others wanted and would stop at nothing to get, including causing his family public disgrace. Nor would the embarrassment be mine to privately endure. My family and friends would suffer, not to mention the media blitz this could cause.

My own epiphany slapped. Only one option remained for me now. I had to leave Jordan before something happened that couldn't be undone. But first, he deserved the truth.

"You may not like me after I tell you," I replied quietly, my voice fracturing as my emotions chased the fear building inside me.

His arms hugged me tighter. "Marli, trust me, that's impossible."

Warily, I divulged the guarded story surrounding my entrance into the high profile Program, airing my family's dirty laundry before the son of the President of our nation. When I finished the story about the slice to the bottom of my foot and the one to my heart by my own mother, I was bawling and Jordan had grown silent.

He lifted my face and swiped the tears from my cheeks. His face glowed in the firelight, his eyes warm and compassionate, with no sign of judgment hidden in the flecks of gold edging his pupils. A single tear drew a shimmery trail over his cheek.

"Babe, I'm so sorry." His soft voice rang with sincerity. "How did you survive and stay so sweet? I'd be madder than hell. I *am* actually. I hate that someone hurt you like that. You were a child."

"I've learned to keep the anger buried." I twisted to look him in the eyes. No more hiding.

"Jordan, I came into The Program illegally. Chuck and Rick have worked hard to keep this confidential, but knowing your real identity and your father coming into an election year, if this information got out, it could ruin everything. Face it. I can't be your assigned candidate anymore. I'll call Mike in the morning to make arrangements to return home before this becomes public."

I touched the face mirroring my pain. "I'll always love you—to the moon and back."

Cautiously, I balanced on the least painful side of my foot. Jordan reached for me, but I hopped away from his outstretched arms. His brow twisted, a sudden look of horror washed over his face.

"You can't walk out of my life because of a damn technicality!" He tossed the lounger onto its side and clutched my shoulders, "You belong with me! I can't lose you again. Don't you understand, Marli? I'm not letting you go!"

I shrugged out of his grip. "You have to. It's better for everyone."

"I don't give a shit about anyone but you and me! The bastards in The Program can go straight to Hell along with whoever else thinks otherwise."

"Even your father? Are you that selfish, Jordan, to destroy his political career over me?"

"Don't you dare guilt me into agreeing with your crazy rationalizations. Besides, *they* can't hurt him if I drop out of The Program, which is exactly what I'm doing first thing tomorrow."

"You're not dropping out of The Program! I won't let you. Your position is too important. Mine's not. I'm merely a 'means to an end.' You'll find someone better—more *qualified*." He stepped forward and I backed away.

"Marli, I don't want anyone else. I want *you*!" His angry voice echoed across the bay. He yanked me back in his arms. "Your leaving will be the 'means to *my* end.'"

"You can't have me, Jordan," I stated quietly and severely. The truthfulness of my statement stung both of us, and to deepen the wound, I added, "I can't have *you*."

The slam of the screen door pierced the night, stopping our argument mid-breakdown. Jordan's father stood on the back patio, his acute expression reflected in the orange glow.

"You two okay out here? I heard shouting."

I pled with Jordan in the smallest voice I could find. "Jordan, please. I've suffered enough humiliation. Let me take this secret with me. If you truly love me, you'll let me go."

He dropped his arms and my heart stopped. He *agreed*!

When I reached the porch, Jordan's father offered a supportive arm, which I refused. By the time I limped to the top of the stairs, I couldn't hide the tears. Jesse opened his bedroom door and reached out to me, but I swatted his hand away and told him to leave me alone.

He bolted down the stairs yelling Jordan's name, and even buried beneath several pillows, I could hear them argue.

I'd ruined their relationship, too.

I gathered the crumpled bedspread around me, the fabric still damp from this afternoon's seductive teasing. The trust was out—the shock wave starting its devastating roll.

## 28
# FULL DISCLOSURE

Cloaked in darkness with only the light of a crescent moon filtering through the lace drapes, I rocked back and forth, the chair's wooden rungs grinding dust into the floorboards. Under the door, a ribbon of gold light stretched across the hardwood toward me. Several times I watched the shadow of Jordan's feet under the door, stopping, waiting, and disappearing, only to return a few moments later. He didn't knock or venture into the room. I wasn't sure I'd let him, if he did.

I pulled my knees to my chest and dropped my head against them. The tears dried up, but airy sobs still painfully punched my lungs. Earlier, I packed my bags and set them beside the door. When dawn colored the sky pink, I'd call Mike. I wanted to call Dad, but a phone call this time of night would give him a heart attack and cause him unnecessary worry. Nothing could be done to change things.

Soon the light under the door disappeared and a door shut at the end of the hall.

Silence.

Jordan gave up and my heart ached.

The sound of scraping metal outside piqued my curiosity. I rose from the rocker to peer out the window. Bright red glimmered beneath a skeleton of blackened cinder logs. A stubborn single flame licked one end. A long yellow band of light from the kitchen stretched onto the sand. To the side of the fire pit stood Jordan's father, hands deep in his pockets, studying the glowing embers. Soon he disappeared under the eaves of the patio. The screen door squeaked and the light turned off, leaving the fire nothing but a glowing ruby circle in the sand.

Emotionally exhausted, I moved onto the bed, pulling the afghan from the rocker over me. Tomorrow I'd return home and leave Jordan and his family to begin the process of finding a new candidate. The pain in my heart at the realization that someone else would spend their life wrapped in Jordan's arms, crushed me.

Once safely in Ohio, I'd call Chuck. Hopefully he could find a way to have me discreetly released from The Program so my secret stayed hidden. I wanted a fresh start at living life free of any further expectations or requirements. From now on, the complications and consequences of life would be of my own choosing and not from some manipulative plan. I was tired of existing as the square peg constantly pounded into a round hole.

Someone crept on the bed behind me and an arm slipped over my shoulder. Warm legs curled under me. I knew the feel of the hair on his arms, the size of his feet under mine, and the rhythm of the heart beating against my back. A gentle kiss on my bare shoulder confirmed my visitor's identity. I relaxed into Jordan's arms, drawing them tight around me one last time. Neither of us uttered a word nor moved a muscle. A hot, stray tear trickled over the bridge of my nose.

Jordan's breath blew warm against my neck, slow and steady inside a deep slumber. Carefully, I slipped from under his arm and crawled off the bed. Quietly slipping into the small walk-in closet, I changed into the khaki shorts and black shirt I laid out the night before. A pang of guilt hit me as I buttoned my shirt over the purple bra he teased me about yesterday.

Watching through the slit in the door at Jordan sleeping soundly, the edges of my dry eyes stung with unshed tears. Today, I'd leave the best thing to ever happen into my life, *again,* only this time, I couldn't return.

I took my "spy receptor" from the nightstand and tiptoed downstairs to make the dreaded call. The gurgling sound and rich aroma of freshly brewed coffee beckoned. I poured a cup to take out to the front porch and heard a flat clunk on the wooden kitchen table behind me. I wasn't alone.

"Marli? Could we talk before you make your call?" Jordan's dad scooted his chair away from the table and came to the side of me, topping his cup with fresh brew. "Let's go outside where we won't disturb anyone."

I slapped my chest to keep my pounding heart from leaping out. "You've got to quit scaring me! And what makes you think I'm calling someone?"

He smiled. "You're holding a receptor." He lifted the medical bag from the entry table and followed as I hobbled to the door. "I should also check your sutures." He dismissed the bodyguard standing erect to the side of the front door, although I felt certain more eyes watched.

The rockers from the front porch sat at the edge of the lawn, overlooking the ocean from above the stone breaker wall. I paused, suspicious of what appeared to be a planned discussion. Jordan's father surmised my tense demeanor.

"Yes, I've been waiting for you. I knew you'd wake early to make arrangements for your departure before anyone could sway you differently."

I gave him a wary, sideways glance.

President Banks grinned. "I make it my business to read people, Marli. Also, young love is very predictable, as are the parties involved." He held his arm out gesturing toward the intimate seating area, "Shall we?" He secured my elbow as I teetered off the steps.

The wind blew a few knots stronger this morning and a cool spray of water occasionally hit our faces when the waves splashed against the rocks below. "Looks like another storm brewing," he stated, making small talk.

He turned to me, resting his mug of coffee on the grass by his feet. "Marli, I want you to hear me out and then if you still want to leave, I'll personally take you to Miami this afternoon. I wanted to talk with you last night, but when I came upstairs, I saw Jordan sneak into your room. I decided to leave things be, hoping he could persuade you to change your mind."

I blushed at the thought of him knowing Jordan snuck into my room, and with everything else he seemed to know, he undoubtedly knew Jordan spent the night.

"Sir…Mr. Mason…I mean President Banks…*what* do I call you?"

"Whatever *you* are comfortable with is fine."

"Jordan and I…we're not, you know…*doing* anything."

"Marli, you're both adults and I trust, smart enough to keep things appropriate. It also appears Jordan didn't succeed in changing your mind."

"We didn't talk. When I left him by the fire, I begged him to let me go." The hurt look on Jordan's face would forever burn in my memory. "Trust me, Sir, you don't know the whole story, and it's best for everyone if it remains between Jordan and me. I don't want to leave Jordan. I love him, but I can't be a part of his life anymore."

Jordan's father shifted in his chair, both of us staring out at the foamy rolls of aqua blue heading for the shore. He took a long sip of coffee.

"You're wrong, Marli. I do know. Maybe not your version, but I've always known the circumstances surrounding your entrance into The Program. That's why we need to talk. I need to explain *my* side of your story."

Shock stole my breath and I dropped my mug on the grass. I watched the dark liquid bubble between green blades before disappearing into the sand.

"What?" The word carried on a whisper, lost in the wind.

President Banks lifted my toppled cup and leaned closer. "As I explained last night, Marli, I gave my children their mother's maiden name to protect them from the dangers associated with being a high profile public figure. My predecessor's family was murdered while he was in office."

Being only six years old when President Banks first took office, I didn't remember, but our history syllabus referenced the tragedy.

"Their birth certificates show 'Banks,' but those are the only documents reflecting their true name and they're sealed," he continued. "Anything of public record says 'Mason' and that's how the world knows them. Marli, you're now part of an elite circle knowing the truth, and whether you decide to stay with Jordan or not, I trust you'll keep this secret. Their lives and possibly *yours* depend on you taking this information to your grave, if necessary."

"I would never say anything. But if you know my secret, why did you allow Jordan to request me in the first place?"

He rocked gently, regarding me. "Marli, I know you understand the numbers game in The Program and their significance. When your impressive numbers entered the system, it alerted the upper echelon in The Program, the reports inevitably coming to me. I held a particular interest in the young ladies, knowing one of them may be matched with my sons.

"Jesse told me he discussed Kate's situation with you. If I'd paid closer attention as a parent, I might have averted that catastrophe. Now, it's a heartbreak I bear, and the guilt weighs heavily on me for not being a better father to my daughter."

He paused, finishing the last of what had to be cold coffee. "Marli, when I heard of your father's strong opposition to your entrance in The Program, I was intrigued. Most parents are thrilled to have a child selected. Your father's simple reasoning for you to live a normal, uncontrolled life humbled me. "

An unexpected tear escaped. "He's pretty amazing. My mom's betrayal crushed him. I don't think I can ever forgive her."

Jordan's father stopped rocking, his warm brown eyes considering. "Marli, please don't blame your mother, or even your grandmother. I have a confession to make, one no one is aware of, and I hope one you won't hold against me for too many years. Marli, dear, *I* played a part in manipulating your enrollment in The Program. I knew about your forged application, but I chose to look the other way."

My mouth and eyes competed for widest with surprise. He didn't pause for my reaction.

"You were raised with a set of principles and values almost lost to this world. When I discovered the uncanny similarities to yours and Jordan's genetic codes, I made the decision to circumvent the genetic selection pool and pulled your file. I personally entered your information through my private database, making your alignment with Jordan appear random on The Program's. Granted, the database would probably have made the same selection, but I couldn't chance it."

President Banks grinned at my reaction, "Don't get me wrong, I love my children more than life itself. Jesse's numbers were impressive, but his rebellious tendencies would eventually be his downfall. Jordan has always been our strongest child and I knew it would take a special girl to be his equal. *You.*"

He stared at the water. "When he acted so impetuously and all but handed you to Tony Peterson's son, I damn near died. Jesse would have been a better choice."

I reached over and touched his arm. "Why does everyone freak out about Jesse?"

Jordan's father moved to the ground in front of me, taking my foot in his hands. The medical bag clicked open and I winced in anticipation. He sprayed my stitches with some foam, dissolving them. He didn't look at me, but offered an explanation. One that shocked me.

"Marli, if you were, pardon me, intimate with Jesse and a child was conceived with perfect markers, The Program would have no jurisdiction to test the child."

I tried to yank my foot away—a reflex action to his shocking statement.

"*Test* a child?"

He relaxed his grip, but kept hold. "Genetic testing—for cloning."

"Clone a baby? What makes you think Jordan or I would allow it?"

"No, not an infant, and yes you will. It's in your contract."

"So that's the real purpose of The Program? To make a *fake* generation."

"No, to create an 'advanced civilization.' I'm sorry, but I can't discuss it further. I can assure you though, no harm would come to the child and as the parents, you'd become famous."

"I don't want to be famous. I want to be normal."

"My dear, a life with Jordan under any circumstances will never be *normal*. I have a hunch, however, your heart will never be content with anyone else."

"Jordan doesn't like the cloning idea."

"I know, but he's wise and takes commitment seriously. He'll follow through."

He re-bandaged my foot and set it on the cool grass. "I know I've given you a lot to think about, some things you probably don't like. Just keep in mind, Marli, it doesn't matter how you came into Jordan's life. It only matters that you did, and regardless of all the manipulation, Jordan falling in love with you happened naturally—no strings attached. He loves you hopelessly and last night he was prepared to throw away all his dreams to keep the only one he cares about, or wants—*you*."

When he stood, his shadow blocked the sun. "Promise me you'll consider what I've told you in a positive light. The boy upstairs in your bed will perish without you, Marli, and judging by the look in your eyes every time he comes near you, your life will be just as empty without him."

President Banks walked away, leaving me to process the information flooding my brain. I felt more confused than ever. Curling my legs under my chin, I stared at the waves turning over each other.

Could I ever be happy with anyone else living outside of The Program? Knowing Jordan would be living his life with someone else, sharing his lips, his body…giving her *his* kids, sent a frightening chill rippling through me.

But could what his father said about Jordan's willingness to throw away the life he carefully planned to be with me, be true? Could we be happy together *outside* of the government's clutches? No, not from what I overheard yesterday. Jordan would feel guilty about letting his father down.

My decision became clear. I'd stay with Jordan as long as he'd have me, even if my heart ended up broken…inside or outside of The Program.

The gentle touch of fingers stroking the side of my neck had me bend my head toward the sky. A beautiful angel peered down at me, his bronze hair aglow in a halo of sunlight.

"Hi," I whispered.

Jordan kissed me upside down on the lips. "Hi yourself."

He pulled me from the chair and onto the soft grass beside him. I nestled into the side of his neck, my senses swamped with his cologne. I pressed my lips to his warm skin, still damp from a morning shower, and his arms folded tenderly around me.

"I panicked when I woke this morning and you were gone," he said. "I almost called Mike to threaten his life if he didn't bring you back, but when I came downstairs, I saw you through the window sitting out here with Dad. Tell me you're staying, Marli. Please don't leave."

"I'm not leaving. Your father's pretty persuasive." I looked up, meeting Jordan's eyes, the color of rich emeralds in the morning sun. "He already knew." A wrinkle furrowed his brow and I brushed the crease to release the tension.

"What do you mean?"

"He knew my story—how I came into The Program. Jordan, did you know he hand-picked me for you?"

Jordan kissed my palm. "He told me he'd found someone special and someday, I'd meet her. At the time, I only cared about finishing high school, not finding a wife. When Mom pulled your portfolio for an interview, I figured my life was over and I'd be assigned some girl my parents believed appropriate. You looked cute, but digital images can be enhanced. Then Jesse sent me that picture of you in Kate's swimsuit and my knees buckled."

"You're such a sucker for girls in bikinis."

"Only for one girl." His fingers wrapped the back of my neck and drew my lips onto his. "So what else did you two discuss? It looked intense."

"Cloning."

Jordan rolled to the side. "Oh." We didn't say anything, just stared at the puffs of white clouds drifting across the cornflower blue sky. Jordan kissed my hand. "Puppies first, no matter what, I promise."

"Okay," I answered, feeling an instant rush of relief.

## 29
## CLOSE CALL

Leaves showered us in brilliant hues of oranges, blood reds, and neon yellows, each unique in shape, falling silently and turning crunchy under our steps. Autumn snowflakes that blanketed the earthen floor in a carpet of color—a carpet that covered the roots trailing from the base of trees, cording thick along the riverbank and across the trail.

"Ouch!" I stumbled over one such wooden snake, landing on my knees, the palms of my hands smacking the ground hard.

Jordan, who walked the path a few feet ahead of me while I lagged behind taking in the wonders of Fall, ran back and helped me to my feet. He brushed dirt and shredded bark off my kneecaps while I did the same off my hands, finally giving in and swiping my palms down the sides of my jeans. He plucked a golden oak leaf from the top of my head.

"You all right?" he laughed lightly.

"Guess I should pay better attention to where my feet are landing than the autumn leaves overhead. They're just so pretty with the sunlight peeking through."

He cranked his neck skyward as if seeing the explosion of color for the first time. "Wow. You're right. It's rather spectacular."

I linked my arms around his waist through the circles his made with his fists pressing his hips. "Close your eyes and tell me what you hear." He gave me a quizzical look. "Go on. You've spent way too much time inside lately. I want you to become 'one with nature' for a moment."

Jordan's mouth wiggled with a smirk, but he shut his eyes, his long dark lashes feathering in the creases of his laugh lines. "'One with nature,' huh?" he repeated sarcastically. He inhaled deep, his chest pushing against mine. "I hear the river washing over rocks behind us; a couple of birds chirping like they're arguing in the tree branches above; the buzz of a lawnmower because some poor schmuck still thinks you need to mow your lawn in October, and Brittany shrilling up by the falls, probably because a bee buzzed her."

"Or Gabe made a pass at her."

"That too." He pecked the tip of my nose. "Okay, your turn. Shut your eyes and tell me what you smell."

"Hmm, besides my favorite cologne on the skin of some hot guy standing close?" Jordan's laugh rumbled against my chest and a naughty thought flashed, one where we take a side trail into the thicket and never quite make it to Ithaca Falls.

Jordan jiggled me. I swear he read my mind. "Focus, Davis. 'One with nature,' remember?"

*One-on-one in nature sounded better.*

"Fine. The 'scents of autumn.' Well, I can smell the cut grass, now that you mentioned hearing the lawnmower; damp bark, but that may be from my knees, not the trees; something smoky—burnt wood…no, someone burning leaves." I inhaled another deep breath. "Dirt, but not dusty, more like wet soil; the musty scent moss has, and a spicy fragrance—something between cloves and sage."

Suddenly, an unwelcome scent, pungent and coming closer attacked my nose. "And a—"

"Skunk!" we both shouted. Jordan grabbed my hand. "Dammit! Run!"

By the time we'd raced far enough up the trail to be out of range, we were out of breath and laughing hard enough I worried I'd pee my pants. We hobbled up a small slope to a large rock and sat to catch our breath. The crashing sound of the falls in the background meant we weren't far from our destination.

I hadn't heard Brittany's voice for a while and wondered if Gabe had found a way to quiet her girly shrills, or if she'd fallen in the river and drowned. Knowing Jordan's friend and cloning research partner, Gabe Andrews, had a major crush on Brittany and this hike was an attempt to get her alone, I figured he may have succeeded in getting some personal attention.

"So do you think Gabe and Brit will hit it off?" I asked, reaching in my backpack for the orange slices I'd brought.

"I'd like to see her end up with someone decent. Gabe's a good guy, but he knows he's got to interview someone quick, or they'll make the decision for him."

"The Program can do that?" Jordan shoved an orange quarter in his mouth, smiling back at me with the rind bulging between his lips. "So mature. You look like a monkey." He started scratching under his armpits to prove my point and I slapped his arm. "Enough already!" He pulled me onto his lap, then deposited the eaten orange in my recycle bag.

"He's almost twenty-one and only interviewed two other girls, neither of which he liked. I know you hate when I remind you of the five-diamond thing, but if he thinks Brittany could be 'the one,' he'll probably do something about it before too long. Otherwise, yes, the 'forces that be' will choose his partner—probably another quinate-stoned princess."

"Oooh, I love it when you use big words!" I teased. "Maybe he could get assigned Heather."

Jordan kissed the side of my head. "Let's not go there, Marli. Leave the past buried, please, for both our sakes." Before I could object, he placed two fingers over my eyes and pulled my lids down. "Okay, one more nature challenge. Tell me what you feel."

"Feel?"

"Yes. Describe what Fall feels like."

I leaned against him, turning my face to the afternoon sun and pulled his arms tighter around me. Perched on a rock next to a river only a couple of miles from my new apartment, living independently and hundreds of miles from my worrisome father, wrapped in the arms of the boy I loved with all my heart, I couldn't feel anything but contentment.

My dreams were starting to materialize. Cornell's veterinarian medicine program was top in the nation; my best friend agreed to be my roommate so I didn't get homesick; and Jordan and I were finally at a place in our relationship where our future looked solid—a place I could accept as my forever-after, even if under the scrutinizing eyes of The Program.

"Crisp," I answered. "Cool, frosty, yet warm, mostly because I imagine sitting by a fire sipping hot chocolate. The air feels 'settled.'

"Settled?" Jordan asked, setting his chin on top of my head, his focus also on the river weaving a wrinkled path down the canyon a few feet away.

"Yeah, settled; calmer. Summer is jam-packed with activity and so much energy that when Fall finally comes around and everyone gets back into a routine with school, or whatever, it's like Mother Nature takes a deep breath and cuddles under a blanket to wait for winter."

"Wow, babe, that sounds amazing. You sure you don't want to be a writer instead of a vet?"

"I need money. Authors struggle for a long time before making any money, if ever."

"Marli, you know—"

"Don't, Jordan. We talked about this at the beach house. Like you said, let's not go there."

He heaved a heavy sigh. "Just know the option is there."

A long silence followed his statement, neither of us moving. The sun slipped behind a wandering cloud and the river changed from a sparkly clear ribbon to a dark, mossy one. Brittany and Gabe's voices, along with several other hikers taking advantage of the unseasonably warm October Saturday, echoed through the canyon.

Jordan's lips caressed my ear in a soft whisper. "I love you."

I turned and straddled his hips. "Close your eyes."

He did, but his mouth pushed his dimples deep with a mischievous grin. His hands cupped my butt and held me against him, a familiar stirring evident. "I'm really starting to like this game."

"Shhh. We only have a few minutes left before we're discovered." I kissed his mouth, then each eyelid. "Tell me what Fall *tastes* like." I grazed my teeth along his jaw. I knew Brit and Gabe might reach us shortly and Jordan wouldn't be able to act on any sudden urges, which made my seductive tease all the more fun. I loved moments when I wielded power.

"Apple cinnamon crumble," Jordan squeaked, his voice dropping from soprano to bass on the word *apple*. He cleared his throat, the hard swallow rolling between my lips as I nibbled his neck. "Meg's pumpkin pie with real whipped cream." A couple more hard swallows dropped when I licked his earlobe. He widened his legs a tad and adjusted our position. I smiled and pressed a light kiss to the sensitive skin in front of his ear.

"What else, I whispered, watching the shiver of gooseflesh pebble up his neck.

"Oatmeal."

I pulled back. "Oatmeal?" His hand wrapped the back of my neck and he crushed his lips to mine. I'd been outsmarted.

"*You* are my all-season-favorite-flavor.'"

Our brownstone apartment building was located 2 miles off campus, the perfect distance for a brisk walk to school when Jordan had early lab classes and couldn't give me a ride. He had a pass to park on campus where I, in the interest of saving money, chose to forgo the cost until winter quarter. Brittany's class schedule only matched mine two days of the week, so she caught a shuttle most mornings.

Farther up our quiet street sat Jordan's apartment building—slightly more upscale than ours. Turned out Jordan's building, mine, and two fraternity houses were included in the real estate portfolio held in SpringCor. Jordan's apartment had also been the private residence for his grandfather and father during their attendance at Cornell, which explained the professional decorating not common to the majority of college students.

"Dinner's ready," Brittany called out, carrying the pan steaming with her signature spinach lasagna. I followed with the tossed salad, placing it on our small round kitchen table, next to the garlic bread.

"Smells wonderful," Gabe commented following behind Jordan.

We'd shooed the two of them out of our tiny kitchen to discuss whatever guys talked about in our living room while we cooked and chatted about them.

Gabe brought a six pack of beer to share, but I knew Jordan to be a bit of a beer snob and had only drank half his bottle to be polite. Gabe downed his first and currently worked on a second. Brittany nursed some from a glass as she worked on the lasagna, which Alex would have loved. I stuck with my diet soda.

Jordan had a bottle of red wine chilling in the refrigerator and he poured everyone a glass, including me, to breathe while we put dinner on the table. One of the many forms of social etiquette I'd come accustomed to with Jordan's lifestyle, even though he knew I wouldn't drink mine.

"Brit is quite the gourmet cook," Jordan touted, holding my chair for me. "Next to playing Marli's guard dog, I'd say it's her second strongest talent." Gabe stood looking confused and Jordan quickly grabbed Brittany's chair to give him the hint before explaining his comment. "She's worried I'll steal her best friend's innocence with my lecherous tactics."

I scooped some salad, avoiding Brittany's glower and smiled at Gabe. "Jordan's exaggerating. It's my father who wants me to be the oldest virgin to ever live." Everyone laughed, but when Jordan sat next to me, I kicked him under the table.

Jordan and Gabe insisted on doing the dishes after dinner. Brittany excused us to do laundry while they finished up—an obvious ploy to get me alone. I followed her lead and gathered my dirty clothes, shrugging my shoulders at Jordan when his brows pulled together. Gabe droned on about football stats, probably unaware we'd even left the apartment.

Once we each loaded our clothes in separate washers, I perched on an empty one, crossing my dangling legs. "So, what's up? Don't you like Gabe?"

She eased a hip on the folding table. "He'd nice enough and an okay kisser, but that's not the problem."

I focused instantly on his kissing abilities. "You kissed him?"

She waved her hand dismissively. "Yeah, well, it wasn't like you and Jordan were going to join us anytime soon at the falls."

"We made it to the falls."

"Yeah, for like two seconds before it started getting dark. Point is, when Gabe did make a move, I thought what the heck? Beats standing here watching a waterfall for hours."

"You made out with him? Like *made out*?"

Brittany blew a loud sigh. "No, not like you're thinking. We just kissed…a lot. But nothing else. Besides, I just pretended he was somebody else."

I jumped off the washer and planted both hands on the stainless steel table. "Brittany Johnson, you're holding out on me. What's going on?"

Her fingernails nervously tapped the metal between us and she gazed about the fluorescent lit room. "While you were at Jordan's beach house, I sort of interviewed with someone."

"Sort of?"

She twirled circles on the shiny surface. "A video interview, due to geographic distance. Nothing's set in stone, although we've kept contact."

Brittany's last interview—the one right after her eighteenth birthday—didn't happen because her father insisted she graduate from high school first. Even though she was at the age of consent, because she still went to high school and lived at home, The Program respected her parents' wishes. She briefly told me of one she did in Chicago for some law student, but never elaborated on the details. She received the standard impersonal rejection letter, so I never pushed to find out more. Alex said she wouldn't talk about it with her, either. To discover she'd had another interview and appeared all starry-eyed, gave me hope her self-confidence had returned.

"Brit that's awesome!"

She leveled her eyes to mine and something in her obsidian irises made me uneasy. "You may not think so after I tell you with whom." She waited a beat and took a big breath. "I interviewed with Doug."

"Peterson?" Jordan bellowed from the doorway.

"Shit," Gabe said under his breath behind Jordan. He pushed off the doorframe. "I'm going to take off."

"No!" I glared at Brittany before grabbing Jordan's hand. "You stay and we'll leave. You two need to talk."

When the elevator doors closed, Jordan turned to me. "How could she?"

"It's none of our business, Jordan."

He leaned back, his fist punching the wall behind him. "I don't want him in your life, not even by way of a third party. How did he find her, anyway? Her numbers aren't remotely close to Doug's. His dad would never allow him to interview with anyone else, especially with you still available."

I released Jordan's hand immediately and stared at our reflections in the doors we faced. "Well, that is a problem. Still, it's Brittany's life." I hung my head and scuffed my shoe against the floor. "I gave Doug Brittany's candidate number when I left Italy. Now that I know more about him, I wished I hadn't."

Jordan reclaimed my hand. "Me too."

The old water pipes clanked in the wall separating my bedroom from the bathroom, jolting us awake. We'd crammed for finals every night this week until after midnight. The last two nights, however, exhaustion won out and we'd fallen asleep in our clothes.

"Damn! I fell asleep again." He stretch his six-foot-three body out with a loud groan. "Remind me to call someone about that pipe."

I reached across his chest and hugged him tighter. "Five more minutes," I begged, refusing to open my eyes. "If you fix the pipe, we'll never wake up."

Jordan rolled me beneath him. "And that would be a bad thing?"

He pulled the quilt over our heads and nuzzled into my neck, his unshaven whiskers pricking my skin. "You're tickling me," I giggled, rubbing my hand against his bristly cheek.

He kissed my palm. "Let's go someplace this weekend, just the two of us."

"And what kind of flowers would you like on your grave when Rick finds out? Did you forget I'm driving Brittany home to pick up her car? Rick's last call also sounded like he could use a visit, and if I go to Florida with you for Thanksgiving, I won't see him until Christmas." Jordan flipped on his back curling me into the crook of his arm. I traced the letters spelling *Cornell* across his chest. "You could come with us. There's plenty of room."

"I'm not sure my manhood would survive riding in your pink car."

His statement felt more like an insult than a tease. "If you truly loved me, the color of my car wouldn't matter."

Jordan leaned toward me and pushed his fingers through my tangled hair, his tone serious. "You know how much I care for you. Of course I'll go with you. I don't give a damn if your car is covered in sequins as long as I'm in it with you." A dangerous grin slid sideways and a hand slipped under my T-shirt. "Then again, we could go buy you a new car. An early Christmas present?"

I tightened my fingers around his wrist. "You're crazy if you think I'd ever accept something so expensive from you."

Little puffs of air blew against my neck from his chuckling. "I'm joking, babe," he whispered. "But you should know," he warned over the shell of my ear, "I intend to spoil you rotten..." his hand moving to a familiar place that made my body buzz, "seduce you every chance I get..." his mouth sliding over mine, "and someday..." his lips sealing over mine, "paint your car black."

Rick's face revealed his disappointment when I walked through the backdoor of the clinic, towing Jordan. He and Karen were in the middle of making bottles for a kennel full of whimpering puppies. I dropped to my knees, opening the cage door. Four furry balls toppled over each other in their escape. I wrangled a solid black one, but the other three scampered across the slick tile floor. Dad shot me a disapproving glower.

"Thanks. Now I've got to round them up again."

"Where's 'momma?'"

"She's got an intestinal infection I'm trying to clear up. She's sedated in a kennel in the back."

The wandering mutts wriggled out of Karen's hands as fast as she gathered them. Jordan managed to corner two, another little rascal pulling the corner of his T-shirt with his teeth. He laughed, rolled a brown spotted critter on his back and rubbed his tiny tummy. Not wanting to be left out, the others tumbled in Jordan's arms where he corralled them until Karen placed them in a warming box for feeding.

Jordan cradled the spotted puppy he held close. "Not this one. He's my fav."

Rick handed him a bottle. "If you're holding, you're feeding." I raised a brow to my dad, who returned my scowl with another bottle. "Same goes for you, Pumpkin."

"Hand me another pup," Jordan challenged, ignoring Rick's curt tone.

Karen placed another wiggly one in the bend of Jordan's free arm and once his fingers pressed the bottle to his snout, the puppy settled next to his brother and ate.

Rick regarded Jordan carefully, his knitted brows relaxing. "You're a natural. Next spring, I'll take you out to the Miller farm and you can help me castrate sheep."

"Dad!"

"Rick!" Karen scolded.

Dad's eyes watered he laughed so hard, and once Jordan caught on, he joined in. To me, the joke meant he'd officially accepted Jordan.

Jordan slept in Daniel's old room in the basement and I lay restless twenty-three stairs and thirty-one footsteps away on the second floor. We exchanged steamy instant messages most of the night and napped together in the overstuffed chair, basked in afternoon sun pouring through the front window.

Sunday, before the gunmetal gray shadows yielded to the sherbet spray of dawn, my bedroom door creaked slightly. Half asleep, I pulled my pillow over my head. "I'm not putting Muffy out," I grumbled, waiting for Rick's plea. I drifted back to dreamland before hearing the reply…but not before I felt the kiss on the back of my neck.

"Okay, you don't have to put Muffy out."

Jordan slipped my camisole strap off my shoulder and his lips caressed the vacant spot. I turned in his arms, our legs braided together and lips engaged in sultry wake-up kisses. Only when oxygen became necessary did we stop to breathe. My hands pressed his bare chest, feeling his lungs swell.

"We're playing a dangerous game, Jordan."

"You mean with Rick asleep across the hall?" His hands cupped my head, another mind-blowing kiss stealing my breath.

"I mean it's getting harder to keep from going too far," I whispered against his mouth.

"Shhh. Give me five more minutes to convince you I don't give a damn."

My guardian angel stood watch because Rick's alarm sounded, icing down the fire smoldering. "You better get back downstairs."

Jordan pecked my lips one last time before climbing out of my bed. I snuggled into the pillow still holding the smell of his hair and curled into the warm spot where his body had been moments ago.

*Too close.*

# 30
## BARTERING

The eleven o'clock hour flashed on the dash readout when we pulled off the interstate. Jordan tugged my hand to his mouth when we started down the street toward our apartments.

"Marli, stay with me tonight. I'll wake you early enough to go home and get ready for school."

The soft touch of his fingers drawing tiny circles on the back of my neck didn't help my resolve. After this morning, the thought of being alone with Jordan conjured up several devilish thoughts, all surrounded with caution tape. However, I'd reached a point under his touch where I no longer cared and parked the car against the curb in front of his complex.

He leaned over the console and seared my lips with a victorious kiss.

"Promise to behave?" I felt his smile on my mouth. His arm circled my shoulders and drew me against his shoulder while he pursued his persuasion technique. Summoning my last shred of willpower, I pushed away. "Jordan, I'm serious."

"I'll agree to anything, just don't go home." My pulse quickened at the husky tone of his voice.

"You get to call Brittany."

The light rain showers that started earlier in the evening had turned to sheets of water waving sideways in the headlights. "Stay put. I'll get your door."

He was soaked in the few seconds it took to get from one side of the car to the other.

We ran across the front lawn, so saturated it actually splashed. The gray and white marble floor inside qualified as an ice rink. I grabbed the sleeve of Jordan's shirt when my leg precariously flipped into the air. He latched onto me, wrenching my shirt sideways. Loose buttons scattered everywhere.

"Blue, my favorite color." Too late to cover my exposed bra.

"They're all your favorite color." I joked, knotting my shirttails across my chest.

Once inside his apartment, I placed my soggy shoes next to Jordan's on the gray drip mat protecting the granite entry floor. Jordan tugged his wet polo shirt over his head and dropped it onto the arm of one of the overstuffed burgundy leather chairs that faced a small white leather sofa. I doubted I'd ever be comfortable in the lavish lifestyle Jordan lived. He was completely unaware how what felt normal to him, intimidated everyone else.

My damp bare feet sank into the heavily-padded gray carpet and I contemplated staying rooted where I stood when Jordan turned on the fireplace and dimmed the lights. The firelight bounced off his naked torso as he lit a smattering of candles encased in colorful red and turquoise glass jars lined across the mantle. Music played softly from various speakers hidden in the room. He glanced at me, a calculated smile holding a promise to push limits, linked between dimples.

The hormonal side of my brain locked away the common sense side immediately.

Jordan lowered onto the black fur rug in front of the fire and tipped his head in an invitation for me to join him in the intimate setting. A shiver shimmied over me, more from nervousness than the chilled air when I eased down beside him. He fingered a damp curl draping over my brow.

"You're soaked, babe." Another quivering tremble snaked over my body. "And chilled." His arm circled my shoulder and he tried to pull me close, but I pressed my hand to his chest. A warm chest. Even the soft dusting of hair that started between his pecs and trailed South, felt hot and dry beneath my fingertips—fingertips that seemed to have a mind of their own as they drew slow circles across Jordan's upper body. His eyes took on a dreamy haze, his mouth pulling into a small, sexy bow that deepened the dimples.

A throaty voice I didn't recognize spoke through my mouth. "My shirt's wet. And you're dry."

Jordan leaned in, his gaze locked on my lips, which suddenly felt dry. I licked them, pulling my bottom lip back into my mouth with my tongue's retreat. Jordan's thumb tugged it from my teeth and stroked the sensitive skin in a lazy caress. His dark eyes locked me in a sexy stare as he laid his mouth softly against mine—still slack and open. The tip of his tongue traced the inside of my lips and I couldn't remember taking a breath, nor did I want to and break the spell.

"You could take the shirt off," he whispered, beckoning my tongue to come play. He undid the two buttons that hadn't popped off. The shirt lay open, his hand wrapping the back of my neck and eyes holding mine hostage. "Or I could."

I think I mumbled *okay,* although it may have been my thoughts begging him to. Without stopping the seductive tease between our mouths, he slipped his hands inside my blouse and eased the fabric off my shoulders. Fingertips caressed my arms encouraging flickers of heat to ignite places his hands didn't touch. One lone finger drew a line from the shell of my ear, slowly down my neck, meeting the swell of my breast and dipping under the edge of my lace bra.

His touch, soft, yet deliberate, became my sole focus. The warmth inside my body overpowered the heat of the fire blazing a few feet away. Moist lips tasted my bare shoulder, my bra strap now hanging in a loose sling on my arm and Jordan's hand splayed between my shoulder blades, waiting permission to remove the blue lace contraption straining against my heavy breaths.

Jordan had seen me in a bra, explored my chest with tender hands many times, always with consent, but over fabric, fingertips sweeping barely beneath lace-trimmed edges. Never had his palms touched the sensitive skin or his mouth traveled beyond where his fingers traced. At this moment, however, with the firelight illuminating the dewy sheen glittering on Jordan's naked chest; his dark eyes holding mine hostage in visual foreplay, and hungry kisses I wanted feasting on my body, *any* fabric barrier was subject to removal.

I pulled Jordan on top of me as I lay in the furry cushion beneath us. Snap. One hook released.

"Jordan, wait," I panted against his mouth.

"What if I can't?" he asked, his breath on my neck triggering a rush of gooseflesh. The hard ridge pressing my stomach hinted this might be true. He pulled his hand from behind my back leaving one tiny metal bracket as the only guard to the lace barrier separating my skin from Jordan's searing touch—something I suddenly craved.

Jordan's mouth moved over my ear. "I want you, Marli. All of you."

He always teased, but his tone, the way the words filled me, told me this time it was for real. Jordan wanted to go all the way—break all the rules.

"I-I'm not sure—"

He stroked between my legs—something he'd *never* done before and I knew he felt the lie I'd spoken when my body rose to meet his touch. My eyes disappeared deep their sockets and I mashed a hungry kiss to his mouth when my body responded to the awakening flames of heat licking every nerve ending.

Suddenly, I understood the sensation of *need* I'd only read about on steamy pages of romance novels, or listened to Alex drone on about in hushed whispers to David on her cell receptor when she thought no one listened. I wished I'd paid attention because I'd entered uncharted territory without any direction other than to follow uncontrolled impulses—like smoothing my hand over the bulge in the front of Jordan's jeans.

The moan traveling over my tongue from somewhere deep in his chest sent shivers bubbling over my skin. When my fingers stilled, he begged me not to stop, his ragged breathing only encouraging the fervor holding me hostage.

Jordan popped the top snap of my jeans open and tugged the zipper down, but when his fingers dipped into the lace edge of my panties, the common sense subconscious I'd buried deep, broke free and rushed forward.

*Stop Marli!*

*I don't want to*, I mentally argued, unzipping Jordan's pants.

*You want more—the whole fairytale—hearts, roses—the promise of something beyond tonight—*

Two more seconds and my sanity would surrender and I'd give in to Jordan, to my body, to whatever I had to do to douse the scorching fire before it consumed me and turned me to ash.

*You want the happy-ever-after—something special—a "forever love."*

I clamped Jordan's hand and shut my lips against his. The words "I can't" were barely audible and I took the first deep breath I remembered inhaling since I walked in the room. Jordan said nothing, his body heavy over mine and breath hot on the nape of my neck. His arms spread outward over the carpet; wings holding prey in place. Slowly, he rolled off to the side, silent and gaze fixed on the ceiling.

Unaware my jeans had slipped, or been pulled down, exposing part of my backside to the woolen rug, I felt an unexpected blush of embarrassment and tugged them back over my hips. Jordan's chest still rose and fell with exaggerated breaths; the only sign of "life" given he remained motionless.

I crawled to the sofa, pulled off the lap quilt his grandmother had made him, and wrapped into a cocoon in the corner. My body ached, possibly with regret, and the tingles eased, but the feeling of where Jordan's hand had caressed still burned. Curling into my familiar protective position, I squeezed my thighs, not to erase the sensation, but to keep it trapped.

Jordan lie a few feet away, a *sizable* change in his silhouette against the fire resurrecting the memory of the first time we talked about sex. The fear that my first time could, in all likelihood, be painful appeared a real possibility.

He yanked his zipper closed and turned his head my direction as if reading my thoughts and my cheeks warmed. "You okay?" he asked, his voice raspy but full of genuine concern.

The sting of tears pricked my eyes. "I'm sorry," I mumbled. "I know I frustrate you, and tonight I really—"

Jordan was next to me before I completed the sentence. After spending the summer together, he knew better than to unfold me when my knees pressed beneath my chin. Cautiously, he reached out and fingered a loose curl.

"Marli…babe, I don't want you to ever feel guilty about shutting me down. I will never push for more than you're willing to give, got that?"

"I know," I answered into the fabric bunched around my face.

He leaned against me, perching his head on my knees. "Sweetheart, when the time is right for *both* of us, it will be amazing. Tonight, just isn't that time." His thumb swiped my wet cheeks. "I love you, Marli Davis, but more important, I respect you."

Jordan stood and held out his hand. "Come on." I let him tug me into his bedroom, dragging my quilt cape as I walked. The bed had been neatly turned down with not so much as a crease in the pillowcases. He turned on the lamp sitting on the night table before walking over to his dresser and retrieving a navy blue T-shirt from the drawer for me.

He pressed a light kiss to my forehead. "I'm sleeping on the couch." His finger pushed my lips when I started to object. "Lock the door behind me."

"Jordan, what are we going to do about us?" I risked asking before he closed the door.

He scrubbed a hand through his unruly locks. Only a ghost of a smile moved his lips, which worried me. "I've got an idea, but it's late and I don't have enough hearts and roses. Now lock the door and get some sleep."

When I'd walked out Jordan's bedroom the next morning, he'd already showered and was in the process of making my favorite mocha frappe. I raised my hand as a signal for silence, relishing the first delicious sip, loudly slurping the whipped cream bubble through my lips.

"I don't want to talk about last night," I announced.

"But we need to discuss what happened, Marli. This thing between us is..."

"What? Spinning out of control?"

He removed his espresso from the beverage maker and took the seat across the table from me.

"I was going to say 'amazing,' but apparently we share different points of view."

I sensed him edging me into a deep discussion, slash, argument, but all I wanted was to go home. My stomach had that weighted, gassy feeling, and I couldn't think of anything more humiliating than experiencing an attack of diarrhea in Jordan's immaculate bathroom. Some things could definitely wait to be shared until we'd been together like a hundred years.

Mocha droplets spattered the placemat when I suddenly planted my cup on the table. "I think I better go home."

Of course Jordan jumped to conclusions. "Why? You still have a half hour. Did I do something?"

Gross gurgling sounds stirred between my spine and belly. "No, I just don't feel well. The heaviness settled lower in my abdomen and I sensed time running out. I left the front door open in my hasty retreat and didn't even stop to kiss Jordan goodbye—just made a beeline for my car.

When I barreled through the door to our apartment, Brittany jumped.

"You scared the crap out of me!"

"Don't use the word 'crap' and 'out' together right now." She giggled with understanding until I doubled over from a sharp pain. Diarrhea apparently wasn't my issue. "Damn! I forgot my stupid shot!" Another severe pain gripped my insides. "My stupid period just started."

Menstrual shots lasted three months, but if you forgot one, you suffered a monstrous cycle. There were meds to counter the effects of a mindless blunder, shortening matters to a mere three days, but the first twenty-four hours were murder. My shot due date passed two days ago while we were in Maple Heights. The tiny syringe of magic serum still sat in bathroom drawer.

"Marli Davis, where's your head? How hard can it be to remember a measly shot? Now you'll be sick all day."

"I guess with finals coming up and studying to the point of exhaustion, I just forgot.

"More like studying Jordan Mason, if you ask me. Nice shirt by the way. Do I even want to know what happened to yours?"

*Probably not.* When the next cramp cinched, I felt the wetness and raced for the bathroom. *Next life, I'm coming back as a guy!*

"At least you're not pregnant," Brit hollered through the bathroom door.

*Not yet* my judgmental conscious chanted. I peeled my soiled clothing off, tossed them in my hamper and programmed the shower for fifteen minutes. Remembering I had one last report due tomorrow before the quarter ended, I cracked the door and called out to Brittany.

"Hey, can you call Jordan and have him download my psych lecture?"

Brittany's face filled the crack and I squealed. "*I* can get your assignments. Take a day off from Jordan and rest. There's some cramp medicine in the cabinet. I'll cook dinner tonight, but no Jordan, got it?"

"Yes Master," I snipped, shutting the door and hurrying for the sanctuary of warm water.

The medicine kicked in almost instantly, dulling the pain somewhat and making me sleepy enough I decided to go back to bed. I wound in a towel, walked out of the bathroom...and screamed.

"Jordan!"

His dark eyes swept over me standing in the doorway, wrapped in nothing but terry cloth. "Damn Marli. I think I've lost the feeling in my legs."

My heart bounced in my chest and my body felt weird, in a hot way. I clutched the towel tighter. He kept staring, slowly moving his eyes from my bare toes to my blue eyes so intimately, I squirmed.

"You ran out so fast you forgot your cell receptor. When no one answered the door, I let myself in and was laying it on the counter when you walked out."

"You should have yelled out before walking in the apartment uninvited. You scared me. And what if Brit had been home?" She had no idea Jordan had a key so he could bypass the security system and sneak in after lockdown.

Jordan scrubbed the back of his neck. "In my defense, she instant messaged your phone asking if you wanted chicken noodle or vegetable soup, so I figured you must be really sick and wanted to check on you." His eyes lifted slowly, undressing me as he stepped closer. "When I walked in, the place was quiet and I thought you might be asleep."

I backed against the wall and he leaned on his arm to the side of my head. His fingers traced a water droplet trickling over my naked shoulders.

"Are you contagious?"

My head felt dizzy, either from the medication or Jordan standing so close. "Would it matter?"

His Adams Apple bounced several times. "Not really."

"Trust me, I'm safe," my voice fading when he leaned down, lips parted and almost on mine. When they finally touched, they felt like they were on fire, and my mouth melted against them.

He broke the kiss and spoke in shallow breaths, hot against my cheek. "You're making me crazy, here. Tell me you'll be better by this weekend."

"Yes, Mr. 'One-Track-Mind.' Only a temporary situation."

"I'm hurt," he grinned. "While kissing you is my favorite pastime, there's something else I want to share with you." He laughed when I quirked my eyebrows. "Now who's got the dirty mind?" He kneaded my hips. "Skydiving, Miss Davis. For my birthday present.

I jumped back, smacking the wall. "Ouch! Skydiving? No way! Something else—anything."

His knee pushed between my thighs. "Anything?" I gulped hard and his lips curled. He'd won. "We'll tandem jump. You'll be fastened to me and I'll control the parachute." His lips found the sweet spot below my ear and I turned to putty in his hands. "For me? Please?"

"Fine, I surrender, but for the record, you play dirty. Skydiving? I must really love you!" I'd have to come up with something monumental before the weekend to change his mind.

*Silly girl. You're asking for a miracle to happen.*

He placed the sweetest kiss on my lips, his voice genuinely humble. "I certainly hope so, and 'thanks for playing,' babe. You won't regret it, I swear."

*Too late.*

Jordan's arms wrapped me to him and I leaned into the curves of his body. His lips burned against mine, urgent and demanding.

My current predicament nudged a reminder when a cramp clenched deep, freezing the embers of heat starting to build. I crumpled against Jordan gasping.

"Marli?"

"I need to lie down."

"What's wrong? You're pale as a ghost."

No way to avoid the embarrassing revelation. "I'm fine, really. Just a consequence for my absentmindedness." His forehead wrinkled. "My period started, okay? I forgot to take my shot and now I'm paying royally."

Instead of recoiling from the grossness of my situation, he wrapped an arm around my shoulders and ushered me to my bedroom. "Put on your sweats and I'll make you some tea."

"No, you need to get to school."

"For once, let me take care of you—please? Dressed. Tea. Jordan leaves and worries about you all day, in that order. Okay?" I managed a weak smile and nodded before he pulled my door closed.

When I stumbled sleepily out of the bedroom, the teapot sat on the table alongside a cup and saucer. A hand-drawn sketch of a tulip stuck out of a glass in the center and I smiled at Jordan's romantic creativeness, feeling tender emotions building. The note tucked in my teacup summoned hormone-driven tears.

*Feel better my sweet girl. Love ya—to the moon and back.*

## 31
## EXPECTING THE UNEXPECTED

Paralyzed. The perfect description of my present state of being, with Jordan's birthday fast approaching and some idiotic promise looming I'd made in a hormone-crazed moment. I couldn't believe I agreed to tether myself to Jordan's body and plummet to the earth from an airplane.

*No more making promises when only wearing a towel and kissing Jordan...or fully dressed and kissing Jordan...or while kissing Jordan, period.*

Later this afternoon, we'd board an air train to Florida for the Thanksgiving holiday, combined with celebrating Jordan and Jesse's birthday. I had one hour to finish packing before Jordan's class ended and my attention demanded elsewhere.

Anxiety carved a niche in my already overloaded brain. This would be my first visit to the penthouse since my interview. I wondered if Jordan would act different there compared to the beach house. We would undoubtedly be under more scrutinizing eyes, but my biggest worry? I wouldn't fit in with his family.

My car seemed to go on autopilot when I pulled into my apartment complex, naturally heading for the parking stalls behind the first building. I rounded the corner and slammed on the brakes. Parked in *my* space sat a black monster jeep with *Alaska* license plates.

Damn! Douglas Peterson kept reappearing like a bad penny. He leaned against the jeep dressed in black jeans and a flashy ski coat—dazzling. I'd barely climbed out of my car before he hovered too close for comfort.

"Doug, why are you here?"

"Ouch. Missed you too. Sorry 'Ice Princess,' but I'm not here for you." His gaze slowly roved my body, a brow arching with his tweaked-up mouth, probably following a disgusting thought. "Then again…"

"Seriously, what brought you down from the arctic?"

"First, I didn't come from Alaska. I'm attending Dartmouth—decided to expand my major and take some pre-med courses. Second, not that it should matter to you because you've made it very clear I don't *matter*, but I'm here to see Brittany—Number 4233, remember? We've kept in touch since our video interview."

*Why hasn't she said anything?* Because Jordan and I jumped down her throat when she revealed who she interviewed for. Why would she say anything and risk being attacked again?

"I didn't know you two had a thing going." *Brit said "kept in touch"….not involved.*

He reached around me, his hand sliding over mine and grabbing the cloth bags with my purchases. I hated the surprise prick jangling my nerves when he touched me.

"We don't. We're keeping things casual."

He motioned to the doors requiring my key code to open. Once inside, he took inventory of the cameras positioned in the corners of the entry—ones I'd never noticed being there before. When he followed me into the elevator, he made a point of facing the one over the keypad.

"Brit hasn't talked about the interview. I assumed neither of you were interested."

"We don't want to rush into something we'll regret later," he answered, his eyes trained on me.

"Nice payback." He smirked at my acknowledgement. "What does your dad think?"

"He doesn't know."

"Don't let him hurt Brittany."

"My father isn't an animal, Marli." I lifted a brow in disbelief. "Let me handle my own life—the one you want no part of, remember?"

"Brittany is my friend."

"And mine. She's a big girl and perfectly capable of making her own decisions...unlike someone else we both know."

The elevator bumped slightly and opened.

"You can stop the personal attacks." He followed me into the apartment without an invitation, placing the bags on the counter. "And I've got Brit's back, like it or not."

"I don't doubt it. Just keep in mind your boundaries, now that you *know*," he warned.

My lips folded under tightly in frustration. I knew I couldn't say anything to Brittany about Tony Peterson's manipulative tactics without raising questions I'd sworn to never answer.

I tensed when Doug tugged the collar of my jacket, helping me shrug it off. When I turned, I found myself trapped between him and the entry wall. He gently touched my cold cheek.

"*Rude* becomes you."

I slapped his hand away.

"Brit shouldn't be too much longer."

He settled back on a kitchen chair with exaggerated casualness, one leg crossing the knee of the other in a smug posture. His jutted chin and arrogant smirk radiated superiority. He knew me to be too polite to kick him out, although that would be the smart thing.

"I have a confession. I knew Brittany would be late and hoped to find you alone so we could catch up."

"It appears I don't have a choice…again." Hardly two months had passed since the ninety-day freeze ended, formally releasing me from Doug's hold. "Something to drink?" If his hands held something they'd be less likely to reach for me.

"Tea sounds great."

I programmed the beverage maker and carried the personal items I'd bought to the suitcase lying open on the sofa. He followed, dominating my personal space again.

"Going somewhere?"

I moved a half-step, exposing the contents. "Florida for Thanksgiving. It's also Jordan's birthday this weekend."

Doug reached into my suitcase, retrieving the top to my little black bikini, the bead accented ribbon ties dangling between his fingers. "I can only imagine how hot you look in this. Jordan must go crazy when you wear it."

He played with a ribbon streamer while his mind drifted elsewhere. Unfortunately, I knew the memory he walked through. "Reminds me of another bikini—one with ties similar to these. The kind that slip apart easily. Remember Marli?"

My heart pounded as I recalled the same moment. "Yes, I remember," my tone clipped. I hated that he still rattled me. I ripped the swimsuit top from his hand and put it in the suitcase, zipping it and the memory closed. "That was a dangerous afternoon."

Doug caught my arm. "Marli, I think about that day all the time." He pulled me closer. "I remember every detail from the salty taste of your eager lips to the way your body responded to my touch." His arms circled me, his lips at the corner of my mouth.

"Doug, stop—" I didn't finish before his mouth covered mine, the kiss more demanding than expected—my kissing him *back* scaring the hell out of me.

The timer on the beverage maker dinged, recovering my sanity. I wiped his kiss from my mouth. "Damn you Doug!"

He laughed shamelessly. "What are you angry about? My kissing you, or *you* kissing me back? There's still something there, sweetheart."

"Shut up! There's nothing between us, understand? Nothing!"

"*You* kissed *me*, Marli, and if Jan hadn't knocked on the door that afternoon, you'd be with me, not Mason. I know it and so do you."

"I know I love Jordan. Not you."

Angry tears burned hot in my eyes. I didn't need this. I took a deep breath and steadied, reaching for the hot carafe before facing Doug.

"There's never been anything between us other than my overactive hormones and your need to please your father. I was hurt and acting on the rebound. You took advantage of the opportunity."

"That's not true. I wasn't the only one having a good time on the bed that afternoon."

The heat on my face felt so intense I was surprised my skin didn't melt off. Doug's tone softened.

"Sorry. I shouldn't have said that. But Marli, you meant more to me than some way to gain my father's approval."

"Did I? Tell me your father doesn't still blame you for my leaving Italy? Deny he wouldn't be thrilled if I was with you?"

Doug boxed me in the tiny kitchen, taking the kettle from my shaking hand. "I can't deny either. But you've got to believe me, I never thought of you as some pawn in a power play. Not in Italy." He drew me into him, ignoring my head shaking in protest.

A hot tear dampened my cheek. "Doug, let me go. I don't belong to you."

"Marli, I know you're not mine. However, for one precious moment, I tasted our future on your lips—"

The front door opened and in walked Brittany *and* Jordan.

"What the hell?" Jordan snapped.

Brittany's expression wavered between confusion and anger, tinged with a bright green streak of jealousy when our eyes met.

"Doug? Marli? What's going on?"

Jordan and Doug squared off. Déjà vu. Let the chest pounding begin. I rushed to Jordan before things worsened. He turned, really looking at me for the first time since entering our now very small apartment.

"You're crying. Did he hurt you?"

"No, I didn't hurt her!"

"I didn't ask you Peterson," Jordan snarled, still watching my eyes. I knew he looked for the lie behind them. "Marli?"

"I'm okay, honest. Let's go."

"Wait," Brittany interrupted, cocking her head the direction of her bedroom. "Marli, could I talk to you?"

She didn't pause for my answer and I took her cue to follow, leaving Jordan in an alpha-male standoff with Doug. If Doug used the opportunity to brag about what happened moments ago and ruined things with Jordan, Brittany would have to deal with the blood-stained carpet because I'd murder him.

Brittany closed the door and stood guard, trapping me in a direct, probing glare. "Do you get off on guys fawning all over you? I know you and Doug shared something, but you wanted nothing to do with him. Then I walk in and find you tangled up with him and by how swollen your lips are, I'm pretty certain you weren't *talking* about old times."

My fingers immediately flew to my guilty lips. If Brit noticed my mouth, undoubtedly Jordan did too. Doug didn't have to tattle. Jordan surely figured it out on his own. I hated Doug all over again...and myself for letting him get to me. But worse, I despised him for coming between me and my best friend—a friend I thought knew me to be better than some boyfriend stealer. Hurt linked with anger that Brit made such a judgmental assumption. Even more frustrating? She played for Doug's team now.

"How dare you! Of all people, you know how I hate attention and especially how I struggle with affection. Nothing in my life has shown me how to handle all these new feelings, let alone trust that any of them are real. Jordan is the only boy I've ever let get this close, Brit, and I'm frightened every day I'll lose him too." I couldn't stop the tears running over my cheeks. "Brit, I'm sorry for what it looked like when you walked in. There's nothing going on, trust me. *One* kiss happened, but it shouldn't have."

"Doug kissed you, didn't he?"

"Yes, and...I kissed him back. I didn't mean to and I swear it will never happen again."

Brit pushed the back of her hand under her nose the way she always did to keep from crying. "I hate being jealous. It's so 'high school.'" She folded her arms tight about her waist. "He's going to hurt me, isn't he?"

"I hope not. Just swear you'll be smart, okay? Deep down Doug might be a nice guy, but the person he hides behind shouldn't be taken at face value." And I wasn't talking about Doug. I wished I could tell Brit about his father, however, my new life dictated secrecy.

A double pound sounded on the door. "Marli? We need to go."

I hugged Brittany and begged for understanding, not forgiveness. I had to earn that.

Jordan helped me with my coat and grabbed my suitcase. His arm wrapped protectively about my waist. "Peterson, as always, it's never good to see you."

A thick silence loomed on the short drive to Jordan's apartment. We pulled into a spot in the underground parking and Jordan turned off the Porsche, but didn't get out. Music played quietly in the background and I watched him nervously pick at the leather wrapped steering wheel.

"Marli, please tell me I don't have to worry about Doug Peterson."

"What? No! Doug is a stupid blip from my past." I took his hand, pressed a kiss to his knuckles. "You're my future. He'll never be more than a friend, if that."

"His wants more than friendship from you, Marli."

"Then he's alone on a one-way street because I don't."

Jordan smiled for the first time since I saw him this morning. The kiss he placed on my mouth held a gentle frailty as if I'd break if he pressed too hard.

His beautiful eyes glistened. "I don't know what I'd do if I lost you. The thought frightens me."

"I'm not going anywhere. You're stuck with me."

His hand cradled the back of my neck the way I liked, holding my lips to his for a long kiss. "I'll grab my bag and be right back so we can get out of here. I won't relax until I have you far away from Douglas Peterson. I don't trust the guy where you're concerned, or me around him."

He wasn't the only one. I decided to keep the news about Doug now living in New Hampshire a secret. The kiss, however, I had to confess or I'd lose Jordan's trust too.

Jordan tossed his bag in the trunk and bounced into the driver's seat. I grinned sheepishly. "I-I need to tell you something."

The dark mood from the apartment returned instantly and I wondered if Doug had already told Jordan what happened. Jordan programmed the car's heater. Obviously, we weren't going anywhere anytime soon.

"What," he demanded in an icy tone.

I inhaled deep as if it might be my last breath. "Doug kissed me." Jordan's head snapped sideways and anger flared in his eyes. "And I kind of reacted."

Jordan angled to face me. "Explain *reacted*."

"I kissed him back."

"You *what*? Why?"

Avoiding eye contact, I concentrated on my twisting fingers. "Honestly? I don't know why." He slammed his fist on the steering wheel. "Jordan, it meant nothing, I swear! The kiss caught me off guard and, of course, Doug misinterpreted everything. That's why I was crying. We were arguing about it when you and Brit walked in."

"Does Brittany know?"

"Yes. I told her and she's angry with me."

"Seems a bit extreme. They've only interviewed."

"Doug said he's been communicating with her behind his father's back. Brit hasn't said anything because she knows I wouldn't approve, but I'm worried she likes him."

Jordan pressed his head against the steamed window and pinched the bridge of his nose. "Damn. Their relationship is doomed."

"Please don't say that." I carefully reached for his hand. "What about ours?"

He kissed my knuckles. "We're solid. But the next time Doug touches you, Marli, I have grounds to kill him, understand?"

"I'll help you." My answer triggered a grin to slide off the side of his mouth. "And there won't be a next time because the only one I want touching me is you."

Jordan's thumb gently stroked my cheek. "Forever?"

"And beyond."

# 32
# THANKSGIVING

The elevator ping rivaled a cathedral bell, announcing our arrival at one o'clock in the morning, and separating our fused bodies from the corner. It had been a long nine hours trapped in separate seats and only able to hold hands in our very public setting. We hadn't shared so much as a chaste kiss and now craved each other like addicts needing a fix to survive.

"Maybe we should have stayed at a hotel," I whispered inside our brass box.

"Mom would have had a fit if we did." A wicked grin curled Jordan's mouth. "Alone with you in a hotel room would also guarantee we'd be late for Thanksgiving dinner…if we even showed up at all."

The doors opened washing us in brilliant light. I stepped onto the glossy floor, forgetting all about the rainbow of emotions churning inside me. Deep violet radiated beneath my feet and Jordan eyes checked off mine, my feet, before back to my eyes. A most disarming smile formed on my favorite mouth, reaching eyes holding a familiar glimmer. When I looked at the floor again, two large bright violet puddles merged, but a hot pink tinge also rimmed the edges of Jordan's feet.

"What are you afraid of?" I asked.

His grin screwed sideways. "You know about the colors?"

"Yep."

"Then you also know there's no way we can be alone together tonight. According to the lovely purple shade pulsating under our feet, we'd be in serious moral trouble."

"Aren't we always?"

"Exactly." He took my hand and tugged me toward the entrance. "I'll have to erase the security tapes before anyone sees."

The goodnight kiss pressed to my mouth outside Jordan's bedroom, proved the floor to be right. A slow burn snaked through my body as Jordan's tongue moved languid strokes against the sensitive hollow on the top of my mouth, his hands pinning mine to the wall to the side of my head. His hips rocked with mine in rhythm to the dance happening between our lips until I finally broke the kiss.

Jordan's lips moved to the hollow of my throat. "Stay with me," I whispered.

"Not the best idea given how weak my self-control is at the moment."

We giggled against each other's mouths, taking familiar deep breaths to slow racing hearts in preparation of unwanted goodbyes. When I asked about the pink highlights again, Jordan refused to answer, opening the door and pushing my reluctant body inside. Worry plagued my thoughts as I changed into my pajamas. If Jordan was afraid of something, then I should be terrified.

Unable to fight the morning rays filtering through the blinds and warming my face, I stretched my arms over my head, letting one drop off the side of the bed

"Ouch!"

I rolled to the edge of the bed, finding Jordan on the floor rubbing his nose. "When did you sneak in here?"

"After I tossed for hours with steamy thoughts of you spinning in my head. I couldn't sleep knowing you were on the other side of the wall in my bed. Besides, this floor is much more comfortable than the sofa in the office."

Jordan caught my arm and pulled me on top of him. I squealed in surprise and his hand immediately covered my mouth. "SHHH!" he chuckled.

I perched my chin on my arms folded across his chest, taking in his beautiful eyes—a glittery mossy green in the morning sunlight. "I missed you last night."

"I hate when you're not in my arms." His hands eased over my hips and stroked my bare thighs. "Next semester we're going where the weather is warm so I don't have to ever see you in another pair of flannel pajamas."

I reached behind and stopped his roaming hand. "Behave."

"I'm tired of behaving," he grumbled. "I swear we're the only two people on the planet who sleep in the same bed without having sex."

Jordan rolled me under him, burying his head in my hair, one hand moving slowly under my T-shirt. I smiled on his mouth when he shifted his body.

"Everything okay?" I teased, feeling his body sell him out.

"You know I'm not." His lips barely grazed mine before stopping, his shoulders going rigid beneath my fingertips. "I smell coffee. Someone's awake. I can't be found in here with you, at least not this morning. My grandparents are here and I don't want them to get the wrong impression before they get to know you."

He scrambled to his feet and paused in the doorway, speaking in a hushed tone. "Warning. Mom is taking you shopping later, so be a good sport. I'll see you in the kitchen for breakfast." He blew me a kiss and quietly shut the door.

After smoothing the crisp gold sheets and black down comforter over Jordan's bed, I stepped back and let my eyes loiter around his room—a private gallery of Jordan's life. Trophies and ribbons recognizing his feats as an athlete over the years lined shelves and bookcases.

I couldn't help but admire how closely the décor matched his personality. Rich tones and luxurious fabrics showed his classy, gentlemanly traits. The room's organized and neat appearance matched his driven, goal oriented thinking, while notes of rosewood and spice lingering in the fabric particularly told of his sexy prowess.

The bright red stuffed dog with floppy ears hanging from a navy silk tie noose off his desk lamp, and an old Mr. Potato Head with goofy oversized ears, however, definitely represented his playful side. Several body parts belonging to Mr. Head lay scattered in a small box. I added curly eyelashes and earrings, connecting him with his "feminine spud" side.

When I closed the door, the part of me that should be locked away wondered what I'd find if I crossed the hall and opened Jesse's bedroom door. I imagined bright colors, chrome instead of wood; contemporary versus traditional, along with guitars on stands, citrus fragrance, and framed, overly-endowed beach beauties in bikinis dotting the walls. I decided that door must never be opened.

I'd forgotten about the breathtaking view of the ocean beyond the glass wall comprising the southeast wall of the living room. I strolled leisurely past and into the formal dining room. China, crystal goblets, and stacks of silverware filled the center of a long table. At the far end of the room the delectable smell of coffee drifted from behind the door.

The kitchen felt warm with the morning sun beaming through the large window. The facets of leaded glass surrounding the window sprayed the kitchen with tiny rainbows. Meg's silhouette against the morning light completed a picture perfect scene.

"Awesome," I said, touching one of the multi colored splotches shimmering on the marble counter. I pulled a stool from under the center island and Meg handed me a cup of coffee fixed the way I liked it at the beach house.

"I'm so glad you came, girl. I've missed you." She grinned mischievously. "We haven't had such drama between the boys since they were small."

After pouring herself a cup of coffee, she leaned on her elbows. Her brows waggled. "The last gnarly fight I remember was when Jordan smacked Jesse with a wooden oar, knocking him out of the dinghy they floated in. They tussled on the beach until they both had bloody noses." She sipped her coffee. "They were eleven years old. Wow, I can't believe nine years have passed."

She returned to preparing the batter for blueberry waffles—the traditional Thanksgiving Day breakfast, I'd been informed. Dinner would be later this evening, but the smell from the freshly baked pies cooling on the counter already had me drooling.

I soon discovered this kitchen, like the one at the beach house, was the morning gathering place. A puff of air blew across my back when the door opened.

"Pretty women in a kitchen is every guy's dream."

Meg muttered something under her breath and snapped a dishtowel at our half-naked guest, who yelped when it hit his back. A kiss on the side of my head and a playful hug from a familiar arm gave me an instant rush. Jesse.

"Mars, you're a sight for sore eyes. How's my brother treating you? If he's not spoiling you rotten, I want you to leave him and come back to me."

Jesse straddled the stool at my side, sorting through the blueberries and picking the best ones to add to the batter.

"I've tried, but she's stubborn about letting anyone fuss over her," Jordan answered from behind me.

He at least wore a shirt, but unbuttoned and begging for my hands to slip inside. He kissed my cheek and took the other stool next to me, instantly raising the temperature in the kitchen.

Another swoosh of the door brought Eva Mason. "Oh my, you two!" She patted Jordan's shoulder before taking the cup of coffee Meg handed her. "Marli, please tell them how impressed you are with their manly chests so they'll finish dressing. I'm sure this little peep show is for your benefit."

I reached out and touched both Jordan's and Jesse's chests. They flinched when I pressed my hand to their warm skin and I laughed, hiding my nervousness. I did love both their chests, and had spent time resting against each of them at one time or another. Jordan's hand cupped mine and I felt his heart beating a tad fast. Jesse, however, slithered from my touch.

He quickly recovered, placing a scoop of batter into the waffle iron and pinching Meg's shoulders. "Hey, where's my cup of coffee?"

"Get dressed first. We don't serve naked men in this kitchen," Eva chided before Meg could answer.

I immediately proceeded to button Jordan's shirt and he flashed me a playful smile. I knew that look and returned a warning glint when his fingertips dipped inside the waistband of my jeans.

Jesse wrapped his hands around his mother's waist and nuzzled into her neck. "I bet you wouldn't turn Dad away if he was naked in your kitchen."

"Did I hear my name taken in vain?"

John Banks wiggled his way through the bodies, pulling Jordan's mother into his arms and giving her an enthusiastic kiss. "You wouldn't turn me away if I was naked, now would you dear?"

Without warning, he yanked his T-shirt off, flexing his muscles. Eva covered her face with her hands, while the rest of us cheered him on.

"John! Honestly! Now I know where the boys get it from." She glanced over his shoulder at me. "Consider yourself warned, Marli."

Jordan's grandparents entered and their audible gasp made Eva quickly tug John's shirt over his head. She blushed again at some private look he gave her.

Delectable hors d'oeuvres, side dishes, and an array of desserts covered the dining room buffet. Elegant place settings precisely arranged on the table displayed the colors of autumn beautifully. John and Eva were hosting Thanksgiving dinner for their family and a handful of close friends lucky enough to be included in their circle of trust.

My introduction to those included in this intimate social circle would also be on the menu, serving as an opportunity to appraise my worthiness for Jordan. Both the Thanksgiving turkey and I would be on display before being dissected and devoured. The difference? The turkey was already out of its misery. I, on the other hand, would feel each prick of an eyeball directed my way, and the excruciating pain if I met with someone's disapproval.

As forewarned, Jordan's mother took me shopping earlier in the day, surely to guarantee I wore something she deemed appropriate enough to meet her guests. She treated me to an elegant black chiffon dress with gold threads shimmering throughout the fabric. The skirt flowed in a handkerchief hem touching above my ankles, and the bodice crossed over my chest and tied behind my neck, leaving my shoulders and back exposed. Gold strappy sandals adorned my feet and a pair of flashy hammered gold discs dangled from my uncovered ears.

Eva insisted on doing my hair, slicking it back into some intricate bun. My sophisticated ensemble was very different from the simple floral dress I'd brought. Rick would die if he saw me.

Jordan waited for me beside the pool. He handed me a flute half-full of champagne, which I had no intention of drinking. His arm eased around my waist, tucking me close to his side, but turning me so my back faced away from the crowd. He placed a light kiss on my lips, his fingers seductively stroking the length of my bare back. I understood now his strategic positioning.

"You're gorgeous tonight, babe. This dress makes you look older and insanely sexy. I don't think there's a single male here tonight who can keep their eyes off you. My jealousy issues are seriously being tested."

The touch of Jordan's fingers on my naked skin gave me chills, stronger than the evening ocean breeze. I nestled under his arm to make him stop. "I think that may have been your mother's intention...to make me appear older so you wouldn't look like a cradle robber to her friends," I teased. "And my eyes are only on you."

"I worried I had some stiff competition when you ogled Dad this morning."

"I didn't ogle him," I objected, already feeling the blush on my cheeks.

"Wrong sweetheart. You committed serious ogling."

"Maybe I was checking out what you'll look like in the future?"

"And?" he smiled.

"Looks very good."

We shared a long kiss, Jordan's mouth hot and tasting of champagne. I ran my fingers along his throat to the edge of the collar of his black silk shirt, neatly tucked against the lapel of his camel colored leather jacket. A hard swallow rolled beneath my fingertips. He snugged me closer and moaned softly in my ear.

"We aren't going to make it to the main course, if you keep taunting me. Maybe I should whisk you away someplace private and subject you to my personal torture treatment."

"Don't make promises you can't keep."

"Oh, I plan on making good on my promise. Hot tub at midnight, babe. You, me, and your teensy black bikini." His fingers teased at the side of my dress and I jumped, sloshing champagne.

"*Jordan.* Your grandparents are watching." I tipped my glass in the direction of his grandfather who stood in the doorway, indeed keeping a watchful eye on the two of us. He lifted his glass our direction in return. "See?"

Jordan groaned, releasing me to a respectable hand on my arm, guiding me into the dining room when his father tapped a glass to gather the guests. We found our seats according to elegantly hand-scripted name cards. I sat between Jordan and Jesse. How fitting.

Jesse leaned over while Jordan assisted his grandmother to her seat. "You're beautiful tonight, Mars, which is killing me." He threw back the last of his glass of champagne.

John Banks, which he preferred at home, stood at the head of the table, handsomely dressed in a light gray suit with a dark rust shirt and a comical holiday tie. He held a champagne flute in one hand and a butcher knife poised over the unsuspecting turkey, dressed and steaming before him.

"I want to thank everyone for joining us this evening to celebrate this Thanksgiving holiday, and to meet a certain young lady who's become very special to this family, Jordan in particular. Marli, dear, would you please stand so I can formerly introduce you?"

My knees quivered.

"Showtime babe," Jordan whispered, pulling my chair away from the table. He stood behind me, his hands set at my waist to steady my trembling body while his dad continued.

"Friends, this is Marli Davis, Jordan's candidate, and hopefully more soon."

The familiar warm burn crept from my toes to my scalp under everyone's appraising stares. Jordan kissed the top of my head before letting me sit back on my chair.

We held hands around the table and bowed our heads. Jordan's father offered a prayer for peace and a blessing over our military serving abroad. A pang of longing tugged. This was my first Thanksgiving away from home. Rick would spend the holiday with Karen and probably not miss me. I thought of my mother. The time had come to find her and at least talk, if nothing else. I didn't want any remnants from the past to retain a hold on me any longer.

After dessert, guests lingered poolside or meandered into the living room. A few excused themselves and left early. The evening, so far, had been nothing shy of wonderful. I gathered scattered dessert plates on an empty tray with the intention of taking them into the kitchen, but stopped outside of the doorway to eavesdrop on an intense conversation between Jordan and Jesse.

"Jesse, Dad's going to have a fit if he catches you drinking. We were told two glasses of champagne, and now you've uncorked another bottle?"

"Don't worry, it's the cheap stuff."

"That's beside the point. You've got to stay sober. I need your help tomorrow and I can't chance you flying a plane if you get wasted tonight."

"Always the 'good son.' Don't you get tired of being perfect?"

"I'm not perfect, Jess, but yes, I get tired of covering your ass."

"Mind your own damn business, big brother."

"It's my business when your life keeps spilling into mine."

"You mean, Marli, don't you? You're still worried she'll choose me over you, especially now that she knows why the damn Program is really after her."

"You're an ass. And drunk."

"I'm far from blitzed. It's only my third and last glass. I just needed to dull my heartache. Marli looks gorgeous tonight, and sorry, but that hurts a bit. I love the constant reminder that Dad put her with you. Again, you win, 'golden boy.'"

"Shit, Jess, Dad didn't do it to purposely hurt you. She was fourteen and we were sixteen. Hell, nobody could see the future. He just knew she was special and picked her for us."

"*Us.* Funny how she ended up in the middle, huh? But, the 'win' I'm talking about is *her* choosing *you.* She loves you. Don't worry. I'll be at the airport tomorrow morning, ten o'clock sharp. Treat her right Jordan, because if things don't work out, I have every intention of winning her back."

"In your dreams. There's no way in hell, little brother, I'll not lose her to you or anyone else. I intend on keeping Marli with me forever, if she'll have me."

"*Keeping Marli.* Interesting choice of words, Jordan. Makes it sound like she has no say."

Hands trembling and lips pursed to a painful pinch, I kicked the kitchen door open, stopping the verbal banter. "No one's 'keeping' me. I have as much say as I want and I told you, Jesse, I'm with Jordan because I choose to be. Get a grip."

I placed the dishes on the counter and grabbed the bottle of champagne off the island, tipping it upside down in the sink. They both gasped, but neither dared say a word. I pulled Jordan out of the kitchen before matters escalated. The china looked too expensive to be thrown.

A soft rap came at my door when the clock chimed the midnight hour. I opened it and drank in the sexy sight leaning against the frame. We slinked silently down the hallway and out onto the balcony. The wall of glass we stepped through reflected the candles strategically placed around the bubbling spa. Pale lavender light glowed beneath the churning water and below, the city of Miami spilled to the banks of the harbor in a glittery glow.

I dropped my towel onto the teakwood bench and stepped into the warm water and Jordan's waiting arms. Standing barefoot against Jordan I felt small, my head fitting comfortably under his chin.

"Hey handsome," I whispered, indulging in quick taste of his chest.

"Hi, gorgeous."

His hands caressed my bare skin, more exposed than covered in this swimsuit, pressing me intimately against him.

I became acutely aware of how thin the layers of fabric separating our bodies were and the warm water swirling around us, tucked it close to our skin as if not there at all. I fidgeted on my feet, my body buzzed and squirming. Jordan's physical reaction to my nearness pressed my stomach and I locked my arms behind his neck and concentrated on his moony eyes to deflect my thoughts.

It didn't work.

Jordan drew me closer, my body bending to his touch. His husky whisper at my ear sent a shiver scurrying down my spine.

"I love you so much, Marli."

He moved me through the water, lowering me to the tile bench. Only my shoulders and head appeared above the bubbles. He knelt in front of me, eyes level to mine. His lashes brushed his wet cheeks as our lips touched in a gentle, but extremely intimate kiss.

"Can anyone see us?" I asked between breaths.

"No. The bedrooms are on the other side of the house. We're alone."

The kisses pressed harder and Jordan settled his body between my thighs, his hands exploring my stomach with tentative touches, slowly easing over the curve of my breasts. I swallowed hard, pulling back and studying his face.

Jordan the "ice man" had changed drastically since our summer romance blossomed into something deeper and the need for each other intensified.

Jordan waited for my reaction, his eyes sensually dark and alluring in the flickering candlelight. My breath on his mouth came out in short pants. When his fingers pulled the ribbons apart, I didn't stop him, letting my swimsuit top float away.

"Happy Birthday," I whispered.

The harbor below turned from shades of gray to soft apricot as dawn edged over the Miami skyline and onto the water. Boats sparkled as the first rays of the morning sun struck shiny chrome and brass rails. Waves curled against the breaker walls and rippled through the marina until they flattened to a satiny shimmer.

"Mars?" The voice, barely audible, arrested my heart.

"Jess! You scared me. Why are you up so early?"

"I could ask you the same thing."

"I'm nervous to skydive, but I promised I'd try."

Jesse's fingers threaded through mine. "Marli, about making promises to Jordan."

I turned slightly, my brows knitting with curiosity. Gently, I pulled my fingers out of the braid.

He took my hand again and kissed it. Appearing nervous, he swallowed a hundred times before continuing. "Don't say anything, just listen, okay? You know I love you, even though I shouldn't. The Program aligned you with Jordan, but even so, remember you have options and don't need to bend to anyone's manipulations. You control your destiny and who shares it with you. Promise me when it comes to *forever,* you'll only make choices that match what your heart wants." He pecked my cheek. "See you in a few hours. And don't worry about skydiving. Neither of us would put you in danger."

Jesse disappeared into the shadows, leaving me confused. Why did he think I wouldn't follow my heart, especially when it came to 'forever,' whatever that meant?

And his declaration of love again? Jesse had to understand I loved Jordan, regardless of The Program's involvement—that I chose Jordan of my own free will…over him. I still felt something for Jesse and when he kissed my cheek, my toes even twitched a little.

But I loved Jordan…not Jesse.

Jordan stole behind me, his warm arms wrapping and drawing me against him. I slapped my chest to restart my heart. I really needed to listen for footsteps!

"Sorry," he mumbled in my hair. He rested his chin on my shoulder where his breath whispered in my ear. "Why aren't you sleeping?"

"Because I'm scared about sky-diving today." *And Jesse proclaimed he loved me right before he said some other weird stuff.* "What if something goes wrong, Jordan? Our lives could end today."

"Marli, I'd never ask you to do something that could harm you." He sounded wounded by my mistrust.

"I know. I'm being silly." I yawned halfway through a sniffle.

Jordan towed me down the hall and followed me into the bedroom. "What are you doing?"

"Tucking you back to bed." I opened my mouth to object. "I'll stay with you," he said, delighting me. Maybe we'd oversleep and miss our chance to plummet to our deaths.

"What if someone catches us?"

"Honestly? I don't care." He slipped in the bed beside me. No fabric barriers—only his long legs crossing mine to warm me under the covers we shared.

Strong, caring arms circled my shoulders and my head fell onto my favorite place on his chest where I heard his heart beating every bit as fast as my own. I kissed his warm skin and felt the skipped beat against my ear.

Jordan stroked my hair, letting his fingers run the length of my spine from the ends of the curly tendrils. "No worries, baby. I'll always keep you safe."

"I love you, Jordan," I mumbled, feeling myself sink into a dreamy state. *I can't love Jesse.*

## 33
## HEARTS AND ROSES

So this was how a caged cat felt right before dropped into water.

"I can't do this, Jordan! You can't make me, either!" I shrieked.

"Marli, stop moving so I can get the harness buckled."

Jordan dressed me under constant protest, zipping the flight suit tight to my chin. He forced me into some contraption comprised of a myriad of buckles and snaps, tethering me to his body. His patience wore thin when I whipped around, unexpectedly throwing him to the floor of the plane. His arms immediately locked around my chest.

"Dammit, Marli! Hold still! I swear nothing is going to happen to you unless I murder you inside this plane."

"I'm not jumping. I changed my mind."

Jordan's expression became confused. Hurt? Anger? No...something else. Fear? Of what? According to him, he skydived all the time. A childlike innocence crept into his tone.

"But you promised."

"Yeah, well...I make a lot of promises where you're concerned."

"Are you saying you don't mean to make them, or I pressure you to think you have to?"

"Of course I mean them. I just don't know about this one. I'm scared. *Really* scared."

His voice faltered, tone flat. "Fine, don't jump. I told you I'd never force you into anything."

Damn. An argument brewed, one I didn't want to have. It was his birthday and I did promise. I reached for his dangling hand. "Okay, I'll jump," I conceded inside a whine, secretly hoping he wouldn't make me. He hugged me hard and kissed my hair with a loud smack. *Damn, damn, damn.*

Mike slid the doors open and the deafening sound of air rushing the sides of the plane sucked the last of my oxygen. Panic gave way to fear. Below, far away, lay a patchwork of various colors of green, brown, and gray. I wanted to avoid the grays. *Concrete.* A ribbon of blue curled between—*water.* Water would be good, or green, preferably light green—*grass.*

Jordan brushed my hair to one side and placed a tender kiss on the back of my neck. "Marli, trust me, please. I would never purposely hurt you."

Tremors took possession of my body and if not fused to Jordan, I would have crumpled to the floor of the plane.

Jesse yelled to us from the cockpit. "You guys ready? We're coming up on the target field."

They chartered a plane specifically used for skydiving. The open cockpit allowed me to not only hear, but see Jesse laugh hysterically at the physical struggle between Jordan and me. His wide smile, however, didn't cover up the anxious look in his eyes. Our strange conversation in the middle of the night not only plagued my dreams with thoughts of Jesse, but apparently still lingered in his head as well.

Jordan's voice in my ear evaporated Jesse from my mind and resurrected the terror zigzagging inside me.

"Babe, pay attention to what I'm saying when we're out there. Lean your head against my chest. We'll drop backward so you see the sky above instead of the ground. That way you'll get used to the sensation of falling."

*Falling?* How could anyone get used to the feeling of falling?

Mike came toward us with the helmets. "I can't!" I cried. "Jordan I'll let you buy me any car you want, if you won't make me jump." All my begging wouldn't work. I'd tumble to earth with Jordan strapped to me. I prayed for the angels to take me before I felt the impact.

"Marli!" Jordan hollered in frustration, locking the helmet under my chin. "Honey, you'll be fine and I'll be holding you in my arms all the way. Now, please relax." He moved us onto a small platform, my feet teetering on the ridge of the door frame. "Ready, set..."

Jordan stepped back, pulling me out of the plane and into the sky. My screams echoed to the planet Jupiter, my face froze in horrified angles with my stolen breath. I clenched my teeth so tight I waited for them to crumble so I could choke on them and die before I smacked the ground.

The plane moved away and a cornflower blue color extended upwards as far as I could see. Jordan's arms remained tightly wound around my waist. "Marli—breathe," he called over my shoulder, his tone level and soothing. I managed to suck a couple deep pockets of air before my next lesson. "Arch your back, babe."

I obeyed not realizing the effect of this simple movement. Without warning, we rolled forward and I spied the earth below. My screams returned. The skin surrounding my mouth billowed, exposing my tonsils. I didn't realize I cried until Jordan started laughing.

"I need windshield wipers for my goggles!" He gave me a reassuring squeeze. "Sweetheart, relax."

"Jordan, open the chute!" I shrilled.

"Not yet." His fingers wound into my hands and he pulled my arms out to the side, slowly shifting our weight from side to side, dipping our bodies in an airborne dance.

"Jordan, I'll promise you anything—*do* anything, just pull the cord and open the chute!"

"Anything Marli? Are you telling me there isn't anything more frightening than this?" He mocked me now and the ground appeared to rise faster.

"Nothing is scarier than this. Please? If you love me, open the stupid parachute!"

"What guarantee do I have you won't promise me something again, only to take it back when we land safely?"

"I won't! Cross my heart! Please open the damn chute before I kill you Jordan Mason!"

"There's that feisty temper. Good thing I'm the one in control here." To prove his point, he swung our bodies into a spin and my screams intensified.

"You're loving this, aren't you?"

"Holding you hostage? Call me an ass, but yep!"

I decided to try a different approach. "Jordan?" I asked sweetly. "Baby, please open the parachute and when we are safely back on earth, your wish is my command." I swore I could count blades of grass and closed my eyes.

Suddenly, we jerked upward. Silence enveloped us unlike any quiet I'd ever experienced.

*Am I dead—spared the pain when my body slammed the ground?*

Something ruffled in the wind and I glanced upward. Overhead, a bright yellow and royal blue striped safety net floated us toward earth.

A bracketed smile widened on Jordan's face. "Remember, Miss Davis, once our toes touch solid ground, my wish is your command. Understood?"

"Okay, I get it." I let go several deep breaths, my heart rate slowly returning to normal. "This is kind of nice. Peaceful."

"I told you. Too bad you were so busy screeching you didn't enjoy it."

"I'm enjoying it now."

Jordan played with the cords, pulling the chute in different directions as we danced toward earth.

"All right, babe, here comes the tricky part. See that pink patch below? Our goal is to land in the middle. I'll maneuver the chute, so stay still."

"Pink patch?" Below, in the middle of a bright green field, was a definite vivid pink...patch? No—wait. Patches were square. This one curved in the shape of a *heart*.

"Lift your legs and I'll guide us in." As we got closer, I saw variegated shades of pink, red, and violet clustered together.

"Feet up, Marli, and one more thing—close your eyes."

I lifted my legs and let out another shrill, but shut my eyes as instructed. Jordan's legs came up under mine and we slid onto the ground, the landing surprisingly soft. Jordan released the chute and I heard it rustle off to the side. Two clicks and we separated.

"Stay put one more second, and keep those baby blues shut."

I was so relieved to be alive and sitting on hard ground I would promise the world as long as no one moved me. My hands gathered what I sat on, feeling velvety, fragrant particles.

"Can I open my eyes yet?"

"Patience, Marli. I promise it will be worth it, at least I hope so." Jordan lifted me to my feet, keeping his hands securely on my waist. "Can you stand? Your legs aren't wobbly?"

"No I'm fine. Just let me open my eyes."

Jordan took my hand in his and I felt the wetness of his lips kissing my palm. "Remember you said nothing else would ever be scarier than what you've survived. Plus, you promised me anything if I brought you safely to earth."

I could hear the smile in his tone, but his voice shook, heightening my nerves. "Yes, I remember. I'll keep my word." *Maybe.*

"All right. Open your eyes."

My lungs seized. Thousands of rose petals surrounded me.

"Jordan? What's all this?"

"Hearts and roses. I hope it's romantic enough because I need all the romance I can get right now." His eyes shimmered.

Then the ultimate happened—a surprise topping everything I'd experienced so far in my eighteen years of life. While keeping my left hand in his, Jordan dropped to one knee, holding a tiny white satin box. The diamond ring inside caught the sun's rays and sent a rainbow-edged beam into outer space.

I studied his handsome face, holding a most fragile expression. The world around me disappeared behind a sudden veil of water.

"Marli, I need you in order to breathe. I love you and never want the sun to rise on another day without you beside me for the rest of my life. Please...marry me?"

## 34
## BITTERSWEET

$C$ool water lapped against my shins, the top of the pool covered in a shimmer of sunbeams.

"You can't avoid me forever," I shouted to the body slipping beneath the surface again. Ten laps without so much as a pause to acknowledge my presence.

Jesse resurfaced across the pool, propping his elbows on the edge and shaking his head like a wet dog. His stare cut through me.

"Why so shocked? You helped Jordan, didn't you?"

"You didn't have to say 'yes.'"

"But, I wanted to. I love him, Jess." I looked around, wondering whose ears tuned in to our argument. Jordan had been behind closed doors with his father since our return, making me nervous.

"You're compromising, Mars, like you always do—taking the easy way out."

"*Easy*? You think this is easy? I just made a major life decision! Why can't you support us…me?"

"You know why." Jesse dropped beneath the water again. Suddenly, he popped up in front of me, placed his hands on pool deck to the side of my thighs. He hoisted his upper body out of the water and I tried to ignore the fact his wet torso pressed my legs, or his face close enough I could see the tiny scar cutting through his left brow.

"You're officially trapped."

"If you'd move—"

"I'm talking about The Program. You'll never escape their control once you marry Jordan." He pushed back into the water, treading a few feet from me. "Have you called Rick to tell him the good news?"

"Not yet."

"Love to be a fly on the wall when you make that call."

"Why? He likes Jordan."

"He hates The Program more. He won't want this for you, Mars."

I flicked my foot, showering Jesse's face. "Rick wants me to be happy."

Jesse swam closer, lowering his voice. "I can make you happy. You could drop out of the damn Program. I told you last night to choose with your heart." When I tried to lift my legs to get out, he caught them, pulling me slightly forward, his fingers wrapped around my calves. "Tell me I don't stir feelings inside you when I get close."

I yanked my legs out of the water, kicking him away. "I thought we settled this already."

"Settled what?" My heart banged my spine when Jordan appeared behind me. Jesse dipped back under the water. "Am I missing something here?"

He pulled me to my feet when I extended my arm. "No. Let's go inside."

Jordan followed me into the bedroom, shutting the door behind us. Suddenly, I felt self-conscious standing in *his* room clad in only my infamous black bikini, especially when Jordan's eyes slowly swept the length of my body and his swim trunks became noticeably tighter.

"You shouldn't be in here. Someone might find out."

After closing the distance between us, he lifted my left hand. The large diamond sparkled in the light streaming through the window. "*This* changes things."

Jordan captured my mouth, the kiss intense and urgent. His hand smoothed over my hip, his thumb hooking into the side of my swimsuit bottoms. When his other hand reached for the ties to my top, I broke the kiss and stepped out of his arms.

"What's wrong?"

"I'm not in the mood."

"Not in the mood? Since when? You've never—"

"I've shut you down plenty of times. Giving me a diamond doesn't give you anything else. I told you, I want to wait."

Jordan scrubbed the back of his neck. "I've never said it did. What's going on, Marli?" A ghost of a smile appeared on his mouth and he rubbed his bottom lip. "An hour ago you'd have sucked these puppies off my face." A stormy expression dissolved the sexy smirk when I didn't respond. "Jesse said something, didn't he?"

"What were you doing in your father's office for so long?"

"Don't change the subject. What did Jess say? You seem different."

"Jesse has nothing to do with this. I've just got a lot to process and I need to call Dad."

"Are you worried he'll be angry?"

Tears threatened and I turned away. Jordan gently pulled me to him.

"Rick loves you and he's not going to like giving you up now, or in fifty years. But, he'll be okay after the shock wears off."

"He'll accuse me of compromising my future. He wants to believe I only have a crush on you."

"You mean you don't?" Jordan asked in a playful lilt.

"I passed 'crush' a long time ago." I nestled under his chin. "I love you." *Not Jesse.*

"Let me make the call."

"No, I have to be the one to tell him."

"I know, but let me talk to him first. I want to properly ask for your hand."

I looked up at the handsome boy whose fingers toyed with the strings on my bikini bottoms. A teasing grin curled a corner of his mouth when I pulled his hands away and balled them inside my own under my chin. I figured this conversation was a distraction from his real purpose.

To get me naked. New ground rules needed to be established, and quick.

"Jordan, that's so old fashioned. Nobody does that."

He wiggled his hands free and commenced to tug on the ones to my top, kissing my mouth before I could object. The damp material slithered to a crumpled lump between our torsos and the sensation of Jordan's bare chest crushed against my own, stirring feelings I hoped would never fade during my mortal existence.

"Your dad's an old-fashioned guy. Besides, I want to give you the whole fairytale, Marli."

Surprise tears burned trails over my cheeks. Jordan stopped trying to undress me and cupped my face in his hands. "Babe?"

"I'm scared. What if—"

"Shhh." His thumb flicked away a salty droplet. "For once in your life, trust your heart. Trust *me*. I know love doesn't come with a warranty, but right now, holding you, I feel like 'Superman.' Invincible. Nothing can hurt us."

"There's always Kryptonite."

"Love's stronger. Marli, your parents' fate doesn't have to be ours. We'll make our own story, good or bad, but it will be ours—not some screwed up karma thing you believe."

I stared into the same eyes that mesmerized me almost a year ago from a video feed, feeling the same thrill chase my racing heart, my bones turning spongy and my body tingling. I watched the lips hovering close, remembering all the thoughts that raced through my brain back then—what they'd feel like touching mine, soft or hard? Would I be a good kisser? Even the worry about my breath passed, the memory leaving the taste of bubble gum on my tongue. All those questions answered in our first kiss an eternity ago, against my kitchen counter.

Now I stood in Jordan's bedroom months later, wearing a bikini I knew drove him wild, feeling his warm skin press the length of mine, arms wrapping me tenderly, protectively, holding all these emotions inside me, plus a few new ones I'd discovered when we're this close. My dream had come true, despite everything I did to fight it happening.

Jordan Mason, Candidate 2255—my *assigned* destiny, the one, if given the chance again without interference, I'd still choose. My prince charming came to rescue me after all. I just didn't know he'd be clad in surf shorts with hypnotic hazel eyes playing hide-and-seek between damp locks of bronze colored hair. His only armor…strong brawny arms meant to fit perfectly around my body.

So why couldn't I pin my faith to him? Because the same day an innocent kiss rocked my world, a boy begged me not to break his heart.

A light knock on the door broke the spell between us. "Dinner in thirty minutes, Miss Davis."

"Thank you, Burton."

Without realizing, I'd stepped from Jordan's embrace, my arms crossed and shielding my naked chest. The swimsuit top I wore moments ago stretched into a forbidden satin line between our feet. I hooked my thumb toward the bathroom. "I need to shower." Jordan remained fixed in place, an odd expression clouding his face. "You should go. I'll see you at dinner."

Jordan left the room in a huff and an awkward feeling lingered. A few hours ago I rode a wave of elation, but at this moment, I stood on shaky ground.

I fingered the pink princess-cut diamond, running my thumb along the diamond-crusted edge. This ring had to have cost a fortune. A high price to pay for someone who suddenly wondered if she just made a monstrous mistake.

Meg lifted my plate, nudging my shoulder. "You okay, girl? You hardly touched your food."

Eva Mason reached out and took my hand, beaming. "She's probably just worn out from all the excitement, aren't you dear?"

"She didn't sleep much last night," Jesse mumbled, stabbing the last remnants of his chicken with enough force to chip the china plate.

"How do you know that?" Jordan demanded.

"You know I'm right here," I clipped, easing my hand out of Eva's and touching Jordan's arm. "Jesse found me this morning right before you did. I confessed how afraid I was of skydiving and couldn't sleep."

Jordan tipped my chin with his finger and kissed me gently. "But everything turned out okay, didn't it? You survived."

"And engaged!" Eva exclaimed. "I had no idea my son was such a romantic."

"It was pretty amazing," I replied. "I don't think I believe it's all real just yet."

"Well, it is," Jesse snarled, picking up his plate. "Your 'match' is official. Congratulations. The Program will be happy to know their golden couple is tying the knot. A year from now, you can give them the 'golden egg,' too. Tell us, Jordan. How many copies can they make of a kid before—"

Jordan jumped out of his chair, toppling it backwards.

"Enough!" Jordan's father's voice threatened to crack the ceiling. "Jesse, you're out of line. Apologize to your brother and Marli."

"For what? Telling the truth?"

"No, for taking a cherished memory from Marli and turning it into something ugly. Son, you crossed a line. From here on out, keep your personal opinions and feelings to yourself. Understood?"

"Yes, Sir." Jesse put his plate back on the table and leveled his eyes to mine. "Mars, Dad's right. Jordan worked hard to make his proposal special. He wanted it perfect for you and anguished about it for weeks. I shouldn't have spoiled your moment."

"It's all right, Jess," I said, turning away when a tear leaked from the corner of my eye.

"No, it's not. I swore I'd never hurt you, but I just did." His finger traced a swirl on the linen tablecloth. "Bro...I'm an ass." Jesse lifted his head, his face reddened and eyes wet. "God, I'm sorry. Really. How can I make it up to you?"

Jordan picked the chair off the floor and walked around the table. Standing in front of his brother, his expression remained hard, unreadable. "I'm not sure you can, but agreeing to be my best man would be a start. You've been beside me through all the important things in my life, but this one's the biggest. Don't let me down."

Jesse grabbed Jordan by the neck, wrapping his arms tight around his shoulders. Jordan's arms circled back. When they parted, both rubbed their eyes.

"It would be an honor for me to watch you marry the girl of our dreams."

"You're such a loser," Jordan laughed.

"Yeah, this time, I am."

Eva clapped her hands. "See! Everything's just as it should be." She turned my direction, catching me swiping under my eyes with a napkin. "Marli, I'm thinking April. Somewhere on the Cape. The temperature's not too warm then and the flowers will be in full bloom. I'll see if I can rent the grand ballroom at—"

"No!" I shouted over her, silencing the room.

Jordan rushed to me, confused. His voice lowered to where only I heard. "Marli, what's the matter?"

"I don't want to get married at eighteen. Can't we at least wait until after my birthday? Don't I get a say in this?"

John Banks removed a slice of cherry pie from the tray Meg placed on the table. "Of course you have a say, Marli. It's your wedding, right Eva?" he said with an edge demanding obedience.

Eva shot back an equally powerful glower to her husband. "I know the decision is Marli and Jordan's, *dear*. I merely offered a suggestion."

"How about July?" Jordan interjected, deflecting the intensity growing. "We'll still have a couple of months for a honeymoon before school starts." He smoothed my hair back, pulling a handkerchief from his pocket and blotting my cheeks. "Hey, I don't care where or when. I just want to marry you, okay?"

"Okay," I sniffed, threading my hands through his hair and holding his forehead to mine. "I love you," I whispered.

"In spite of my crazy family?"

"Yes, and because of them." I stretched my hand to Eva. "Would you help me plan my wedding? My mother isn't around and I need you."

I meant to finish the sentence with "your help" but somehow, the truth snuck into my words. I needed Eva Mason, in fact, Jordan's entire family. When I called Rick, he accused me of the same things Jesse had. Even Jordan's gallant gesture of asking for his blessing didn't soften his snarky reaction. I hated that my "congratulations" came wrapped in an argument.

"As long as you promise to tell me if I become overbearing. I have a tendency to want to control things."

"You? Controlling? There's no 'tendency' there, Mom. It's a fact," Jordan laughed.

The room erupted in jovial sound, dissipating the tension. Meg passed out pie slices and Jordan spooned vanilla ice cream into my mouth while I sat on his lap, listening to the chatter.

John wandered over and placed a kiss on my cheek. "Welcome to the family, Marli. I'm so glad I picked you."

His reminder, more than any other, dulled the shine from my happy moment.

Jordan and Jesse headed for the media room, arguing over which action movie to watch. I begged out of joining them, telling Jordan I was too exhausted and wanted to go to sleep. He settled for a kiss goodnight at the bedroom door. When I stepped inside, I flipped the lock.

My heavy eyes had barely fluttered shut when my receptor chimed on the night table.

"Hello?" I answered through a sleepy haze.

"Pumpkin? It's your old man. Got a second?"

I leaned against the headboard, rubbing the slumber from my eyes.

"Yeah. What's up?"

"I didn't handle things very well, did I?"

Painful tears circled my eyes. "You hurt me, Daddy."

A couple of large sighs sounded on the other end. "I'm sorry I let you down. Hell, it's not like I didn't see this coming. Watching the two of you in California—the tender way he treated you through everything, and then showing up on the porch that morning when you were in Italy, I knew the poor sap was hopelessly in love with you and not going away. To be honest, I couldn't ask for anyone better to take care of my little girl."

"You should be telling this to Jordan."

"I did. I called him a few minutes ago to apologize. He said you'd gone to bed, but I had to talk to you."

A wide yawn made a squeaky sound in my jaw. "Sorry. Today kind of wiped me out."

"Sounded pretty spectacular." A silent moment passed. "So, when's the big day?"

"July."

"Good. I get custody of you for Christmas."

"And Jordan."

"Yes, and Jordan. Guess I'm going to have to get used to the package deal. Are we okay? I really am sorry and happy for you. I love you, Pumpkin."

"Yeah, we're good, and I love you, too." We were about to disconnect when I remembered my earlier thought. "Dad? I need to find Mom."

After tossing and turning for what felt like hours, I climbed out of bed to walk off the restlessness. A full moon pressed against a black velvet backdrop and its radiance cast the kitchen in a lustrous grayish white, giving the room a sterile appearance. The white marble counters glowed, the dark cherry cabinets ebony black in the muted shadows. Even Meg's favorite teakettle on the stovetop lacked the depth of its blood red brilliance.

I pulled out a stool and settled at the work island with a cup of instant herbal tea. My toes curled over the brass foot bar on the stool, the cold metal sending a chill up my bare legs. I stared at the glowing orb, distorted through the faceted glass, imagining myself on the edge of a deep lunar crater, ready to leap. When I lifted my mug, the pale amber ring left behind looked odd, glaringly out of place on the countertop, just like the ring on my left hand.

*July.* Eight months from now, I'd be Mrs. Jordan Mason. Marli Davis would become past-tense and the idea played havoc with my heart. Since the notorious day my candidacy became official, life had been a roller coaster ride and this last turn brought me to an abrupt halt.

I twirled the sparkling stone garnishing my finger. By accepting Jordan's proposal, I surrendered much more than my heart and soon, my body. I became submissive to whatever fate The Program decided.

When the door creaked, I turned expecting Jordan. Not Jesse.

"Are you stalking me?"

"I couldn't sleep."

He tore open another tea packet, filled a mug with steaming water, and perched on the stool next to me. He blotted the tea stain with a paper napkin, cleaning up another one of my messes.

"Sorry about dinner," he muttered before a noisy slurp.

"Don't beat yourself up. You're forgiven."

"Am I?"

Jesse took my hand, slowly rolling my engagement ring between his fingers. His eyes were hooded, his expression hard as stone, and his whispered breaths heavy on my skin.

"He must have spent his entire trust fund on this rock. Such a beautiful 'trap.'" I tried to pull my hand away, but Jesse's grip tightened.

"Let go, Jess."

"Of your hand or you?"

I chewed my lip, not realizing I'd curled my fingers around his hand.

"Is that a 'yes give me freedom, Jess'….or 'hang on tighter because I've really screwed up?' I can do both, you know."

"Stop with the games."

His hand skimmed my cheek. "Who's playing games, Mars? Me? You?" He eased his hand down my neck and drew a lazy line across my collarbone with his index finger. "Or Jordan?"

I slapped his hand away and he chuckled quietly, angering me.

"Jordan doesn't play games."

"You're right. He manipulates."

Tears fill my eyes, but I forbade them to fall. "Why are you being cruel?"

"I'm being honest, something no one else is being right now." He pushed his mug away and leaned closer, dropping his voice to barely above a whisper. "Jordan loves you, I get that. I do too, which we all hate, but the fact is, I can give you what Jordan can't. Freedom."

"I'm going to marry Jordan."

"And then what? Have mind-blowing sex and pump out perfect babies for the fucking Program?" he hissed.

"Keep your voice down."

"Why? Are you worried there'll be another brotherly brawl and you'll really get hurt this time?"

Careful to remain out of Jesse's reach, I moved off the stool. "You're being a jerk. I'm going back to bed." I barely got two steps towards the door before Jesse attacked my Achilles Heel.

"You'll never go to veterinary school, regardless of what Jordan promises. *They* won't let you." He moved beside me when I didn't answer, his voice quiet. "Marli, you have no idea what pressure The Program will inflict on you, especially to get pregnant."

"Jordan promised no kids until I'm ready."

Jesse stroked the side of my arm. "I hate to be the one to pop your fantasy bubble, but that's not a promise he'll be allowed to keep."

The heartbeat I once felt vanished and fear settled in the empty chamber. Surely Jordan wouldn't let me down. He knew the importance I placed on fulfilling my dreams. I swallowed the lump bouncing in my throat.

"Why do you say that?"

Jess held my chin, forcing my eyes to lock on his. "Because my father wants a human successfully cloned before he leaves office and he wants that *clone* from his grandchild."

His lips hovered over mine and my breath stilled, but my body trembled. "Don't—"

The kiss felt sweet, tender…terrifying.

"Marry *me*, Marli. Not Jordan."

I pushed away when he leaned in for a second kiss. "Goodnight, Jess."

I didn't say "no" and Jesse caught my mistake by returning the sentiment through a wide, triumphant smile.

I checked the hallway, relieved to find it empty. I needed to escape somewhere to think. Dawn's lavender rays sprinkled the living room in ghostly shadows. I tiptoed to the entry and paused, my nervous heart clamoring for release. The blinking green light on the security panel assured me no silent alarms would sound when I opened the door. There was no escaping the magic floor, recording my bright pink footsteps as I bolted for the stairwell, avoiding the elevator. The chime announcing its arrival would also herald my departure.

Exiting through the back entrance and into the private gardens, I ran the winding path around gurgling fountains and fragrant flower gardens to the iron gates holding back the noise of the city. I waited until the security camera swept to the other side of the vestibule, then sprang forward, entered my pass code and slipped out. Once around the corner of the building, I hailed a taxi shuttle.

"Where to Miss?"

"The marina, but drop me a block away." He glanced in the rearview mirror, a curious expression on his face. I didn't want him to think I jogged the waterfront alone. "I'm meeting my running group." He dropped his gaze and whistled to the song playing out of the crackling speakers.

Remembering all the security codes in Jordan's life proved no easy task. When the dock supervisor walked away to make rounds, I fumbled three times before finding the right number sequence allowing my access. Another stupid keypad stumped me for a second before I gained entrance to the gangplank leading to *Her Majesty*.

The high pitched whine when the gate opened repeated across the marina and I panicked I'd be discovered. I stooped below the rails until I could steal around to the stern of the boat and drop into the galley.

Gulps of cool water slithered down my throat from the bottle I stole out of the refrigerator. I deposited the empty container into the recycling tube and eased a hip onto a barstool.

Yesterday still seemed surreal. Nevertheless, the large diamond on my left hand reminded me it did happen. Jordan and I were officially engaged.

*Marli, what have you done?*

This morning when I woke, dread swamped me. All the confusing feelings I thought had settled, resurfaced. After Jesse cornered me in the kitchen earlier with his formal proposal of marriage—of a life outside of The Program, confusing thoughts swirled in my brain.

Could he be right about Jordan giving me an empty guarantee to keep The Program at bay and not force me into an unwanted pregnancy? Would Jordan bend to his father's pressure?

Damn. Did I make the wrong choice by accepting his proposal?

Marriage to Jesse wouldn't be awful. We shared something, only somewhere along the way, Jesse's feelings turned to love where mine never grew beyond lust. Over time, surely my feelings would deepen…wouldn't they? Regardless of whether I came to love Jesse or not, I'd always love Jordan.

Suddenly, I realized a life with Jesse would be anything but *free*. Our relationship would be forever haunted by my feelings for Jordan. He held the key to my caged heart.

I jerked at the sound of screeching metal from further up the marina. Someone walked—no *ran* down the boardwalk. I peeked out a small porthole. Jesse! Damn! He found me.

I hustled down the dark hallway, banging my shoulder against the door jamb when I turned into Kate's old cabin. I locked the door and childishly hid in the corner, hoping he'd go away. A couple of light taps sounded on the door.

"Mars? It's Jess. Please open up."

He cautiously pushed the door open when I unlocked it, gathering me in his arms. My nose pressed his warm neck and the scent of his cologne, the same as Jordan's, filled my senses. Overwhelming guilt rushed me, acknowledging the crossroads I faced.

We returned to the galley where Jesse managed to scrounge up some instant coffee that didn't taste half bad. The morning air held a slight chill and he draped his jacket over my bare shoulders when an involuntary shiver rolled over my arms. He pulled his receptor out of his pocket and I grabbed his arm.

"No, please. Not yet."

"You know Jordan probably has the FBI looking for you."

A sudden thought popped in my head. "Why are you here and not Jordan?" The touch of anger surprised me. Jordan should be my hero, not Jesse.

"Jordan saw you in your jogging suit on the security camera and figured you'd gone for a run. Nice *pink* floor by the way. He was in the shower when a call came regarding a possible stowaway on the yacht. When Jordan asked Meg if you'd returned yet, I put two-and-two together and figured you were the stowaway."

His brow arched. "I'm just curious why. Having second thoughts?" Jesse leaned closer. "Reconsidering my offer?" His lips pressed my cheek lightly, but I didn't turn my face to accept a kiss in return. My lips pressed my coffee mug instead.

"Sort of," I confessed. Another sip warmed my throat and bought me a couple of seconds. My heart clanged in my chest. I faced Jesse, taking his hand. "I needed someplace quiet to sort through the confusion."

Jesse's fingers wrapped my wrist and he drew me closer, but I pulled back.

"No more seduction tricks, Jess. It's important you listen to me."

"Okay, you have my attention. What?"

"This morning I realized something. I care for you Jess, yes, but nothing close to what I feel for Jordan." I placed my hand to the side of his face to keep him from turning away. "I did consider your proposal, more seriously than you think"

"What changed your mind back to Jordan?"

"The other night you told me to choose my happy-ever-after with my heart. Jess, Jordan holds my heart. He always has. I don't care who holds the strings to my future, as long as he shares it with me."

Water pooled in Jesse's chocolate eyes. "But is love enough, Mars? When you wake up someday not having realized your dream, will that love for Jordan be all you need?"

"Jordan *is* my dream. He's the prince charming I've fantasized about my whole life. We've already survived enough drama for me to realize that together, we're strong. Our love grows with our problems…not fades. I know life holds no guarantees and believing otherwise would be foolish. But I want the chance to prove the odds wrong…with Jordan. I love him, Jess. Not you."

Tears dripped from Jesse's eyes and my heart wanted to hurt for him, but too much joy filled it. I threw my arms around him and he crushed me to him.

"Damn this hurts."

"Like hell," I validated. "But I can't take it back, Jess. I don't want to."

He pulled away and heaved a couple of large breaths. "I won't believe it's over until a preacher says so." He handed me his receptor. "I think there's someone looking for you." He brought my hand to his lips, softly kissing my knuckles. A tear splashed and rolled off my wrist, its origin unknown. His or mine. "Be happy."

He trudged down the boardwalk, his hands stashed deep in pockets, head hung low. He never looked back.

I leaned against the bar, closing my eyes against the golden rays bending into the galley and warming my face. The forgiving voice answering on the other end of the receptor sent my heart racing.

"Hey, baby, I miss you. Are you all right?" Jordan asked, pensive.

"I will be as soon as I'm in your arms. Come get me?"

The voice suddenly sounded close. "I'm already here, but until I'm holding you, I'm not complete."

I drank in the image of faded jeans riding hips in such a way my mouth parched. My gaze followed the lines of the narrow waist to the broad chest testing the threads of a heather gray Cornell University T-shirt. A hard swallow bounced down a tan neck, and my eyes drifted over the square chin to the heart-shaped lips that knew how to turn my bone marrow to hot liquid.

Dimples framed the corners when they tweaked upward and when I locked on eyes the color of a deep, still pond, my heart leapt with excitement. Every nerve ending in my body pinged.

Jordan lifted me onto the counter, hands firmly on my hips and moved his six foot three inches of unbelievable gorgeousness between my legs in an extremely intimate embrace.

I locked my hands around his neck. "What are you doing?" I asked unable to mask my needy tone.

He pulled me tighter and I sucked my lower lip against the surge of excitement rocketing through me. Jordan took my chin in one hand, pulled my lip from my teeth with his thumb and settled his mouth gently on mine.

"Research for a future project."

I blushed hot enough to combust. "You're terrible."

He kissed me again and laughed lightly against my lips. "Let's hope not."

I threw my head back with a wicked laugh and Jordan bathed my neck with tiny nips, turning my laughter to moans. My fingers twisted into his silky bronze locks, still damp and smelling of fruity-scented shampoo. I circled my legs around his hips, keeping the sensuous feel of him pressed against somewhere soon to be only his.

Jordan's fingers trembled as they smoothed over my face and his secret weapon lips claimed my mouth hard, possessive, and greedy. He released my hair from the twisted bun, tangled his fingers into the loose strands. His other hand pressed my lower back, pushing out any molecules of air remaining between our bodies.

I swam deliriously in the intoxicating kiss, relishing the rush of feelings awakening more frequently and stronger, chipping away my self control.

Jordan broke the kiss, rested his forehead against mine and struggled for air through ragged breaths. The torture I put him through mirrored in his blackened eyes.

I ran my thumb slowly over his lips watching them dilate further. "Marry me?" I whispered.

He kissed me again, slower, softer. "You're really going to make me wait, aren't you?"

"I believe page four of our contract says we're sworn to celibacy," I teased, knowing full well from this moment on all laws would be broken, boundaries crossed, and the only limits that mattered were those Jordan and I set ourselves. To hell with The Program.

"Marli, when I'm with you there are no rules. Everything and everyone fades away. It's only you and me. What do you say? Want to fool around?"

I bit his bottom lip…hard.

"Damn, girl."

*Turn the page for a glimpse into Book Two of the Designer Genes Saga.*

# Prologue

"Son, have a seat."

Out of instinct, I chose the black leather wingback closest to the door. When Jess and I were younger, being summoned to our father's private office generally meant we'd been caught doing something we shouldn't, or some parental decision had been made—one we wouldn't like. Once the announcement was delivered or punishment rendered, you wanted out of the room before anyone witnessed your emotional reaction. Like tears.

The heavy wooden door closed behind me, silencing the room. Dad paused at the wall of windows showcasing a picturesque view of the harbor, and cerulean ocean stretching to infinity beyond the border patrols. His shoulders rose and fell with deep, contemplative breaths, and mine turned shallow in response with panic rooted deep in my stomach.

"Jordan," he began, his back to me and his serious tone resonating off the bullet-proof glass. "I can't begin to describe how pleased I am with your decision to marry Marli Davis. The choice has been yours to make from the beginning, but I'm proud of the way you let the relationship evolve into one of trust and mutual admiration, instead of exercising dominance." He glanced over his shoulder. "Her eyes tell how much she loves you."

"I love her so much, but I'm afraid to trust in how happy I feel."

He angled my direction, a questioning air about his demeanor. "Why?"

"Because of The Program." An honest answer. "I fear she'll be taken from me any moment. I almost wish we'd had sex so they'd be forced to consider the match official."

A small smile bent his mouth, but disappeared before settling permanently. The heavy breath expelled through his nostrils offered little comfort. He lowered into the chair behind his massive desk and drummed his knuckles against his mouth. A trace of weariness bracketed his eyes.

"I see. I'm somewhat relieved to know you haven't, although I'd never render judgment. You and Marli are old enough to understand the responsibility behind such a choice. If, however, by 'they' you mean Tony Peterson, a moral compromise won't matter."

Not the answer I needed.

Nervously, I punched my fist softly against my palm below the desktop. "Maybe after our engagement is recorded in the database, the Petersons' obsession with Marli will end."

Dad's mouth twisted and he gave me a worried look. Bad news coming.

"I wish the solution was that simple." He leaned forward, eyes dropped to an ivory envelope. "Jordan, I need you to hold off contacting Marv for a bit."

Marvin Gomez, my counselor, would be the first step in notifying The Program of my decision to make my relationship with Marli permanent. He would, in turn, notify Marli's counselor once he met with me and finalized matters. In the meantime, neither Marli nor I were allowed to share our news outside of immediate family until The Program officially changed our candidacy status.

The fact Marli didn't want to call Rick when we returned to the penthouse to share something so important, worried me she second-guessed her answer. If I postponed changing our status, I risked my worst nightmare coming true because I'd give her the escape hatch she already appeared to search for.

The muscles in my shoulders roped tight. I lifted my arms, locked my hands behind my skull, and studied the carved wooden tiles covering the ceiling. "Why would I want to wait?"

From my peripheral vision, I watched Dad push the envelope across the desk. I dropped my hands, twisting them in to a tight knot between my knees. I slumped close to the desktop, refusing to touch what I assumed contained another control agent I'd despise.

"What's this?"

"Jordan, The Program is struggling to find eligible candidates. Moral standards are almost non-existent. Personally, I'm saddened to see that even the academic numbers have fallen drastically. Traditional educational options are being discarded for false hopes of attaining big money by working for corporate conglomerates, in particular, those promising fantasy positions on one of the three operating space stations."

"Careful. SpringCor is one of those corporate monsters."

Dad scrubbed his hand across his chin. "Don't remind me."

"So back to the reason why I have to put my life on hold? Marli's going to freak, especially if she thinks I'm keeping something from her." Again.

"Well then she's really going to hate what I'm about to ask of you."

The hackles raised on my neck. "*Me?*"

He tapped the envelope I still hadn't picked up. "New Year's Eve, the two governing districts in The Program will host a ball. Six hand-picked candidates, three girls in the West and three boys in our section, will play hosts and hostesses to a select few candidates, for promotional purposes. All staged and, hopefully, enticing to those potential candidates gleaned from the database in February. I'm not comfortable with the advertising stunt, nevertheless, I'm not in the control seat. You, Jordan, along with Ambassador Kirk's son, and…"

"Shit! Doug Peterson?"

"Check you language, son. Even between us. And yes, Douglas Peterson. Each of you will be given an assigned dance card of sorts with the young ladies you are to dazzle for the cameras."

"Marli? Is she on my card?"

When Dad didn't answer, I bolted from the chair and stood at the window, neck craned sideways to see if I could spot Marli by the pool. Flashes of sunlight bouncing off the ripples told me someone swam, but all I could see were a couple of deck chairs resting in puddles that had splashed on the deck. At least I hadn't lied about anyone seeing us in the hot tub last night.

The memory kicked my lower regions into action and my pants suddenly felt snug. Marli's satiny skin running the length of mine underwater, a free pass to explore parts of her previously forbidden, and her granting permission to such intimacy, tore down the remaining wall between us. For the first time, I believed I'd earned her complete trust. Now, I risked losing it again.

"Jordan?"

"No. I won't do it," I declared, the defiance rising in my chest. "I'll never lie to Marli again."

The chair squeaked behind me when the man I loved, respected, and loathed at the moment, left it to cross the room and join me at the window. The words spoken next were the same ones I'd heard over and over all my life, but this time, cut deep. Anger, fear, and frustration melted into a heavy ball weighted in my gut.

Dad shoved his hands deep in his pockets. I braided mine behind my back, my feet shoulder-width apart in an all too familiar military stance.

"You don't have a choice, son."

"I see." Quiet but tense. "Tell me, *Father*, when will the choice be mine? At what point in *my* life will I have control?" Remaining rigid and facing forward, I turned my head, jaw set hard, and throat tight. "If anything happens…" Tears burned without warning and I swallowed them down. "If I lose Marli because of this asinine Program, I will hold *you* personally responsible."

I turned back to the world moving beyond the plate glass, unaware of the control subtly manipulating innocent lives.

"And…I'll hate you forever."

# ACKNOWLEDGEMENT

It's been said it takes a village to raise a child. The same holds true for publishing a book.

The Designer Genes saga has been over four years from concept, to publication of this first book. Every change in this story stood subject to scrutiny by wonderful critique partners, beta readers, and finally through an editorial fire that brought the characters to life. Thank you "my village" for sacrificing endless hours to help Designer Genes go from sticky notes to something I'm proud to share.

To my husband who stands at my side with pocket book open and tissues in hand, I love you.

To Kaye, Karla, and Sascha. Thank you from the bottom of my heart for sticking with me once again, and not letting me wave the white flag as I threatened countless times during this process. Your friendship is priceless.

To my mentor and editor, Lynne. You made me laugh when I wanted to cry. Your blatant, somewhat colorful, honesty regarding my characters' flaws, and unfailing perseverance in helping me develop them into stronger, three dimensional individuals, is what makes Designer Genes shine.

Lastly, to my fans. Thank you for your support. Without you, my dreams would never come true.

You rock!

# ABOUT THE AUTHOR

**Harley Brooks** dreamed of being an astronaut when she grew up, but when she entered her teens she discovered boys, and her quest for the stars turned to finding her prince charming. Vivid memories of the emotional rollercoaster called "life" during those years, influenced her decision to write teen romance.

Known for writing racy, edgy, and emotionally charged stories filled with unforgettable characters who can't seem to get out of their own way, Harley Brooks untangles superheroes from their capes.

When she's not writing, she's exploring scenic byways on her Harley Davidson. She still wishes on the first star of the night and the last one sparkling in the morning.

Fans are what make her world go round and she loves to hear from them. You can find her at the following hangouts:

www.harleybrooks.com

harleybrooks.author@gmail.com

Facebook – Harley Brooks, Author

Twitter - @_harleybrooks

**Other award-winning books by Harley Brooks**

*Riley's Pond*

www.ingramcontent.com/pod-product-compliance
Lightning Source LLC
Chambersburg PA
CBHW070752280626
47162CB00016B/161